P9-DMP-832

THE ANDALUCIAN FRIEND

THE ANDALUCIAN FRIEND

A NOVEL

Alexander Söderberg

CROWN PUBLISHERS
NEW YORK

Published in the United States by Crown Publishers, an imprint of the Crown Publishing Group, a division of Random House, Inc., New York. This translation published by agreement with the Salomonsson Agency.

www.crownpublishing.com

Originally published in Sweden as *Den Andalusiske Vännen* by Norstedts, Stockholm, in 2012.

Library of Congress Cataloging-in-Publication Data

Söderberg, Alexander.
[Andalusiske vönnen. English]
The Andalucian friend : a novel / Alexander Söderberg. —1st ed.
p. cm.
"Originally published in Sweden as Den Andalusiske vönnen by Norstedts, Stockholm, in 2012."
(alk. paper)
1. Organized crime—Fiction. 2. Police corruption—Fiction. 3. Nurses—Fiction.
4. Sweden—Fiction. I. Title.
PT9877.29.O34A5313 2013
839.73'8DC23
2012023775

ISBN 978-0-7704-3605-6
eISBN 978-0-7704-3606-3

Printed in the United States of America

Book design by Elina D. Nudelman
Jacket design by Ben Wiseman

10 9 8 7 6 5 4 3 2 1

First Edition

CAST OF CHARACTERS

THE SWEDES

Sophie Brinkmann
Albert Brinkmann
Jens Vall
Lars Vinge
Gunilla Strandberg
Erik Strandberg
Anders Ask
Aron Geisler
Hasse Berglund
Sonya Alizadeh
Svante Carlgren
Tommy Jansson

THE RUSSIANS

Mikhail Asmarov
Dmitry, Gosha, Vitaly

THE SPANIARDS

Hector Guzman
Adalberto Guzman
Carlos Fuentes
Leszek Smialy

THE GERMANS

Ralph Hanke
Roland Getz
Christian Hanke
Klaus Köhler

THE ANDALUCIAN FRIEND

PROLOGUE

She kept looking between the rearview mirror and the road ahead. She couldn't see the motorcycle, not just then. It had been there a moment before, looming up behind her, then it disappeared. She pulled into the inside lane of the highway, trying to seek cover from the cars behind her.

He kept looking back, trying to direct her driving from the passenger seat. She couldn't hear his words, just the panic in his voice.

The outline of the motorbike appeared in the shaky rearview mirror, disappeared for a few moments, then reappeared—it kept going like that as it cruised between the cars behind them. She pulled out into the left-hand lane, which lay open ahead of her, and put her foot down, and the car vibrated with the rapid revolution of the engine as she put the car into fifth gear, the highest. She felt sick.

There was a draft around her feet, the bullets must have hit somewhere down there. The holes made a whining noise that merged with the sound of the straining engine, a terrible noise that cut into her consciousness. She couldn't remember how far she had driven before the shots came—sudden and unreal. She had time to see that the man riding the motorbike was wearing a blue helmet with a dark visor, that the gunman behind him had a black helmet with no visor; she had seen his eyes for a moment, she had seen the emptiness in them.

They had been shot at from the left; the sound came out from nowhere—rattling in quick succession. The clatter inside the car sounded like someone was hitting the bodywork with a heavy chain. At the same time she heard a yell, but she couldn't tell if it had come from her or the man beside her. She glanced quickly at him. He was different now: his nerves and fear were shining through, showing themselves as anger. That much was clear from his face: furrowed brow, staring eyes, every now and then a twitch in one of them. He pressed one of the speed-dial numbers on his cell phone again—he had done this once already since the shots were fired—he waited, staring intently ahead of him, no answer this time either, he hung up.

The motorbike was heading toward them at high speed, he yelled at her to drive faster. She realized that speed wasn't going to save them and neither would his yelling. She felt the metallic taste of fear in her mouth as a white noise buzzed feverishly in her head. Her panic had crossed a boundary, she was no longer trembling, she just felt a terrible weight in her arms, as if driving the car were somehow heavy. And like an invincible enemy, the motorbike was suddenly alongside them. She glanced to the left and saw the snub-nosed weapon in the gunman's hand again as he raised it toward her. She ducked instinctively as the gun spewed out bullets: hard cracking sounds echoed as the shots hit the bodywork, the crash as the side window shattered, throwing a cascade of glass over her. She was slumped down with her head to one side, foot hard on the accelerator. The car was driving itself, she had no idea what was happening ahead of them. She had time to notice that the glove compartment by his knees was open, that there were several magazines in there, that he was holding a pistol in his hand. Then a loud bang, metal against metal. A loud scraping sound from the right as the car slid into the barrier along the side of the highway. There was a shrieking, scraping sound, the car was juddering, and there was a smell of burning.

She sat up, turned the wheel, and straightened the car, and pulled out into traffic again. A quick look over her shoulder; the motorbike was off to the side behind her. He swore loudly and leaned across her, firing the gun through her window, three shots in quick succession. The explosions from the gun echoed improbably inside the car, the motorbike braked and disappeared.

"How much farther?" she asked.

He looked at her as if he didn't understand the question, then he must have heard it as an echo in his head.

"I don't know. . . ."

The accelerator pedal was still on the floor, the needle of the speedometer was quivering as the car lurched around curves in the road. Another quick glance in the rearview mirror.

"Here it comes again," she said.

He tried to open his own window but the collision with the barrier had buckled the door and the window was stuck. He leaned back toward her, took aim with his right foot, and kicked at the window. Most of the glass fell out. He cleared the rest with the barrel of the gun, then leaned out and shot at the motorbike, which pulled back once more. She realized how hopeless their situation was. The motorbike was in control.

Then everything fell silent, as if someone had switched off all sound. They sailed along the highway, staring ahead as if they were both trying to reconcile themselves to their approaching death, faces pale, incapable of comprehending what was happening to their lives at this precise moment. He looked tired, his head was hanging, his eyes sad.

"Say something!" She uttered the command in a loud voice, both hands on the wheel, eyes on the road, speed unchanged.

At first he didn't answer; he seemed to be thinking, then he turned toward her.

"Sorry, Sophie."

PART ONE

STOCKHOLM, SIX WEEKS EARLIER, MAY

1

There was something about her that made some people say she didn't look like a nurse, and she could never figure out if this was a compliment or an insult. She had long, dark hair and a pair of green eyes that sometimes gave the impression that she was about to burst out laughing. She wasn't; that was just the way she looked, as if she had been born with a smile in her eyes.

She went down the stairs, which creaked beneath her feet. The house—a fairly small, yellow wooden villa built in 1911, with leaded windows, shiny old parquet floors, and a garden that could have been bigger—was her place on this earth, she realized that the first time she saw it.

The kitchen window was open to the still spring evening. The smell coming through the window was more summer than spring. Summer wasn't supposed to arrive for several weeks, but the heat had come early and not wanted to leave. Now it was just hanging there, heavy and completely still. She was grateful for it, needed it, enjoyed being able to have her windows and doors open—being able to move freely between outside and in.

There was the sound of a moped in the distance, a thrush was singing in a tree—other birds too, but she didn't know their names.

Sophie got out the china and set the table for two, with the best plates, nicest cutlery, and the finest glasses, avoiding the workaday as best she could. She knew she would be eating alone, seeing as Albert ate when he was hungry, which seldom coincided with her timing. She heard his steps on the stairs—sneakers on old oak wood; a bit too heavy, a bit too hard—Albert wasn't bothered by the noise he was making. She smiled at him as he came into the kitchen; he smiled back boyishly, yanked open the fridge door, and stood there for far too long, staring at the contents.

"Shut the fridge, Albert."

He stood where he was; she ate for a while, idly leafing through a newspaper, then she looked up, said the same thing again, this time with a hint of irritation in her voice.

"I can't move . . . ," he whispered theatrically.

She laughed, not so much at his dry sense of humor but more because he was just funny, which made her happy . . . proud, even.

"How was your day?" she asked.

She could see he was close to laughter. She recognized the signs, he always thought his own jokes were funny. Albert took a bottle of mineral water from the fridge, slammed the door, and jumped up onto the kitchen counter. The carbon dioxide hissed as he unscrewed the top.

"Everyone's mad," he said, taking a sip. Albert started to tell her about his day in small fragments as they occurred to him. She listened and smiled as he made fun of the teachers and other people. She could see he enjoyed being amusing, then suddenly he was done. Sophie could never figure out when this was going to happen; he would just stop, as if he had gotten fed up with himself and his sense of humor. And she felt like reaching out to him to ask him to stay, carry on being funny, carry on being human, friendly, and mean at the same time. But that wasn't how it worked. She'd tried before and it had gone wrong, so she let him go.

He disappeared into the hall. A short silence; maybe he was changing his shoes.

"You owe me a thousand kronor," he said.

"What for?"

"The cleaning lady came today."

"Don't say 'cleaning lady.'"

She heard the zip of his jacket.

"So what should I say?"

She didn't know. He was on his way out through the door.

"Kiss, kiss, Mom," he said, his tone suddenly gentle.

The door closed and she could hear his steps on the gravel path outside the open window.

"Give me a ring if you're going to be late," she called.

Sophie went on as normal. She cleared the table, tidied up, watched some television, called a friend and talked about nothing—and the evening passed. She went up to bed and tried to read some of the book on her bedside table, about a woman who had found a new life helping the street children of Bucharest. The book was dull; the woman was pretentious and Sophie had nothing in common with her. She closed the book and fell asleep alone in her bed as usual.

Eight hours later, and the time was quarter past six in the morning. Sophie got up, showered, wiped the bathroom mirror, which revealed hidden words when it steamed up: *Albert*, *AIK*, and a load of other illegible things that he wrote with his finger while he was brushing his teeth. She had told him to stop doing it, but he didn't seem to care, and in some ways she rather liked that.

She ate a light breakfast on her feet as she read the front page of the morning paper. It would soon be time to leave for work. She shouted up to Albert three times that it was time to get up, then fifteen minutes later she was sitting on her bicycle and letting the mild morning air wake her up.

He went by the name of Jeans. They seriously believed that was his name. They'd laughed and pointed to their trousers. *Jeans!*

But his name was Jens, and he was sitting at a table in a hut in the jungle in Paraguay together with three Russians. The boss's name was Dmitry, a lanky guy in his thirties, his face still looked like a child's—a child whose parents were cousins. His colleagues, Gosha and Vitaly, were the same age—and their parents may have been siblings. They kept laughing without showing any sign of pleasure, their eyes wide, half-open mouths letting on that they didn't really understand anything at all.

Dmitry was mixing a batch of dry martinis in a plastic container. He tipped in some olives and shook it around, poured it into some rinsed-out coffee mugs, spilling it, then proposed a toast in Russian. His friends roared; they all drank the martinis, which had an undertone of diesel.

Jens didn't like them, not a single one. They were repulsive: dishonest, rude, twitchy.... He tried to not show his distaste but it shone through; he'd always been bad at hiding his feelings.

"Let's take a look at the goods," he said.

The Russians lit up like children on Christmas morning. He went out of the shed toward the jeep that was parked in the middle of the dusty, poorly lit yard.

He had no idea why the Russians had come all the way to Paraguay to look at the goods. Normally someone ordered something from him, he delivered, got paid, never met the customer. But this time it was different, as if the whole business of buying arms was a big deal for them, something fun, an adventure in itself. He had no idea what they were involved in either, and he didn't want to know. It didn't matter; they were there to look at their purchases, test the weapons, snort some cocaine, fuck some whores, and pay Jens the second of three installments.

He had brought one MP7 and one Steyr AUG with him. The rest were packed away in a warehouse by the harbor in Ciudad del Este awaiting shipment.

The Russians grabbed the guns and pretended to shoot one another. *Hands up...hands up!* They were shrieking with laughter, jerking about. Dmitry had a white smear of coke in his stubble.

Gosha and Vitaly were arguing over the MP7, pulling and tugging at the gun, punching each other hard in the head with their fists. Dmitry separated them, brought out the container of dry martinis.

Jens watched from a distance. The Russians would get out of hand, the Paraguayans would come back with some whores as a gesture of goodwill. The Russians would get even more wired and drunk and then they'd start firing live rounds. He knew what was going to happen and he couldn't do anything to stop it, and it would all be terrible. He wanted to leave, but he had to stay until sunrise, stay alert and sober, to take his money whenever Dmitry decided it was time to hand it over.

"*Jeans!* Where the fuck is the ammo?"

Jens pointed to the jeep. The Russians ran over, tore open the doors, and began searching. Jens put his hand in his pocket, he only had one piece of nicotine gum left. It was two months since he had stopped using chewing tobacco, and three years since he stopped smoking. And now he was in the jungle twenty-five miles from Ciudad del Este. The nicotine synapses in his brain were screaming for attention. He pulled out the last piece of gum, chewed hard on it, looked over at the Russians with ill-concealed disgust, and realized that he was about to start smoking again.

Once she was at the hospital, she worked. There was rarely time for anything else, and besides, she didn't enjoy drinking coffee with her colleagues; it felt uncomfortable. She wasn't shy, but maybe there was something missing, preventing her from socializing over coffee. She was mainly there for the patients' sake, not because of any particular piety or a specific desire to look after other people. She worked at the hospital so she could talk to them, spend time with them. They were there because they were ill, which meant that they were basically themselves. Open, human, and honest. And that made her feel safe and functional. That was what she wanted, that was what kept her coming. Patients rarely talked nonsense, except when they were getting better, and that's when she left them, and they her. Maybe that was why Sophie had chosen this as her career in the first place.

Did she wallow in other people's misfortune? Possibly, but it didn't really feel to her as if that was what she was doing. It felt more like she was dependent. Dependent on other people's honesty, dependent on their openness, dependent on the chance to see glimpses of people's inner selves shine through every now and then. And when that happened, those patients would often become her favorites on the ward. Her favorites were almost always imposing characters. "Imposing" was the word she used. And when they appeared before her, she would stop and think, impressed, maybe, and filled with an indefinable sense of hope. Straight-backed people who dared to face life with a smile, the ones who were imposing on the inside: she had always been able to see them, right from the very first glance, without being able to explain how or why. As if these few people let their souls blossom, as if they chose the very best over what was merely good, as if they dared to see all sides of themselves, even the shady, hidden aspects.

She was walking down the corridor carrying a tray, heading for Hector Guzman in Room 11. He had come in three days earlier after being knocked down on a pedestrian crossing in the city center. His right leg was broken below the knee. The doctors thought they'd discovered something wrong with his spleen, so he was being kept in for observation. Hector was in his mid-forties, good-looking without being handsome, large without being fat. He was Spanish, but she thought she could see hints of something Nordic in his features. His hair was fairly dark, with a few lighter hints. His nose, cheekbones, and chin were sharp and his skin verged on the sandy brown. He spoke fluent Swedish and he was *imposing*—perhaps because of the observant eyes that lit up his face, possibly because of the lightness of his movements even though he was a large man. Or possibly because of the natural indifference that made him smile every time she went in to him—as if he knew that she knew, which she did, and that made her smile back at him.

He pretended to be absorbed in a book as he sat up in bed with his reading glasses on his nose. He was always doing things like that when she was with him, pretending not to see her, pretending to be busy.

She sorted out the pills and put them in little plastic cups, then handed him one. He took it without looking up from his book, tipped the pills into his mouth, accepted a glass of water, and swallowed them, all without taking his eyes from the book. She gave him the second dose and he did the same with that.

"Always just as tasty," he said quietly, then looked up. "You're wearing different earrings today, Sophie."

She caught herself about to raise one hand to her ear.

"I might be," she said.

"No, not might be, you are. They suit you."

She headed for the door and pulled it open.

"Can I have some juice? If that's OK?"

"It's OK," Sophie said.

In the doorway she bumped into the man who had introduced himself as Hector's cousin. He wasn't like Hector—thin but muscular, black-haired, taller than average, with alert blue eyes that seemed to notice everything going on around him. The cousin nodded to her curtly. He said something to Hector in Spanish, Hector said something back, and they both started to laugh. Sophie got the feeling that she was part of the joke, and forgot about the juice.

Gunilla Strandberg was sitting in the corridor holding a bunch of flowers, watching the nurse come out of Hector Guzman's room. Gunilla studied her as she came toward her. Was that happiness she could see? The sort of happiness that a person doesn't themselves know about? The woman went past her. On her left breast pocket was the little pin that showed that she was a "Sophia Sister"—a graduate of Sophiahemmet University College. Beside the pin was a name badge. Gunilla had time to make out the name *Sophie*.

She watched Sophie go. The woman's face was beautiful. Beautiful in the way that privilege bestowed: narrow, discreet... and fresh. The nurse moved easily, as if she let each foot merely graze the floor before taking the next step. It was an attractive way of walking, Gunilla thought. She watched until Sophie disappeared into another patient's room.

Gunilla was left thinking, her thoughts based on emotional equations. She looked once more in the direction where Sophie had just disappeared, then toward Room 11, in which Hector Guzman lay. There was something there. An energy... an emphasized form of something invisible to the naked eye. Something that woman, Sophie, had brought out of the room with her.

Gunilla got up and walked down the corridor, then peered into the staff room. It was empty. The week's roster was on the wall. She looked around the corridor before going in, then went over to the roster and ran her finger down it as she checked the names.

Helena...

Roger...

Anne...

Carro...

Nicke...

Sophie... *Sophie Brinkmann,* she read.

Stuffing the bunch of flowers in an empty vase on a portable table, she left the ward. In the elevator she pulled out her cell, called the office, and asked for an address for a Sophie Brinkmann.

Instead of heading back to the station on Brahegatan, she drove over the highway from Danderyd Hospital and turned off into the villas of Stocksund. She got lost in the maze of little roads that seemed actively to want to stop her from reaching her destination, and ended up driving around in circles. It felt like she was driving up and down hills at random, until eventually she found the right road. She checked the house number and pulled up outside a small, yellow wooden villa with white detailing.

She sat for a while behind the wheel, looking around. It was a quiet area, leafy, birch trees about to flower. Gunilla got out of the car and the scent of bird cherry hit her. She did a full turn, looking at the neighboring houses. Then she looked at Sophie's house. It was beautiful, smaller than its neighbors, and she got the impression that it was less tidy than the others. She turned around again, comparing them. No, Sophie Brinkmann's house wasn't untidy, it was normal. It was the neighboring houses that were odd: a sort of perfectionism—dull, soulless order. Sophie's house again: more *alive*; the woodwork hadn't just been painted, the grass hadn't just been cut, the gravel path hadn't just been raked, the windows hadn't just been cleaned.

Gunilla took a few tentative steps through the gate and walked carefully up the gravel path. She peered in through the kitchen window facing the road. What she could see of the kitchen looked tasteful. Old and new styles in an attractive combination; lovely brass faucets, an Aga stove, an old oak counter. A ceiling lamp that was so lovely, so unusual and well-chosen, that for a moment Gunilla felt a pang of envy. She went on looking, her gaze settling on the cut flowers in a large vase in the hall window. She backed away and looked up. She could see another beautiful arrangement on one of the upstairs windowsills.

In the car on the way back to the city her brain started working at high speed.

2

Leszek Smialy felt like a dog, a dog with no master. He got anxious when he wasn't close to his master. But Adalberto Guzman had told Leszek to go, had told him what to do. Leszek had gotten on the plane and landed a few hours later in Munich.

He hadn't left Guzman's side for ten years, apart from one week every third month. His life was made up of three-month shifts, work followed by a week off. During those weeks he usually booked himself into a hotel, stayed in his room, and drank himself into a stupor, day and night alike. When he wasn't too drunk or sleeping he would watch television. He didn't know any better. He just waited for the week to be over so he could get back to work again. Leszek never understood why Guzman insisted on making him take the time off.

He had just concluded one such week. The first days back after his vacation he had been unfocused and shaky from the hangover, and had cured it with exercise and eating properly, and now he felt like he was on his way back up again.

Leszek was sitting behind the wheel of a stolen Ford Focus in the fashionable town of Grünwald, outside Munich. Large villas in big, enclosed gardens, not many signs of life anywhere.

Guzman had given Leszek some photographs of Christian Hanke, twenty-five years old, good-looking, short dark hair. Also in the enlarged black-and-white photographs was his father, Ralph Hanke. Leszek thought they looked nice: successful smiles, tailored suits, and neat haircuts.

He had been watching the young man through his binoculars but hadn't been able to build up a clear picture of him, except that he came home at around eight o'clock in the evening, parking his BMW on the road outside the villa. He had female company, a housekeeper, and the light in his bedroom was on until two o'clock in the morning. Then, at half past seven the following morning, he walked from the front door down to the iron gate in the wall, crossed the road to his car, and drove off into Munich. That was all Leszek had to go on, that was what he had seen during twenty-four hours of surveillance.

The car radio was playing southern German Europop. Some guy was singing, through a broad smile, it sounded like, and there were electronic strings in the background, a predictable melody. Leszek picked up words like "mountaintop," "family ties," and "edelweiss." There was something sick about this country that he could never quite put his finger on.

He sat there with his hands in his lap, breathing calmly. It was a beautiful morning, mist in the air. The sun's rays were shining through the foliage, casting a yellowish glow over the scene. He thought it was beautiful, almost painfully beautiful.

He looked down at his hands, they were dirty. Installing the bomb had been a messy job. He'd done it before, a long time ago during his years in the security service. It had been easier then, less time consuming, easier to get at compared to today's modern, self-contained engines. He stretched and shut his eyes for a moment.

When he opened them again he could just make out the shape of someone coming out of Christian's house, behind the trees, down toward the road. Leszek tried to make out who it was. He grabbed the Swarovski binoculars from the passenger seat and raised them to his eyes. The person behind the trees was a woman, a fairly young woman. Leszek glanced at his watch: quarter to eight. The woman opened the iron gate in the wall and stepped out into the road. Leszek found the focus with his index finger. She was blond, maybe twenty years old, maybe twenty-five, with long hair, large, dark sunglasses, ripped designer jeans, and high-heeled boots, and she was walking toward the car, a handbag over her shoulder. She looked expensive. Leszek quickly trained the binoculars on the house. Where the hell was Christian? He looked back at the woman, who was crossing the road toward the BMW. Instead of getting in the passenger side she opened the driver's door and slid in easily behind the wheel, putting her handbag on the passenger seat. Leszek turned the binoculars toward the house again, no sign of Christian Hanke anywhere.

The seconds that followed ticked past slowly. Leszek felt an urge to blow his horn, open the door and wave at her, get her attention by doing something dramatic, something odd. But instead he just sat there, aware of how pointless it would be to try to change an already predetermined course of events. With his field of vision enlarged ten times through the lenses of the binoculars, with the smarmy German's voice singing in the background, he watched as the beautiful fair-haired woman did that little thing you do when you start a car, one hand on the wheel, leaning forward slightly to turn the key.

In the millisecond that the electricity traveled from the battery to the starter motor, an electrical wire captured it along the way and ignited a detonator, which in turn set off the explosives fastened beneath the car.

The force of the blast threw the woman up against the roof and broke her neck as the car lifted almost two feet off the ground. And at that moment the container full of napalm that he had fixed inside the car ignited and transformed the twisted wreckage into a blazing inferno.

Leszek watched through his binoculars as the woman caught fire. Sitting there completely still, burning inside the wreckage. How her beautiful hair disappeared, how her lovely fair skin disappeared... How her whole being slowly disappeared.

Leszek made his way out of Grünwald, found a deserted spot in the forest where he could set fire to the stolen car. Then he made his way into Munich and called Guzman, leaving a short message to say that it hadn't gone according to plan, that Guzman should stay alert and have friends at his side. He dumped the phone in a drain in the street, then meandered aimlessly around the city for a while to reassure himself that he wasn't being followed.

When he felt safe, he flagged down a taxi and went to the airport. A few hours later he was on his way back home to his master again.

From the day he first arrived, Hector had asked Sophie questions, about her life, her childhood, her teenage years. About her family, what she liked, what she didn't like. She found herself answering all his questions honestly. She liked being the focus of his attention and in spite of the flood of questions she had never felt that he was being intrusive. When he got too close to something she didn't want to talk about, he stopped, as if he understood where her boundaries lay. But the more they got to know each other, the shier he became with her. Anything medical that was too intimate had to be dealt with by one of her colleagues. Which meant that Sophie didn't have much reason to go into his room. She had to sneak in to see him, pretending to work.

He asked if she was tired.

"What do you mean?"

"You look tired."

Sophie folded a towel. "You certainly know how to flatter a woman."

He smiled.

"I don't think you're going to be here much longer," she went on.

He raised an eyebrow.

"Well, I'm not supposed to say things like that, of course, that's up to the doctors.... But I just did."

Sophie opened a window, letting the air in, then went over to him, gesturing with her hand that he should sit up, pulling out the pillow from behind his head and replacing it with a fresh one. She made her duties in his room look like routine, tidying up, airing, making sure his notes were in place before the doctor's round. She could tell from the corner of her eye that he was watching her. She went over to his bedside table, was about to pick up the empty water jug when he suddenly caught hold of her hand. Her reaction should have been to pull it away and walk out. But instead she left it where it was. Her heart was pounding. They stayed like that, as if they were two shy teenagers touching each other for the first time, not even looking at each other. Then she pulled away and went over toward the door.

"Was there anything you wanted?" she asked. Her voice was thick, as if she'd just woken up. Hector looked at her, then shook his head.

She wanted to tell herself that he wasn't her type, but who was? She'd liked so many different types over the years, and there hadn't been many similarities among them. She persuaded herself that it wasn't a physical attraction, he was just someone she liked being around. Not as a father figure, not as a lover, not as a husband, not as a friend, but somehow all of those mixed together.

She spent the rest of the day working down in the ER. When she came back to the ward later that afternoon Hector and his belongings were gone from Room 11.

Everything had gone completely to hell. The evening had deteriorated just as he had predicted. The Russians had started shooting after spending their minutes with the poor Paraguayan whores. They were wired, shooting the automatic weapons uncontrollably. Bullets flew in all directions. Jens had been forced to punch Vitaly. Dmitry and the other one were killing themselves laughing.

The next morning they met up again in the hut and went through all the preparations one more time. Delivery date, logistics, and payment. The Russians didn't seem bothered. Dmitry offered him some coke and asked if Jens would like to go to a cockfight with them. Jens declined and said good-bye to the Russians.

He got a lift back to Ciudad del Este from one of the Paraguayans. The drive took two hours. They bounced along on poor roads. The seat had no cushion. The man driving was taciturn, and, as always in this country: the ever-present radio. Always poor reception, turned up too high, with an annoyingly shrill treble that in this instance howled from two speakers in the thin doors of the car. It was OK,

Jens was used to it. He had time to go through his plans. It felt good, not perfect, but good—as was usually the case. He couldn't remember the last time it had felt perfect.

He wasn't quite forty yet. Six-foot-two, blond, thickset with a weather-bitten appearance and a dark, low voice that was the result of premature puberty together with a vast number of cigarettes over the years. His way of moving was heavy rather than agile, and he seldom said no to anything, which was clear from the look in his eyes; a curiosity that shone through the creases of age that were starting to show.

The automatic weapons the Russians had bought from him would be transported by truck from Ciudad del Este, east to the port of Paranaguá, in Brazil, where they would be loaded onto a ship and taken across the Atlantic, then unloaded in Rotterdam. From there they would be driven to Warsaw, and Jens's work would be done.

The business with the guns had begun two months before. Risto had called from Moscow to say that he had been asked for MP7s, and something more powerful.

"How many?"

"Ten of each."

"That's not much."

"No, but this is an ambitious group. They'll be needing more help from you in the future. Try to look at it like that."

It was a small job, ought to be fairly easy to put together.

"OK . . . I'll have a look 'round and get back to you."

He contacted the Dealer. The Dealer was anonymous down to his very marrow, he had a website about model airplanes where you could contact him by typing a password on the site's discussion forum. He was an expensive but reliable resource who thus far had never said no or failed to fulfill any of Jens's requirements. The Dealer organized the deals with a seller whom Jens didn't know. That way there were no leaks, and no one could rat on anyone else. Jens asked for MP7s and Steyr AUGs—a not-too-old-fashioned Austrian submachine gun. The Dealer had gotten back to him, saying yes to the Steyr AUGs and no to the MP7s, but said the seller could offer MP5s instead. Risto's clients had been clear, they wanted MP7s. And as usual the matter had resolved itself, almost. A full set of the Austrian guns plus eight MP7s and two MP5s. Good enough, Jens thought.

Risto had told him to go to Prague and meet the clients. Jens was taken aback.

"What for?"

"No idea. It's just what they want," Risto replied.

The meeting in Prague had turned out to be pointless. The only reason for it was so they could get a sense of who he was, he realized. Dmitry, Gosha, and Vitaly behaved as if they were stuck in some sort of malevolent adolescence.

They drank vodka in Jens's hotel room in Malá Strana. Vitaly pulled off the bathroom mirror and laid it on the coffee table, then cut out a load of fat lines with a badly worn Diners card with its laminate hanging off. Then came the hookers—several far too young—spaced-out girls from some former Soviet republic. Dmitry wanted to take everyone to dinner. They went to a modern, soulless place on Václav Square. Chrome, leather, and molded plastic décor. The hookers were strung out on heroin; one of them kept picking at a tooth at the back of her mouth, another kept rubbing her cheek with her index finger, and the third was scratching her lower arm far too hard. Dmitry bought Champagne for them all, and ended up having a pointless argument with Gosha. Jens realized that he had nothing in common with Dmitry. He snuck out and went to the Roxy, a nightclub on Dlouha. He sat there drinking and watching people dance until the sun came up.

The next day Dmitry and his hollow-eyed gang came to his hotel again and suggested they take some LSD and go and watch a football match between Sparta Prague and Zenit St. Petersburg, who were in town for the game. Jens said that sadly he couldn't go, he had to head home early. They laughed mirthlessly, as usual, took their drugs in his hotel room, came up on the drugs and messed about with him for a while, then went off yelling and brandishing a fire extinguisher they'd pulled from the wall in the corridor.

Jens took an earlier flight back to Stockholm.

When Jens got back to his apartment he had a message: *Buenos Aires in two days*. He repacked his bag, slept badly, then went back to Arlanda Airport the next morning and flew to Buenos Aires via Paris. He landed at Ezeiza, slept a few hours at his hotel, ate lunch with a self-satisfied idiot of a courier. Jens paid off the courier, who handed him a set of car keys and told him that there was a van waiting in the hotel garage. He checked the boxes in the back of the van, the weapons were there, everything was going according to plan.

He was feeling tired and decided to stay an extra day before driving the goods to Paraguay. He went to a boxing match, but the fight disintegrated and ended up more like a case of grievous bodily harm than a fair contest. Jens stood up and walked out before the referee stopped it. Instead he spent the afternoon looking at tourist attractions. He wanted to feel normal but realized almost immediately how dull that was.

He found a decent restaurant, had a good meal, and read a copy of *USA Today* that he had taken with him from the hotel.

At first he didn't react to his name. But when he looked up he recognized Jane at once, Sophie Lantz's younger sister, as she stood there beside his table. She looked just the same as the last time he had seen her, when she had been just a child.

"Jens?...Jens Vall! What are you doing here?"

Jane's smile turned to laughter. He stood up, infected by her laughter as they hugged each other.

"Hello, Jane."

The silent man standing behind her was named Jesus. He didn't introduce himself, Jane did. They sat down at his table and Jane started talking before her backside hit the seat. Jens listened and laughed in turn, realizing early on why she had picked a silent type like Jesus. She told him that she and Jesus were in Buenos Aires to visit his relatives, that they didn't have any children, and that they lived in a three-room apartment near Järntorget in Stockholm's old town.

He asked after Sophie and was given superficial information about her life: that she was now Sophie Brinkmann, that she was now a widow, had one son, and worked as a nurse. Jane realized that she'd come to a halt and started asking questions back. Jens lied with an honest face—said he was a fertilizer salesman, that he had to do a lot of traveling for his work, that he didn't have a family yet but maybe that would change in the future.

They ate and drank late into the evening. Jesus and Jane took him to places in the city that he would never have found on his own. He saw the real face of the city and liked it even more.

Jesus's silence remained unbroken all evening.

"Is he mute?" Jens asked, entirely reasonably.

"Sometimes he talks," she said.

The next morning, in the taxi back to the hotel, he felt melancholic. Melancholic at that moment because of his past. He slept badly that night.

The car lurched toward Ciudad del Este. He could see the city in the distance and was relieved to be rid of the Russians. He would make the preparations necessary before departure, then the cargo could be loaded into the truck.

—

There was a message waiting for Sophie in the staff room. A small, white, stiff envelope with her first name written on the front in black ink. She opened it while she waited for the coffee machine, read it quickly, and then put it in her pocket.

She carried on with her duties all morning, hoping she would forget what she had just read. She couldn't. At a quarter to twelve she went into the changing room, took off her nurse's uniform, grabbed her handbag and summer jacket, and went down to the entrance hall.

The cousin was waiting for her, nodding to indicate that she should follow him outside. She did so, feeling somehow rather uncertain, as if something inside her was telling her that this was the wrong decision. But behind any notion of uncertainty was a delight in doing something spontaneous and not thought through. It had been a while.

The car was new—one of those environmental Japanese cars. There was nothing special about it, it was just new. It smelled new and was comfortable to sit in.

"We're heading for Vasastan," he said.

She met his gaze in the rearview mirror. His eyes were blue, clear, and intense.

"You're cousins, aren't you? On which side?"

"All possible sides."

She laughed. "Really? How do you mean?"

"All possible sides."

He sounded as if that were his final word on the subject.

"My name's Aron. . . ."

"Hello, Aron," she said.

They sat in silence the rest of the way into the city.

Tables, chairs, and a swing door leading to a kitchen. The lighting was too bright, there were landscape prints on the walls, and there were checkered paper napkins. A standard lunch restaurant, nothing more.

She found herself smiling when Hector waved to her from a table toward the rear of the room, and she tried to erase the smile as she made her way through the tables toward him.

He stood up and pulled out a chair for her.

"I would have picked you up myself if it wasn't for my leg."

Sophie sat down. "It was fine, Aron was good company, if a little quiet. . . ."

He smiled.

"You came," he said.

He slid a laminated menu toward her.

"We never said good-bye," Hector went on.

"No, we didn't."

His tone of voice changed. "I come here for the shellfish. The best in the city, but hardly anyone knows about it."

"Then that's what I'll have."

She didn't touch the menu, kept her hands in her lap. He made an almost invisible nod to someone standing behind the bar.

Meeting Hector outside the hospital was different. She had a giddy sense that she was about to eat lunch with someone she really didn't know at all. But he noticed her uncertainty and started talking, telling little anecdotes about what it was like to have your leg in a cast in Stockholm, about the process of slicing up your favorite trousers, and how much he missed the hospital food and instant mashed potatoes. He was good at seeing the funny side of everyday life, turning a strained situation into something light and entertaining.

She listened to him with half an ear. She liked the way he looked, and her gaze kept getting caught by his alert eyes, which seemed to be two different colors. The right one was dark blue, the left dark brown. In a certain light the color of his eyes seemed sharper, as if he became a different person for a while.

"So is it empty without me at the hospital?" he asked.

Sophie laughed and shook her head.

"No, it's the same as usual."

A waitress brought over two glasses of wine.

"Spanish white. Not our finest achievement... but perfectly palatable."

He raised his glass in a relaxed toast. She left the wine where it was, picking up the water glass instead and taking a sip, then she did the Swedish thing of tilting her glass slightly and seeking eye contact with him. He didn't notice, had already looked away. She felt foolish.

Hector leaned back, inspecting her calmly and confidently, then opened his mouth to say something. A fleeting thought seemed to stop him. He was left searching for words.

"What?" she wondered with a little laugh.

He shifted on his chair. "I don't know... I don't recognize you.... You're different."

"In what way?"

He looked at her.

"I don't know, just different. Maybe because you're not in your nurse's uniform?"

"Would you prefer that?"

Her words seemed to embarrass him, which amused her.

"But you do recognize me? You know who I am?"

"I'm starting to wonder," he said.

"About what?"

"Who you are..."

"You know who I am."

He shook his head. "Well, I know a bit... but not everything."

"Why would you want to know everything?"

He stopped himself. "Sorry, I didn't mean to be intrusive."

"You're not intrusive."

"I think I probably am...."

"How do you mean?"

Hector shrugged. "Sometimes I'm in a hurry to get what I want. That can make me a bit pushy. But let's not talk about that. Instead I'd like us to carry on where we left off."

She wasn't quite with him. "Where did we leave off?"

The food arrived, and plates were put in front of them. Hector set about the shellfish with his fingers, peeling them with a practiced hand.

"Your dad had passed away, and you spent a few years being lonely and sad. . . . Then your mom met Tom and you moved into his house. Wasn't that it?"

At first she didn't get it, then it struck her that his questions while he was in the hospital had been about her life, from childhood onward. She had told him everything chronologically, or rather he had asked his questions chronologically. She was surprised she hadn't realized before.

He met her eyes as if to say go on. Sophie thought, searching her memory, then picked up the story where she had left off. How she and her sister had felt brighter as time passed after their father's death. How they had moved into Tom's villa with their mother, just a few minutes away from their childhood home. How she started smoking Marlboro Lights in year nine, how life seemed brighter.

They ate oysters, saltwater crayfish, lobster. Sophie kept on talking. Told him about her exchange trip to the United States, her first job, her travels through Asia, how hard she found it to understand love when she was young, and the lingering anxiety of growing up—a feeling that had clung to her long into her thirties. She picked at the food, absorbed in her own story. The time passed and she realized that she had been talking nonstop without giving him any chance to interrupt. She asked if she was talking too much, boring him? He shook his head.

"Go on," he said.

"I met David. We got married, had Albert, and suddenly the years ran away with us. I don't really remember that well."

With that she didn't want to go on, it felt uncomfortable.

"What don't you remember?"

Sophie picked at her plate.

"Some periods in your life seem to blend, merge together."

"How do you mean?"

"I don't know."

"Yes, you do." He smiled.

She poked at her plate with her fork.

"Passiveness," she said quietly.

The word seemed to make him even more curious.

"In what way?"

She looked up. "What?"

"Passive, how?"

She emptied her glass, thinking about his question, then shrugged.

"The way most moms are, I guess. Children, loneliness. David worked, traveled a lot. I stayed at home. . . . Nothing happened."

She could tell what her face looked like, she could feel the furrow in her brow and straightened herself out and tried to smile. Before he had time to ask another question she went on.

"The years passed and David got ill, and you know the rest."

"Tell me."

"He died," she said.

"I know. But what happened?"

This time he didn't seem to pick up on her boundary.

"There's not much to say, he was diagnosed with cancer. Two years later he passed away."

The way she said this last sentence stopped him from milking the subject further. They ate in silence. After a while things picked up again in the same way. He asked more questions, she replied, but resisted saying too much. When she found a suitable opportunity she glanced at her wristwatch. He picked up the hint. To hide it, Hector looked at his own watch.

"Time's flying," he said neutrally.

Maybe he realized there and then that he had been too inquisitive, too pushy. He seemed to be in a hurry, folding his napkin and becoming impersonal.

"Would you like Aron to drive you back?"

"No, thanks."

Hector stood up first.

She leaned her head against the window of the underground railcar, staring out into the darkness at the vague shapes flying past before her unseeing eyes.

He wasn't pushy. He just seemed to be trying to understand who she was in relation to him. And she recognized it; she was the same, she mirrored herself in others, wanted to know, to understand. But the similarities alarmed her as well. She had probably always been a bit scared in his company. Not of him, but maybe of something he radiated, something he did to her.

Loneliness was simple and monotonous. She was all too familiar with it, had hidden herself away in it for an eternity by now. And every time anyone got close to her, suggesting that her self-imposed isolation wasn't solid or absolute, she took a step back, pulled away.... But it was different this time. Hector's appearance in her life meant something....

Suddenly there was blinding light. The underground train was rushing over the bridge between Bergshamra and Danderyd Hospital, the sun's rays bombarding the railcar. She was roused from her thoughts, got up, and went to stand by the doors, holding on to keep her balance as the train pulled into the station.

Sophie went up to the hospital and changed back into her nurse's uniform. She worked to keep her thoughts at bay. She didn't have a favorite patient on the ward, and hoped that one would soon turn up.

3

Lars Vinge called Gunilla Strandberg. As usual, she didn't pick up, so he hung up. His cell rang forty seconds later.

"Hello?"

"Yes?" Gunilla Strandberg asked.

"I just called you," he said.

A moment's silence. "Yes . . . ?"

Lars cleared his throat.

"The accomplice picked up the nurse."

"And?"

"He drove her to a restaurant, where she had lunch with Guzman."

"Pull back and come in," she said, and hung up.

Lars Vinge had been watching Hector Guzman and Aron Geisler on and off since Hector was discharged from the hospital.

It had been a slow job, nothing to report. He thought someone else could have done this. Considered himself overqualified. He was an analytical person, and that was why he had been recruited. At least that's what Gunilla had said when she offered him the job two months before. Now he was spending days on end sitting in a car while the rest of the team was busy with the background analysis, potential scenarios, and theoretical approaches.

Lars had been in the police twelve years before Gunilla contacted him. He had been a beat cop in the Western District, where he had been trying to find ways to defuse ethnic tensions. He felt isolated in his work. His colleagues didn't show the same sense of social engagement as he did. Unbidden, Lars wrote an analysis of the area's problems. The report hadn't exactly made much of an impact or received any great recognition, and, if he was being honest, he had written it mainly to stand out from the rest of his factory-farmed colleagues. That was how he perceived the majority of his male colleagues, factory-farmed: their upper arms were too big, their faces too heavy, they were pretty solid, pretty dense, too dim for his liking. And they for their part didn't like him much either; he wasn't considered one of them, he knew that. Within the force, Lars Vinge wasn't the man you wanted as your partner. He was cautious when they were out at night, when things got violent he pulled back and let the big gorillas go in and take charge. He was always getting teased about that in the changing room.

He looked in the mirror one morning and realized how childish he looked. Lars tried to solve it with a new hairstyle, water-combed with a part. He thought it made him look a bit more substantial. His colleagues started calling him Sturmbannführer Lars. That was better than Little Cunt or Front Bottom, the things they used to call him. As usual, he pretended not to hear.

Lars Vinge did his work as best he could, avoiding violent crime and night duty, trying to win the approval of his superiors, trying to make small talk with his colleagues. Nothing went his way, everyone avoided him. Lars ended up having trouble sleeping and developed eczema around his nose.

Two years after his report on local tensions was finished, and probably archived and forgotten somewhere, a woman from National Crime called and introduced herself as Gunilla Strandberg. He didn't think she sounded much like a police officer, and she didn't look like one either when they met for lunch in Kungsträdgården. She was in her mid-fifties and had short black hair with a scattering of gray, beautiful brown eyes, smooth, healthy skin. That was the first thing that struck him, her skin. She looked younger than her years, healthier somehow. Gunilla Strandberg made a calm, stern impression, lightened every now and then with a little smile. The calm that she radiated seemed to be based on circumspection, together with a sort of reflection upon everything that happened. Something she seemed to have actively chosen over impulse and spontaneity. She behaved maturely, like someone who had learned that things could go wrong just because they happened too fast. And all of this was illuminated by a deep intelligence; she was smart and knowledgeable and seldom indulged herself with either exaggeration or understatement. She saw the world in a clear, uncluttered way. He felt *smaller* than her, but it didn't matter, that was just how it was—it felt natural.

She had told him about the working group she had been asked to put together, a sort of pilot project in the fight against organized crime, primarily international, and that they were being given precedence by the prosecutor's office to bring things to resolution. She said she had read his report and had found it interesting. Lars had tried to conceal the pride welling up inside him. He had accepted the job before she finished explaining to him what it would involve.

Two weeks later he was transferred from the factory-farm team in the Western District to the more analytical group in Östermalm. He stepped out of his uniform and became a plainclothes officer at the age of thirty-six, got a raise, and was struck by the realization that this was how he had always imagined his career in the force—that someone would recognize and appreciate his talents and skills, which he himself felt stood out in comparison to all the other officers'.

After shadowing Aron and Hector for a while without any results, the turning point had arrived, as Gunilla had predicted: she had said the nurse would pop up and become one of the focal points of the investigation. He had forgotten her prediction, but that morning as he watched from a distance as Aron held the car door open for the nurse outside the hospital, he realized once again just how good Gunilla was.

He parked outside the local police station on Brahegatan. He made his way through the station, nodding to fellow cops whose names he didn't know, until he came to the tower block behind the single-story police station.

Three rooms in a row, an office like any other; standard-issue municipal furniture, box files on pale pine bookshelves, uninspiring pieces of art on the walls and windowsills; long, striped curtains that must have been there since the mid-'90s.

Eva Castroneves nodded to him as she went past. She was typing on her cell with one hand and had a sandwich in the other. She was always on the move, always going somewhere, moving quicker than everyone else. Lars nodded back, she didn't see. He went in; Gunilla and Erik were in the room, Gunilla at her desk with the phone to her ear. Erik, her brother, his face blood-pressure red as usual, was transferring the chewing tobacco from the little plastic tub it came in into his own brass one with a Viking motif on the lid. Erik Strandberg lived off nicotine, caffeine, and fast food. He made a rather slovenly impression with his scruffy beard and unkempt gray hair. He was a loudmouth and always managed to give the impression that he was a bully, which Lars guessed was the result of misdirected youthful self-confidence that no one had put a stop to early enough. But there was a side to him that Lars appreciated; Erik had welcomed him in a friendly and natural way when Lars started working with them. He didn't seem to judge Lars in any way at all, just took him as he was. That wasn't his usual experience.

Erik brushed the tobacco from his hands, looked Lars in the eye, and nodded, then reached for a Danish pastry from a plate on the desk.

"All right?" he rumbled.

"All right?" Lars whispered.

"Well, shit," Erik said.

"Yes, you could say that," Lars replied, sitting down on the next chair.

"Your call cheered her up."

Erik took a bite of the Danish, opened a file that was on his lap, and started to read.

"Sorry, just have to read this."

"Of course," Lars said, getting up a bit too quickly.

Erik went on chewing behind his beard. "No, stay, for God's sake."

"No, no," Lars said, and went away with a somewhat forced steadiness in his walk.

Lars hated his insecurity, always had. He had a sort of innate sense of awkwardness that seemed to govern everything he did in life. It had now grown into him in some unjust way. He felt it in the way he moved his body, in the whole of his being. From the outside he ought to have been attractive—his fair hair, ice-blue eyes, relatively chiseled facial features—but his insecurity overshadowed all that. In a picture taken from the right angle he could look reasonably OK, but in person he just looked awkward.

Lars went over to the nearest of the room's three large movable bulletin boards. He did that sometimes when he came into the office, mostly to avoid having to stand in a corner looking stupid. He could kill time this way.

The Guzman board was covered with a mass of photographs and findings from the investigation. He stared for a while at photocopies of passports, birth certificates, and documents from the Spanish authorities, looking at photographs of Aron Geisler and Hector Guzman fastened to the right-hand side. Below Hector's there were photographs of his brother and sister, Eduardo and Inez, as well as an old picture from the late '70s of their mother, Pia, originally from Flemingsberg. She was pretty, blond. She looked like she was straight out of a shampoo ad Lars had seen at the cinema when he was young.

A red line connected Hector to two other black-and-white photographs on the left-hand side of the board. Two men that Lars didn't recognize. One was a suntanned elderly gentleman with thin, slicked-back white hair—Adalberto Guzman, Hector's father. The second picture was an enlarged passport photograph of a man with short hair and hollow eyes—Leszek Smialy, Adalberto Guzman's bodyguard.

Lars read extracts from the summary of Smialy below the picture. Leszek Smialy had been in the security forces in Poland during the communist era. He'd had a number of different bodyguard jobs since the fall of the Soviet Union. Probably started working for Adalberto Guzman in the summer of 2001.

Lars moved on to Aron Geisler, and read the scant information about him. He attended the Östra Real Secondary School in Stockholm in the 1970s, was a member of Östermalm Chess Society in 1979. He spent three years doing military service in Israel during the

'80s.... He joined the Foreign Legion and had been part of the team that was first into Kuwait during the Gulf War. His parents lived in Stockholm until 1989, when they moved to Haifa. Aron Geisler spent parts of the 1990s in French Guyana. There were large gaps in the timeline.

He backed away from the bulletin board, trying to take in the big picture but understanding none of it. So instead he went to get himself a cup of coffee from the kitchen, pressing the buttons for sugar and milk, and a pale brown sludge trickled into a cup. When he came back into the room Gunilla hung up the phone. She raised her voice.

"Today at 12:08 Aron Geisler went and picked up the nurse and drove her to a lunch restaurant, Trasten, in Vasastan, where she spent an hour and twenty minutes having lunch with Hector Guzman."

Gunilla put on her reading glasses.

"Her name is Sophie Brinkmann, a registered nurse, widow, one son—Albert, fifteen years old. She goes to work, comes home from work, she cooks. That's pretty much all we know right now."

Gunilla took off her glasses and looked up.

"Eva, you look into her personal life, see if you can dig up friends, enemies, lovers... anything."

She turned to Lars. "Lars, drop Hector for now, and concentrate on the nurse."

Lars nodded, took a sip from the cup.

Gunilla smiled and looked around the group. "Sometimes God sends a little angel down to earth."

And with that the meeting was evidently over. Gunilla put her glasses back on and got back to work, Eva began typing on her computer, and Erik kept on reading the file as he tapped a blood-pressure tablet from a bottle of pills with a practiced hand.

Lars wasn't keeping up, he had a thousand and one questions. How did they want him to proceed? How much information did Gunilla want? How long should he work, evenings and nights? What did they do about overtime? What exactly did she want him to do? He didn't like having to make that sort of decision himself. He wanted clear guidelines to follow. But Gunilla wasn't that sort of boss, and he didn't want to draw attention to his uncertainty. He headed for the door.

"Lars. There are a few things I'd like you to take with you."

She pointed to a large box over by the wall. He went over and opened it. It contained an old Facit typewriter, a fax machine, a digital system camera—a Nikon with matching lenses of various sizes—and a small wooden box. Lars opened the lid of the little box and saw eight pin-button microphones resting in molded foam rubber.

"We're surely not going to bug her?" he said, then immediately regretted it.

"No, you just need to keep those handy. You can start using the camera right away, get photographs, keep an eye on her. We need to gather as much information as we can, as quickly as possible. Write up your reports on the typewriter and fax them to me. The fax is encrypted, you can just plug it into your normal phone jack at home."

Lars looked at the equipment, and Gunilla saw the quizzical look on his face.

"Everyone here writes their reports and evaluations on typewriters. We don't leave any digital fingerprints anywhere, we don't take any risks. Bear that in mind."

He looked her in the eye, gave a quick nod, then picked up the box and left the office.

Leszek came walking toward him, unwilling to look Guzman in the eye.

Adalberto Guzman, or Guzman el Bueno as he was sometimes known, had just emerged from the sea. There was a glass of freshly squeezed orange juice on a small table on the beach. A towel was folded over a chair, a dressing gown hanging over its back. He dried himself off, sat down, and drank the juice as he looked out across the sea.

As a child he used to swim alongside his mother as she swam in the same water he had just climbed out of. Every morning they would float there together. The swim remained the same, but the view from the return leg had changed over the years. In the early 1960s, around the time when he met the love of his life—a Swedish tour guide, Pia—he had bought all the available land around the villa, flattened the other houses, and planted cypress trees and olive groves. Now he owned the water he swam in and the beaches he landed on.

Guzman was seventy-three years old, a widower and father of two sons and a daughter. Over the past three decades he had donated vast sums to charity without having any business interest in them whatsoever. He had built up an organization that had made him a wealthy man. He was known for his generosity, for his concern for those who were less well off; he was a friend of the church and a regular celebrity guest on the local television cookery shows. He was Guzman el Bueno—Guzman the Good.

Guzman gave Leszek a brief pat on the arm when they met. Leszek allowed a suitable distance between him and Guzman before following him up toward the villa.

"Sometimes things go wrong, Leszek, my friend."

Leszek walked in silence.

"They got the message, didn't they?" he went on. Guzman started to climb the stone steps up to the villa.

"Not in the way we wanted," the Pole muttered.

"But they got the message, and you've come back unharmed, that's the most important thing."

Leszek didn't answer.

The large glass terrace door was open, and the white linen curtains inside were swaying in the breeze from the sea. They went inside the house, and Guzman took off the dressing gown as a servant came in with his clothes for the day. He got dressed, unembarrassed, in front of Leszek.

"I'm worried about the children," Guzman said, pulling on his beige trousers. "Hector's got Aron and can look after himself, but sort out security for Eduardo and Inez. If they make a fuss . . . well, they can't make a fuss."

Eduardo and Inez lived their own lives, far from Adalberto Guzman. He had practically no contact with them at all but always sent birthday presents—presents that were too large and far too expensive for his grandchildren's birthdays. Inez had told him to stop. Guzman took no notice.

On the other hand, Hector, his firstborn, had always been by his side. At the age of fifteen Hector had started to take an interest in his father's business. At eighteen he was running everything together with Adalberto. The first thing Hector did was to wind down the heroin trade between North Africa and Spain, seeing as the police had stepped up their efforts to stop drug trafficking. Instead he had devoted a lot of time and energy to building up a money-laundering operation. They laundered drug money, arms money, stolen money, anything that needed freshening up. It turned out to be almost as lucrative as bringing heroin into southern Europe. The Guzmans became renowned for being open to pretty much anything. During the '90s, when the United States started to take its war on drugs seriously, which raised the price of cocaine to an all-time high, there was no question of them sitting on the sidelines looking on.

They visited Don Ignacio in Valle del Cauca, in Colombia, to look into the possibility of setting up their own pipelines to Europe. Adalberto and Hector identified a few good smuggling routes, but it was difficult, expensive, and risky work. They switched pipelines a number of times and lost several shipments to both customs and theft. They gave up and let the idea drop. Adalberto and Hector's legal businesses started doing worse after the year 2000, and it took them a while to recover. But they were never quite able to drop the idea of how valuable a well-run cocaine pipeline could be. They tested a route between Paraguay and Rotterdam, a relatively secure line that turned out to be their best yet. They leaned back, earned a lot of money, and everything was fun again.

Then suddenly the Germans marched in and stole everything out from under their noses. Adalberto was reluctantly forced to admit that he had been caught napping. But his dealings with Ralph Hanke hadn't started there. They had encountered each other indirectly during negotiations surrounding the construction of a viaduct in Brussels some years earlier. Hanke tried to buy off everyone involved, he was desperate to win the contract. But Guzman got the contract as Hanke stumbled at the finish line. In itself it wasn't much of a contract, but the first time Hanke stole their cocaine Adalberto knew who he was dealing with: an idiot who had to win at any cost.

Setting up and maintaining the pipeline between Paraguay and Rotterdam had taken a lot of effort. Bribes, bribes, and more bribes, that was how you established a pipeline and kept it going. The money wasn't the problem, the hard part was finding people who were prepared to accept it. With time they had found good people who did what they were paid to do: customs officers, dockworkers, and a Vietnamese captain with his own ship—an old tub with a crew that he could vouch for. Everything had been relatively painless, and perhaps that was why Ralph Hanke one day stepped in and helped himself to everything. Hanke marched in and raised the price of every single person Guzman had bought off, threatened the courier who met the ship in Rotterdam, then took the goods and used his own network to distribute the cocaine throughout Europe.

Adalberto Guzman had received a letter by courier, handwritten. It was well formulated, polite, formal, on expensive ivory writing paper. He read between the lines that every attempt at confrontation would be met with violence. He sent a reply, also handwritten, but less formal and on slightly cheaper paper, informing them that he would recoup his losses, with interest. As a response to that letter, it was extremely likely that Hanke had dispatched someone to Stockholm to run Hector down on a pedestrian crossing. It had been hit-and-run, the Swedish police had been unable to trace the car.

Adalberto gave in to his first emotional instinct and sent Leszek to Munich to kill Hanke's son. But that hadn't gone according to plan. Maybe that was just as well, now that he came to think about it: at the moment it was a no-score draw. It could stay that way for a while.

There was the sound of small paws on the floor. His dog, Piño, a ball in his mouth, showing the same delight and enthusiasm that he always did. Piño was a stray who had turned up on his doorstep five years ago, wanting to come in. Adalberto had let the dog in, and since then they had been good friends.

Guzman el Bueno took the ball and threw it. The dog raced to fetch it, caught it, and ran back to his master. Always just as much fun.

If the peace held, he could concentrate on planning how to retake his pipeline, because there was no question that he was going to, and in some style.

The evening was still warm, the cicadas were loud, and a Paraguayan television show was echoing from somewhere nearby.

Jens was packing boxes in an old warehouse. He had dismantled the automatic rifles and put their bolts in a packing case with steel pipes of various shapes and sizes. He packed the butts between vacuum-packed watermelons.

The past few years had been hectic. He had spent time in Baghdad, Sierra Leone, Beirut, Afghanistan. It had been dangerous. He had been shot at, he had shot back, he had met people he never wanted to see again.

Jens had decided to take some time off after this job, go home, take it easy. He didn't usually accompany his goods, it was too risky. But this time he had decided to go along. He had booked passage for the goods from the Brazilian port on a Panamanian registered freighter that was heading for Rotterdam. The Vietnamese captain had his wits about him, said that another customer had already arranged for the unloading in Rotterdam to be risk-free, and that the price would take that into account. It would take two weeks to sail to Europe and he felt he needed to wind down a bit, get some rest—and even test his patience, see how bad his restlessness really was. The boat would give him no chance to escape. Which is what he usually did once he'd seen the same view twice.

He nailed the boxes shut, wrote fake customs declarations, and loaded the goods onto an old truck that would be taking him and the weapons to Paranaguá the following morning.

When everything was ready Jens went out into Ciudad del Este. It was total chaos. Filthy, noisy, crowded—and over everything there lay a thick stench that seemed to contain all the world's smells in one. So thick that it sometimes felt like the whole city was losing its oxygen. The poor ran barefoot, the rich had shoes, everyone wanted to sell, a few wanted to buy—Jens loved it there.

He kept himself awake with drink and some female tourists from New Zealand in a local bar but soon grew tired of their company. He crept away to another bar. There he found a dark corner and drank alone until he was very drunk.

The drive to Paranaguá the next day was an eleven-hour nightmare. His hangover kept him awake, and the driver shouted and blew his horn all the way to Brazil.

The ship was an old hulk from the '50s, blue in the places where the color was still visible. It was some two hundred feet long, with diesel engines whose throbbing could be heard through the whole of the hull and right up to the quayside where he was standing looking at it. It was steered from the bridge, which was toward the stern of the vessel. Half the deck was open. Some shipping containers had been lashed down in the middle of it all. Then boxes, crates, and other half-successful attempts at packaging. It was a freighter whose best days were behind it—no more, no less.

Jens went aboard via a rickety gangplank and looked around when he reached the deck. The ship felt larger up there.

He found his cabin after wandering about for a while. It was more like a cell. Just wide enough for him to get inside without having to turn sideways. A narrow bed fixed to the wall, a small cupboard, and nothing else. But he was happy with it. Partly because the cabin had a window and lay above the waterline, but mainly because he didn't have to share it with anyone.

He stood at the railing as the ship pulled out. The sun was over the horizon as Jens watched the container port of Paranaguá disappear into the distance.

Lars Vinge was finding the days long and dull. He had photographed Sophie as she cycled home from work. He had sat glowering somewhere nearby, trying to pass the time; he had taken a walk under cover of darkness, then took a few grainy pictures of her as she passed a window inside the house. He had followed Sophie and her son, Albert, as they drove into the city and went into a bar and then a cinema. Then two days when she ate dinner alone. Why he was doing this was a mystery to him, it felt utterly pointless.

Lars was getting tired and cross, and because he didn't have anyone he could share it with he kept going over it, again and again, as he always did.

The evening before he had written a report for Gunilla about Sophie's activities and had concluded it with a sentence in which he suggested the surveillance be suspended.

Lars's partner, Sara, was sitting in the living room of his apartment watching a television program about environmental destruction. She was upset, some professor in England had said everything was going to hell. Lars was leaning on the doorpost watching the program. Statistics and convincing arguments from well-educated people scared him.

His cell received a text message and he read it on the screen. Gunilla wrote that he was important and valuable to the investigation, and that he couldn't end the surveillance yet. She had ended the text with the word "Hugs."

Even though Lars realized that her flattery was a ploy to get him back in line again, he couldn't help feeling a bit more cheerful. He made up his mind to carry on doing his job. In time he'd get other things to do, in time Gunilla would give him better duties, she'd promised him that—duties that better reflected his intellect than sitting in a car all day and all night watching a nurse who seemed to live an unusually routine-bound existence. Then he would understand what he was doing, then the others in the group would realize that he was unbeatable in his work.

He sat down on the sofa beside Sara and watched the end of the program, which explained that it was partly his fault that the world would soon be coming to an end. He felt a pang of guilt and grew as annoyed as Sara at the information the reporter was presenting. Sara said she was thinking of not flying anymore, that she'd travel by train from now on…if they ever went abroad. Lars nodded, he felt the same way.

"I've got to go back to work later this evening. Shall we go and lie down for a bit?"

She shook her head, her eyes glued to the television.

At half past seven that evening he parked the Volvo a short distance from Sophie's villa and took a stroll along the roads around her house, trying to find a way of getting closer. As usual, he saw nothing that struck him as odd, and he returned to his car. He sat there for a while, staring out into space, then went for a drive, making sure he knew the neighborhood for the tenth time. Then he parked in a different place, took a few indistinct pictures of her house, made a note of something that didn't need noting. At nine o'clock Lars sighed to himself once more, started the car, and decided to swing past the house one last time before heading home.

He passed the villa just as Sophie emerged and walked over to a taxi that was waiting outside her gate. She was wearing a thin, unbuttoned coat, an evening bag in her hand, and she got in the back of the taxi and it drove off.

He had watched her for a few short seconds as he passed by in the car. Time had felt stretched, slower—as if everything had stopped for a while. In those short moments he had experienced her as something perfect, something ideal. Lars was struck by a strong impression that he knew her, that she knew him. He shook off the peculiar feeling, turned the car around farther down the road, and followed the taxi.

Lars maintained a safe distance, nervousness throbbing inside him, and he wanted to pee, as if the two things were connected in some unfair way. He never let the taxi out of his sight as it passed Roslagstull and went on down Birger Jarlsgatan before turning left onto Karlavägen, past Humlegården Park. Eventually it pulled up on Sibyllegatan. He cruised past as she got out of the taxi, and watched her in the rearview mirror as she disappeared through a doorway.

Lars parked farther down the street in the bus lane and waited for a minute before jumping out of the car.

He shone his pocket flashlight through the door and wrote down all the names on the board inside the hall.

It was eleven o'clock before she came out with a female friend. They walked arm in arm toward Östermalmstorg, laughing; her friend eventually had to stop and lean over in a fit of giggles. Lars stared for a while, then left his car and followed them on foot.

Sophie and her friend went to three different places that evening. Lars was denied entry to two of them and had to show his police ID.

Sophie and her friend were sitting at the bar. Several times men of various ages went up and tried to talk to them, but the women showed no interest. Lars was standing farther along the bar, drinking a Virgin Mary and feeling out of place. He seldom went out, and when it did happen it was to a restaurant, never a club, and absolutely not in the smartest part of the city. He watched her, realized he was staring, looked away, and finished his drink. The tomato juice tasted of tomato juice and the celery was bitter. Her proximity was knocking him off kilter. He glanced at her again, noting how attractive she was, how beautiful. He saw details he had never noticed before: the little, almost invisible wrinkles by her eyes, her bare neck, her hair, which seemed to have a life of its own . . . the nape of her neck, which he glimpsed every now and then, a perfect nape that seemed to hold up her whole body... her forehead, the shape of which made her look tasteful and beautiful as well as exuding an intelligence that radiated around her. He was close now, almost too close. But still he stared, peering at her like a teenage boy seeing someone naked for the first time.

Sophie and her friend suddenly burst out laughing again. Lars was infected by her laughter and for a moment she turned to look at him, maybe alerted by the intensity of his stare. Their eyes met for a second, she smiled mid-laugh, he smiled back, but her gaze slid past him.

He felt her smile on his face, let it fall, turned, and quickly left the bar.

At home in the light from a low-energy lamp he wrote his report about the evening's events, about Sophie's friend, listed the names he had read in the hallway, then faxed the report to Gunilla.

Sara was asleep. He crept in beside her; she moved in her sleep, woke up.

"What time is it?" she whispered, confused.

"It's late... or early," he said.

She pulled the duvet around her and turned away. He pressed close to her, seeking intimacy, a feeble attempt at foreplay. He was useless at stuff like that, no finesse or feeling.

"Stop it, Lars." She let out an irritated sigh and pulled even farther away.

He rolled onto his back, stared at the ceiling for a while, listening to the muffled sound of traffic down in the street. When he realized he wasn't going to get to sleep he got up and went and sat in front of the television, which showed him Sophie Brinkmann's face on every beautiful woman who flickered past on the screen.

The music in the department store was beautiful, calming. She was looking at the underwear in the women's department, looking and feeling the quality and material. She carried on toward the makeup, buying some cream that was far too expensive and promised something unlikely.

"Sophie?"

She turned around and saw Hector with his stick and his leg in a cast, behind him Aron with two paper bags from a men's clothes shop in his hands.

"Hector."

The silence that followed was a second too long.

"Have you found anything you like?" he asked.

"Some cream, so far."

She raised her little bag. Hector nodded.

"How about you?" she asked.

Hector looked at the bags in Aron's hand, nodding to himself.

"I don't know," he said quietly.

He fixed his eyes on her.

"We never had coffee," he said.

"Sorry?"

"We didn't have time for coffee after lunch the other day. There's a decent place downstairs, by the food hall?"

Sophie took her coffee with milk, Hector did the same. The girl in the checkered apron behind the counter had offered them all sorts of different coffees but they had rejected her suggestions, they just wanted ordinary, reliable coffee. Aron sat down a short distance away and waited patiently, looking around the room.

"Doesn't he even drink coffee?"

Hector shook his head. "He doesn't like coffee. He's not like other people, Aron."

They sat in silence for a moment until Sophie broke it. "So how are things in the book world?"

Hector smiled at her stillborn question, didn't bother to answer. "How are things in the sick world?"

"Same as usual. People get sick, some get better, everyone's brave."

Hector nodded when he realized that her answer was serious.

"That's the way it is," he said, taking a sip of his coffee. "It's my birthday soon."

The look on her face showed that she liked that.

"I'd like to invite you to my party."

"Maybe," she said.

Hector glanced at her quickly. She had time to note a change in him. As if the humor and happiness had gone, and some sort of opposite emotion had replaced them—something ordinary that she didn't recognize.

"It's an invitation. It's not very polite to say *maybe* to an invitation. You can say yes or no, just like everyone else," he said quietly.

Sophie felt stupid. As if she had been playing a game—as if she were assuming he had been flirting with her and that she should play hard to get. Maybe he wasn't flirting with her at all. The longer she looked at him, the more she realized that he wasn't courting her. He was doing something else, maybe he was just a friend who was fond of her. That was what he seemed to be saying; anyway, he hadn't implied anything else.

"Sorry," she said.

"You're forgiven," he replied just as quickly.

"I'd love to come to your birthday party, Hector."

Hector smiled again.

4

There was a ripple of flashbulbs. Ralph Hanke smiled for the cam-eras as he shook hands with a short man with thinning hair and a mustache.

One journalist asked the local politician if he thought it was wise to build a shopping mall on a site where there was believed to be unexploded ordnance from World War II. The politician started to ramble and after just a couple of sentences was left fumbling for words. Ralph Hanke stepped in.

"That's a ridiculous idea. We've spent a lot of time and money making sure that this site is absolutely safe. . . ."

The journalists fired a torrent of questions at Ralph. None of them concerned the impending building project or the munitions. Now it was about everything from his fortune to his rumored romance with a Ukrainian model.

Ralph Hanke never gave interviews and only showed himself in public very occasionally at small, unexpected places where there was little at stake, such as the construction of this small shopping mall in a Munich suburb.

His right-hand man, Roland Gentz, stepped in front of him and thanked the journalists for their interest, then shepherded Ralph away from the podium.

They got into the car driven by Mikhail Sergeyevich Asmarov, a big Russian whose neck was almost as broad as the seat he was sitting in.

"He doesn't know when to shut up. The problem with that moron is that he thinks he's working for the people," Roland said from the passenger seat.

Ralph was looking out the window. Buildings glided past, houses, shops, and people—all unknown to him, and that would always be the case. In recent times he had started playing for high stakes, and he liked that. His construction company was getting all the contracts he wanted. Building shopping malls, docks, parking structures, and office buildings looked good, it made him legitimate. He provided a lot of work and earned a lot of money, clean money.

Ralph Hanke lived a life he had created for himself, no one could say otherwise. As the only child of a poor family he had grown up in the former German Democratic Republic. His then wife gave birth to his son, Christian, in 1978, but he divorced her two years later when she developed an unhealthy taste for heroin.

He spent the years before the Wall fell working in the post office, where he informed on his colleagues to the Stasi. His activities as an informant gave him advantages that he went on to exploit later. He got to know some security officers who were smart enough to predict the collapse of East Germany. He resigned from the post office and prepared a coup with his friends in the Stasi to steal archive material about informants in order to sell it back to them after the Wall fell.

He spent the last year working solely for the Stasi, where he was part of Kommerzielle Koordinierungs—KoKo. The purpose of the department was to use the security service to acquire Western currency to keep the bankrupt country afloat a bit longer.

Ralph Hanke and his friends sold small arms from the East German Army to anyone who wanted them. The first time he ever went abroad it was to General Noriega's Panama. Noriega paid for the guns in cash, with dollars, and for the first time Ralph realized he had found his role in life. On November 9, 1989, he walked free as a bird into West Berlin, his son, Christian, by his side. The sun shone behind him, lighting up the way ahead as they walked through the opening at the Brandenburg Gate.

He lived for a while with an old friend in West Berlin, waiting a few months before he started selling the files to the former informants. The longer he waited, the more money he could get for them. He used this small fortune to buy stolen supplies from the collapsed army: vehicles, weapons, and other equipment that could be snapped up for next to nothing; then he resold them and earned back his money tenfold. He kept copies of the Stasi reports he had sold back to the informants, many of whom went on to occupy positions of power in the new Germany.

In the late 1990s, when most of these men and women felt that their secret was safe, they received another visit from Ralph Hanke, this time with young Christian by his side. But this time Ralph didn't ask for money. This time he wanted other services, all designed to build up a sphere of power and wealth around them.

Ralph and Christian traveled the world, establishing contact with governments and big business, paying bribes and selling planes, vehicles, and radar equipment to warring countries through intermediaries and fake companies. Within the space of a few years they had built up Hanke GmbH and were raking in profits.

The view from the car window had changed. They were now in the center of Munich. There was a sparkle to this city, he thought. A sparkle that was a mixture of success and common sense.

The leather seat creaked as he changed position.

"Have you got hold of Christian?" he asked Roland.

"Yes...," Roland replied.

Ralph waited.

"And?"

"He's at home, drowning his sorrows. Evidently she meant a great deal to him."

"Yes, she must have."

Ralph looked out the window. His reaction when Christian's car had been blown up had been one of relief—relief that Christian hadn't been sitting inside it. He had been trying to figure out if that really was Guzman's response. Were they aiming at the girlfriend or

Christian? Or was it a message from someone else, and in that case, who? No, it was Guzman, but he was surprised by the approach he had taken. Did they think the girlfriend was somehow a fitting response to the injuries Hector suffered on the pedestrian crossing? Or was she an accident? Had they been trying to get Christian to show that they meant business?

They were passing the Frauenkirche. Ralph looked up at the domes and started thinking again: curious at how the Guzman affair would develop, curious at how Adalberto Guzman would react when he had brought him to his knees. Because he would, mainly because he wanted to find out who Guzman really was. Because that was the only time you got to see what a man was really worth, when he was lying beaten on the floor, only then could you judge. Some just lay there pathetically, begging for forgiveness. Some got up and let themselves get knocked down time after time. Others got up, blamed someone else, and sold their souls to the devil. Some would call it the survival instinct, but Ralph called it fear of life. But there were also a small group of people who hit back with full force. They demanded respect, and maybe Guzman was one of those?

After a while Roland broke the silence and started to run through the rest of the day's schedule. He had been working for Ralph for eight years. Roland Gentz made sure that most things that could be seen as problems for Ralph were turned to his advantage. He was an economist, lawyer, political adviser, and knew no boundaries. Ralph appreciated this aspect of his personality. He was the right hand that Ralph couldn't do without, he did things that Ralph himself couldn't do: contacting people, negotiating, and making sure that everything ran as it should. He had an almost minutely detailed overview of everything that was going on. If anyone made a fuss, Roland took a step back and Mikhail stepped up in his place. Ralph had built up a small but highly efficient organization around him.

"Mikhail, you're off to Rotterdam, aren't you?" Roland said.

"What are you going to Rotterdam for?" Ralph interrupted.

Roland turned in his seat.

"I've decided that we should always have someone there to receive the goods, at least for the first six months. It's just routine, just to make sure. Guzman's people may start to get ideas."

"Why Mikhail, haven't we got anyone else?"

"They're all busy elsewhere. This will have to do."

Mikhail said in his broken German that he had prepared everything, it would be him and two others, and it would be fine.

"Which others?"

"We served in Chechnya together."

"Are they OK?"

Mikhail gave a crooked smile and shook his head.

"No, not remotely."

Ralph liked Mikhail's attitude, he'd always liked the Russian. There was something straightforward about the way he worked; he seldom questioned anything, did as he was told, and when things didn't go as expected he used his own initiative to sort things out.

"OK," Ralph said, sitting back and relaxing. He closed his eyes, a few minutes' sleep would do the trick.

Sophie tried a number of different styles in front of the mirror. She thought she looked too dressy, and got around it by putting on a pair of jeans to even things out.

"Where are you going?"

Albert was sitting on the sofa in the living room. She looked at him as she came down the stairs.

"To a party."

"What sort of party?"

"A birthday party."

"Whose?"

She stopped in the hall, looking at her reflection in the mirror hanging above the hall cupboard.

"A friend."

"A friend?"

"His name's Hector."

She leaned closer to the mirror and put on her lipstick.

"Hector? Who the hell's named Hector?"

Sophie pressed her lips together. "Don't swear."

"So who is he then?"

She applied some finishing touches. "He was a patient."

"You're not really that desperate, are you, Mom?"

She could hear the irony in his voice and had to make an effort not to smile. He got up from the sofa and went past her toward the kitchen.

"You look really great, Mom," he muttered.

She'd noticed him trying to boost her confidence on the rare occasions when she went out.

"Thanks, darling," she said.

The taxi dropped her off outside the Trasten restaurant. When she opened the door to go in she was met by a young man in a white shirt and black trousers who held the door open for her, took her thin coat, and walked her inside. Sophie felt suddenly nervous, not sure she was right to come. She could hear voices and laughter from within the restaurant.

The room was lit by candles rather than lamps. People were sitting around different tables, laughing, talking, drinking. Several more streamed in behind her. Sophie glanced at how they were dressed. She couldn't figure out if she was too fancy or too plain, something in between, she guessed, exactly as she'd hoped. A woman passed her carrying a tray, Champagne glasses filled to the brim. Sophie took a glass and looked for Hector in the crowd, and found him sitting farther into the room with a small boy on his lap. The boy was laughing fit to burst as Hector bounced his good leg, making the little boy bob up and down. She started heading toward him as someone clinked a glass. She stopped and went to stand by the wall, and looked on as a man who was probably in his fifties, heavily built and bald, with a white shirt that was half unbuttoned, waited for the noise in the room to subside. He tapped his glass again, a voice from one of the tables said something loudly in Spanish, and several people laughed. The man who had called for silence let the laughter die out, then started to speak in Spanish. Every now and then he would turn and look at Hector, and after a while the man began to speak more quietly and seemed almost sentimental. His voice kept breaking. Hector listened calmly, something that the boy in his lap seemed to sense in some subconscious way, as he sat completely still, leaning back in Hector's arms. The man concluded his speech, raised his Champagne glass, and proposed a toast to Hector. The other guests joined in. As she drank, Hector caught her eye and waved her over to him. The boy in his lap disappeared. The noise of the party returned and Sophie headed toward him as Hector whispered something into the ear of a young girl sitting on the chair next to him. The girl got up and offered her seat to Sophie, who thanked her with a smile. Hector got up as well, and seemed to get stuck just looking at her. Then he pulled himself together and kissed her on both cheeks.

"Sophie, welcome."

"Happy birthday, Hector."

Sophie handed over a small parcel and he took it without opening it. He looked at her briefly once more.

"I'm glad you're here."

She smiled in response.

"Come with me, I'd like you to meet my sister."

They headed toward another table. Sophie saw Aron sitting at the bar at the far end of the restaurant; he nodded warmly to her.

A woman stood up from the table, short, dark hair, dark freckles on olive skin, alert eyes that were curious and happy at the same time—she looked very well.

"Sophie, this is my sister, Inez."

Sophie held out her hand. Inez ignored it and gave Sophie a hug, kissing the air as their cheeks met. Hector said something in rapid Spanish to Inez. Inez said something as she looked at Sophie.

"She says thank you for looking after her useless brother."

Sophie was told that Inez had two children who were back home in Madrid with her husband. Inez said she was glad to have met Sophie, patted her arm, and disappeared.

"My brother couldn't come, he lives in France. He's a marine biologist and seems happiest when he's underwater. Not that I blame him," Hector said.

The man who had made the speech came over and hugged Hector, then turned to Sophie. His bulky frame and large nose seemed even bigger close-up. He had bits of gold all over him, a thick bracelet around his wrist, a chain around his neck, and two heavy signet rings, one on the ring finger of each hand.

"Sophie, allow me to introduce you to Carlos Fuentes, this is his restaurant."

"It's a pleasure to meet you, Sophie. I saw you before, very briefly, when you had lunch here with Hector."

Carlos spoke with a strong accent.

"I understand you're a nurse? Maybe you could mend my broken heart one day?"

Carlos put his hand to his chest, smiled at her, and left them.

"Why has he got a broken heart?"

Hector shrugged. "He wants women to see him as a hopeless romantic. He hasn't got a broken heart, just two broken marriages, and he broke those himself."

Hector watched Carlos walk away. For a moment Sophie caught a glimpse of something dark in his eyes.

A couple, possibly from the West Indies. He was tall, skinny, and powerful at the same time. She was attractive, with a round ball of hair on her head and a proud posture, and she swayed as she walked. They were walking toward Hector arm in arm. It was as if they owned the whole world, but wanted to share it with everyone else. The tall man patted Hector affectionately on the shoulder and gave him a wrapped parcel. Hector lit up at once, and the man took Sophie's hand.

"My name's Thierry, and this is my wife, Daphne."

Sophie introduced herself, and Daphne smiled at her. They talked to Hector, then Thierry and his wife went off, wrapped around each other, to say hello to people they knew.

Someone clapped their hands and asked the guests to take their seats for dinner.

Hector asked Sophie to sit at his table. There was no seating plan, people seemed to know where they were sitting. She found a spare chair and sat down.

Next to Sophie was a man who appeared rather dry; he was one of the few wearing a suit and tie, a gray suit with a blue, checkered tie. He had short hair, was fairly trim, wore thin-framed glasses, and seemed rather awkward, as though he'd rather not be there. He introduced himself as Ernst Lundwall, then he sat in silence until it became unbearable, perhaps he became aware of it himself.

"How do you know Hector?" he asked.

She talked about the accident, which Ernst was already aware of, how they had met in the hospital and now she was sitting here. She returned the question.

"I help Hector's publishing company with legal matters. I'm a lawyer by training, most of the time I work as a solicitor and adviser in matters of copyright law."

His voice was nasal and monotonous. The meal turned into something of a trial for her. Ernst Lundwall replied to all her questions in monosyllables without asking her anything, without picking up any threads or behaving in the usual, functional social way. The man on the other side of her was no help, he couldn't speak English or Swedish. In the end she gave up and decided to sit in silence.

She concentrated on the food, glancing occasionally at Hector, who was engrossed in a conversation with his sister, who was his dinner partner. Alongside him, on the other side, was a beautiful woman in her thirties, Sophie didn't know who she was. The woman looked up, caught Sophie's eye for a moment, then looked away. Sophie realized she was staring.

Sometimes people would get up to go out and smoke. She made use of that, excused herself to Ernst, got up from her chair, and went outside.

She stood alone outside the entrance to the restaurant, smoking. She felt slightly drunk after a few glasses of Champagne, and the cigarette tasted good. The door opened behind her and Aron came out, followed by two men.

"Hello, Sophie."

"Hello, Aron."

He looked around. One man went down the street to the left, the other went right. Aron turned to her.

"Can I ask you to go in for a moment?"

Sophie was taken aback, but his attitude implied that the question was completely natural.

"Of course."

A car was coming up the street. The man who had gone right waved to Aron. Aron took a couple of steps out onto the street. The car came closer. Sophie went in.

During her cigarette break a vague sense of chaos had descended on the party. Everyone had changed places and was sitting and talking over coffee and liqueurs. Someone else was sitting in her chair at Hector's table. She found a spare place at another table, and it wasn't long before Ernst Lundwall came and sat down beside her.

"They took our places!"

He seemed upset. The front door opened and a short-haired, muscular man came in. He surveyed the room quickly, then an elderly, well-dressed man with white hair and a deep suntan followed him inside, followed lastly by Aron, who locked the door behind him. Hector stood up; he looked surprised, almost bewildered. The elderly man made his way over to him and the two of them embraced.

"Guzman el Bueno!" someone in the room cried, and everyone began clapping their hands.

Sophie saw Hector and his father exchange a few words as they patted each other on the cheek. A waitress helped Adalberto Guzman to take off his coat, chairs were moved, people changed places, and Adalberto sat down next to his son. They immediately fell into conversation. Adalberto held Hector's hand in his the whole time.

Ernst Lundwall had suddenly gotten drunk. He was more talkative than before, telling Sophie what music he listened to when he was younger, and what music he chose to listen to now. Sophie tried to look interested but she kept glancing over at Hector and his father. There was something truly joyous, intense about them.

"Excuse me a moment," she said.

He didn't hear her, just continued droning on about his uninteresting youth.

"This is my father, Adalberto Guzman."

Sophie shook his hand while Hector explained who Sophie was to his father in Spanish. Adalberto didn't let go of her hand, but looked her in the eye and nodded at what Hector was saying.

Hector stood up and offered Sophie his arm. They did a circuit of the room and Hector introduced her to a mixed group of people, and she thought that her walk through the restaurant with Hector's arm in hers gave the impression that they were in a relationship, as if Hector wanted to show her off to his friends. She pulled away from his arm and went back to her place, where to her delight she couldn't see Ernst anywhere. Music started playing from the speakers, people got up and started to dance. Hector came over after a while and sat down next to her.

"Do I scare you?"

She shook her head. He looked out over the dance floor.

"I didn't mean anything by introducing you to my friends."

"It doesn't matter," she said.

He took her hand in his. "Is this OK?"

She nodded.

They stayed there holding each other's hands, watching the dancers. His hand was large and warm. It felt good to hold it.

Toward two o'clock in the morning the guests began to leave, and half an hour later the music was turned down and there were just a dozen or so people left in the room, most of them gathered around one table. Hector, Adalberto, Inez, Aron, and Leszek—the short-haired man who had arrived with Adalberto—as well as Thierry and Daphne. And, beside Hector, the beautiful woman. Sophie was sitting next to Aron and had been chatting to him about nothing much. Then she had started talking to the short-haired Pole, Leszek. She looked at the people around the table. She saw Inez talking to Adalberto—she looked like a child who had decided to be cross with her father, while Adalberto looked almost pained, like a father who didn't want his daughter to be cross with him. Thierry and Daphne were huddled together. She looked at Hector. He wasn't talking to the woman beside him, he had only exchanged a few words with her all evening. Sophie realized she was staring at her again. There was something chilly about the woman, something chilly and beautiful, not cold but almost sober and sensitive. She seemed sad, introverted, without being shy. But above all there was something grand about her, "beautiful" was too small a word. Sophie felt a pang of envy.

She bumped into her in the bathroom, perhaps she had followed her. They stood next to each other, inspecting their faces in the mirrors above the two washbasins. The woman was touching up her makeup.

"My name's Sonya," she said quietly.

"Sophie."

Sonya left the bathroom.

When Sophie came out she was met with music and dancing again. Everyone who had been sitting around the table was now dancing energetically. A young waiter came over to her with a tray. She saw a load of white pills.

"Please, help yourself," Hector said behind her.

"What is it?"

"Ecstasy. I've taken one of these every birthday since I was thirty. It won't kill you."

She hesitated, looked at the happy guests, looked at Hector.

"Have you taken one tonight?"

He nodded. "Just now."

"Can you feel anything?"

He stared into the middle distance, searching his emotions to see if anything had changed.

"It probably hasn't had time to work yet... I think. But I'm not sure," he said with a wide smile.

Sophie took a pill and swallowed it.

She discovered that she loved dancing more than anything, that what had seemed like an unremarkable restaurant was one of the most beautiful places she had ever been, so beautiful in its exquisite furnishings. Time kept twisting on its axis and suddenly they were all sitting at the table again, the music was quieter now, like the most perfect backdrop.

Sophie looked on. The others around the table were talking and laughing in turn, smoking and drinking. It seemed that every subject of conversation was a link that bound everything together in a far greater context. Inez leaned over and started talking to her. Hector interpreted as best he could, but he and Inez kept bursting out laughing in Spanish. Sonya wasn't laughing, she just smiled—a gentle smile that settled over her beautiful face, as if she was finding everything agreeable for a while, as if she had chosen to enjoy the moment instead of giggling. Hector was acting with boyish confusion; he was having a great time, she could see that, everyone was. Adalberto had become a child, chattering away in a Spanish that no one seemed to understand but that everyone found funny. Daphne and Thierry seemed even more in love now, sitting closely entwined, holding each other tight. Sophie felt as if the whole world were perfectly composed and comprehensible.

At half past three in the morning she left the restaurant; she didn't really want to go home but realized the party would carry on long into the following day.

Hector followed her out to her taxi and opened the door for her.

"Thank you," she said.

"Thank *you,*" he said.

She leaned forward and let him kiss her. His lips were softer than she had imagined. There was something very careful about him. He slid out of the kiss.

She couldn't sleep when she got home, so she sat on the veranda instead, listening to the birds singing to her, breathing in the magical smells of the early morning and absorbing all the beauty before her. The fresh, dark, early-morning green of the lawn, the dense foliage of the trees, the interconnectedness of the whole. She knew she was high, but didn't feel at all guilty.

She asked herself why she had so suddenly dropped her guard, and why she had willfully crossed so many boundaries in her life recently with such an intense inward smile.

Lars was leaning against the wall watching Erik, who was sitting with his feet up on an open desk drawer, poking his ear with a pen. Eva Castroneves was making tiny half-inch turns on her office chair and Gunilla was reading a document with her glasses perched on her nose. She put down the sheet she had been reading, took off her reading glasses, and let them dangle on the cord around her neck.

"OK, Lars, you start."

Lars shuffled on the spot as if he were trying to find a hole to crawl into, always this anxiety whenever he was asked to speak in front of other people. He searched inside himself for the part of his personality that could help rescue him from this. Maybe the slightly angry one, maybe the slightly vacant one, or perhaps a mix of the two. He found something, plugged it in, and started to explain to his colleagues in a more or less clear voice about how Sophie Brinkmann had met Hector Guzman at the NK department store and how last night she had gone to a party at a restaurant in Vasastan.

"But I've written all that in my reports."

Gunilla took over.

"Sophie and Hector have some sort of relationship, we know that now. What sort of relationship it is will doubtless become clear in the future. The party, Lars, tell us about that."

He cleared his throat quietly, clasped his hands, let them go; his arms were hanging awkwardly, his legs couldn't find a relaxed posture.

"I didn't see or notice anything unusual except that two men took up position outside the restaurant after an elderly man arrived there late in the evening, probably Hector's father. Sophie got in a taxi at 3:28, which in all likelihood drove her home from the city."

"Thank you," Gunilla said, and nodded toward Eva.

"I took photographs of the other guests as they left the venue," Lars added. "The pictures are a bit grainy, but maybe you'd like to take a look, Eva?"

Lars noticed that his voice was sounding higher than normal, and didn't like it.

"Good... let Eva have the pictures," Gunilla said.

He scratched his neck.

Eva went back to her papers, looking through them, then leafing a bit further.

"Sophie Brinkmann, born Lantz, seems like someone who lives a good life, probably on the inheritance from her husband, socializes sporadically with her friends and occasionally her mother. There aren't really any question marks in her past. Normal school career, marks slightly above average, she spent a year in the United States as an exchange student, traveled in Asia for a few months with a friend after graduating from high school, then had a number of jobs before studying nursing at Sophiahemmet University College. She met David Brinkmann and gave birth to Albert two years later, they got married, moved into a villa in Stocksund from an apartment in Stockholm. When David died in 2003 she sold the villa and bought something smaller for her and her son in the same area...."

Eva stopped, leafed a bit further through her notes, then continued: "She's close to her son, Albert, she doesn't seem to have any hobbies or particular interests. The social side of things is difficult to interpret; we don't know much about her circle of friends yet, apart from her best friend, Clara. That's the woman she was out with that time you followed her, Lars. That's what I've got for the time being."

Gunilla thanked her and went on: "Was she like this before we came across her? A woman who goes out with men? Or has she been the grieving widow sitting at home, and Hector is the first to draw her out of her shell?"

"That's probably how it is," Eva said.

"Which?"

"That Hector's the first."

"What makes you say that?" Gunilla wondered.

"There's nothing to suggest that she's seen any men since the death of her husband, but I'll keep looking."

"Erik?" Gunilla said.

Erik was cleaning under his fingernails with a toothpick. "In and of herself she's not of any interest, but the question is whether the Spaniard has fallen for her. Because if that's the case then she has a role, but otherwise the question is irrelevant."

The room fell silent, as if everyone but Lars was thinking. He looked at them with a sudden feeling that he was alone in the room. Gunilla woke from her thoughts first.

"Lars, can you give me a lift?"

They drove through the lunchtime traffic. Gunilla was sitting in the passenger seat, applying lipstick, looking in the mirror on the back of the sun visor.

"So what do you make of it?" she asked, pursing her lips together.

"I don't know."

She put the lid back on the lipstick and dropped it in her bag.

"I'd like your opinion, Lars, not an evaluation or analysis, just your opinion."

He thought for a moment as they got stuck behind a bus on Sturegatan.

"It feels flimsy," he said.

"It *is* flimsy. It's always flimsy, often we don't have anything. So I feel the opposite about this case, I think we've got a lot."

Lars nodded. "You're probably right."

He was staring ahead, there was a lot of traffic.

"You don't have to agree with me, Lars," she said flatly.

Lars coughed for some reason, he really wanted her to trust him.

"I think I've got more to offer you, Gunilla."

"What do you mean?"

"That I can do more than just surveillance. I'm analytical, I've got a lot to offer, I think. We talked about it when you offered me the job. . . ."

Gunilla indicated that he should pull over a little way ahead.

"You're important to the group, Lars, you're making a valuable contribution. I'd like to bring you in closer, but for that to happen we need something to go on, and the person who can come up with that is you. I'll take full responsibility if anything goes wrong, but we have to increase the level now, the level of surveillance. Do you understand what I mean by that?"

"I think so."

Lars found a gap in the traffic, pulled over to the curb, and stopped.

"We're on the right track," she went on. "Have no doubt about that, just do whatever you can to take this a step further."

She closed her handbag. "I'm going to send you a number, Lars. It belongs to a man named Anders. He'll help you. Anders is good."

Gunilla patted him lightly on the arm, opened the door, and got out of the car.

Lars stayed where he was for a few minutes, thoughts flying through his head—somewhere there was a little bit of euphoria about what Gunilla had just said, about how valuable he was. But there was also a feeling of discomfort, but on the other hand that was always there. Gunilla could continue to be correct in her analysis of him. He wasn't going to disappoint her.

He pulled out into the heavy traffic again. His cell beeped and the screen asked him if he wanted to save the contact *Anders*.

The sea was rough and cascades of water were washing over him. He was standing at the prow of the ship, looking at the flat mainland in the distance. Holland.

The ship's engines suddenly shut off, then a rumbling, thudding sound ran through the hull as the helmsman put the ship into reverse. It wasn't particularly noticeable, the ship was still moving forward at the same rate. It took time to stop a ship of this size. Jens looked around to find the reason why the captain had decided to stop this far out to sea.

On the horizon he could see a relatively large open motorboat with a central console bouncing over the waves, heading directly toward the ship. He screwed up his eyes, trying to find anything that could tell what sort of boat it was, or who was steering it. He couldn't see anything and left his position at the prow, crossing the deck back over to the metal staircase leading up to the bridge.

He dragged the door open. The captain and helmsman were drinking tea, smoking foul-smelling cigarettes, and were in the middle of a game of backgammon.

"There's a boat coming."

The captain nodded.

"Customs? Police?"

The captain smiled, shaking his head.

"Passengers," he said, taking a sip from his mug of tea.

Jens was suddenly nervous—and it was evidently noticeable, because the captain turned to his helmsman, said something brief in Vietnamese, and they both burst out laughing.

There was a great commotion when the motorboat pulled up alongside the ship. A rope ladder was thrown down and two men climbed up, one short-haired and muscular, the other dark-haired with a black, waist-length jacket. The short-haired one was carrying a cloth sports bag. As the motorboat pulled away and accelerated back toward shore, one of the men went up to the bridge. The other man, the short-haired one, waited below.

Jens watched them from his position on deck, the way one of them spoke to the captain, who gesticulated in a submissive way, as though he regretted something he had done, as if he were trying to explain. The conversation was short, then the man walked out, onto the metal staircase.

"Leszek!" he shouted to the short-haired man, and waved at him to move toward the front of the ship. Leszek did as he was told and disappeared.

The diesel engines belowdecks started to rumble again and the ship slowly chewed its way through the waves along the same course to Rotterdam. Jens went back belowdecks.

The captain had forbidden him to go into the hold during the voyage, but Jens had no intention of asking his permission.

He broke open two crates, put the guns back together, and repacked them into two smaller boxes that would be easier to shift over to the van he had ordered to be waiting on the quayside. The price he had paid for passage across the Atlantic included a promise that customs wouldn't do any spot checks during the first hour they were in port. Jens wanted everything to be ready, so he could leave the ship as quickly as possible and get away from there.

A few hours later the ship was piloted into harbor. Jens was sitting on the roof of the bridge, drinking bad coffee and smoking a cigarette. The sea was calm, the sun shining behind the fog. He could hear foghorns out there somewhere. Then Rotterdam harbor emerged clearly. It was enormous, everything was enormous. Cranes, containers, huge, brutish ships alongside vast docks. Jens felt very small as they made their way through this oversized world.

After an hour the ship docked alongside a concrete quay in a remote part of the harbor. The captain ordered the hold opened from his position up on the bridge, cranes reached over the ship, and the crew began fastening straps and cables around the containers, which were slowly hoisted ashore.

Just as Jens was starting to wonder when his rented van would show up, a car came driving along the quayside and parked beside the ship. It couldn't be the one he had ordered, it was far too small. Three men got out. One was large and thickset, the other two somewhat smaller. The men walked quickly toward the ship and up the gangplank, onto the deck. Jens studied them from his position on the roof. The largest of the three kept going toward the bridge while the other two stayed on deck.

Leaving the coffee mug on the roof, Jens clambered down and walked across the deck past the two men. He nodded to them—more like someone at a golf club than on a Vietnamese smuggler's ship. Neither of them nodded back. He got a quick look at them as he passed. From close up they looked rough: skinny, hollow eyes, pocked skin... the look of addicts.

Just as Jens put his foot on the metal staircase leading down into the hold he heard one of the men behind him shout.

"Mikhail!"

Then three distant bangs followed in quick succession. Somewhere he thought he heard a scream and at that same millisecond came a whining noise combined with the hard sound of something small striking flesh at high velocity. Out of pure reflex he threw himself down the steps into the hold. During the seconds that followed there was complete silence. As if the recent shots had destroyed all the sound in the universe. He clambered up a few steps and peered over the edge. One of the men he had just nodded to was lying, apparently dead, in front of him in a contorted, unnatural position. Jens could just make out a submachine gun under the man's jacket. With the sun against him he could see the outline of the man named Leszek up on the observation deck, on one knee, following the other man, who was running across the deck through the telescopic sights of his rifle. The marksman on the observation deck let off four rapid-fire shots. The man on deck just made it to the shelter of the wall beneath the bridge as the bullets ricocheted off the metal.

Jens's pulse was racing. He watched as Leszek quickly slung his gun on his back and scampered nimbly down and disappeared. Suddenly there were two more shots. They came from inside the bridge, it sounded like a pistol. He saw the door open and the man named Mikhail came out with a large automatic pistol in his hand. He shouted something to the man below him. They exchanged some short sentences in Russian. Mikhail came down the steps, didn't appear to be in any hurry. Then they both disappeared along the length of the ship toward the stern. Jens crawled quickly over to the dead man, lifted his jacket, removed his submachine gun, and then slid backward down the steps into the hold, hurrying into the cover of darkness.

The hold was large, cold, and damp, with packing crates and freezers strapped tightly together. Farther in, the larger containers were stacked on top of one another, seven in total, one of them hanging in the air above him. The cranes and all work on the quayside had stopped when the firing began. He found a safe place, breathing hard, trying to think, trying to pull himself together. No matter how he thought it through, he always came to the same conclusion: neither of the two factions who were shooting at each other—the Mikhail group or the Leszek group—knew who he was, so it was more than likely that they would take him for an enemy. He looked at the weapon he was holding in his hand, it was a Bizon. A Russian submachine gun.

He suddenly felt horribly alone, and fiddled unconsciously with the safety catch with his right thumb. It was making a clicking sound, and he realized that the sound must be carrying a long way and stopped doing it. No further shots had rung out up on deck. Jens stood up quietly and began to make his way through the crates.

The noise came out of nowhere. A hail of bullets slammed into packing crates close to him. He threw himself to the ground, then without thinking he stood up just as quickly, held out the gun, and pulled the trigger. The weapon clicked, nothing happened. He crouched down again, swore at himself and changed the position of the safety catch that he had been fiddling with earlier. He took a deep breath, realized that he had used up his only chance and that the gunman knew his position now. He got to his feet and ran a few yards across an open space until he reached the rear part of the hold, then kept going, throwing himself behind the shelter of a freezer. His breathing was quick and shallow, and Jens was listening so hard that after a while he thought he could hear things that weren't really there. He glanced out, saw nothing, and was about to get up and move when a voice whispered in English behind him.

"Drop your gun."

He hesitated and the man repeated the words, and Jens put the Bizon on the floor.

"How many of you are there?" the voice asked quickly.

"Just me."

"Who are you?"

"A passenger."

"Why are you armed?"

"I took the gun from the dead man up on deck."

"Did you see the men who came on board?"

"Yes."

"How many of them were there?"

"Three. One got shot. One went up to the bridge, the third one joined forces with him. I think they headed back toward the stern."

Jens swore to himself in Swedish, then said to the man in English: "Were you the one shooting at me?"

Now the man addressed him in Swedish: "No, it wasn't me, it was the others shooting at you, not us."

At first Jens thought he must have misheard.

There were noises from the open section of the cargo hold. Jens tried to look, then turned to face the man. He was gone. Jens picked up his gun once more.

5

Anders Ask was the name of the man Gunilla had told Lars to call. Anders turned out to be a cheerful soul, more cheerful than Lars could handle. He had picked him up in the city center and they had driven out to Stocksund.

Anders was sitting comfortably in the passenger seat, going through the microphones in his lap.

"So, who's Lars, then?"

Lars glanced quickly at Anders. "Oh, well, what can I say, nothing special."

Anders held up a microphone to the light, examining it for a moment.

"God, they're tiny," he whispered to himself. He smiled at this, then tucked the microphone back into the foam rubber. "What were you doing before?"

"Western District," Lars said.

"Crime?"

Lars cast a quick look at Anders. "No . . ."

Anders waited for more, then laughed. "No?"

Lars shifted in his seat, a small frown on his brow.

"Law and order," he said quietly.

Anders smiled broadly. "A beat cop. Fucking hell. I'm in a car with a beat cop! That doesn't happen every day. What the hell did you do to get a job with Gunilla?"

"She called and asked."

"You're kidding me," Anders said theatrically.

Lars shook his head, unsettled by Anders's attitude, which he was finding very hard to come to grips with. Anders put the box of microphones on the dashboard in front of Lars. Lars took it down and put it in his lap.

"What about you? Who are you?" Lars countered.

"I'm Anders."

"Who's Anders?"

Anders Ask looked out through the window.

"None of your damn business."

It was just after one in the afternoon when Lars Vinge was standing on the terrace at the back of Sophie's house, watching as Anders had picked the lock, and he wasn't the whispering type.

"Terrace doors are like fat girls," Anders said, smiling at his own analogy.

The door slid open. Lars was nervous. Anders was too loud, too fearless. Anders saw how nervous he was.

"Poor little Lasse?" he sang from the old song. He gestured with his hand that Lars could go in. "Welcome home, darling," he whispered.

They were wearing disposable shoe covers and latex gloves. Lars stood in the living room, his stomach simultaneously clenching and churning. He wanted to get out, and his nervousness wasn't helped by the fact that Anders was not only calmness personified but also had the bad habit of whistling loudly as he worked.

"Stay away from the windows," Anders said, opening his bag and rooting around in the bottom. "Have you got the mikes?"

Lars didn't like this. He pulled the little wooden box from his jacket pocket and gave it to Anders, who wandered off, inserting an earpiece and switching on a receiver, then testing the little microphones.

Lars looked around. The living room, large and airy, bigger than he had imagined when he had been sitting some distance away looking in. It was open-plan, leading into the kitchen at the far end. A wide step running the whole width of the room separated the two spaces.

He took out his digital camera and took a series of pictures of the room. The furnishing was a mixture of styles, in a way that he'd never seen before. But everything fit together. A low, old pink armchair next to the large sofa. Colorful cushions on the sofa... then an antique wooden chair with a light-brown seat. They ought to clash, but somehow didn't. The wall behind the sofa was covered with pictures. Their subjects were varied but the overall result was... wonderful. There were flowers and healthy-looking potted plants here and there. The room had been furnished tastefully, intelligently, and thoughtfully... in spite of the variety. The colors and shapes made the house feel warm, made you feel you wanted to be there, to stay.... One shelf was full of framed photographs. He could see Albert, her son, from a happy little boy to the unfair face of puberty. To the right was a black-and-white portrait of a man, a solid fellow from the look of him. Lars thought he could detect a similarity to Sophie in his brow and eyes, it was probably her father. Lars glanced at several other pictures, one smaller photograph of a man in his thirties, Sophie's husband, David, standing behind a small boy, Albert. Then a picture of the whole family, David, Sophie, little Albert, and a dog, a golden Labrador. They were standing close together, smiling at the camera.

Behind him Anders was pulling a length of tape from a roll over by the sofa. Lars kept on looking. Sophie laughing on a white garden chair, the picture looked fairly recent, from the last year or so. She was wrapped in a blanket and her knees were pulled up. Her smile was infectious, as if it were aimed at him. He stood like that for a moment.

Lars set his camera to macro mode, put the lens close to the photograph of Sophie, and took a series of shots.

Anders called to get Lars's attention, and pointed to a lamp by the sofa, then at his ear. Anders got up and headed toward the kitchen, still humming "Little Lasse."

Lars stared out over the living room. He wished that Sara had the same taste, the same sense of what went well together, not that bohemian style where everything for some reason always had to be Indian, cheap, and... irregular.

There was a blanket folded over the sofa. Lars picked it up and felt it. It was soft. And without thinking he held it up to his face and smelled it.

"Are you a pervert as well?"

Anders was looking at Lars as he stood in the middle of the living room. Lars put the blanket back on the sofa.

"What do you want?" Lars said, trying to look angry.

Anders laughed. His laughter turned into a crooked smile, a smile that was evidence of his distaste.

"Oh, little Lasse, you seem completely daft," Anders whispered.

Lars watched him go as he tramped up the creaking wooden staircase. Then he left the living room and went down the step into the kitchen. That too was clean and tidy. He noticed a large vase of cut flowers in the window, the high, rough island unit in the middle of the kitchen... and the dark green door to the little pantry. Dark green in a way he didn't know existed, didn't know it was permissible to have anything so beautiful in a kitchen. Someone with the flair and understanding to decorate a room like this probably understood a few other things. All of Lars's senses came alive, as a thousand thoughts and feelings raced through him. There was a lot about life that Lars Vinge didn't understand. He realized that now. He wanted to know. He wanted the woman who lived here to tell him....

He went upstairs, trying not to make the treads creak beneath his feet. Anders was crouching next to a bedside table in her bedroom. Lars leaned against the doorpost.

"Can we go?" Lars whispered.

"Have you always been this irritating?"

Anders checked his work, stood up, and play-tackled Lars on the way out with one shoulder before disappearing back downstairs with far-too-heavy steps.

Lars stayed where he was in the doorway, looked into the bedroom. A large double bed, covered with a bedspread. There was a beautiful iron lamp on the bedside table where Anders had just attached a microphone. The floor was covered in carpet, and the walls were pale, with just a few pictures, most of them in dark frames. Mixed subjects: a single large butterfly, a woman's body in charcoal on light brown paper, one unframed picture, with just a deep red color to make you aware of something that wasn't there. Then an oil painting of a large, leafy tree. It all worked. Lars tried to understand.

At the back of the bedroom were ivory-colored double doors over in one corner, smaller than a normal door. He stepped into the room, his feet sinking into the soft carpet, and went over to check them, letting them swing out slowly. A large closet, almost like a little room. He stepped inside and found the light switch. Soft, warm light lit up the room.

Blouses and other clothes hanging in rows from wooden hangers. Below them were drawers, new drawers made of oak. He opened one and found jewelry and watches. He opened the drawer beneath, folded scarves and more jewelry. He bent down, the third contained underwear, panties, and bras. He closed it quickly, then opened it again at once, looking down into the drawer, with an awareness that he had long since broken all his ethical rules, so he may as well carry on now.

Lars reached out his hand and felt the underwear. Silk... soft, he couldn't stop touching them, stroking them with his fingers, felt suddenly aroused, hard. He wanted to take a pair with him—keep them in his pocket so he could touch them whenever he felt like it. Noises from downstairs snapped him out of it. He closed the drawer, left the closet and the bedroom.

Outside the room he took several deep breaths. He headed toward Albert's room, pushed the door open with his fingers, looked in. It was a boy's room, furnished as if the boy didn't know if he was grown up or still a child. Grown-up pictures on the walls, and a yellow and black AIK football banner with the slogan "We Are Everywhere." An electric guitar with only three strings leaning against the desk, an empty candy bag on the floor. The bed made yet still unmade, but at least the bedspread was straight. Under the bed an old telescope but no stand. He knelt down, saw some books and a black guitar case farther in.

Lars took a few pictures, then looked at his watch; the time had gone quicker than he had thought. He left the room, heading for the stairs. He didn't pause outside Sophie's room, just acted on impulse. Into the bedroom again, open the closet, open the third drawer, take a pair of panties, stuff them in his pocket. Close the drawer, close the closet, out again.

Anders was sitting behind a computer in what looked like an office.

"Time's getting on," Lars said from the doorway.

"Shut up," Anders said, his eyes on the screen.

Anders went on typing on the computer.

"Anders!"

Anders looked up. "I said shut up! Have a look 'round, do whatever the hell you like, just leave me alone."

He returned to tapping at the keyboard. Lars felt like saying something else, thought better of it, and walked out.

He wandered about, went into the kitchen, looked at the floor to make sure they hadn't forgotten anything. Everything looked the way it should, and he backed away toward the terrace door, where they had come in, then retraced his steps. He could feel that he was breathing shallowly, high in his throat, and his forehead was wet with sweat. Anders came out of the office.

"I just need to go to the toilet. Then we can go."

"No, please," Lars begged quietly.

Anders smiled at Lars's anxiety, picked up a newspaper from a sideboard, and padded off toward the bathroom. Anders took his time, whistling the theme from *Bonanza*.

Lars hid in the hall next to the kitchen door. No one would see him there from the outside. He stood next to a row of coats and jackets, taking deep breaths, then leaned his forehead against the wall, closed his eyes, and tried to rediscover a sense of calm. He tried to take deep breaths, but they were only reaching the top half of his chest. He attempted breathing through his nose, the same thing there—just half breaths. He felt as taut as a string on a violin. His heartbeat was thudding in his ears, his stomach felt tight, his hands were cold, his mouth dry.... A sound outside, footsteps on the other side of the door... a key inserted into the lock. Lars turned around and stared at the door, frozen to the spot. Nothing in his body made any attempt to react and run away. He just stood there immobile, scared as a small child, incapable of action, and struck with such an overwhelming sense of panic that for a moment he seriously believed he was going to die just from the emotions raging inside him.

The lock clicked, the handle was pushed down, the door was pulled open. Lars shut his eyes, the door closed, he opened his eyes. In front of him was a short, unfamiliar woman in her sixties; she put a handbag down on the floor and started to unbutton her coat. He looked sideways at her; she met his gaze and jumped with fright, put a hand to her chest, muttered something in some Eastern European language, and her fear was replaced by something calmer. She laughed, then gabbled something in Swedish about not knowing that there was going to be anyone at home.

She held out her hand and introduced herself as Dorota. Lars, from the vacuum-filled universe of bewilderment, took her hand.

"Lars."

He heard a thunderous burst of laughter behind him and turned around. Anders was shaking with laughter, one hand over his face. "You really do take the prize!"

Dorota looked at the two men with half a smile, suddenly unsure about who they were.

Anders went up to her, grabbed her arm, picked up her bag from the floor, pulled her into the kitchen, and sat her down on a chair. He turned and looked at Lars. "What now?"

Dorota was scared.

"We'll just go. Come on," he said.

Anders stared at Lars with a look of contempt on his face.

"Great idea. We'll just go." He turned to Dorota. "Who are you?"

She glanced between the men. "I'm the cleaner."

"You're the cleaner?"

Dorota nodded. He tossed her handbag into her lap.

"Give me your wallet."

Dorota looked at Anders as if she hadn't heard what he said, then fumbled nervously in her handbag until she found her wallet. Anders took it, pulled out an ID card, and glanced quickly at it.

"Where do you live?"

"Spånga," she replied in a whisper. Her mouth was completely dry.

Lars looked at the woman, suddenly feeling very sorry for her. Anders put Dorota's ID card into his pocket.

"We'll keep this. You never saw us here."

Dorota was staring at the floor.

Anders leaned closer to her.

"Do you understand what I'm saying?"

She nodded.

Anders turned toward Lars, a dark look on his face, then started to walk toward the terrace door. Lars didn't move for a moment, looking at Dorota, who was still staring down at the floor.

Anders was striding toward the car, Lars jogged behind him to catch up.

They sat in silence as Lars drove out of the suburb, making sure he kept to the speed limit. Suddenly Anders grabbed Lars's collar, slapping him across the face with the palm of his hand. Lars braked sharply and made an attempt to defend himself. Anders kept on slapping him.

"You fucking idiot... Are you completely fucking useless?" Anders was shouting now. Then he stopped abruptly, sat back in his seat, and sighed as his rage subsided.

Lars stared ahead of him, huddled up, unsure whether the abuse had stopped. His ear was stinging and his legs felt like jelly.

"What would you have done if I wasn't there? Given up, told her what you were doing? You introduced yourself to her with your real name.... Haven't you understood anything about what we do?"

Lars didn't answer.

"Fucking idiot," Anders muttered to himself.

Lars was incapable of figuring out what to do.

Anders looked at him, then pointed ahead at the windshield. "Go on then, drive!"

They drove into the city in total silence, Anders still furious, Lars suffering terribly.

"We don't have to tell Gunilla any of this," Anders said eventually. "It all went fine, the microphones are in place. You'll have to test that everything's working next time you're out there. If not, I'll go in on my own next time. Just keep quiet about the cleaner."

He got out at Eastern Station, leaving a bag containing the receiver on the car floor. He pointed at it.

"Test that as soon as you can."

Then he slammed the car door and vanished into the crowd of people.

Lars didn't move. His whole body was full of fear and anxiety. His thoughts didn't dare venture back to what had just happened, and instead a fury found its way into him, a fury that told him that he hated Anders Ask more than he had hated anyone in his entire life.

The stranger who had spoken Swedish to him was gone. Jens was sitting and listening from his position by the hull of the ship, his eyes darting about, the submachine gun ready to fire at any moment. The sound he had just heard had come from over near the open part of the hold. Otherwise everything was quiet. The men working on the quayside and the Vietnamese crew must have fled when the first shots were fired. That felt like a lifetime ago, but it was really only a few minutes. Long, tough, elastic bloody minutes. He hated minutes. Minutes were always when the shit happened.

He was starting to hear things that weren't there again. Someone getting closer, a quick whisper, footsteps, a gust of wind... His body was pumping sweat and adrenaline, and his shirt was stuck to him.

Once again he was filled by a sudden and intense desire to get away from there, a feeling of panic that he could remember from childhood—the urge to run.

He was debating with himself whether he should stay hidden or fight. Then he heard a movement and a shape flashed quickly across the deck some distance away. Instinctively Jens raised the Bizon to his shoulder and fired a few shots toward the shadow. Then he took cover. The question he had been pondering just now had gotten its answer, he was going to fight. There was no going back now. Jens waited, no sound apart from his own heartbeat pounding inside him. He would have to move, but got no farther than standing up. The weapon sounded like a chainsaw as it rattled off bullets toward Jens. He threw himself to the ground. The bullets hit all around him and the sound was deafening, followed by absolute silence. He could hear a weapon being reloaded some distance away. Jens got up and threw himself over the crates, moving forward, trying to find the person who was shooting at him.... There, up ahead, movement! He could make out half of a body behind a stack of crates, just visible. Then a submachine gun, like the one he was holding, being raised in his direction. But Jens was quicker, firing a burst at the man, who ducked behind the crates. Jens kept moving. The man peeped out quickly again. Jens was some thirty feet away, fired, hit the man in the shoulder; he spun around but still managed to raise his weapon toward Jens, who was now in the middle of the deck with no chance of any cover.

Two guns aimed at each other. And then time stopped, as if someone had grabbed the second hand measuring the movement of the universe. Jens had time to see the man's empty eyes, the barrel aimed toward him. Was he about to die? He couldn't accept that. No fleeting images of his childhood, no mom smiling at him in the light of creation. Just a dark, empty sense of pointlessness about the whole situation. Was this ugly bastard going to kill him?

The thoughts went through his mind during the long moments as he sank to one knee with the butt of the gun to his shoulder, the Russian in the crosshairs.

Jens fired, the Russian fired.

Their bullets must have passed each other in the air somewhere halfway between them. He could hear the whining sound as they passed him on the left, then the burning pain as one of them hit his upper arm.

The three bullets that he had managed to fire were better aimed, and hit the Russian's chest and neck simultaneously. His carotid artery had been punctured, blood was squirting straight out, and the man fell back limply, dropping his gun and hitting a packing crate, dead before he hit the floor.

Jens stared, then heard steps behind him and spun around with his gun raised. The Swedish-speaking man had his pistol aimed at Jens's forehead. Jens's Bizon was aimed straight at the man.

"Lower your weapon. . . . I'm not going to hurt you," he said calmly.

"Lower your own weapon," Jens said, completely foolhardy because of the adrenaline coursing through his body.

The man hesitated, then lowered his gun, and Jens did the same.

"Are you hurt?" he asked, staring at Jens's shoulder.

Jens took a look, felt the wound, it seemed to be superficial. He shook his head.

"Come on! Leave him."

Jens looked at the man he had just killed. Thoughts involving luck, fate, gratitude, angst, guilt, and distaste were flying around his head without finding anywhere to go.

"Come on!" the Swedish-speaking man repeated. Jens followed him.

He noted that the man had a microphone by his chin and an earpiece in his left ear. He said something in a low voice, then stopped abruptly.

"We have to wait," he whispered.

No activity anywhere, no sound, just waiting. Jens looked at him; he was calm, evidently used to this sort of thing.

"My name's Aron," he said.

Jens didn't answer.

The man put a finger to his earpiece, then stood up. "It's clear now, we can go up."

In the middle of the deck Mikhail was on his knees with his hands behind his head, with Leszek standing behind him, an HK G36 with telescopic sight in his hands.

Aron gestured to Jens to follow him. They went past Mikhail and up the steps to the bridge, into the cabin, where they found the dead helmsman lying in a pool of blood. The captain was hiding under his desk, pale and shocked, clutching a large monkey wrench in his hand. He got up, looked at the dead helmsman, then out the window. He saw Mikhail kneeling on deck, and a flash of hatred crossed his eyes. The captain pushed past Jens and Aron as he hurried from the bridge, down the steps, and across the deck. Mikhail didn't have a chance to defend himself before the captain hit him with the wrench and he collapsed. He stared down at the big Russian, who was now trying to protect himself as the captain hit him over the arms and legs again and again, all the while cursing him in his own language. Jens and Aron watched the attack from the bridge.

"What are you doing on board?" Aron asked.

Mikhail had curled up into a ball down below. "I was getting a lift home from Paraguay."

"What were you doing there?"

"All sorts of things."

"How do you make a living?"

Jens looked away from the violence.

"Logistics," he replied.

"Have you got any goods on board?"

"Why?"

"Because I'm asking."

The captain was working hard with the wrench.

"I think that's enough now," Jens said, gesturing with his thumb toward the attack below.

Aron didn't seem to understand, then he let out a short whistle and signaled to Leszek, who intervened and put a stop to the captain's brutal attack. The captain spat at the bleeding Mikhail, who was lying unconscious on deck. He headed back toward the bridge.

In that short instant everything seemed to relax. Leszek dropped his guard, Aron was about to repeat the question he had just asked Jens. Mikhail took the opportunity to get to his feet with some primordial force. It all happened in a flash as the body full of broken bones ran the short distance across the deck to the railing and jumped, managing somehow to heave itself over. At that moment Leszek let off a burst with his automatic weapon. Mikhail vanished. Jens heard him hit the water below.

Aron and Leszek leaped into action. They rushed toward the railing, taking aim and moving in opposite directions, peering at the water and talking between themselves. Every now and then they fired off some shots toward the water. The search went on for ten minutes, then they realized there was no point going on. The man must have drowned. Either because of the injuries inflicted during the beating or because one of their shots had hit him.

The diesel engines throbbed impatiently belowdecks. The ship was at the quayside, but everyone wanted to get moving. Shots had been fired, everyone had fled, and the police were probably on their way. Rotterdam was one of the world's largest ports. If they could get away from the quay, they would be able to hide among the other traffic in the harbor.

They worked together to loosen the heavy ropes securing the ship to the quayside, then hurried on board. The gangway fell into the water as the ship pulled away.

Lars had gone home, where he found two bottles of red wine in one of the kitchen cupboards. He drank one immediately, then opened the other and forced himself to drink another couple of glasses. He was soon drunk, his face hot. He glanced out at the rear courtyard, feeling sorry for himself and the cleaner, wondering what she was doing now. The alcohol shifted into second gear and stopped him from cursing himself.

The sun beating down on the windows was making the apartment unbearably warm.

He pulled off his shirt and drank more wine. He went into the living room, where he threw his shirt on the floor and poured himself a glass of the vintage cognac on the bookcase; it tasted crappy but he forced himself to take several deep gulps, fighting the urge to throw up. He curled up on the sofa and stared out into thin air.

A quarter of an hour later, the change hit Lars Vinge. He turned bitter, and his insides took on a crooked smile as he thought about all the morons he had been surrounded by over the years. His mom and dad, his childhood friends, everyone he'd worked with, everyone he'd met... Anders Ask. He cursed them all, feebleminded and infantile, unlike him.... This was pretty much the extent of the information washing around his marinated head. That was why he didn't often drink, he lost control and went temporarily mad. It had been that way since the very first time he had ever gotten drunk, but he didn't pause to consider that now. He was fully occupied making excuses for the darkness inside him.

An hour later Sara came home and glanced disinterestedly at him.

"Are you ill?"

He didn't answer. She went into the kitchen, then came back shortly after.

"Have you been drinking wine?"

There was an accusing tone to her voice. Lars didn't move, just went on hugging his naked torso.

"Are you drunk?"

He didn't answer.

"What's the matter, Lars?"

He stood up, picked up his shirt from the floor, and pulled it on.

"None of your business," he said, then went out into the hall and put on his shoes, and left the apartment.

In the nearest bar he ordered a vodka and tonic, and got into a debate with an alcoholic retiree about whether Sweden was too soft about sending people to prison. Lars flared up and embarked upon a confused discussion about rehabilitation versus punishment. It didn't take long for him to lose his train of thought. The obvious line of argument wasn't coming to him the way it usually did. The drunk old man and the bartender burst out laughing at Lars's reasoning.

The bar closed and Lars wandered the city streets in the middle of the night, taking an unsteady piss against a parking meter. He was giggling at nothing, pulling faces, and giving the finger to passing cars and people. Then everything went black.

He woke up in a doorway on Wollmar Yxkullsgatan at half past four in the morning when a paperboy stepped over him. He slowly lumbered home with his hands in his trouser pockets, drunk and hungover at the same time. Back home, he saw in the hall mirror that he had a cut on his forehead and completely empty eyes. He fell into bed like a log beside Sara, waking her up. She got up, taking her duvet with her, hissing that he stank of drink.

Three hours later Lars woke up with the morning sun in his face. Sara was gone, her side of the bed unmade as usual, he hated that. He pulled the covers over his head and tried to get back to sleep, but he had ants crawling around deep in his soul.

He drank his morning coffee with trembling hands, trying to pull himself together and remember who he was. He found nothing, it was empty, everything was gone.

"I still want you to help me!" Sophie called upstairs, wiping her hands on a kitchen towel.

"Coming!" he called, sounding irritated.

She looked at the towel, decided it was too old to hang back up, and threw it in the bin.

Albert came downstairs as she was putting aluminum foil over the steaming potato gratin. She pointed at a gift box on the table. Alongside it was wrapping paper, tape, and some yellow ribbon. Albert sat down and started cutting the paper.

She moved the ovenproof dish from the stove to the counter, hurrying when the heat started to come through the oven gloves and letting the dish drop the last half inch onto the counter.

Albert measured the paper against the box. "Who's it for?"

"Tom."

"Why?"

"It's his birthday."

He started folding the paper neatly but applied the tape messily. She got annoyed and took over, doing it properly...then regretted doing so.

They drove the few miles to her childhood home. The thick green foliage made everything feel lush and verdant. The houses were surrounded by oaks, birches, and apple trees. She liked the way the evening sun was casting a golden glow over everything.

On the drive leading up to the house they were met by Rat running toward them. Rat was a little white dog, no one knew what breed, it was just small and white, and barked at anything that moved, and occasionally bit someone.

"Run it over," Albert said in a low voice.

Neither of them liked the dog.

"Would you be sorry if Rat died?" he went on.

Sophie smiled without replying.

"Would you?" he asked again.

She shook her head and Albert smiled at her conspiratorially.

Tom was mixing drinks in the sitting room—Sinatra was singing Jobim songs.

"Hello, Tom."

With his mouth full of olives he gestured to Sophie to wait, but she didn't. Yvonne came to greet them. She kissed Albert on the forehead, then pressed Sophie's lower arm and disappeared. She had white sneakers on her feet, as usual. At the age of seventy, Yvonne still moved as though she thought of herself as an extremely attractive woman.

Jane's boyfriend, Jesus, from Argentina, was sitting on the rug in front of the television, watching something with the sound turned down.

"Hello, Jesus."

She pronounced it *Hessuss*. He said "Sophie" in a friendly tone, then went on watching the television, cross-legged.

Jesus was different. She didn't know how, exactly, but every time she found herself judging his behavior, or trying to figure out his rather odd attitude, she turned out to be wrong. Jane was happy with him in a way that Sophie didn't understand but was jealous of. They left each other alone, and when they met up they smiled at each other. Whether it was when they were reunited after Jesus had been in Buenos Aires for three months or when they met in the kitchen after she'd been on the phone, the smiles were always the same, so big and wide that they both looked like they were about to start laughing.

Sophie went into the kitchen. Jane was sitting at the table trying to slice vegetables on a chopping board. She was a hopeless cook. Sophie put the potato gratin that she had brought with her in the oven, kissed her sister's hair, and sat down beside her. She looked on as Jane made heavy work of dicing a cucumber. The resulting pieces were all shapes and sizes, and Jane swallowed her frustration and pushed the chopping board across to her big sister, who took over.

"Where have you been?" Sophie asked.

Usually at dinner on Sundays there was Sophie and Albert and Sophie's mom, Yvonne, and Tom. Jane and Jesus came when they came, there was no pattern to their visits, only joy when they did show up.

"Nowhere, here and there," she replied, shaking her head. "I don't know."

Jane leaned her chin on her hand, half lying over the table, resting on her elbow. She always sat like that. The posture seemed to have a calming effect on her. She watched Sophie as she sliced vegetables on the chopping board.

"Look at me," she said.

Sophie turned toward Jane.

"Have you done something?"

"Like what?"

"With the way you look?"

Sophie shook her head. "No, why?"

Jane was staring at her intently. "You look... more relaxed, happier."

Sophie shrugged.

"Has something happened?" Jane wondered.

"I don't know."

"Are you seeing someone?"

Sophie shook her head. Jane was still looking at her.

"Sophie?" she whispered.

"Well, maybe."

"Maybe?"

Sophie met Jane's look.

"So who is he, then?"

"A patient... a former patient," Sophie said quietly. "But we're not seeing each other, not like that."

"So how are you seeing each other?"

Sophie smiled. "I don't know...."

She swept the vegetables into a large bowl. It looked messy, she felt like trying to tidy it up but stopped herself. She hated anything that could be seen as showing what a good girl she was when she was at her mother's. Jane was still sitting in the same position, watching Sophie as she worked. Suddenly she jumped as she remembered something.

"Of course, God, we've been in Buenos Aires! I don't know what's up with me, I'm all over the place. We went to visit Jesus's family. We got back on... Thursday."

She hesitated over which day, then decided that that was right. Jane was a fairly chaotic character. At first glance it was easy to assume she was playacting, but that wasn't the case at all. She was disorganized and occasionally far too happy, which sometimes alarmed the people around her, who tended to judge her as being rather false. But those who weren't scared by her tended to like her, the way people who aren't scared usually do.

They sat down at the table, Yvonne and Tom at either end, the others spread out around it. As usual, Yvonne had set the table nicely, she was good at that, one of her better skills. Dinner passed much as it usually did: small talk, laughter, and silent concentration from everyone present, to make sure that things were kept in check and no old injustices or misunderstandings bubbled up.

After dinner Sophie and Jane settled into a couple of easy chairs on the veranda. Jesus disappeared into the library, where he sank into an English book. Albert was upstairs playing cards with Tom to the sound of the Goldberg Variations, which Tom put on the worn-out old gramophone whenever he got the chance.

In their wicker chairs under the infrared heater, the sisters drank their way to intoxication and chatted into the small hours. To start with Yvonne had eavesdropped on them, pretending to be busy with something just inside the terrace door. They caught her red-handed a few times, but she refused to admit she was listening—she was a bad liar. Eventually Tom came and told her to leave them in peace.

Yvonne had been a bit neurotic throughout Sophie's childhood. Her hysteria had avalanched after Georg's death. She went from smiling housewife to disillusioned egotist, dragging them all along with her. Sophie and Jane were permitted to mourn their father, as long as they recognized that Yvonne was bearing the greatest loss. Her mood swung from anger and depression to sudden demands for understanding and way too much love from her daughters. Jane and Sophie didn't know what to do, and their relationship with their mother became distorted, based upon a somewhat confused image of consideration and care. One consequence of this was the deterioration of their own relationship. Yvonne's unhealthy behavior became a barrier between the sisters. They seldom shared any happiness or laughter, and spent most of their time alone in their rooms and competing for their mother's attention.

Then Tom showed up in their lives. They moved into his house a few blocks away. A larger villa with big windows, impressive paintings on large walls. Thick, white down quilts on big beds made of cherrywood. Tom drove them to school in his green Jaguar with pale-brown leather seats, and a vague smell of tobacco smoke and aftershave. Yvonne spent her days at home, painting talentless pictures. She changed over time, emerging from her grief and becoming something like a mother again, but still focused on not giving up her role as victim, to which she had become so attached.

Over the years, once Sophie was grown up and Yvonne reached her fifties, Sophie started to like her again, which she hadn't for a very long time. Occasionally Yvonne could be wise, human, and warm all at the same time—which was when Sophie recognized her. But all too often she behaved as if an old, unresolved aspect of herself was trying to get out—full of hysteria, irritation, and an unhealthy curiosity, a fear of being left out, of losing some invisible and unfathomable sense of control. A few weeks ago she had gone around to Sophie's, had a cup of tea, and asked Sophie how she was. The question had come out of nowhere and had left her bewildered. Out of habit, Sophie had replied that everything was fine, but she could see from the way her mother looked that the question was genuine. That made her stop and think, and without realizing why she had started to cry. Yvonne had held her in her arms. It had felt simultaneously nice and wrong, but she let herself stay, close to her mother, crying over something she didn't understand. Maybe it was just some sort of tension inside her letting go, or maybe Yvonne had realized something that only a mother could understand. Sophie had felt lighter afterward. They never spoke about it again.

The heating and the wine they had drunk warmed them from different directions, creating a wonderfully centered concentration of heat. They shared a pack of cigarettes they had found in the freezer. Yvonne had always kept her supplies there, and that was where the sisters had always stolen them from. They chain-smoked until the pack was gone, then ordered a taxi, which arrived with another pack and two bags of salt licorice. Tom wandered past and clucked at the fact that they had drunk a bottle of wine he had been saving for years. They burst into laughter, gasping for breath. Then they got sentimental as they remembered summers when they were little, the smell of toasted bread and tea in the kitchen of their summer cottage, their days by the shore and Grandma's gentle questions that always seemed designed to strengthen their self-confidence. They talked about their dad, then sat in silence for a while. That always happened when they talked about him, as they were left wondering mutely why he had died and left them so early. Georg had been kind, handsome, and safe, that was how Sophie remembered him. She often wondered if he would still be the same if he had lived. Georg Lantz had died in a hotel in New York during a business trip, dropping down dead in the shower. She only remembered the good things about him. His laughter, his jokes, and how thoughtful he was—how big and relaxed, and that attractive thing she always noticed in older men who had never let themselves be tempted into the murky swamp of bitterness. As if he radiated a desire for things to be well, as if that had been his gift to his wife, his two girls, and God. She still missed him badly, and sometimes talked to him when she felt lonely.

The alcohol and lateness of the hour took their due. Jane went up to the guest bedroom and her very own Jesus. Sophie tucked Albert up in his guest bed, kissing him on his forehead and letting him sleep on.

She asked the taxi driver to take a detour. She sat in the backseat, looking out at the villas gliding past, enjoying being alone and drunk. She liked the affluent suburb she had grown up in, and recognized most of the houses that went past, aware of who had lived there once, and who among them was still living there. This was her place, her fixed point. But even so, she couldn't help feeling rather melancholy as she watched the world going by outside the taxi's windows. It all looked the same, but the time she associated with it was long gone. Now it was something different, somewhere she didn't feel any real sense of belonging.

On the veranda Jane had told her that she and Jesus had met Jens Vall in Buenos Aires. She had been surprised when his name came up, hadn't thought of him for years. *Jens Vall*... They had met one summer when they were still in high school, out in the archipelago, and hadn't let go of each other until they had been forced to. She could half remember the way she felt back then. At the end of the summer vacation she had gone to visit him. He lived on Ekerö, way out on the other side of the city; his parents were away and Jens had the house to himself.

She had spent most of the time lying with her head on his chest, that was her main memory of that week. They talked constantly, as if they had been saving up all those years. Occasionally they would go to the shops in his parents' big, wallowing Citroën—loud music and no driver's license, as if they were practicing being grown-up and free.... They used to hold hands when they were brushing their teeth in the bathroom. God, she'd forgotten all that. In spite of her age, she had realized that she loved him even though she knew that the end would hurt her. And it did. Over the years she had come to think that he had probably felt the same, acting with the same reluctance to avoid the punishment of love.

The taxi driver dropped her off and she went inside her house, reluctant to let the intoxication fade. It was too good for that, too precious. She went down into the cellar and fetched a bottle of wine, opened it in the kitchen, poured a large glass, and sat down at the table. She drank a few sips, then found a couple of crumpled cigarettes tucked in a packet. She lit one without bothering to put the extractor fan on or open a window. The delicious intoxication faded with the last of the wine, the lightness of her thoughts started to take on a darker tone, and the cigarette began to taste bad.

She ended her evening with a strong sense that the last part of it had been unnecessary, wrong. She took that feeling with her into the night, and into her empty dreams.

She woke up the next morning feeling guilty.

6

The cargo ship had headed north from Rotterdam, moving slowly along the Dutch coast. The sea was calm, the sun blazing bright when it appeared between large cirrus clouds. Jens got up from his place in the shade and crossed the deck, letting the rhythm of his own body carry him forward, then went down the metal steps into the hold.

He went through his goods belowdecks, unwilling to do anything but sit and stare, with the image of dead men still on his retinas. He heard steps behind him and Aron appeared. Jens made no attempt to conceal the contents of the boxes.

Aron looked down at the weapons, then sat on a crate beside Jens. "We're heading north for a bit, then east toward Bremerhaven. But before that we'll meet up with a boat off Helgoland where we can unload. You and your goods can go on the other boat."

Jens looked at Aron. "Why?" he asked.

"Because you won't be able to unload any weapons in Bremerhaven. Customs would steal your shipment."

"You can do better than that."

"Yes, and so can you. . . ."

They looked at each other.

"Take the offer. You know how this works."

Yes, Jens knew how this worked, he understood the deal. By accepting the favor he would be tied to Aron. Jens had seen it all. It was an implicit threat. Jens would be stuck. That was how it worked.

"And where will the boat we're going to meet be going later on tonight?"

"Denmark," Aron said. "We'll find some quiet stretch of Jutland and put ashore under cover of darkness."

"And then?"

"I can help you get a car. That's all."

Jens peered at Aron, then looked away and went back to his crates.

Night came, and the ship's engines shut off. Everything was quite still as it rocked in the darkness with all lights extinguished.

He had spent the past few hours going through all his options in his head. Leaving the weapons in Denmark, trying to get them into Germany. Even calling the Russians and telling them that they'd have to pick the goods up themselves somewhere. But they wouldn't go for that. He'd be obliged to do what they had agreed. The weapons were going to Poland. He could figure out how later. Now they had to avoid being boarded before they reached Denmark. They might even have the coast guard on to them already.

Jens took out his cell phone and saw that it had a weak signal. He dug out a number from his address book and let it ring a few times. He brightened up when someone at the other end answered.

"Grandma! It's me, I can hardly hear you but I'm in Denmark, yes, Jutland . . . for work. I'll call in and see you tomorrow or the day after. . . ."

He had lugged his two crates up on deck. Aron and Leszek turned up. Leszek had his automatic rifle slung over his shoulder. The only difference was that this time he had a Hensoldt night sight mounted on the gun.

Leszek heard the boat first.

"It's coming," he said, and disappeared up to the bridge, where he lay down on the roof and followed the approaching vessel through his telescopic sight.

The sea was calm, the engines were now clearly audible whirring out there in the darkness. Jens could just make out a large fishing boat approaching.

It pulled up alongside the ship. A voice from the trawler shouted for Aron, who shouted back something Jens couldn't quite pick up. A man, mixed race, came up onto the ship and gave Aron a broad smile, throwing his arms out.

"So what are we doing out here, Aron, in the middle of the sea?"

Aron smiled back and pointed at Jens. "This gentleman's going to be traveling with you for a bit. Along with a few boxes that belong to him."

The man turned to Jens and looked him quickly up and down. "Welcome aboard, I'm Thierry."

Jens said hello.

"What have you got in your boxes?" the man asked.

"He's shipping automatic weapons," Aron said.

Leszek came over to them, rifle over his shoulder, exchanged nods with Thierry. Then Thierry inspected Jens as if he were trying to see something of the gunrunner in his face, then turned to Aron.

"OK... Aron, have you got what I asked for?"

Aron held up a bag, smiled, and passed it to Thierry, who weighed it in his hand for a moment before putting it down on deck and unzipping it. He pulled out an object that was wrapped in a piece of velvet cloth, carefully put it down, and opened it. Jens could almost hear the man gasp for breath as the little stone statue was revealed. It looked fairly unremarkable to Jens. Small, gray, and shapeless. Thierry held it up to the light from a lamp above him. He began to give an animated explanation of how old it was, that it was a cultural treasure from the Incan empire, that it was impossible to put a value on it, that it was probably priceless.

"Thank you, Aron," Thierry said.

"Don't thank me, thank Don Ignacio. He's the one who managed to get it for you."

Leszek and Aron disappeared belowdecks.

Thierry was gazing at the statue.

"Are you going to sell it?" Jens asked.

"No, you don't sell something like this. I'm going to keep it at home, to look at." He turned to Jens. "But I sell a lot of things rather like it, if you're interested?"

Jens smiled and shook his head.

"Besides, it'll be a good counterweight to your weapons and the cocaine on our journey once we land. This has good energies. It will help us."

Jens had gotten his answer to the question of what Aron and Leszek were doing on the ship.

A Volkswagen LT35 was what Lars had bought with the money Gunilla had transferred into his account. A large white van without a single distinguishing feature. There was an internal wall dividing the driver's cab from the large space at the rear, and a single window in one of the rear doors, with mirrored glass.

The van was parked seventy-five yards from Sophie's house on a small gravel track that overlooked the area. He had fitted out the back of the van with a shabby old armchair, and there he sat with a set of headphones attached to a receiver, which in turn was attached to a recording device, listening in stereo to the Brinkmann family eating dinner. Every word that was said, every inference, taught Lars a little more about Sophie and the world she lived in, how she thought, how she felt. . . .

He had been watching her for two weeks, and it felt like an eternity. During this timeless stretch of days, evenings, and nights during which he had been following her, photographing her, wondering about her, and writing content-free reports for Gunilla, something had started to happen inside him. For some unfathomable reason he had started to feel a bit freer, a bit stronger, and a bit quieter in his otherwise constant internal questioning of himself.

He didn't know where this change had come from, maybe it was just coincidence, maybe it was his new job, maybe the fruit of his isolation during the day? He kept fretting about it—was it something to do with Sophie Brinkmann? Her appearance in his life had told him something, her femininity had somehow spoken to his masculinity. She had enlightened him about what he wanted, and how he wanted it. She had opened up something to him and he felt that if she was capable of doing something like that for him from a distance, without even knowing him, then he ought to be able to do something similar for her. He knew they were connected somehow. And he knew that she was somehow also aware of it....

Lars could hear an openhearted dialogue between Sophie and Albert through his headphones. A conversation between them that showed that their relationship was unforced and loving, and it amazed him; he had never heard anything so natural before.

He spent the last few hours of his shift half lying in the armchair, clipping his fingernails with an imitation Leatherman, listening to Sophie lying in bed reading a book. All he could hear was her turning pages occasionally. He shut his eyes. He was lying in bed beside her, and she was smiling at him.

He drove home through the night with the window open to the Swedish summer, which had suddenly taken the place of spring—the air warm and clear at the same time.

At home in the apartment he wrote up his report on the old typewriter.

"Why are you using a typewriter instead of the computer?"

Sara was standing in the doorway, newly woken, wearing her hideous washed-out nightdress. He looked at her, got up, and slammed the door in her surprised face, locked it, and went back to the desk.

"What the hell's wrong with you?!" Her voice was muffled by the door.

He wasn't listening to her, and just kept on tapping at the machine. In his report to Gunilla he reproduced the majority of the conversation at the dinner table. The sheets slid through the fax machine and then into the shredder. He didn't feel like going and lying down beside Sara. The cognac was finished, the bottles of wine empty. Lars had a go at the sherry on the bookshelf. He had no idea where it had come from, it had always been there. He drank straight from the bottle as he waited for the computer to boot up. Sherry, what a load of crap... insipid and disgusting at the same time, which was hardly worth making a fuss of, was it? He forced it down. The misery around him eased a fraction and his brain heated up to a vaguely tolerable temperature. The computer screen flickered into life, showing the desktop. He clicked to open a file, highlighted the contents, and selected "slideshow." Then he opened the classical music folder and began watching pictures of Sophie to the sound of Puccini. He had several hundred photographs of her, playing in front of his eyes at five-second intervals, enlarged to cover the whole screen.

Lars leaned back in his office chair and watched as Sophie cycled to work, as she put her key in her front door, as she appeared hazily through the kitchen window, as she fetched the newspaper from the mailbox, as she cut suckers from the roses along the side of the house. He knew where she was, how she felt, what she was thinking about, every nuance of her face. It was like a film, the film of Sophie Brinkmann's inner life. He couldn't help laughing at the miracle, amazed that he, who so rarely thought things like this, had happened by chance to encounter the woman he knew everything about. Or was it actually chance? No, it couldn't be, maybe fate had finally dared show its face to him?

Lars printed out his favorite pictures of her, put them in a folder, drew a flower on the front, and hid it in a drawer.

She wasn't thinking about anything in particular as she walked along the cor-ridor looking at the floor, but looked up when she heard footsteps in front of her.

A woman in her fifties was trying to get her attention. Sophie recognized her, she'd seen her before. She was related to someone on the ward, she didn't know who.

"Sophie?"

Sophie was surprised that the woman used her name, that rarely happened in spite of the name badge on her chest.

"My name's Gunilla Strandberg, I'd like a few words with you."

Sophie nodded, smiling her best nurse's smile. "Of course."

Gunilla looked around and Sophie realized that she didn't want to talk in the corridor.

"Follow me."

Sophie showed Gunilla into an empty room and let the door close behind them.

Gunilla opened her handbag, took out a leather wallet, searched through an inside pocket, and found what she was looking for among some old cash register receipts and banknotes. She held her ID up toward Sophie.

"I'm a police officer."

"Yes?"

Sophie folded her arms.

"I just want to talk to you," Gunilla said calmly.

Sophie realized that she was standing defensively.

"Maybe you recognize me?" Gunilla asked.

"Yes, I've seen you here before. You're related to one of our patients."

Gunilla shook her head. "Can we sit down?"

Sophie pulled a chair over for Gunilla, who sat down. Sophie settled on the edge of the hospital bed. Gunilla was silent, she seemed to be searching for words. Sophie waited. After a while Gunilla looked up.

"I'm running an investigation."

Sophie waited. Gunilla Strandberg still seemed to be trying to find the right words.

"You're friends with Hector Guzman?" she said calmly.

"Hector? No, I'm not sure I'd say that."

"But you do see each other?"

It was more a statement of fact than a question.

Sophie looked at Gunilla. "Why?"

"Nothing much, I'd just like to ask a few questions."

"What for?"

"How close are the two of you?"

Sophie shook her head. "He was a patient, we talked. What do you want?"

Gunilla took a deep breath, smiling at her own clumsiness.

"Sorry, I don't mean to be intrusive, I never learn." She collected herself and looked Sophie in the eye. "I... I need your help."

7

Mikhail had hit the water. He had escaped being hit by the shots being fired off at him by a hairbreadth. On his way down through the dark sea he heard the whirr and hiss of the projectiles as they slowed in the water. After a while he turned and swam back underwater toward the ship again, then lack of oxygen forced him to the surface. The wedge-shaped design of the ship saved his life. The men up above couldn't look both down and inward. Mikhail stayed there beside the hull, moving the whole time. When the engines started up he took a chance and swam toward the concrete quayside, aiming for its far end. The quay was high. If there weren't any steps or something similar for him to climb up, he'd drown. His body was aching, he wouldn't be able to manage much longer. But after the exhausting swim he rounded the end of the quay and found a rusty old cable that he clung to until the ship was on its way out to sea. With a fair amount of effort and a great deal of pain he managed to get himself up on the quayside, then clambered into the rental car, soaking wet, pulled the GPS and cell phone from the glove compartment, then called Roland Gentz. He said they had encountered armed resistance, that both his men were dead and that there had been three men on the ship—two he recognized as Aron and Leszek, and a third, unknown man, apparently Swedish.

Roland thanked him for the information and said he'd get back to him within the next few hours. They ended the call.

The Vietnamese captain hadn't held back with him. Broken nose, broken ribs, but he could live with that. He didn't blame the captain—after all, he had shot and killed his helmsman in front of him. He had been forced to make an example of him, because at the very moment shots started to ring out he knew the captain had broken his agreement with Hanke's people. The helmsman was the punishment, and he hadn't hesitated for a second.

Mikhail seldom felt any resentment toward people who beat him up or fired at him, they were just doing the same as him. He'd taken part in serious wars against both Afghans and Chechens; he'd been pinned down under heavy fire, on the very edge of what the human psyche could stand. He'd seen friends get shot, blown to pieces, burnt up. And he for his part had done the same to the enemy, but his actions had never been about anger or vengeance. Maybe that was why he had survived.

He had already had this attitude toward his life and his way of treating people when he started work for Ralph Hanke. The same attitude no matter whether he was shooting and killing someone on Ralph's orders, beating someone up, or going to Stockholm and driving into Adalberto Guzman's son.

He never reflected on whether he'd done the right or wrong thing, his years as an active frontline soldier in bloody and meaningless wars had given him an awareness that things like right or wrong didn't actually exist in this world at all. All that did exist were consequences, and if you were aware of these, then life could rumble on in something like a manageable fashion.

He stopped the car at a shopping mall. People stared at the big, bloodstained man as he limped through the shops. He bought all that he needed, bandages, Band-Aids, cotton balls, antiseptic, and the strongest painkillers he could find. The shop smelled nice, a mixture of pharmacy and perfume counter. He paid for his goods and the pretty, white-clad woman at the counter avoided looking him in the eye.

Mikhail drove to a roadside bar, went into the bathroom, and patched himself up as best he could, then swallowed four painkillers.

He sat at a table at the far end of the restaurant and washed down his food with three glasses of beer. Then he stretched, feeling his joints crack, and noted that his whole body was still aching like hell.

While he waited for the bill he checked his GPS receiver. He had attached a transmitter to one of Guzman's crates of cocaine in the hold of the ship. The screen said there was no signal, so they were probably still out at sea.

Mikhail got a room in a roadside motel, clean sheets in hideous colors that smelled of way too much fabric softener. He took all his clothes off and examined himself in the mirror, looking at the blue bruises on his upper body, rolling his shoulders and clicking his neck into place. His body told its own very clear story: a mass of scars, four bullet wounds, shrapnel injuries. The scars were evenly spread over his body, some inflicted by direct force, others by accident, but every injury to his body had a strong memory attached to it. Some of these memories he would prefer to have avoided, but that wasn't how it worked; he was obliged to carry them with him the whole time. Whenever he looked at his body he couldn't help seeing the sort of person he really was.

His cell phone rang. Mikhail crossed the carpet and picked it up from the bedside table. Roland on the other end, asking what the options were.

"We've got a transmitter to follow, but that's all."

"Ralph's angry."

"Isn't he usually?"

"You have to strike back, if only to avenge your dead colleagues."

Mikhail understood that Roland was trying to play on his emotions, but he didn't have any feelings of that sort. Mikhail didn't give a fuck if his colleagues were dead, they were both wrecks, and their deaths probably came as a release for them.

"I'll see what I can do. Are you sending anyone?"

"You'll manage fine on your own."

Mikhail looked at himself in the big mirror, stretched his neck to the right, and something slid into place in his shoulder with a click. "OK, but be more specific."

Mikhail could hear Roland clicking his mouse, he was evidently online.

"Ralph's mad as a hornet, just do something, anything; he won't sleep until they've understood that they've lost, you know what he's like."

Mikhail didn't answer, just clicked to end the call.

He took a shower and then called an escort agency. He ordered a big girl, not too young, not too skinny, one who could speak decent Russian. The woman arrived, she was from Albania, very short, with knee-high white boots, a pink top, wide hips, exactly to his taste. She introduced herself as Mona Lisa, which he didn't like, and he asked if he could call her something else, maybe Lucy?

Mikhail and Lucy lay in bed, sharing a bottle of Genever and watching a Dutch talk show. He began to like her as they lay there laughing at the fact that neither of them could understand a word of what was being said on the television.

"Can you stay the night?"

She reached for her cell in her sparkly gold handbag and called someone, then read out Mikhail's credit card number to the person on the other end.

That night he slept with his head on her chest, holding her like a child holding its mother. At four o'clock in the morning his alarm went off. He sat up and rubbed the tiredness from his eyes. The pain was still there, it would be for a while yet. He turned around; Lucy was snoring quietly.

He switched on the GPS receiver, got up, and went into the bathroom. There he rinsed his face with cold water, washing himself as best he could in the little washbasin. When he emerged again the transmitter was active. He looked at the map. The boxes were in western Jutland.

Mikhail got dressed and left a big tip for Lucy on the bedside table.

He closed the door gently behind him, got in the rental car, and headed out onto the highway, disappearing into the early-morning mist.

—

The little half-timbered house with its thatched roof lay isolated and sur-rounded by a mass of trees a hundred yards or so from the old main road. He turned the car onto a pitted gravel track that led through an avenue of trees, with wheat fields behind the trees on both sides. The sun was shining in that golden color that Jens remembered from summers here when he was small—gold, orange, and green all at the same time.

After getting off the ship the previous night, he had headed up the coast of Jutland in the fishing boat that Thierry had arrived in. They had moored in an isolated inlet and unloaded their cargo under cover of darkness. Three cars had been waiting for them there, one of them allocated to Jens, and he had driven off quickly.

He parked the car in front of the house but didn't get out at once. It was a beautiful morning, the birds were singing, the dew was drying up as the temperature rose. A door surrounded by climbing roses opened and an old lady with white hair and an apron smiled broadly at Jens. He smiled back at the almost absurdly picturesque image, then opened the car door and got out.

They hugged, and she kept hold of him.

"Fancy, you coming and surprising me like this . . . how lovely!"

Grandma Vibeke made tea for them both, serving it in the same old chipped blue china that she always used. He looked at her. She was old, unbelievably old, but her age never seemed to slip into that stage when old people got tired and introverted. He hoped she would be able to leave this earthly life with the same attitude she had always had, that she would be permitted to die in this house.

He looked around the kitchen, picking up a photograph from the mantelpiece: Grandpa Esben with his drooping mustache, wide-brimmed hat, and a rifle on a leather strap over his shoulder.

"I could stare at this picture all day. I used to think it looked like he was standing out on the savannah, out on the veldt. On his way to hunt elephants or poachers. But he wasn't, he was standing on a new-mown wheat field outside this house ready to hunt rabbits."

Vibeke nodded.

"He was a grand man."

Jens stared at the photograph. "But we didn't get on that well, did we, Grandpa and me?"

He put the photograph on the table and sat down.

"I don't know, he used to say you knew no boundaries. And for your part you always said he was crazy and should keep out of things. You always ended up arguing for one reason or another."

Jens smiled at the memory, but there was something serious about his relationship with his grandfather. He had never understood why they always argued.

She came over with the teapot and filled their cups.

"Every summer when you arrived you used to get along fine to start with. You would go hunting with Esben, or go fishing down at the river, as if you were testing out your relationship. Then after a few days you'd stop spending time together, you always found something of your own to do, and Esben kept himself to himself."

She sat down.

"One year, I think you were fourteen, you went into town to go shopping. There was a gang of boys on mopeds, a few years older than you. . . . They picked a fight with you. You came home with a black eye and Esben blamed you for something you hadn't done, he'd made up his mind that you were at fault. I tried to tell him, but he wouldn't listen."

Jens remembered. Vibeke drank her tea.

"The day before you were due to go home you set off into town on your own, found out where the boys were, and gave all four of them broken noses. You were positively glowing when you got back, but you didn't say anything. I only found out about it after you'd gone, one of the mothers came 'round and wanted an apology."

Vibeke smiled.

"Esben was always worried about you, said you never backed down even when you knew it was all over."

"No, I probably didn't."

"What about now?"

He thought for a moment. "I probably still don't."

They ate dinner out in the garden, at an old wooden table in the arbor. Jens and Vibeke sat up late talking; he didn't want to go to bed, wished he could have stayed longer.

"Thanks for coming, you're a good boy."

Jens looked at her, drained his glass of wine, and put it back on the table. "I used to be so eager to get here every summer, and it always felt so empty, having to go home again.... It was the same each year. You're the only person who knows me, Grandma."

Her eyes filled with tears. Tears of old age, containing neither sorrow nor disappointment.

That night Jens lay awake in bed for hours just staring at the ceiling. The bed was as deep as a bathtub. He tried to remember the nights he spent in that same bed as a child. The memories came as emotions, good emotions. He slept flat on his back for the first time in a very long time.

His dream was sweeping him closer to the abyss. He was alone, unable to get away. There was a layer of darkness covering everything. He tried to shout but no sound came out. Lack of oxygen to his head brought him back to consciousness. He opened his eyes.

On the edge of the bed, with one hand around his neck and the other holding a pistol, its barrel resting against his chin, sat Mikhail, staring at him. The look in the man's eyes was empty but curious, as if he were trying to read something from Jens's eyes. Mikhail's battered face was made worse by the white light of the moon illuminating the room, the look of a pallid, sick person.

His deep voice said, "Car keys."

Jens tried to think. "In my pants pocket."

Mikhail turned around and checked the pants that were hanging over a chair. He turned back toward Jens and struck him on the head with the butt of the pistol. There was an unlikely metallic echo, and Jens fell into empty unconsciousness.

The lawnmower was making its way through the grass. It was heavy and So- phie was sweating in the heat. The little motor that was supposed to drive the front wheels was broken, she'd ordered a new one but it had never arrived. Maybe it was just as well, seeing as she had no idea how to install it.

Since her meeting with Gunilla she hadn't stopped thinking. She had gone for walks, bike rides, runs, trying to find some peace of mind. She had tried writing in the evenings when she was alone, she had looked inside herself—thinking, reasoning, evaluating.

Anger had been a constant, that had been there from the start, in the question Gunilla had put to her. Or perhaps not in the question itself but in the reply that she hadn't been able to avoid, angry because she had known all along what it would be. A yes, there was no other choice open to her. She was a nurse. A police officer had contacted her, asking for help.

Sophie cut the grass in straight lines; now there was just a thin line of taller grass running from one end of the garden to the other, and she aimed the lawnmower at it and let it cut the tops off the blades of grass.

When she was finished she let go and the dead-man's handle automatically switched the engine off. The lawnmower clicked quietly in the heat, her hands were warm and red from the vibration—and somewhere deep inside her ears was a high-pitched squeaking. She glanced at her work, the lawn looked symmetrical.

Sophie poured herself a glass of iced water from a jug in the fridge, and her cell buzzed anxiously on the counter and the screen lit up. She stopped drinking, took several deep breaths, trying to slow her pulse rate.

UNKNOWN NUMBER it said on the display. She clicked to open the message.

Thanks for your message. Have been busy. Meet up? Best, H.

She had sent a text to his cell the day before, after wondering what to write. In the end she had kept it brief: *Thanks for the party.*

Now she wasn't sure about replying, her fingers hovered above the buttons. The car horn sounded anxiously outside, interrupting her thoughts. Albert was sitting in the front seat, and she glanced at the clock on the wall and realized that she had lost track of the time. She put the phone in her pocket. Albert blew the horn again, and she called out angrily that he'd have to be patient. She would have to go as she was, scruffy, all sweaty in her jeans, gardening boots, and washed-out sweater. On the way out she managed to pull her hair up and grab her handbag.

Albert was sitting beside her in the car wearing a green tennis shirt, white shorts, white tennis shoes, holding a tennis racket in a case on his lap. The air-conditioning wasn't working. Sophie had the window open. The heat outside had a cooling effect once they were going faster. They didn't talk, Albert was always quiet before a match. A mixture of nerves and concentration.

She headed straight over the roundabout by the main square in

Djursholm, drove up past the castle and down the little hill beside the water tower. She turned off into the garage in front of the red and utterly tasteless tennis hall.

"You don't have to come in." He opened the door, saying this more out of politeness than anger.

She didn't answer, just took the key out of the ignition and got out of the car. They went in together, Albert a few steps ahead.

There were matches under way on the courts inside the hall. Albert found some friends sitting in a group a short distance away and went over to join them. They fell into amused conversation. She liked his friends, they were always laughing when they were together. Sophie found a spare seat and sat down to watch the match in front of her. The ball moved back and forth between the two girls who were playing, she thought they were pretty good. The match kept up an even pace as Sophie's thoughts drifted off. She pulled out her cell and reread Hector's message, her finger hovering above the Reply button. Albert's name and that of another boy were called out over the loudspeaker. She put the phone back in her bag and discovered that she was smiling as she watched Albert step onto the court. His walk was confident, and he looked relaxed as he shook hands with the umpire, then focused as he threw the ball in the air and hit the first serve of the match.

Albert won one of his matches and went through to the semifinals, due to be held at the outdoor courts over by the castle. People began to get up and leave the hall. She went with the flow out to the garage, and saw Albert looking for her in the crowd. He indicated that he was going to go ahead with his friends.

In the garage she got stuck with another mom, who was going on about a collection for a teacher at Albert's school. Sophie avoided another mother who was renowned for thinking that every child apart from her own daughter was heading in the wrong direction in life. She pretended not to see the red-wine club, a gaggle of over-the-hill women who had once been attractive. Slender legs, bulging stomachs, expensive makeup, and an easy social manner at first acquaintance but with whom just minutes later the conversation slid onto other people's faults and shortcomings.

She got in behind the wheel, feeling no connection to any of the people she had just encountered. She asked herself why she chose to live among these peculiar people who never ceased to amaze her.

She drove the car toward the castle. Without quite knowing why she took out her cell, found Hector's message again, and wrote *Whenever.*

Mikhail had driven south from Jutland, across the unmanned border into Germany.

When he arrived in Munich he parked the car in the garage of one of the empty villas that Hanke owned.

The villa was on a sleepy, middle-class road where all the houses looked the same—brick-built, heavy doors. He guessed he had about ninety pounds of cocaine in the trunk of the car. In spite of the intermezzo on the boat he was pleased with the way things had turned out, and he knew that Ralph would be too. They had got the last word and, thanks to Mikhail's last-minute intervention, some of the cocaine as well, just as Ralph wanted.

He reversed into the garage and closed the door.

The boxes, two of them, wooden, were sitting on top of each other. He pulled one out, found his transmitter, pulled it off the box, and put it in his pocket. He pulled the other box out and opened it with a crowbar, pushed the wooden lid off, and found a load of sawdust. Mikhail brushed it aside and put his hand in, and found the butt of a machine gun. He pulled it out and recognized the model, a Steyr AUG. He evaluated it quickly. Relatively unused, good condition. Mikhail found another nine of the same model, recently greased and with their bolts in place. He broke open the other box and under the sawdust he found eight brand-new Heckler & Koch MP7s and two MP5s.

He scratched under one eye with his index finger.

Hector was sitting in the backseat of the car that was waiting outside So-phie's gate. He watched as she came down the little gravel path. They looked at each other. When she came out of the gate he leaned across the seat and pushed the door open for her.

"Welcome, Sophie Brinkmann," he said.

She got in beside him and shut the door. In the driver's seat Aron started the car.

"Hello, Aron," she said.

Aron nodded and pulled away.

"You have a nice house," Hector said.

"Thanks."

Hector raised a finger.

"I like yellow houses," he said.

"Really?" she said with a smile.

"How long have you lived here?"

"Quite a while."

He was searching for a follow-up question. "Do you like the area? Is this a good place to live?"

Now she looked at him as if she were about to start laughing, wondering where this sterile small talk was going. He realized.

"Well, good," he said after a pause.

"Mmm." She smiled.

They kept on driving.

"Thanks for your present, I like it a lot. I've been using it," he said.

She had given him a money clip, possibly because it was suitably impersonal but really nice.

The car journey turned out to be straightforward. Hector talked in his assured, calm way, telling her things, asking questions, and steering them away from small silences and other awkward moments. He was good at it—one of his accomplishments. She didn't know if he was aware of it himself, but throughout the drive his leg kept nudging hers.

Aron turned into Haga Park and drove up to the Butterfly House.

"Have you been here before?"

She shook her head. They got out of the car and went inside the large greenhouse. A man offered to take her jacket. It was damp and warm, and there were birds singing and the sound of running water, and—as the name suggested—butterflies fluttering about, apparently oblivious to everything, possibly even their own beauty. She realized that she liked butterflies a lot, had always liked them.

In one part of the tropical room there were several rows of wooden chairs set out in front of a single larger chair, placed a step up from the others. Behind the single chair sat a four-man orchestra. One cello, two violins, and a flute.

A few people were already sitting, waiting. Sophie sat down. Hector walked in, and called for everyone's attention. He began in Spanish, then switched to Swedish, introducing a Spanish poet whose work had been translated into Swedish. Applause broke out in the tropical heat.

The poet, a short man with a cheerful face, came in and sat down on the chair, said a few words of Spanish, then began reading his poetry to the accompaniment of the quartet behind him.

To begin with, Sophie wasn't sure what to think. She almost started giggling, but after a while she got caught up in the solemnity of the moment. She listened to the beautiful music, to the beautiful words the man was intoning with calm concentration. It was as if he were transmitting some sort of harmony even though she couldn't understand a word he was saying. The butterflies were fluttering about, seemed to be showing themselves off to the audience. Her thoughts began to wander: Gunilla Strandberg, Hector, herself, to and fro without settling. And all the time the feeling that had been running through her since her encounter with Gunilla in the hospital, something along the lines of *Follow your heart*...But when she tried to do that, she realized that she had more than one heart. There was the one that Gunilla had played on, *Do the right thing*—her moral heart. But there was also the one that Hector had somehow brought to life, the passionate heart that had lain dormant within her for so long.

Do the right thing, Gunilla had said during their conversation in the hospital. *Do the right thing.* With the subtext: tell them all about Hector Guzman, that's the right thing to do. We're on the right side, she had said, and he's on the wrong side. Had Gunilla understood who Sophie was? Someone who couldn't say no to a request from the police. A nurse—someone who wanted to do the right thing.

Sophie opened her eyes, the poet was still reciting his work. She looked at Hector, who was listening intently to the poet's voice. She liked watching him when he looked like that, private, concentrating, impenetrable. Her eyes fell to her hands in her lap. No matter how she might want to look at it, contact with Hector was already established, the game was afoot. And what, according to Gunilla, ought to feel right really didn't at all.

The Spaniard read, the orchestra played, the butterflies fluttered about, and tears started rolling down her cheeks. She found a handkerchief in her bag. Hector turned to look at her, possibly thinking she was crying because of the intensity of the moment. She managed to smile as though she were embarrassed by her tears, then wiped them away and pretended to concentrate on the music and poetry again. She could feel him still looking at her.

When the poet finished the audience applauded. Hector stood up and showed everyone the bilingual book that his publishing company had produced in both Swedish and Spanish, telling them about it and thanking the poet for coming.

They headed toward the garage, Hector walking slowly with his stick, one leg still in a cast.

"Beautiful? Lovely? Good?" he asked.

"All of those," she said.

They stopped at a waiting taxi. He paid the driver to take her home. The door closed and the taxi drove off and she realized that she was smiling. She was rather scared of how much she liked being in his presence.

"Stocksund, please."

The driver muttered something.

Her cell buzzed to let her know she had a message. She pulled it out of her bag and read: *Well done. Meet me at once in the multistory garage on Regeringsgatan, 4th floor*, from an unknown number.

She read the message several times, debating with herself.

"Sorry, I've changed my mind. Regeringsgatan, please."

For some reason the taxi driver sighed.

She took the elevator up to the fourth floor of the garage. Gunilla was waiting for her in her car, and gestured to Sophie to get into the passenger seat.

"Thanks for coming."

Gunilla started the car and pulled away.

"Was it nice? The Butterfly House?"

Sophie didn't answer, and fastened her seat belt.

"We don't follow him all the time, it's called sporadic surveillance."

They drove down the spiral ramp that took them to the exit onto

Regeringsgatan. She was driving a fairly new Peugeot, and the seat was too far forward, too close to the steering wheel. It made her look like a little old lady. As usual, the traffic was heavy but Gunilla drove better and more safely than Sophie had feared when she saw the position of the seat.

"I realize that you must have done a lot of thinking since our conversation, and that your decision has been difficult."

Music was playing quietly on the radio. Gunilla leaned over and switched it off.

"You've made the right decision, Sophie. If that means anything."

She pulled out to pass a double-parked truck.

"You can help us do something good. Our work combined with your observations will help us get results.... It will feel good, I promise you."

Gunilla looked at Sophie. "What do you think?"

"It doesn't feel like that right now."

"What?"

"Good. It doesn't feel good."

"And that's entirely natural," Gunilla said quietly.

They got stuck in traffic. There was something unforced about Gunilla Strandberg, something grounded and normal. She had a calm about her, a calm that never let her get out of balance. The traffic eased and they pulled out onto Valhallavägen, heading toward Lidingö.

"I saw something in you when you came out of his room. I was sitting on a bench in the corridor. You didn't notice me, but I noticed you."

Sophie waited.

"I checked you out. A widow with one son, a nurse making ends meet with the inheritance from her husband. She seemed to live a fairly comfortable, quiet, retiring life. But perhaps meeting Hector Guzman has changed that?"

Sophie was feeling uncomfortable. Gunilla noticed.

"How does that feel?"

"What?"

"That I know that about you?"

The question surprised Sophie. She automatically replied with the opposite of what she was feeling. "It feels fine, it doesn't matter."

Gunilla drove on for a bit.

"I'm going to be honest with you, Sophie, otherwise this isn't going to work. And that honesty includes explaining how I work, and what you can expect from me."

"What I can expect from you?"

They were passing a truck in the inside lane, and it let out a loud hissing noise as it changed gears.

"I'm a widow as well, although my husband died many years ago now."

Sophie glanced at her.

"I know that your father's dead as well. So are my parents. I know how it feels, I recognize the emptiness that never really goes, the feeling of loneliness. . . ."

They were crossing the long bridge out to Lidingö, with motorboats and yachts on the glittering water below them.

"And that loneliness contains something that I've never understood, a little hint of shame."

Gunilla's words hit home heavily inside Sophie. She kept her eyes on the view.

"Do you know what I mean, Sophie?"

Sophie didn't want to answer, then nodded.

"Where does that come from?" Gunilla went on. "I mean, what is it?"

Sophie's eyes were glued to the world outside.

"I don't know," she whispered.

They sat in silence for the rest of the journey.

They turned into a maze of little roads, and Gunilla made her way through them with ease, eventually pulling onto a gravel track that led to a little wooden house in the middle of a grove of trees.

"This is where I live," she said.

Sophie looked at the house, it reminded her of a summer cottage.

Gunilla showed her around the garden, pointing out her peonies and roses. Told her their names and how she'd got them, how they behaved in different soil, at different times of the year. How she kept them free from various diseases and pests, how she was genuinely affected by their well-being. Sophie was left in no doubt about Gunilla's genuine interest, it was fascinating.

They passed an arbor and Gunilla invited Sophie to sit down on a white wooden chair. Gunilla sat down opposite her with a file on her lap, Sophie couldn't remember if she had been carrying it the whole time.

Gunilla was about to say something but changed her mind. She handed the file to Sophie.

"I'll get us something to drink. Take a look at this in the meantime."

Gunilla got up and went off toward the house. Sophie watched her go, then opened the file.

The first thing she saw was a report of a murder investigation that had been translated into Swedish from Spanish. Hector's name appeared on every other line.

Sophie kept looking through the file, leafing past other official documents. They were followed by a number of translated documents about other murders. She read a bit more. They went all the way back to the '80s. Each document had two photographs attached to one side. One was a picture of the corpse, the other a picture of the murder victims when they were still alive. She leafed through the cases, looking at the pictures of the victims. A dead man lying on the floor in a pool of blood. A man shot inside a car, his head at an odd angle. A man in a suit hanging from a noose in a tree in a forest. The bloated body of a naked man in a bathtub. Sophie went back through the file, looking past the photographs of the crime scenes and staring instead at the family photographs. Men with their wives and children. Different settings, mostly vacation snapshots, but a few pictures of dinners, barbecues, Christmas parties. The men were happy, the children were happy, the women were happy. . . . But the men were dead. Murdered.

She turned a page and saw an enlarged photograph of Hector; he was staring straight at her and she stared back.

Sophie closed the file and tried to take some deep breaths, but found that she couldn't.

PART TWO

8

Sonya Alizadeh was on all fours on the large double bed. Svante Carlgren was taking her from behind. He was many years older, and many years uglier. Sonya faked an orgasm, screaming into the pillow. Svante felt a surge of pride.

He really preferred more elaborate things but today he was in a hurry, they only had half an hour before his lunchtime meeting. He liked sneaking away for a fuck every now and then. Sonya was his sexual fantasy, possibly even better than a fantasy. Her long black hair, her quiet, mysterious attitude, and of course her breasts, which in his opinion sat perfectly on her nicely curvaceous body.

He had met her a year before when he was attending a theatre premiere with his wife. They had bumped into each other during the intermission by the bar, and she had spilled champagne on his trousers. His wife had gone out to the car to get a cardigan, she was always cold. All that bloody freezing got on his nerves.

Svante and Sonya had gotten to talking after the mishap, before his wife returned, and when they separated she gave him her phone number, offering to pay to have his trousers dry-cleaned. He said that that was out of the question, and she said he could call anyway if he felt like it. Those words had made Svante go weak at the knees for a moment. Never before had a woman been as candid as Sonya, never before had a woman of her caliber made contact. She was sexy, she was an animal. She didn't ask for much, apart from an agreed fee—she was perfect. And he had noticed that she found him interesting, just as he himself did; he saw himself as one of the elite, one of the big boys.

After studying economics in Gothenburg, Svante Carlgren had joined Volvo during the years when Gyllenhammar was in charge, but when the great man resigned and moved to London, Svante went to Stockholm instead and worked his way up in Ericsson, the telecom company. The firm was so large that only a very few people had a good overview of how it all worked. Svante was one of them. The only thing he was missing was the occasional mention in one of the business papers, getting some sort of public recognition for his work, but he was also aware that the day that this happened would be the day when his sphere of influence began to shrink. He made do instead with the appreciation he was shown by his colleagues, and sometimes got to join in with the big boys, even flying on the company jet.

As usual, Sonya had offered him cocaine before they went to bed. He thought the drug was fantastic, it made him feel fit, alert, and self-aware in a way that was completely new to him. In all of his sixty-four years he had never taken any drugs, but the combination of cocaine and energetic sex with Sonya was such a heady mix that nothing could make him abstain from it.

Sonya was talking dirty, the way he liked so much, he whimpered as he came, and she said how *biiiig* he was again.

Svante left the money on the bedside table, along with a silver and gold bracelet. Svante had long since realized that women liked getting presents, he knew pretty much everything about the way women worked.

Sonya said good-bye at the door in her silk dressing gown, smiling appreciatively at the bracelet that she had put on her right wrist. She said she didn't want him to go. He replied that he had to, that his work and responsibilities were greater and more important than she could possibly understand. He pinched her cheek and headed downstairs. She could hear him whistling something tuneless before he vanished out the front door.

She let her smile fade, went into the bedroom, switched off the video and sound-recording equipment behind the mirror, and tore the sheets from the bed. She squeezed them into a black garbage bag, the way she always did after seeing a man, then dropped the tasteless bracelet in as well and left the bag by the door of the apartment.

In the bathroom she stuck her fingers down her throat and threw up in the toilet, then rinsed with mouthwash and brushed her teeth carefully. Then she took a shower and washed off as much of Svante Carlgren as she could.

When Sonya was clean she dried herself carefully with a fresh towel and rubbed her skin with various lotions for different parts of her body. She couldn't smell him at all once she was finished. All the while she was careful not to look at herself in the bathroom mirror, it would be several days before she could do that again.

Sonya now had eight hours' worth of material showing Svante Carlgren taking cocaine, her whipping him, his shouting perverse crap. Showing him with a rubber ball in his mouth, showing him pretending to be a handyman, a slave, or head of Ericsson.

He had requested a meeting with Gunilla, but she had said it would have to wait. He had called her voice mail and asked for some feedback on his surveillance at least, on the analysis of Sophie that he had been sending her. She hadn't replied. Then he had e-mailed her. A long, well-formulated e-mail in which he reminded her that when they had first met she had said she appreciated his analytical skills, so how was she thinking of using them? No response to that, either.

Lars was boiling over in his isolation as he thought about the way he was being treated. He had only asked for a conversation, no more, no less. He went over it again and again, having long discussions with her in his head where he explained that he wasn't just anyone, he wasn't made for sitting in a van for days on end.

Gunilla was at her desk when he walked into the office; she was talking quietly on the phone, met his gaze, and gestured to him to wait. Eva and Erik weren't there. Lars pulled out an old, low-backed office chair on wheels from Eva's desk and sat down to wait patiently for Gunilla to finish her conversation.

A few minutes later she hung up and turned toward him.

"I don't appreciate getting that sort of e-mail or phone message from you, Lars."

"Surely I have to be able to express the way I feel?" His reply sounded feeble.

"Why?" she asked.

He had no answer to that and wove his fingers together, dropping her gaze.

"What do you want, Lars?" she asked.

He looked down at his hands. "What I wrote in the e-mail, what I said in my message." He looked up. "What we talked about when you gave me the job. That I can do other things. I can help Eva with analysis, possible scenarios, and approaches, I can work on profiling.... Well, anything."

He was stressed and nervous. She was calm and observant.

"If that were the case I would have contacted you."

Lars nodded reluctantly. Gunilla adjusted her position on her chair. A heavy silence filled the room.

"Can I ask you something, Lars?"

Lars waited.

"Why did you join the police?"

"Because I wanted to."

His answer came out far too quickly. She showed that she thought the same and gave him a second chance.

"Because... Well, it was a long time ago. I wanted to help."

"Help with what?"

"What?"

"What did you want to help to do?"

He rubbed the corner of his mouth. A telephone started to ring on a desk some distance away. He looked over at it. She didn't move a muscle, the look in her eyes was waiting for his answer.

"Well, society, helping the weak," he said, and regretted it again. Gunilla looked at him critically. Lars could feel he was splashing about in deep water.

"Helping the weak?" she asked quietly, almost with distaste.

He took the chance to repair the mess he'd just made. "I wanted to be part of something bigger."

His voice sounded more honest now.

She nodded almost imperceptibly for him to go on.

Lars thought. "And because I wanted to make a difference. It might sound silly, but that was what it felt like."

"It doesn't sound silly. And you do, anyway."

He looked up.

"You are part of something bigger... and you do make a difference, I just wish that you could see that yourself."

He waited.

"We're a group. We work the way people do in a group, everyone does their best to contribute. I'm not always happy with my role in it, I'd change places with you several times each week if I could. But this is the way it is. We do the jobs we have, Lars."

She let a few moments pass.

"If you want to carry on working here with us, then you have to be clear about that. I'm being honest with you, and I expect you to be honest in return."

"I want to work here," he said, and swallowed.

"I can help you to move on, if you like?"

He didn't understand.

"If you stop working here, that doesn't mean that you have to go back to Husby or the Western District, I could try to help you to get somewhere else, something better?"

He shook his head. "No, no... I want to carry on here."

She looked at him hard. "So carry on."

Gunilla didn't smile that little smile the way she usually did at the end of a meeting, instead she just looked at him, letting him understand that this was something else. Lars gathered his thoughts, stood up, and began to walk toward the door.

"Lars."

He turned around in the doorway. She was reading a sheet of paper.

"Don't do this again."

Her voice was low.

"Sorry," he said hoarsely.

She was still looking at the document.

"Stop apologizing."

He was on his way out the door.

"Wait a moment," she said.

She opened a drawer, pulled out a car key, and held it out to him.

"Erik said you need to switch cars, back to the Volvo, it's parked out in the street."

Lars went over to her, took the key to the Volvo from her hand, and left the office.

He was driving the car through the city at random, feeling that he had been emotionally raped. Lars tried to think, tried to feel, tried to see where he was going... nada.

He needed to talk to someone, he knew exactly who: the woman who never listened. He turned the car around over the median.

Rosie was sitting in the corner of the sofa watching television in her dressing gown. She always sat there. Lars had brought a bunch of flowers that he'd pinched outside the old-people's home. The nurses in Lyckoslanten used to leave the senile patients' flowers in the same place, because otherwise they'd eat them.

Rosie didn't belong to the Alzheimer's gang, she was one of the younger residents in the home with her seventy-two years, part of the group that had just given up.

"Hello, Mom."

Rosie looked at Lars, then turned back to the television again.

The room was warm, Rosie had a window open slightly. He looked at his mom and noticed that her collarbone was damp with sweat. The volume on the television was turned up loud. That wasn't because her hearing was bad, it was because she couldn't understand what they were saying. She was anxious by nature, Rosie Vinge. As was Lars, he guessed she must have infected him early in life. Her anxiety had always been there, but when Lennart died it shifted into a complete terror of life. She had kept herself shut away in the apartment, scared of the immigrants moving in, afraid of the noises coming from the fridge, afraid that there'd be a fire if she left the lights on for too long, afraid of the dark if you turned the lights out.

He hadn't known what to do with her, for a while he contemplated just forgetting all about her, letting her rot away inside the apartment, but his conscience got the better of him and he put her in the old-people's home eight years ago. The staff stuffed her full of tranquilizers and she had been there ever since, in her bubble, watching afternoon television.

"How are you?"

He asked the same question each time he went. She smiled in reply, as if he would understand what the smile meant, which he didn't. He looked at the sorry scene for a while before going out into the little kitchen, boiling some water, and making himself a cup of instant coffee.

"Do you want coffee, Mom?"

She didn't answer, she never did.

He took the cup into the living room and sat down on the sofa beside her. The television was showing a quiz program where you had to call in with the answer, and the host was young and awkward. They sat there in silence, mother and son.

He took a sip of the coffee and burned his tongue. The youthful host was trying to talk fast, but kept stumbling over his words.

Lars got up and went into her bedroom.

It was dark, the bed wasn't made, and there was a musty smell. He began hunting through her drawers, sometimes he found money that he pocketed for himself. He'd been taking money from her for as long as he could remember, as if he harbored a constant feeling that she owed him something. But this time he didn't find any money, just a load of prescriptions among her revolting underwear. He grabbed three of them, one of them looked different; he folded them up and put them in his pocket. Did he know? Did he know they would be there?

He left the old-people's home and got back in the car, then headed off through the lunchtime traffic. He got stuck in traffic on Karlbergsvägen and felt the prescriptions in his pocket, they were damp with the sweat from his hands. The radio was playing hard rock from the '80s, and the singer sounded like a total wimp. A few raindrops hit the windshield, a sudden shower—light, easy rain, warm and damp without any of the cooling effect everyone expected. He leaned forward and peered up at the sky, thick black clouds gliding slowly in across the city. The colors around him shifted into a sort of orangey turquoise tint. The air pressure became heavy and thick. Lars started to get a headache and massaged the tip of his nose, letting the car roll forward a few feet. Suddenly the thunder broke, not rumbling the way it usually did but exploding in short, violent bursts above his head. It scared him and he crouched instinctively, then the skies opened properly and the rain poured down on the people dashing for cover outside the car. The windshield wipers were working as fast as they could and the windows were fogging up, turning the world outside hazy.

He put the key in the door. The top lock was unlocked, Sara was home. Lars stepped into the hall and closed the door quietly behind him, crept into the office, opened one of the desk drawers, and hid the prescriptions.

Sara was sitting in the living room writing an article about the precarious finances of female artists who didn't have partners. Something with the heading "The Socioeconomic Stranglehold." She had been working on it for ages. He didn't understand why she persisted with it. Who wanted to read that sort of thing?

Lars looked at Sara, trying to remember what he had ever seen in her, what he had found attractive. He couldn't remember anything, maybe he had never seen anything, maybe they'd only ended up as a couple because there weren't that many left to choose from. Maybe they became a couple because neither of them wanted children. Or because they were so enamored with feeling guilty; he thought he was beginning to understand that now, that most of his life he had been driven by guilt, and that this had been reflected in her sitting there writing something that no one wanted to read. Lars hated anything to do with guilt, mainly because he had no idea where it came from.

"What are you doing?" he said, leaning against the doorframe.

She looked up from her computer. "Guess."

Why did she have to answer like that? He looked at her with disgust, struck by how ugly she was. So vacuous, so empty, so unattractive—so unlike Sophie. Her way of sitting with her back hunched, curled up, her legs all tangled. That revolting teacup that she kept using without ever washing it properly. Her reluctance to make an effort with her appearance if there wasn't a good reason, the whole fucking tawdriness that she tried to hide behind a sort of intellectual drivel—the personification of the opposite of everything he wanted.

"Who's going to move out, you or me?" he asked.

"You."

Her answer came too quickly.

"No, you move out, it's my apartment. I'll move into the office for now."

He left the doorframe and went into the office, picking up a bag and his camera.

As he walked past the living room he saw Sara standing with her arms wrapped around herself, looking out the window.

"What's happened?" she asked, far too loudly.

He didn't answer, and left the apartment.

When Jens got up to his apartment on Wittstocksgatan he slumped down on the sofa. He had hoped to be able to take a breather for a while. Instead he found he could scarcely breathe at all.

He stared at the ceiling, listening to the muffled sound of the distant traffic on Valhallavägen. His body ached with restlessness and he got up and opened a window, then went out to the cleaning cupboard in the kitchen and fetched his bow and a quiver of arrows.

The apartment was 1,400 square feet, and he'd had most of the internal walls removed, to let more air through and to give him space to use his bow.

At the far end of what had once been the living room stood the target, a big round thing made of reeds. He shot several rounds of five arrows from his position in the old dining room. The music center was playing '70s salsa—two tough guys in white bell-bottoms singing in Spanish about male loneliness and girls with big breasts. He was drinking beer in between the rounds, then tired of the beer and switched to whiskey, went on shooting, then got fed up with the salsa lads, fed up with music in general, fed up with the whiskey, and switched to cognac. He went on shooting, then tired of the whole thing and ended up doing pull-ups until his arms ached.

He recognized the pattern, never feeling happy no matter how much he tried to fill himself up with music, drink, or whatever else was at hand. Always wanting to feel something more. Spoiled, his mom would call him. Addict, his dad would say, and maybe they were both right.

He had contacted the Russians to say that the goods had been delayed, and the Russians had replied that that was his problem, and that they wanted their purchases at the time they had agreed. They gave Jens one week, after which they would demand a refund and Jens would be left needing hospital treatment.

He lay on his back on the rug with one thought in his head: how to find Aron or Leszek, who, with a bit of luck, might be able to tell him how to find Mikhail.

He got up and put some coffee on, then got to work. Finding Aron turned out to be easier said than done. Jens tried all the ways he could think of. First he checked through all the Arons in Stockholm, then the whole country, using directory inquiries and various search engines. The next morning he contacted the police, the tax office, the county council, and everyone else he could think of. But he only had a first name to go on. Aron, around forty, sharp features, black hair... something of the gentleman about him. That didn't get you very far.

Aron had mentioned Stockholm when they parted, but there was nothing to say that he was necessarily still in the city. Maybe he lived somewhere else, maybe not even in Sweden. The walls started to creep in. He moved on to Leszek instead, had he said anything? No... what about Thierry? The stone statue, could that be something? What had he said? Something about being able to sell him similar items.

Jens tried to find stone statues online. Hopeless. He called the Museum of Ethnography and tried to describe the statuette, although it had really just looked like a lump of rock. The woman at the other end tried to be helpful, but it was useless. He printed out the addresses for all the antique shops, art galleries, and ethnic shops in the whole city. It ran to several pages.

Jens left the apartment, bought cigarettes instead of chewing tobacco, and set off into the city to look for Aron, Leszek, Thierry, and stone statues. He cruised about the various districts, walking, catching the bus and subway, visiting shops and asking the same vague questions everywhere, always getting the same vague no in response, searching without getting any result. He hadn't expected anything else, and tried to convince himself that this was a sort of vacation, a way of winding down after everything that had happened lately, but it didn't work. The clock was counting down, and he was getting more and more stressed.

"Sophie, are you having fun out in your comfortable suburb?" he had asked over the phone.

She had tried to work on her nerves in the car on the way out to the marina at Biskopsudden. Her anxiety kept climbing up into her throat. She didn't want to. That was pretty much all she felt: *I don't want to....* But that wasn't entirely true. Part of her wanted to, and another part of her felt obliged to do it. Not forced, exactly, just that the meeting was somehow obligatory and she would have to go through with it.

So she had met him. He had been standing on the jetty. And in spite of everything she now knew about him, his presence made her feel calm. And as usual he took charge of the moment in his own way, making it simple, relaxed, and that made her feel safe. As if he knew that this was just what she needed.

The boat was big and open, with a blue awning. It said BERTRAM 25 on the side.

They cast off, the boat's engine hummed, and Hector steered out through the channel. Sophie looked back to shore, the way she had come, and saw a Volvo in the garage with a man sitting inside it.

When they got out into open water Hector accelerated to top speed as the sun shone down on them.

They had been going for a quarter of an hour when he lowered the speed and steered the boat into a deserted inlet, reading the depth from his echo sounder, then dropped anchor and switched the motor off. Water was lapping against the hull and a yacht passed their stern, the people in the cockpit waved to them and Sophie waved back. Hector looked critically at the waving people, then turned to her.

"Why do people do that?"

She glimpsed an irritation in his eyes, as if he thought the people waving were making fools of themselves, and she smiled at his reaction.

"You said you wanted to show me something. This?" she said, gesturing at the archipelago surrounding them.

He seemed to consider, then shook his head, got up, and opened one of the seats. He pulled out a bag, opened it, and took out two old, leather-bound photograph albums, one dark green and the other dark brown with gilded edges. He sat down beside her.

"You said you wanted to know more about me."

He opened the first page of the dark-green album, and the pictures, apparently from the '60s, showed a smartly dressed couple standing in front of the Spanish Steps in Rome.

"This is my dad, Adalberto, you've met him of course. And that's my mom, Pia, standing next to him."

Sophie looked closer. Pia seemed happy, not just her face but also her posture. Relaxed and upright at the same time, and obviously very beautiful. Adalberto had thick black hair and appeared proud, proud and happy. Sophie looked back to Pia again. She was blond, she was pretty, skin tanned by the Mediterranean sun. She was the Swedish ideal of the time.

Hector went on, showing pictures of his siblings and himself when he was little. He talked about those early years, about growing up in the south of Spain, about his loneliness when his mother died, about his relationship with his father, about friends, enemies, feelings, hidden and otherwise, about relationships. She listened attentively.

He pointed to a picture of himself as a ten-year-old together with his brother and sister, the three of them in a row, laughing, wearing Indian headdresses.

"They made the best of life, my brother and sister. They've got children, they're married, they've found their own peace. I haven't quite managed that."

He seemed to get caught up on that thought, as if the words he had just said became a reality that he had never wanted to put his finger on before. Sophie looked at him, she liked this side of him, the reflective, hidden side, with a depth that he didn't want to admit to himself, that he didn't feel he had access to.

Hector turned the page, and there was a picture of his sister, Inez, five years old, holding a doll in her arms. Hector smiled. Then another page. He lit up when he saw himself as a boy, standing in front of a tree, his arms by his sides, one front tooth missing. He pointed at the picture.

"In the garden back home, I remember that picture being taken. I lost my tooth when I fell off my bike, and I told my friends I'd been in a fight."

He laughed and moved the album onto Sophie's lap, leaned back, and took a cigarillo from his breast pocket, lit it, and held the smoke in his lungs for a moment before letting it out.

"Things were better before, weren't they?"

Sophie went on looking through the album, more pictures of him as a little boy, a photograph of him sitting fishing with the evening sun on his face. She paused at that picture; he must have been about ten years old, but the expression on his face already suggested that he was a very determined individual. She compared the photograph with how he looked now, leaning back and smoking the cigarillo: they weren't much different.

She switched to the other album, and found more pictures of his mother, Pia. There was a picture of her washing her three children's hair in a tin bath on a lawn somewhere. Pia looked like a happy mother. Sophie went on. A picture of a young, dark-haired Adalberto Guzman sitting and smoking a cigar on an old stone veranda with cypress trees and olive groves in the background. Pictures of the children playing, having parties. A few pictures of Adalberto and Pia in various locations with the celebrities of the day. Sophie recognized Jacques Brel, and possibly Monica Vitti. An artist whose name she couldn't remember. Then a family trip to Tehran in the mid-'70s. Dinners with friends, happy memories. Adalberto, Pia, and the children. The pages that followed were full of a mix of family pictures, unknown friends and relations, happy pictures—Madrid, Rome, the French Riviera, Sweden and the archipelago. The album stopped in 1981, the rest of the pages were empty.

"Why does it stop here?"

Hector looked at the album.

"That was the year my mother died. We stopped taking pictures after that."

"Why?"

Hector thought for a moment.

"I don't know, maybe because we were no longer a family."

She waited for him to go on. He noticed.

"Instead we became four people trying to manage on our own. My brother hid himself away beneath the sea in his diving suit, Inez disappeared into a life of partying in Madrid for several years. I followed my father into the family business. Maybe I was the one who dealt with Mom's death worst, clinging to Dad like that."

He went on smoking and looked away from her. She kept trying to catch his eye, he felt it and turned toward her.

"What?"

She shook her head. "Nothing."

Sophie went back through the album, looking at the pictures again.

"Which one's your favorite?"

He leaned over and picked up the second album, then leafed through to a picture of him at age eight, standing bolt upright and staring into the camera with an alert look in his eyes. There was nothing special about the picture. He pointed with the cigarillo in the corner of his mouth.

"Why that one?" she wondered.

He looked at the photograph before replying.

"There's nothing a man likes more than the boy he once was."

"Really?" she said, smiling at his sudden arrogance.

He nodded firmly. "Why are you out here in this boat with me, Sophie?"

The question came out of the blue and she laughed, not because it was funny but because she didn't know what else to do.

"Because you invited me," she managed to say.

He was looking at her intently. She could feel the half smile still on her face after her laughter, and found an almost graceful way to let it fade.

"You could have said no," he said.

She shrugged as if to say, *Of course*.

"Why didn't you?" he asked.

"I don't know, Hector."

She couldn't take her eyes from him; there was something in there, something she was drawn to, something she tried to ignore, to avoid seeing. But it was impossible, it was there, right in front of her, just as it had been since the very first time she had met him. He was honest in that very unusual way, as if his personality didn't have room for lies or games, as if he were incapable of that. She loved that part of him. Honest, open, and true, attributes she valued so highly. But he was also lethal. Open, honest, true, and lethal. She didn't want that to be the case.

"Are we friends?" he asked.

His choice of words felt strange.

"Yes, I hope so."

"We're adults," he said, like it was a declaration.

She nodded. "Yes, we are."

"Adult friends?"

"Yes."

"But you're not sure," he said.

She didn't answer.

"One day you're close. Then you're suddenly distant, cold, holding me at arm's length. As if you can't decide. Are you looking for adventure? A way to pass the time, perhaps? Are you bored with your life, Sophie?"

He was about to go on, ask more questions. But she didn't want to lie, and absolutely didn't want to tell the truth. She leaned forward and kissed him on the lips in the hope of getting him to stop. Hector returned the kiss softly, but instead of allowing himself to tumble into it, he leaned back and inspected her even more intently than before. This time as though he had seen through her attempt to trap him in a kiss, while at the same time trying to understand something involved and complicated.

A motorboat passed by at high speed, Sophie watched it.

"Shall we go home?" she asked quietly.

He was still looking at her, he was still searching for whatever it was he hadn't been able to understand just then. Then he scratched his chin and let out a murmur of agreement, stood up, and tossed the half-smoked cigarillo over the railing and pressed a button on the instrument panel, and the anchor pulled up. He put his finger on the Start button, hesitated, removed his finger, and turned toward her again.

"I've got a son."

She didn't understand.

"I've got a son. I'm not allowed to see him. I want to, but his mother won't allow it. I haven't seen him for ten years."

Sophie just stared at him.

"What's his name?" were the only words that emerged.

"His name's Lothar Manuel Tiedemann, his mother's surname, he's sixteen years old and he lives in Berlin."

A few small waves were making the boat rock gently.

"Now you know all about me, Sophie," he said quietly.

They looked at each other. She tried to make sense of it all. He was on the point of saying something else but decided against it. Instead he started the engine and steered out of the inlet.

Gunilla was walking down the narrow park that ran down the center of Kar-lavägen, designed for pedestrians and dog walkers. It was hot in the sun, the breeze was warm. She crossed over Karlavägen at Artillerigatan. There were people sitting at the little tables outside the Tösse café. She stopped and waited, eavesdropping on the disillusioned housewives revealing in their involved and subconscious way that they didn't feel loved. And on men scattering their speech with English phrases. And on youngsters laughing at things she didn't understand. She did that sometimes, stopping in the middle of somewhere and just listening.

After a few minutes Sophie came walking up from Karlaplan. Gunilla waited until she reached her, then joined up with her and walked off toward Sturegatan with her.

After a while Gunilla began asking questions. As usual, they were all about the people around Hector, their names and roles, what they might be imagined to do or not do. Sophie answered as best she could. When the questions slid toward Hector himself, who he was, what sort of person, she gave Gunilla very little, as if she didn't know Hector, as if she didn't want to break a silent confidence she had just been entrusted with by him.

Some schoolchildren came toward them on the pavement and Sophie moved to let them pass.

"I've met Hector Guzman's type many times in the course of my work. Easygoing, charming, and then they suddenly switch and become the exact opposite. And ruin other people's lives. . . ."

Sophie said nothing, just kept walking next to Gunilla.

"Don't let yourself be taken in, Sophie."

9

He felt like shit. He had a constant feeling that he was doing the wrong thing. Gunilla never got in touch, treating him as if he wasn't there after that last meeting. He felt that he had made a complete fool of himself and had been planning to take it all back, apologize, try to repair the damage. But the more he thought about it, the more he realized that a move like that would only make the situation worse. The confrontation had started something inside him. He twisted and turned in bed at night: sweat, unresolved thoughts, and the street-light through the window all kept him awake. His emotions swung between anger and shame, rage and an angst the cause of which he was unaware.

He had gone to the doctor's that morning. Lars had told him that he worked the evening shift, wasn't getting enough sleep and had a bad back and headaches. The doctor, a man with warm, dry hands, had been helpful and explained that Lars was overworked, and had something called "fatigue symptoms." The doctor examined his eyes with a little flashlight, felt the glands in his neck, and shoved a finger up his backside. Then he prescribed Citodon for his back and the headaches, and oxazepam for the thing that Lars couldn't put into words.

Lars asked to see his medical notes.

"What for?" the doctor wondered.

"Because I want to."

That was evidently enough. The doctor turned the computer screen. Lars skimmed through it, nothing about what he had got up to in the past.

"Happy?"

Lars didn't answer.

"I'll book you in for a follow-up in six weeks' time," the doctor muttered.

Lars picked the prescription up from the pharmacy, then headed through the city in the Volvo.

As a child he had always had trouble sleeping. Rosie used to let him use her sleeping pills. He was eleven years old, and developed an early resistance to them. His mom, Rosie, who was already peddling pills, and was good friends with a doctor she used to sleep with when his dad, Lennart, wasn't home, gave him some anonymous white tablets that knocked Lars out at half past seven every evening. He couldn't remember any dreams and felt an incredible emptiness throughout the latter stages of elementary school, all the way through middle school and into high school.

A school nurse found out about his consumption of pills. She instigated an investigation, tried to conceal her concern by speaking very slowly and clearly, telling Lars that the tablets he had been taking were terribly addictive, terribly strong. That because he had taken so many of these powerful, addictive drugs during puberty, Lars would have to be extremely careful with tablets and other mind-altering substances in the future, and that his system had developed a dependency that could only be held at bay by total abstinence. Lars had nodded without understanding a word she was saying. He always nodded when people spoke to him.

He stopped taking the white pills when he was seventeen years old, and suffered disrupted sleep, mood swings, terrible anxiety, and bestial, black nightmares whenever he did manage to get any sleep. The addiction made itself felt day and night alike. He would twist and turn in his soaking-wet sheets, full of worry, anxieties, and torments.

After a few years the abstinence settled down into a general feeling of emptiness. The longing faded, and the trembling and mood swings gradually disappeared. But the angst was still there, as well as the disturbed sleep. They became part of the daily routine, part of his reality.

He parked the car outside the bowling alley: it was licensed to sell beer and wine.

Lars found a table with a view of the lanes. There were gangs of elderly people bowling. Lars looked down at the palm of his hand, six pills, three from each bottle.

He swept the pills into his mouth and washed them down with some Bulgarian red wine. After a few minutes the pressure in his chest eased and his breathing became more relaxed. He leaned back in his chair and watched the people bowling, feeling delight when they missed and annoyance when they succeeded.

"Hi."

Sara was standing next to him. He looked at her in surprise.

"How did you know I was here?"

"I followed you."

"Where from?"

"The medical center."

Lars turned back to the bowlers and took a sip from his glass of wine. She sat down and tried to catch his eye.

"How are you, Lars?"

"Fine, why?"

Sara sighed quietly. "Please, Lars. Can't we talk?"

Lars pretended not to understand, and let out a little laugh.

"I thought we were.... Isn't that what we're doing now, talking? I mean, our mouths are moving!"

He smiled strangely. Sara looked down at her hands.

"I don't want it to be like this," she whispered.

Lars watched bowling balls rolling down the lanes, pins being knocked over.

"I don't recognize you anymore, you're so angry all the time, you won't say what it is.... Is it something I've done?"

He snorted.

"I want to help you if I can, Lars."

She watched him to see if the words had sunk in.

"You've been here before, Lars," she whispered.

He avoided her gaze.

"When we met, before we decided to move in together, just after you started working in the Western District. You were like you are now.... It lasted a few weeks.... When you came out of it you told me about the medication you were given as a child...."

"You talk so much crap...."

Sara was struggling not to let herself be deterred by his attitude.

"No, I don't," she said.

A skinny old man had just hit a strike, and was doing his best to hide his proud grin when he turned back toward his friends.

"We've done OK, Lars," she said. "We've had a relationship without any arguments or misunderstandings. We've let each other be, but still been together.... We've had the same interests, the same values. We managed to find something...."

He drank some more wine, still avoiding her gaze.

"What do you think's happened?" she asked.

"Nothing's happened, you're just paranoid... and ugly."

Sara tried not to show how hurt she felt.

"In that case, I want us to split up."

His crooked smile was still in place.

"I thought we already had."

Sara's sadness switched to anger, and she stared at him, then got up quickly and walked away. Lars watched her go, sipping the wine, then looked on as a fat old woman rolled her ball into the gutter. The woman made an effort to look cheerful as she walked back toward her friends, as though the whole point wasn't to win but to have a good time together. *Yeah, right.*

When the bowling alley closed he found a bar, an Irish pub that was about as Irish as McDonald's was Finnish. A widescreen television, electronic dart board, a miniature basketball basket with stupid miniature basketballs. And, as the icing on the cake, an Iranian barman who spoke bad English and called Lars "pal." But what did he care? He was there to get hammered, and he succeeded. He drank himself stupid until the place closed, and woke up the next morning in his car, with the windows fogged up and his nose frozen. The world outside was already awake and moving.

Lars sat up, rubbed the sleep from his eyes, scratched hard at his flattened hair, and got rid of the dryness in his mouth with some flat beer.

He drove out toward Danderyd Hospital, somewhere between drunk and hungover. He sat there in his parked car all day, biting his nails, popping his pills, drinking his lunch, and waiting.

When Lars saw Sophie leave the hospital that afternoon he was elated, and felt safe again.

He stayed some distance behind her as she cycled home, then he drove past her and did what he always did, heading toward her house, choosing a spot for the night, then putting the headphones on and listening to her as she lived her life.

This was on the point of becoming his life now, nothing else really mattered. He listened to everything she did, to her steps as she passed one of the microphones, to the dinner she ate alone, to her conversations with Albert.

At eleven o'clock Lars switched to the microphone in the bedroom and listened as she pulled the duvet from the bed and lay down. He had worked out that she slept without covers, he never heard her pull the duvet back over herself again. He visualized her lying there on the white sheet with her hair resting on the pillow, taking soft breaths, maybe dreaming of him. His body was shrieking with longing for her, he didn't understand it, couldn't control it. Lars had another top-up, the pills went down. Everything became natural, even his longing.

When things had been silent for three hours, when Sophie and Albert were sound asleep in their beds, Lars got out of the car and crept slowly into Sophie's garden. The summer night was still and mild. He was feeling calm and harmonious as he stopped by the veranda at the back of the house, then glanced around before going silently up the steps, picking the lock, and carefully opening the door. The hinges made a small squeaking sound. He stepped soundlessly into the living room, listening intently.

She was lying up there asleep, the feeling of being so close to her was intoxicating. Lars crept into the kitchen. Very carefully he opened the fridge and looked inside, letting his imagination run wild, thinking of himself as the man of the house, the man who had gotten out of bed and come downstairs to the kitchen to get something to eat.

Lars got out some bread, butter, and fillings for himself, sat down at the kitchen table, and ate a sandwich. He smiled toward his son as he came downstairs, then got up and kissed Sophie when she came down a little later, showing her that he had prepared breakfast, and she smiled and kissed him again. He said something witty, and Sophie and their son laughed.

Lars left the house, stopping at the gate to wave imaginatively to his little family that didn't exist, then went back through the dark of night to his car.

Back home in the apartment he topped up with pills and slept like a child on the disgusting old mattress.

His knees were rammed against the seat in front. Mikhail thought the air-plane seat was far too small. Beside him sat Klaus. Klaus was forty or so, a German bodybuilder of the more sinewy variety. Klaus had thinning hair and streamlined muscles everywhere, even his face, which was adorned with a big porn-star's mustache. He was a tough guy who knew a bit about a lot of things, but had no specific talent—an all-rounder who rarely turned down a job. They'd worked together before on a couple of home visits that Ralph had ordered. Klaus was good, unburdened by too much conscience.

They had taken off from Munich, on their way to Stockholm. The flight attendant was serving coffee, a child was crying toward the back of the plane, old men were solving Sudoku, and middle-aged women were working on presentations on their laptops. Klaus had earphones in, leaking out the sound of the Bee Gees. Klaus was nodding his head in time and patting his right hand on his trouser leg.

Mikhail thought through what was going to happen. He didn't have a clear plan, and was working through various strategies in his head, weighing them against one another. In the end he kept coming back to the same conclusion—hitting back hard, in a very focused way. Roland had been in Stockholm two days before, he had come back with a grin on his face. *We've got a guy now*, he had said. *He can arrange for you to see Hector....*

There was a ringing sound and the seat belt sign lit up. A female voice came out of the loudspeakers in some Nordic language that he couldn't understand. The plane began to descend for landing. There was a lot of turbulence and Klaus clasped the armrest and raised his feet in reflex each time the cabin shuddered.

"I hate this," Klaus said. "I really hate this."

They approached the runway through strong crosswinds. Klaus was pale. The plane lurched to the left, then back to the right again. Klaus grabbed Mikhail's arm.

"Scheisse..."

The plane hit the ground, the engines reversed. Klaus breathed out.

They took a rental car to Stockholm and booked into a hotel near Hötorget, then headed out into the city. Dusk was falling as they took a bite to eat at an outdoor terrace; it was warm, warmer than Munich.

"As far as I know, he's got three men, so that's what we'll have to assume. Two of them are pros: Hector's bodyguard and the Polack. I don't know anything about the third one."

Klaus listened as he ate his steak tartare, chewing quickly. He was holding his knife and fork strangely as he cut the meat.

"He's got an office here in the city but he doesn't go there much. The last time I was here watching him he spent a lot of time in that restaurant, so that's where we'll strike. We've got a contact, he's going to arrange it."

"Sounds good to me," Klaus said without any emotion, then waved to the waiter and pointed at his empty glass.

They left the restaurant and got back in their rental car, then tapped Sandsborgsvägen, Enskede, into the GPS.

"Perform a U-turn now," the GPS voice said in German, and Klaus did as it said.

They struggled through the Stockholm traffic, made their way to the tunnel under Södermalm, sticking to the left-hand lane as they crossed the Johanneshov Bridge.

"Like a big golf ball," Klaus said as they passed the Globe.

They stopped the car outside an unremarkable villa. They rang the doorbell, and it was opened by a balding, middle-aged man with a beer belly, wearing an unfashionable shirt and a tie that was too short. As if he'd just gotten home from work—unfashionable work.

"Wilkommen... meine herren."

The man laughed at his attempt to speak German.

They followed him down into the basement and the man opened a metal door and indicated for them to go in. Mikhail stepped inside and saw a mass of weapons: revolvers and automatic pistols along one wall, shotguns and high-velocity rifles along the other.

The man smiled excitedly and talked like a presenter on a shopping channel about his darlings—*a gun freak,* Mikhail thought. He interrupted the man's sales pitch and pointed at the wall.

"Give me a Sig and two telescopic batons."

The idiot got the gun down and gave Mikhail a small box of ammunition, then started babbling about how the ammunition was Swiss, how much the bullets weighed, what they were particularly good for. He pulled a box from a shelf and took out two batons. Mikhail passed the gun to Klaus and handed the man a bundle of euros.

They left the basement and house without saying good-bye and got back in the car. Klaus checked a piece of paper, then keyed an address into the GPS. Mikhail tapped the number Roland Gentz had given him into his cell and pressed the green button. A man answered.

"Carlos? I was told to call you, do as you were instructed, we'll be there in"—Mikhail leaned over and checked the GPS—"in twenty minutes."

Mikhail ended the call.

"Perform a U-turn now," the digital woman said once more.

"Shut up," Klaus said.

The antiques shops on Roslagsgatan, the tourist traps in Gamla stan and along Drottninggatan, and all the little shops on Södermalm and Kungsholmen—anything that might be connected to ethnic art, antiques, or just New Age nonsense. Jens had looked everywhere for Thierry. That was pretty much all he had to go on, the guy's interest in a stone statue from South America.... The chances of bumping into Aron or Leszek in the city were fairly slim, but he had been traipsing about for several days now.

Less well-known were the shops in Västmannagatan. Jens had bought a glass globe there a long time ago. The shops lining the street were more focused on curiosities and '50s design. Jens started from Norra Bantorget and worked his way up toward Odenplan. His tiredness was exacerbated by a serious dose of frustration. However, he had no choice but to continue. In and out of the shops, asking pretty much the same question about whether they dealt in South American cultural artifacts. And whether they knew a man who went by the name of Thierry. The same blank faces each time.

After five blocks he passed the shop where he had bought the globe twenty years before. The shop looked just the same, even if the prices in the window were different. Two doors farther on he came to a little shop that he wouldn't have noticed if he hadn't been looking. The window was small and dark, with just a few select items. Boldly patterned blankets, masks, shields, and spears. He stepped inside. A bell attached to the door rang.

The shop was stuffed to overflowing with artifacts from every corner of the world, it was like stepping into several different periods from several different places at the same time. Jens found he couldn't stop looking. There was so much to take in. Old works of art, textiles, furniture, jewelry, statues. It was all beautiful, enticing, and different—imposing, in an inexplicable way. In a glass cabinet in one corner he saw a number of small stone statues, like miniature versions of what he had seen in Thierry's hand on board the ship.

He heard steps behind him and turned around. The woman who emerged from the curtain to the back room was beautiful. Her hair was big and round, and she was upright without being tall. He guessed she was originally from the West Indies.

"Hello," he said.

She responded with a smile.

"Thierry . . . ," Jens said, as if he had suddenly unconsciously realized that he was in the right place.

She hesitated, then turned and went back behind the curtain again.

Jens could feel his heartbeat quicken. It took a few seconds for the man who emerged to recognize Jens.

"You?"

* * *

Thierry had called Aron and given him a brief explanation of the situation, then passed the receiver to Jens.

Aron had told him to go back out into the street, carry on a bit farther, and go into a restaurant.

Thierry opened the door for him, gesturing along the street.

"That way, he's waiting for you."

Jens began walking toward the restaurant. It all felt ridiculous. What were the odds against this? He couldn't even begin to work it out.

TRASTEN, it said on a small sign. Jens stepped in and headed toward the bar, counting a dozen or so people at various tables. He asked for a glass of tonic, then looked around the room as he drank.

After a few minutes Aron came out through the swinging doors to the kitchen, saw Jens, and waved him over.

Jens followed Aron through the kitchen, passed through a little corridor, and was shown inside an office.

The office was very small. A desk with a computer on it, messy, half-full ashtrays, a pile of newspapers, an old stolen road sign leaning against the wall—NO WAITING. Dirty coffee cups and a year planner that was several years out of date. A room that was obviously used by more than one person, and most of them probably men. Men who wanted this to be a free zone, a place where no one needed to take any responsibility.

"Sit down, if you can find a chair."

Jens found one.

"You work here?" he asked as he sat down.

Aron shook his head. "No."

Aron sat down behind the desk.

"So what's on your mind?" he asked breezily, smiling at his choice of words.

Jens composed himself quickly.

"After we separated I drove up through Jutland and stopped at my grandmother's for the night. I woke up with a Glock in my mouth and the big Russian sitting on the edge of the bed."

Aron raised one eyebrow.

"He knocked me unconscious and took my boxes."

"The boxes containing your weapons?"

Jens nodded.

"Who were they supposed to be going to?"

"A customer."

"But not here in Sweden?"

Jens shook his head. Aron thought for a moment.

"Did he know there were weapons in the boxes?"

"No, I don't think so. He must have attached a transmitter to one of the boxes while they were on the ship. It just happened to be one of mine, not yours."

Aron pondered for a moment, then looked up.

"So what can I do to help you?"

"I have to get my goods back, I need to know what you know about him . . . where he is, how I can get hold of him."

The inn wasn't an inn. It was a pizzeria with a sign that read BEER AND WINE in the window. Dark wood furniture and the cheapest possible paper napkins, coarse and thin.

He ate half a pizza, drank four beers and six shots of something stronger. He had felt the need to get drunk. Lars let his thoughts wander, something he'd recently started to enjoy. Previously he had felt guilty if he didn't use his thoughts for something profitable, something useful. Now he allowed himself just to let them go without giving them any particular direction, and simply followed them wherever they went. It was wonderful. New feelings rose up and disappeared. He kept himself topped up on pills and felt as relaxed as a sleeping baby. Maybe this was how everyone wanted to feel, maybe this was the state that everyone was looking for once they'd spent a few years in the grown-up world? He smiled to himself, catching the cook's eye behind the counter. The man seemed worried, and looked away. Lars guessed that he could see his own nirvana-like calm and was upset because he himself wasn't sharing it. Everyone was jealous of him, that had always been the case.

Lars scratched his cheek hard, he had a small pimple that didn't seem to want to go away.

His face was hot and he had narrow tunnel vision when he headed up toward Sophie's house just after nine o'clock. He had eight different places where he could sit and listen to what was going on inside the house, and he alternated between them to avoid attracting too much attention, all of them within a short distance of the house. He parked at number four, unless it was number three? He switched the engine off, pulled on his headphones, and listened. It was silent inside the house. He tried to find Sophie in the soundscape—was she just sitting there? He popped a couple more pills, and the world became more porridgey.

After a while he heard steps in the kitchen heading toward the hall, then the front door opened and closed. He switched to the kitchen microphone, listening to hear if she had gone to open the door for someone or had gone out herself. No sounds in the kitchen, silence in the hall. He waited. She had left the house.

Lars started the car and drove up toward the villa and met her Land Cruiser coming down the hill toward him. He turned the Volvo around at the top.

Being drunk made it harder to follow her; he struggled to stay not too close, but not so far back that he lost her. At least the evening traffic was helpful, there weren't many cars heading into the city along Roslagsvägen. He kept to the middle lane, squinting and using the lines on the road to steer by.

He followed her in to Vasastan, where she stopped outside the Trasten restaurant. Lars found a parking spot farther down and watched in his rearview mirror as Hector walked up to meet her on the sidewalk, then he and Sophie kissed each other on the cheek before going inside the restaurant.

Jens didn't recognize the man who came into the room where he and Aron were sitting talking.

"Is Carlos here?"

Aron shook his head.

"He called me, told me to come down."

Aron shook his head again. "No, I haven't seen him."

The man seemed to think about this for a moment, then dropped it when he saw Jens sitting in the room. He held out his hand.

"Hector Guzman."

Jens took his hand. Hector was a large man, with his leg in a cast, smartly dressed, he looked friendly, and there was a confidence to him—the dog that ate first, not only here, but probably everywhere.

"Jens is the man I was telling you about, on the boat," Aron said. "He has a problem that happens to be ours as well."

"That's good, he can have our share too," Hector smiled. "What sort of problem, exactly?"

Jens told him the story, from when they loaded up in Paraguay to Mikhail's visit to his grandmother's house in Jutland. In the middle of it Hector sat himself down on a chair, looking at Aron, who occasionally elaborated on some detail. Hector thought for a while when Jens had finished.

"That's some fucking story."

Jens waited.

Hector thought some more. "What did your poor grandmother say?"

Jens hadn't been expecting that question.

"She's fine."

A smell of cooking from the kitchen seeped into the office where they were sitting.

"If we help you to get your goods back, you can choose to either pay cash for our services or repay the favor in kind in the future."

"And if you don't succeed?"

"We always succeed," Hector said.

"OK. What do we do?" Jens said.

Aron answered. "We don't do anything yet. We'll have to get in touch with them. It's in our interests that they understand that the weapons aren't ours."

Hector looked at Jens. "We're dealing with very volatile people here, but you already know that."

Hector fell into deep thought, then turned to Aron.

"You're sure Carlos isn't here?"

Aron nodded.

"OK, Jens," Hector said, slapping his hands on his knees, "it was good meeting you. Now I'm going out to have dinner with a lady I rather like. She's been waiting out in the restaurant for long enough." He gestured with his thumb, then stood up and turned to Jens. "Do you have anyone like that?"

"No, I'm afraid not."

"A shame," he said, and walked toward the door.

Jens watched him go. Just as Hector was about to open the door it flew open in his face. He staggered back. Mikhail and another man burst in. Jens had time to see the smaller of the pair hit Hector over the head with a telescopic baton as he was knocked to the floor by a hard blow to the throat. Mikhail flew straight at Aron. It was quick, practiced. Jens leaped instinctively at the smaller man. Head-butted him hard and rained blows down on him, and managed to get him on the floor. But Mikhail had come up behind him once Aron had been dealt with. A hard kick against the side of Jens's head got him off balance. He managed to turn around, started to get up and throw out a fist, but the blows to his head from Mikhail's baton were quick and hard. Jens tried to defend himself. He blacked out.

He could hear muffled sounds, someone was shaking him, saying something he couldn't make any sense of. The sounds were woven together in some indeterminate world where he was swept in and out of consciousness and dream.

Jens opened his eyes. His headache was monumental, with a hint of migraine cutting through everything; the world was sharp and blinding, and he closed his eyes again. Someone was shaking him, harder this time—he felt like protesting, telling whoever it was to leave him alone, but the shaking was relentless. He opened his eyes again and in the harsh light he saw something that made him realize he was dreaming: Sophie Lantz was there, shouting at him. He was happy to see her in his dream, he'd forgotten how pretty she was. She was older now, had little wrinkles around her eyes, but she was still attractive. He smiled at her and rolled over to carry on sleeping. He discovered that he was lying on the floor of the office behind the restaurant, and realized that he had brought part of the real world into his dream. His memory returned, Mikhail had come into the room. . . .

Jens moved his legs, checking them out, then his hands, opening and closing his eyes; he wanted to get out of this bizarre dream.

"Jens?"

He opened his eyes again. She was still there, and Jens tried to focus. It was hard, the world didn't seem to want to stop moving.

"Jens? Can you hear me?"

Now he could see her clearly, and realized that he wasn't dreaming.

"Sophie?"

A quick smile flickered behind her concern. She helped him sit up, crouching in front of him and reading something in his eyes. He looked back, remembering those eyes, remembering the way she looked, the revelation.

"You've got a concussion," she said.

He looked at her. "What are you doing here?"

"Doesn't matter," she replied.

He was finding the whole situation utterly absurd. The door behind them opened and Aron came in, with blood drying on a split eyebrow and bruises on his cheek and around his right eye. He looked focused and stressed at the same time.

"Let's go," he said.

Jens stood up unsteadily.

"Get your car, Sophie. We'll meet you 'round the back," Aron went on.

Sophie left the room.

"We need your help now, Jens," Aron said. "They took Hector, I can follow him with the GPS. Have you got anything with you?"

Jens shook his head.

Aron fetched a revolver from a cupboard, a snub-nosed .45. "This is part of clearing the debt."

Jens took the gun, checked that it was loaded. They hurried out through a rear door and found themselves in a courtyard, walked across it, through another building, and out into the next street. The Land Cruiser came driving up between the buildings at high speed and stopped sharply. Aron opened the passenger door.

"Sophie, stay here for a while. We need to borrow your car."

"You need me," she said. "You and Jens will have your hands free if I drive."

Aron didn't have time to argue. They jumped in the car, Aron in the front, Jens in the back. The car accelerated away.

"The E4, northbound," Aron said, staring at the GPS on his phone.

* * *

Sophie drove quickly past Norrtull and pulled onto the northern link road, accelerating hard when she hit the highway.

That was when she noticed the same Volvo that she had passed on the road when she left the house. It was a little behind her, in the left-hand lane of the otherwise empty highway. The Volvo got closer in the rearview mirror. Sophie debated with herself. Should she let him follow her...help them rescue Hector...Then what would happen?

The Volvo was getting closer.

Sophie maneuvered the Land Cruiser into the right-hand lane as they approached the exit ramp by Haga Park. When they had almost passed the turn-off she waited till the very last minute before wrenching the wheel to the right and accelerating up the exit ramp. The Volvo was too slow to react and kept going, straight up the highway. She managed to get a glimpse of the man driving, she'd seen him before.

Aron looked up from his GPS.

"What are you doing?"

"Sorry, I don't know what I was thinking, I thought I was in the wrong lane!"

She got up to the junction, but instead of going straight over and down onto the highway again she turned left, toward Solna on the Frösunda link road.

"Sophie?!"

Aron sounded upset.

"Sorry, sorry...shit, I have to turn around!"

She sounded stressed and nervous. Aron stared at her, trying to understand her mistake. She went right around the roundabout and headed back the way they had come, then pulled out onto the highway again with her foot on the floor.

It had played out the way she had hoped, the Volvo had turned off at the next exit, at Frösundavik, turned around, and was coming back down the highway again. She saw it coming toward her on the opposite roadway, on its way back toward the city. She didn't look at the driver, just increased her speed.

Common sense had been telling her to go home, to not get involved in this, but now common sense seemed to have deserted her.

She hadn't reacted logically and was governed by just one feeling: concern for Hector. Nothing else mattered at all just then.

She caught sight of Jens in the rearview mirror. She had been alarmed when he had popped up out of nowhere. Now he was sitting there, staring out the window. Older, rather larger than she remembered him. Still the same scruffy blond hair, suntanned like a big kid just back from his summer vacation. She recognized the look in his eyes, an irreconcilable mixture of thoughtful and crazy. He looked up, as if he could read her mind, and met her gaze in the mirror. Aron read out directions from the GPS on his phone.

"They're west of us now, pull off at the next exit."

Sophie left the highway and they emerged onto a main road that led through a patch of forest, and they went on through the darkness until they came to a gravel track leading into the trees. Sophie turned off the lights and drove on in total darkness.

"Stop." Aron studied the GPS. "I'll go. You wait here, keep your phones on."

Aron screwed a silencer onto his pistol.

"I'll come with you," Jens said. "There are two of them."

"No, you wait here, in case one of them comes this way."

Aron got out of the car and disappeared quickly into the dark forest.

Jens and Sophie were left sitting there in a silence that seemed to have taken over the whole car. He felt he couldn't just sit there, and opened the door, taking a few steps into the forest in the direction in which Aron had vanished.

Sophie watched him from behind the wheel.

Mikhail wasn't happy. Klaus had been too brutal with the Spaniard. The plan had been to go into the restaurant, pick off anyone who happened to be around him, then have a quiet word with Hector Guzman, explaining to him that they had no chance against Hanke's organization, forcing him to accept the changes that Ralph wanted, and then leaving. If not, they were to shoot him there and then. But Klaus had knocked Hector Guzman out and they couldn't just sit there waiting for him to come around. And now they were in the middle of the forest, somewhere just west of the highway, you could make out the sound of cars in the distance. Mikhail realized that the situation had changed.

Hector came to after a while. He was sitting on the ground, leaning against the car, beaten up, and he noticed that the top part of the cast on his leg had cracked.

Klaus was standing a few yards away relieving his bladder and quietly whistling Beethoven's Fifth. Hector looked up at Mikhail, who was standing in front of him.

"Hanke?" he asked, his throat dry.

Mikhail nodded.

"What do you want?"

"They want the cocaine you stole, they want the Paraguay-Rotterdam route, they want the setup. They want you to sign up with them and act as a subsidiary group. And for you to do your best to fit in with their wishes as of now. They also want the name of which one of you torched Christian's car and girlfriend. And they want to know why you're getting hold of weapons."

"That's a tall order."

Mikhail didn't answer.

Hector scrutinized him. "Are you the one who ran me over?"

Mikhail was silent.

"Yes, of course it was you," Hector went on, fishing a cigarillo out of his breast pocket and putting it in his mouth.

"So you were in Rotterdam as well? Who are you, Hanke's little brother?"

Mikhail was unconcerned. Hector found a lighter in his trouser pocket, lit the cigarillo, and took a few puffs.

"You seem to be pretty much as stupid as you look. You followed the wrong boxes to Denmark, I've heard all about it. The man with the boxes was a passenger, nothing to do with us. Our things were in similar boxes, the boxes the captain wanted all the goods packed in. You got it wrong... again."

Hector took a few puffs.

"Doesn't change anything," Mikhail said. "Give me what I want and we can get out of here."

Hector shook his head. "Sorry, but you're offering me the worst deal I've ever heard."

"I'm not offering you anything."

Hector met Mikhail's gaze.

"No, you're not," he said quietly.

"Don't be stupid now," Mikhail said.

Hector almost smiled.

"How would you respond to the kind of offer you've just made me?" he whispered.

Mikhail didn't answer, turned to Klaus, asked him in German if they ought to shoot him now.

"I've just had a piss here, and they'll do all that DNA shit..."

"Doesn't matter if we shoot him here, then drive somewhere else and burn him and the car there," Mikhail muttered.

Hector looked down at the ground and stubbed out the cigarillo, which had started to taste bad while he listened to the exchange.

"Why not come over to us, I can offer you twice what you're getting from Hanke." Hector turned to Mikhail. "Besides, you must have noticed that everything you've tried has gone to hell?"

Mikhail didn't answer, just nodded to Klaus, who went back to the car, took out the Sig Sauer, slid the bolt action, and went over to Hector, aiming the pistol at his head.

"You still have a choice...," mumbled Mikhail.

Hector looked up at the big man. The leaves of the trees above him were moving gently.

"Go to hell...," Hector said in a low voice.

The metallic popping sound that followed was unmistakable. It was the first of a series of three. Louder than in films, but still a popping, clicking sound. Hector heard the sound of bullets coming from somewhere behind him, and saw one of them hit Klaus in the stomach, and the look of astonishment on the man's face as he put his hand to the entry hole. He dropped the pistol and screamed in a mixture of surprise and pain. At that moment, out of the dark forest, came Aron, holding his pistol in front of him.

"Back away!" he shouted, aiming the weapon at Mikhail. He hurried over and picked up Klaus's gun from the ground.

"I've been shot, for fuck's sake!" Klaus sobbed.

Aron approached Mikhail and gestured to him to get down on his knees. Mikhail did as he was ordered and Aron kicked him in the throat. The Russian lost the ability to breathe and collapsed, knocked out for a while. Aron checked him over quickly.

He walked over to Hector, holding out his hand. Hector took it and pulled himself up. They looked at the men, then at each other, and Aron asked the unspoken question. Hector thought, then shook his head.

"No, let them go home again with another failure."

A car engine could be heard through the night. The headlights lit up the forest before they saw the vehicle itself. It appeared over a slight ridge and drove up to them fast, stopping in front of Hector.

Sophie hurried over to him.

"I'm OK," he said.

She led him back to the car.

Jens was standing beside the Land Cruiser, staring at the pistol hanging in his hand.

"Can you drive?" she asked Jens without waiting for an answer.

He opened the door for her and Hector.

"He's going to die!" Mikhail shouted.

Sophie stopped and turned toward Mikhail, who was sitting on the ground.

"Is someone hurt?" she asked.

"No, no one's hurt. Let's go," Aron said.

Sophie looked at Hector. He tried to follow Aron's lie, but it didn't work.

"Yes, the man on the ground is hurt but his friend will take care of him. Come on, it'll all be fine, let's go."

Sophie let go of Hector and ran over toward Klaus.

"Sophie!"

Aron, Hector, and Jens called after her in chorus. She didn't listen, and Aron caught up with her, aiming his pistol at Mikhail. Sophie kneeled down beside Klaus. He was clutching his stomach. She began to examine him, and told Mikhail that she wanted his shirt. Mikhail pulled it off and tossed it over to her.

Jens and Hector looked on as Sophie calmly told Klaus to lie on his back, ignoring his screams of pain, then examined his injury with a steady concentration.

"He needs to get to the hospital, he's losing blood. Help me get him in the car."

Silence among the men.

"Help me, he's going to die!" she shouted.

Hector turned to Mikhail. "We'll look after your friend if you go back to your employers and tell them to drop this whole business, if you swear never to take part in anything like this again. . . ."

Mikhail was silent.

"And tell me where my guns are!" Jens said.

Hector shrugged. "And tell this man where his guns are."

Jens and Mikhail helped lay Klaus in the back of the car. Sophie hurried them along, then got in alongside Klaus, pressing the fabric against the bullet wound.

"Drive!"

Jens got behind the wheel. A cloud of dust flew up as they drove off.

Mikhail waited a few minutes before getting in the rental car and heading for Arlanda.

He cleaned the inside of the car at a twenty-four-hour gas station, left it at a rental parking lot at the airport, dropping the keys in the box, then spent the night on a bench in the departure hall of Terminal 5. He passed the time wondering what was going on, who he worked for, what they wanted, what they intended. . . . Their enemies and friends.

He felt guilty in a way he hadn't for many years. Klaus shouldn't have gotten wounded, that wasn't in the plan. He couldn't figure out if the Guzman group was scared or just heavy-handed, they shot first every time.

He would remember that.

"Drive faster!"

She looked down at the bloodstained man, checked his condition again, his shallow pulse, his pale face—blood loss. She couldn't tell how badly injured he was, but the blood was pumping out of his body at a steady rate. He would die if he didn't get medical attention soon. Klaus opened his eyes slightly, but they soon closed again. She slapped him hard on the cheek to keep him awake. The man was going to die in her lap. She would be partly responsible. Another person's life. For what? For Hector? Everything she had ever learned, everything she held dear was the exact opposite of this.

"Jens," Hector said. "You have to let me and Aron out before you get to the hospital."

He met Hector's gaze in the rearview mirror.

"We need to clean the car, have you got anyone who can help us?"

Hector and Aron thought, and talked quickly in Spanish. Aron tapped a number into his phone, then, without saying who he was, said a few words about a friend's car needing to be looked at, and that it needed some new trimmings, mainly in the baggage compartment.

"Sköndal, Semmelvägen," Aron told Jens.

Hector said nothing when he got out of the car, followed by Aron. Sophie watched them walk across Solna Kyrkväg, just outside the Karolinska Hospital.

Jens turned the car and drove quickly up toward the hospital.

"Sophie! We can't go in with him, we have to leave him in the ambulance bay and get away fast. OK?"

She didn't answer, and checked Klaus's pulse.

Jens entered the hospital grounds and found the ambulance bay, which happened to be empty. He drove in and sounded the horn.

"Stay hidden," he said, opening the door.

Sophie left Klaus, clambered over the seat from the baggage compartment, and slid onto the floor behind the front seats, her clothes covered in blood. Jens ran around and opened the back door.

Two male nurses came running out with a trolley, followed by a female doctor. Jens got behind the wheel again.

"Gunshot wound to the abdomen," he shouted to them.

The nurses and doctor pulled out the unconscious Klaus and put him on the trolley. As soon as they had cleared the vehicle Jens put the car into reverse and drove away from the ambulance bay with the back door open. Once they were out of sight he stopped, jumped out, and closed the back door, then got back in. Sophie climbed forward to sit beside him. He looked at her.

"Are you OK?"

"No," she said, her hands and clothes covered in blood.

They drove calmly through the city in silence. He glanced at her. She was pale, deep in thought.

"He'll be OK...," Jens said.

She didn't answer.

"Why did you do this, why didn't you just let me and Aron go?"

"Can you just be quiet?" she said.

The Land Cruiser drove slowly past the houses. He found the right number and drove down the asphalt drive to the garage, and waited a few seconds as the garage door opened. Thierry waved them inside. Jens drove the car in and got out.

"No need to explain," Thierry said. "I've spoken to Aron. Good thing none of us is hurt."

Us, Jens thought.

Sophie got out of the passenger side. Thierry saw the blood on her hands and clothes.

"Hello, Sophie... Come with me, my wife will help you." Thierry looked over the car quickly. "This should be OK."

A door connected the garage to the house. Daphne met them.

"Come here, my dear, let me help you."

She took Sophie by the hand and led her to the bathroom.

Daphne left her alone and Sophie got out of her bloody clothes, leaving them on the floor.

She turned the water on and let it heat up before getting under it. The shower wasn't nice but it wasn't unpleasant either, it was just water running down her body. She soaped herself all over, the blood turned pale red by her feet before running down the drain in the floor.

Afterward she put on the clothes Daphne had laid out on a chair in the bathroom. She wiped the steam from the mirror and looked at herself. The clothes were OK, although the arms of the sweater were too long.

Daphne looked in. "I've made some tea, come."

* * *

Jens had new clothes too, in Thierry's size. He was also wearing a shower cap, dishwashing gloves, and shoe covers. He was wiping the dashboard, the front seats, everything he could reach. Thierry was doing the same in the back.

"Was it the same man who was on the boat?" Thierry asked.

"Yes..."

Thierry drenched the leather seats with disinfectant.

"His name's Mikhail, a Russian. Works for Ralph Hanke."

Jens went on scrubbing everything in sight.

"Who's Hanke?" he asked.

Thierry was emptying a bucket into a grate on the floor, then went and refilled it.

"A German businessman who's picked a fight with us..."

"Why?"

"Good question."

He turned the tap off.

"Who are you, Jens?"

Jens didn't need long to think about his answer.

"I'm just someone who's got caught up in something that has nothing to do with me...."

He got out of the driver's seat.

"What's your view of that?" Thierry asked.

"I want to see it as coincidence... but right now it looks more like fate."

Thierry nodded at his words. There was a knock on the door. Jens looked at Thierry.

"Don't worry."

He opened the garage door. A young man in a hood smiled broadly and handed over a rolled-up rubber mat.

"Land Cruiser, as ordered."

Thierry took it and the young man closed the door. Jens heard a souped-up car engine start outside and disappear.

Thierry went over to Sophie's car and pulled out the blood-smeared rubber mat from the baggage compartment. It was glued down and took a while to come out. He put it down on the garage floor, then held the new one up and compared them.

"It's a bit smaller, but it'll have to do."

* * *

Sophie could hear noises from the garage as she drank from the cup of tea Daphne had put in front of her. The tea tasted different, and after another sip it tasted repulsive. She put the cup on the table.

Daphne took Sophie's hand in hers and Sophie jerked, feeling uncomfortable, the woman was quite invasive. But Daphne didn't let go and after a while it felt better.

"How did you get caught up in this?" she asked.

Sophie had no answer; she shrugged lightly and tried to smile, but failed. Daphne squeezed her hand tighter.

"Hector's a good man," she said. "He's a good man," she said again, her eyes fixed on Sophie.

Then she let go of Sophie's hand, leaned back in her chair, put her hands in her lap, and said in a low voice, almost a whisper, "You've seen something that wasn't meant for your eyes. If you want to talk about what you've been through, come to me, no one else."

Sophie suddenly saw a different side to Daphne, the tone was different, more serious, firmer, almost as if she were issuing a warning.

The door opened and Jens and Thierry came into the kitchen in full regalia. If things had been different she would have laughed.

The Land Cruiser felt like new, smelled new when she got into the passenger seat. Jens climbed in behind the wheel. They drove out of the suburbs and onto the main road back into Stockholm.

He looked at her. She was staring at the world going past outside.

"We have to talk sometime," he said.

"Yes."

They sat in silence, neither of them wanted to start, neither of them wanted to get into small talk.

Jens found a scrap of paper, wrote down his phone number leaning on the wheel, and handed the note to Sophie.

"Thanks," she whispered.

He got out at Karlaplan and Sophie moved into the driver's seat. Their good-bye was short and impersonal.

Albert was fast asleep in his room. She looked at him for a while. Then she went downstairs and turned on the lights, then looked at her hands as she stood there in the kitchen. They weren't trembling, they were still. She was calm on the inside as well. She was amazed, thought it felt wrong. She ought to have been wound up about what had happened, frightened and upset. She looked at her hands again, soft, smooth, and still. Her pulse was beating steadily inside her. She put on a pan of water and got out her English tea, then went to stand by the window as she waited for it to boil. The view was the same as always, the streetlamp lighting up the road, the nightlights in her neighbors' windows. Everything was the way it had always been, but she didn't recognize it; none of what she could see looked familiar anymore.

10

Jens had gotten home to his apartment, packed a bag, got changed. He had walked off to a twenty-four-hour gas station, rented a car under a false name, and set off on his journey down to Munich.

He was sweating in the warm evening, drinking sports drinks to stay awake, smoking cigarettes.

He was thinking about Sophie Lantz... Brinkmann.

Carlos Fuentes was two teeth worse off. His eyes were swollen shut and when he tried to talk, nothing but a gurgling sound emerged because of all the blood in his mouth.

He was sitting on a chair in the office of the Trasten restaurant, a chair that he had fallen off numerous times in the past half hour. He had sobbed, begged, and offered to do anything in the world.

Neither Hector nor Aron was in the mood to listen to that sort of thing. They had picked him up at home. He knew what it was about the moment the doorbell rang, and confessed his involvement with Roland Gentz in the car on the way to the restaurant. Hector and Aron had sat in silence.

Carlos wiped the blood from his mouth with one hand.

"You're confessing too quickly, Carlos."

Carlos was breathing heavily, his body racing with adrenaline. "Maybe I am, but it's the truth, Hector!"

The panic that Carlos was radiating was impossible to miss. Aron gave Carlos a towel to wipe himself with. Carlos thanked his tormentor. Aron didn't acknowledge it.

"Why, Carlos?" Hector wondered.

Carlos wiped the blood with the towel. "Because he threatened to kill me."

"And that was enough for you?"

Carlos said nothing, just stared straight ahead.

Hector wiped something invisible from his eye. He went on in a low voice.

"Carlos, you betray me and lure me into a trap, the trap is sprung, but I get out of it. You confess the moment I ring at your door.... What else have you said, what else have you done, who else have you spoken to about me?"

The tears came, Carlos's heavy body shaking in time with his sobs.

"No one, I swear to you, Hector.... He paid me as well."

"Gentz?"

Carlos nodded without looking at Hector, wiping his nose on his sleeve.

"How much?"

"A hundred thousand."

Hector started. "One hundred thousand? Kronor?"

Carlos looked down at the floor.

"But you could have had that from me! Twice, three times as much if you wanted it!"

Carlos cleared his throat.

"I was scared, he was as cold as fucking ice and he meant what he said! It wasn't the money, of course it wasn't.... I had no choice, he left the hundred thousand in a plastic bag.... I didn't ask for the money, you have to believe me!"

Hector and Aron were staring curiously at Carlos.

"Why didn't you warn us?"

Carlos looked up at Aron, he had no answer.

Hector leaned back in his chair. "What are we going to do with you, Carlos?"

The big man, usually so confident and loud, was now a shadow of his former self, his mouth and face in tatters. Hector almost felt sorry for him.

"Carlos?"

Carlos shook his head.

"I don't know. Do whatever you like," he muttered.

Hector thought for a moment.

"We'll carry on as usual. If you have anything else to tell us, say it now," he said.

Carlos shook his head.

Hector asked himself if he was being too kind, if he'd live to regret this one day. He stood up and walked out. Aron followed him.

"Thank you," Carlos said.

Hector didn't stop, didn't look back.

"Don't thank me."

***

Aron was driving, with Hector in the passenger seat, the Stockholm night outside. The city passed by before Hector's eyes. The car headed down Hamngatan, the neon lights shining even though dawn was approaching. They wove through to Gustav Adolfs torg and crossed Norrbro. Hector was still deep in thought.

"Carlos..." He sighed to himself.

Aron parked the car on the quayside along Skeppsbron.

"I'm thinking of getting drunk, do you want to join me?"

Aron shook his head. "No, but I'll come to the door with you."

They walked up between the buildings of Brunnsgränd, then turned right into Österlånggatan. Laughter, chatter, and music could be heard from up above.

"Hector," Aron said in a low voice.

"Yes?"

"The nurse."

They walked a few steps.

"What about her?"

Aron glanced quickly at Hector, a glance that said something like *Look, just stop that.*

"It'll be fine, she's not a problem."

"How do you know?"

Hector didn't answer.

"She's intelligent," Aron said.

"Yes, she is."

Aron tried to find the right words.

"And she's a nurse.... Presumably a woman with her own values and morals, she seems pretty independent. What she's seen and experienced tonight will have stirred everything up for her. When the dust settles she'll start asking herself questions, weighing right against wrong... looking for answers, moral answers. That's when she might do something hasty, without thinking it through properly."

Hector kept on walking, unwilling to discuss the subject.

They reached Brända Tomten, the little square surrounded by tall houses. They stopped and Hector looked at Aron, at the injuries the beating had left on his face.

"You look pretty terrible."

Aron looked at Hector.

"You seem to have come out of it OK."

Aron glanced down at Hector's dirty clothes, then his leg and the cracked cast.

"But you need to get that fixed."

Hector didn't reply. He patted Aron on the shoulder and walked toward his door.

Aron waited down in the square until he saw the lights go on in the window of the third floor, then he went back the way they had come.

In the apartment Hector turned on the lights in every room, pulled the cur-tains, and put on some quiet music. He opened a bottle of wine and drank half of it in just a few minutes. The stress of the evening subsided slightly.

He called his father and they talked about what had happened. Adalberto calmed his son as best he could.

Hector fell asleep on the sofa with an old revolver on his stomach.

She read the report in the Stockholm section of the morning paper—one of the small items at the bottom of the page, down among the ads.

In the early hours of Sunday morning a man suffering from a gunshot wound was left at the emergency room at Karolinska Hospital by unidentified men who fled the scene in a car. He was operated on during the night and his condition is reported as stable. The man, who is in his forties, has not yet been questioned by the police.

She sat back, relieved. The man was alive.

She heard Albert's steps on the stairs and turned the page.

"Morning," he said.

"Morning," she said back.

"Were you home late last night?" he asked.

She nodded in reply. He reached for the tub of muesli in the cupboard above the stove.

"Did you have a good time?"

"Yes, it was nice," Sophie muttered, her eyes on the paper.

Sophie spent the morning in the garden, weeding and removing suckers from the roses. The birds were singing, people walking past greeted her with a nod or a dignified wave. Everything was lovely, but she didn't find the idyllic scene calming or even appealing, she just felt restless.

She finished up by pruning the roses but let the shears hang limply in her hand as she realized that she couldn't be bothered.

Sophie sat down on a sun lounger, letting the warmth embrace her, letting tiredness take its due, lulling her into a calmer world. She closed her eyes.

She dreamed that her dad was still alive, and that he was helping her with all the things she needed help with.

"Did you have a good trip?"

Leszek met Sonya Alizadeh as she emerged from the gate at Málaga Airport, taking her bags as they headed for the exit.

He had parked outside by the taxi stand. Someone yelled at him that he shouldn't be there. He paid no attention and opened the door for Sonya. They headed out onto the highway toward Marbella.

Adalberto received her in a shirt and beige linen trousers. He was barefoot and suntanned. His thin white hair was swept back, the gold watch on his wrist sparkling ostentatiously.

"Welcome."

He kissed her on both cheeks, as usual, and showed her into the villa.

A large table in the middle of a room filled with light covering the whole inner part of the building had been set for lunch, and the panoramic window showed a view of the endless sea. They sat down.

"How was it?" he asked as he unfolded his napkin.

She drank from her water glass.

"I think it's fine. It's all sorted out, the apartment has been cleaned, I never lived there."

Adalberto ate a mouthful, then looked up at Sonya.

"Is it OK for you to live here?"

She nodded.

"It's wise of you to let us look after you, you never know what men like him might get into their heads, they're the most dangerous, the ones who try to pass themselves off as the right sort."

She didn't respond to his statement, but didn't exactly disagree with it. She was the one who knew Svante Carlgren, she'd had him inside her numerous times. He was genuinely unpleasant. He possessed a sort of chill, an emptiness that she had never experienced in a man before. As if he lacked something other men had, as if he didn't actually recognize that there were other people in the world. And on top of this, there was something stupid about him. Something talentless and moronic, as if he could only deal with one single thing in life—his warped view of himself.

Sonya felt exhausted, and somewhere deep inside she was pleased not to have to be a whore for a while. Yet the choice had been her own. She was the one who put the idea to Hector a long time ago. He was like a brother to her. At least, he was the closest thing to one that she had. Her dad, Danush, had been a heroin importer, had fled Tehran when the Shah was toppled, and had gone into business with Adalberto. Their families became close and, as an only child, Sonya spent a lot of her school vacations in Marbella with the Guzmans. She was like the fourth child of the family. Her parents were murdered in Switzerland in the late '80s. She fled to Asia and fell into severe and protracted cocaine addiction, which intermittently helped her to forget her boundless grief. Hector was the one who tracked her down and helped her get back home. Adalberto and Hector let her live with them in Marbella, helped her to recover. After a while Hector showed her a picture of three dead men. They were lying on a white tiled floor. A public toilet at a roadside café in the south of Germany. They had bullet wounds in their heads, chests, arms, legs. Riddled with holes. The men had belonged to the 'Ndrangheta and they were her parents' killers. She took pleasure in the photograph. She kept it, looking at it whenever life felt tough and unfair. Sonya wanted to repay Hector and Adalberto for all they had done for her. When she suggested the idea to Hector he had tried to dissuade her, telling her that she didn't owe them anything. But she didn't agree, no matter what he said. So she held her ground and went ahead with her plan. Maybe Svante Carlgren would turn out to be the repayment that would help get rid of the sense of obligation that she was keen to escape.

Sonya liked Hector and Adalberto, but she knew that when it came down to it the men in her life weren't so very different, even if the man sitting opposite her now was trying to prove that he was.

Adalberto was looking at her, and almost seemed to be reading her mind.

"I've made preparations for your arrival. A female psychiatrist is at your disposal if you feel like talking. She's a good woman, she'll come whenever we ask her to. You can have whatever you want from me, just say what you need to find your way back again."

He smiled, and she returned a smile that radiated the exact opposite of what she really felt—an accomplishment she had learned early in life.

They ate lunch in silence, the sea sighed outside the open windows, the warm sea breeze caught the white linen curtains and made them move.

Piño the dog came running in and sat down to beg for scraps. Adalberto ignored him, and after a while he settled down at his master's feet.

"I gave him something at the table a few years ago. It's taking him a long time to realize there won't be any more."

He looked at Piño.

"But we're still friends, aren't we, you and me?"

Sonya saw the happiness in Adalberto's face when he looked at Piño. Then the smile faded, as if he suddenly realized how sad it was that the dog was merely a dog.

11

Gunilla looked quizzically at Anders.

"Say that again."

"Two men went into the restaurant after Hector held the door open for the nurse. He never came out again, but the nurse did. Lars followed her."

"And the men?"

Anders shrugged. "Gone, vanished. I went into the restaurant thirty minutes later. None of them was there. There's a back door leading to a courtyard, so that must be how they got out. Through the yard and out onto the other side of the block."

"Then what?"

Anders shook his head. "Nothing. I went home."

They were sitting on a bench in Humlegården. Most of the people around them appeared to be enjoying the summer heat. Anders Ask was the only man in the park wearing a jacket.

"So Sophie and Hector arrived at the restaurant, they went in, two men followed them. How long did you say it was before Sophie came out?"

"About half an hour."

"About?"

"I have the exact times written down, but not on me."

Gunilla thought for a moment.

"And Lars followed her?"

Anders nodded.

Gunilla pulled out her cell and dialed a number.

"Lars, am I interrupting anything? Can you come to Humlegården at once? Thanks very much," she said, and ended the call.

Anders smiled at the friendly tone that left Lars no room to respond or object. She noticed.

"He's coming," she said.

"I know."

Then they just sat there, as if they were two robots on standby mode, completely still, staring out across the park. Anders was the one who moved first. He put his hand in his jacket pocket, pulled out a crumpled bag of candy, and held it out to her. She came to life as well, possibly because of the rustling sound, took two pieces of licorice without thanking him, and chewed on them, deep in thought. One particular thought wouldn't go away. She drifted back to the present, took out her phone again, and looked up Eva Castroneves's number. She put the phone to her ear.

"Eva, can you run a date check?"

Gunilla waited.

"Last Saturday, the fifth, I think it was."

Gunilla glanced at Anders, who nodded in agreement.

"Run the whole day, but pay particular attention to the evening and early Sunday morning. Main focus on Vasastan, but the surrounding areas as well. Anything at all could be of interest. Thanks."

Gunilla ended the call. Anders was looking at her, and Gunilla shrugged.

"Where else can I start?"

He didn't answer.

Lars was approaching along the gravel path from Stureplan. She looked at him. His walk was stiff, as if he had a bad back. Which he probably did, people who felt guilty almost always transferred it to the base of the spine unconsciously.

He walked up to them, there was something hesitant and antagonistic about him.

"Hello?"

Gunilla looked at him.

"Have you cut your hair?"

Lars ran a hand through his hair without thinking.

"A bit," he muttered.

"Thanks for coming so quickly."

Lars waited, put one hand in his jeans pocket.

"If I remember rightly, you wrote in your report for Saturday evening that Sophie drove home after her visit to the Trasten restaurant. Anders here says he saw you outside the restaurant, and that you followed Sophie when she left the restaurant?"

"That's right. She left her house at about eleven o'clock and drove to the restaurant. I seem to recall that she left about midnight. I followed her to Norrtull, then I let her go and went home. I presumed she was driving home."

Gunilla and Anders were looking at him, seemed to be searching for any small signs of lying. Lars scratched his neck.

"Has anything happened?" he wondered.

"I don't know, Anders saw you," Gunilla said.

Lars looked at Anders.

"Oh?"

"And he saw two men go into the restaurant."

Lars was showing signs of impatience, irritation.

"Yes? And?"

"Did you see them?"

Lars shook his head.

"No. Well, maybe, people were coming and going, it's a restaurant."

Lars dug out a cough drop and put it in his mouth, looking at Gunilla. "What is this? An interrogation?"

Gunilla didn't answer. Anders was looking at him intently the whole time.

"The men never came out. Hector never came out. There's an exit from the back. When you followed Sophie, when she left the restaurant, did she stop anywhere?"

The cough drop gave him an excuse to swallow. He did, then shook his head.

"No."

Lars had been insanely wired. He had practically no recollection of that evening. Just a hazy picture of losing her near Haga, then a total blank. God alone knew what had happened or how he had gotten home, and he couldn't exactly ask Him; they weren't on good terms.

It was always a matter of persuading yourself that the lie was true, then you weren't lying, then you didn't betray any signs of uncertainty.

"She drove straight home, and I broke off surveillance when she turned off the highway."

"Which route did she take?"

He made an effort not to show any signs of uncertainty in his posture, visualizing the lie.

"From Odenplan she turned left onto Sveavägen, even though that's not allowed. Then all the way along Sveavägen to the roundabout, then north on the E4."

"Why not Roslagstull and Roslagsvägen? That's closer for her."

Lars shrugged.

"Same difference, really. She must have turned off at Bergshamra and got to the Stocksund Bridge that way. I don't know."

"Why didn't you follow her all the way home?"

Lars sucked the cough drop, and it made a sound as it hit his teeth.

"It was late, not much traffic. I had to be careful."

Gunilla was looking at him, Anders likewise.

"Thank you, Lars, thanks for taking the time to come down here."

Lars looked at the pair of them.

"And?"

The look on Gunilla's face said that she didn't understand what he meant.

"What else? What's happened?" Lars asked.

"Oh, nothing's happened. I just couldn't quite get the evening to make sense."

"What's he doing here?"

Lars directed the question to Gunilla without so much as looking at Anders.

"I don't need tailing, Gunilla," he said in a low voice.

The anger in his voice surprised her.

"No, Lars, and that's not what we're doing. Anders is helping us to identify the people around Hector, and you just happened to be in the same place at the same time. When I couldn't get the evening to make sense I asked to speak to you. But you don't seem to have anything to add that wasn't in your report, so everything's as it should be. Isn't it?"

Lars didn't answer, but the darkness surrounding him eased a little.

"Thank you, Lars.... Continue your surveillance."

He turned on his heel and walked back the way he had come. He only just managed to keep everything under control, inside he was shaking.

Gunilla and Anders sat in silence until Lars had disappeared.

"What do you think?" she asked.

Anders thought.

"I don't know, I honestly don't know. He doesn't seem to be lying."

"But?"

Anders glared out across the park.

"He's insecure by nature. Today he seemed too certain, almost as if he was trying to find a way of hiding a lie of some sort."

Gunilla stood up.

"Come with me back to the station, stay close for a while."

Gunilla was sitting in front of Eva Castroneves's desk. Eva gathered her papers together and read through in silence until she found the right section.

"Saturday. Nothing of note in Vasastan apart from a few drunk and disorderlies, a couple of fights and a robbery from the 7-Eleven on Sveavägen . . . an overdose in Guldhuset in Vasaparken, stolen cars, vandalism. An ordinary Saturday. The only thing I found that stuck out was an unidentified man with gunshot wounds who was dropped off at Karolinska at about one o'clock in the morning."

"Who is he?"

Eva turned to her computer and began tapping at the keyboard. She read from the screen.

"No info about his name. The hospital staff told the police that he spoke German when he was feverish. Nothing else in the file so far, he's probably still unconscious."

"Dropped off, you said?"

Eva nodded. "Yes, by a private car that drove off."

A short while later Gunilla and Anders were standing looking at Klaus Köhler's unconscious body under a white hospital sheet.

"I don't know.... Could have been one of them, the smaller one."

Gunilla waited for more. Anders took his time, looking at Klaus from different angles. Gunilla started to get impatient.

"Anders?"

He shot her an irritated glance, as if her talking was interrupting his concentration.

"I don't know, can we lift him up?"

Tubes, drips, and wires led from the man to a stand beside the bed. Gunilla leaned over and looked under the bed.

"I think the top end will go up."

Anders went over and found the pedal under the bed. He put his foot on it, the hydraulics started to work, and, against his will, the bed started to sink. The needles from the drips and other equipment that were fastened under the skin of Klaus's hand were caught under his arm and popped out when the bed touched bottom. A machine started to beep.

"Shit."

Anders grabbed the needle and drove it back into Klaus's hand and the beeping increased. Eventually he found the right pedal under the bed. Klaus Köhler's upper body rose majestically toward them. The more upright he got, the more noise the machine made. The curve on one screen was lurching up and down. Anders looked down at the floor in an attempt to summon up an image from memory. He looked up again, then repeated the process several times. Then he left the room. Gunilla followed him, the apparatus beeping insistently as the door closed behind them.

"Well?" Gunilla asked.

A nurse was running down the corridor toward them.

"Maybe... probably. Somewhere between the two, leaning toward probably. Seventy percent, I'd say."

* * *

She was sitting on the edge of a concrete flowerbed outside the hospital, phone to her ear, asking Sophie friendly questions, and getting friendly answers back.

"But weren't you planning to have dinner?"

"It didn't work out. Hector had a last-minute meeting, so I went home."

Anders was standing a short distance away. He was killing time by trying to hit an ashtray with small stones, making an annoying ringing sound.

"Has anything happened?"

"There are just a few details that are a bit unclear."

Sophie was silent at the other end.

"Do you know who he was meeting?" Gunilla went on.

"No, no idea."

Anders Ask hit the ashtray several times. Clang, clang, clang.

"Are you sure?"

"Yes. What is it, Gunilla?"

She sat down with the phone in her hand, staring in front of her at the wax cloth on the coffee table in the staff room. The conversation with Gunilla was echoing in her head. She tried to remember what she had said, how the conversation had developed. She tried to remember her tone of voice... *her style.* Had she given anything away? The thoughts were flying around. The phone in her hand rang again, ringtone and vibration at the same time. In her confusion she forgot to check the screen.

"Hello?"

His voice was clipped. He said he wanted to meet her, which surprised her. She asked where Hector was.

"That doesn't matter," he said.

She felt suddenly uneasy. He told her to wait outside the hospital when she'd finished for the day, and that he'd pick her up.

"I can't," she replied.

"Yes, you can," Aron said, and ended the call.

* * *

He stayed behind the wheel, didn't meet her gaze as she opened the door and got into the passenger seat.

Aron pulled away from the traffic circle and drove out onto the highway. But instead of turning toward Stockholm he drove down the other exit ramp, into the lane leading to Norrtälje.

"Where are we going?" she asked.

He didn't answer, so she asked again.

"We're going to have a talk.... Stop asking questions."

He let the car carry them along the highway. It felt never-ending.

"What is it, Aron?" she whispered.

Aron didn't answer, didn't seem to see or hear her. Fear was creeping up on her.

"Can't you tell me where we're going?" she pleaded.

He must have been able to hear how anxious she sounded, perhaps that was exactly what he wanted.

After a while he turned off the highway, sticking to the right-hand lane. A road sign flashed past and she managed to read Sjöflygvägen. He carried on toward the water, found a secluded spot, and switched off the engine. The silence that followed was worse than she could ever have imagined, so dense and almost evil. He was staring straight ahead through the windshield.

"You'll soon start asking yourself questions about that evening. Those questions won't have any obvious answers. And when you don't find any answers, you're going to want to share your questions with someone else."

She didn't answer.

"Don't do that," he said in a low voice.

Sophie looked down at her lap, then out through the window. The sun was shining as usual, and the water was glittering in the distance.

"Does Hector know about this?" she asked quietly.

"That doesn't matter," he said.

She could feel her heart pounding in her chest as the air inside the car seemed to get thinner.

"Are you threatening me, Aron?"

Now he turned toward her and looked at her. The fear she had felt suddenly took physical form in her tear ducts. Tears began trickling down her cheeks, fat and heavy. She cleared her throat, wiping away the tears on her sleeve.

"Am I supposed to take this seriously?"

She didn't know why she asked that question, maybe because she wanted to see if there was an ounce of humanity in him.

"Yes," he said in a measured tone.

She realized that her arms were trembling, just a little, almost imperceptibly, but the trembling was there. Her arms ached. A different pain rose in her neck and she fought against it, trying to swallow, all her anxiety seemed to have gathered in her throat.... She wanted to swallow, her entire body wanted her to. Sophie turned away from Aron and gulped.

"Can we go back?"

"If you say you understand what I've told you."

Sophie stared out through the car window.

"I understand," she said in a hollow voice.

Aron leaned forward, turned the key, the car started.

12

Hasse Berglund was standing in line at a hamburger restaurant. They were running a Mexican theme. The idiots behind the counter had little plastic sombreros on their heads. He ordered an El Jefe—a triple burger with extra everything, including two helpings of fries. Hasse sat down, the feeding frenzy could begin. He took big mouthfuls, breathing through his nose.

A gang of immigrants was sitting a few tables away. Black hair, pale, with stupid little mustaches and black tracksuits. They were noisy, raging with hormones, sinewy, knew no bounds. Two of them started wrestling in their seats. They were yelling, far too loudly, far too intensely, spilling ice and cola on the floor.

Hasse looked at them, unable to understand how they could be so pale when they came from some Arab country. After all, it was sunny there.

He grimaced when it got too noisy. A milkshake got knocked over and spilled across the table. One of them started shouting when the liquid splashed his tracksuit. Another one started swearing crudely, a third started throwing ice cubes from his drink at his friends.

Hasse went on chewing his mouthful and watched the youths. They kept on wrestling. Roughly, hard, thoughtlessly...It turned violent, one of them was getting angry. He started shouting in a language Hasse didn't recognize. Then the whole gang joined in, an infernal choir of breaking voices. Hasse closed his eyes.

Eighteen months earlier Hasse Berglund and his colleagues in the rapid-response unit of the Stockholm Police Department had set about a young Lebanese man in Norra Bantorget. His colleagues knew when to stop, but Hasse didn't. His colleagues had pulled him off. Hasse had calmed down, demonstrated that he was OK...that he was thinking again. His colleagues eased their grip, Hasse pulled loose, and got in that last, satisfying kick. The boy lay unconscious for three days. The doctors found broken ribs, internal bleeding, a dislocated jaw, and a broken collarbone. During the trial Hasse's colleagues testified to his innocence. Two magistrates found no reason for their sleep to be troubled, and the prosecutor was friends with everyone in the room except the boy. A bearded doctor declared that it "wasn't impossible" that the boy had caused his injuries himself, and the boy's lawyer, who was in a hurry to get to another court case, asked stupid and ill-considered questions. Hasse walked free, and the boy was left with lifelong problems. But Hasse's boss had had enough, and offered him a choice: leave the city force for the airport, or leave the city force for whatever-the-fuck-you-like.

Hasse was sent into exile to Arlanda Airport, where he had been stuck for an eternity, trying to pick up the illegal immigrants that so disgusted him.

Then out of the blue he got a phone call. A woman from the National Crime Division, a Gunilla Strandberg, saying she wanted him to meet two of her colleagues. Hasse didn't really understand. But anything was better than the airport.

The youths went on yelling, Hasse finished his mouthful, swallowed, ran his tongue over his teeth, pulled out his police ID, and put it on the table. He took a few deep breaths, then picked up one of the cartons of fries and threw it hard at the young men. It hit one of the wrestlers on the cheek, and fries flew out and hit a couple of the others. They lost their flow and silently stared at Hasse, who took a fresh bite, at the very limits of what his jaw could handle.

One of the young men stood up with a jerk and thumped his chest. He asked something that Hasse couldn't be bothered to listen to. He was so sick of that immigrant Swedish. The young man was on his way over to him. Hasse Berglund shoveled more food into his mouth, chewed, held up his police badge, opened his jacket with the same hand to show the pistol in its shoulder holster, then gestured with his chin.

"Sit down...."

And the young man backed away and sat down. Hasse took aim and threw fries at each and every one of them. The young men put up with the humiliation in silence. Hasse showed neither anger nor joy, just a sure aim as his fries hit them on their backs, heads, arms, and acne-ridden faces.

Anders Ask and Erik Strandberg came into the restaurant, saw the tragedy being played out, and went over to his table.

"You must be Hasse Berglund," Erik said.

Hasse looked at them, nodded, and went on throwing fries.

"I'm Erik, and this is Anders."

Erik sat down with a sigh. He had a temperature that day, a cold sweat, and permanent pressure over his forehead, and his mouth was dry.

Hasse threw another fry that landed on one young man's hood.

"Having a fries war, I see?" Anders said.

"Yep," Hasse said, firing off another one.

Anders joined in, grabbing a few fries and throwing them at the youths. He was also a good shot. The young men stared ahead of them, humiliated.

"You used to be in the city?" Erik asked, breathing heavily through his high blood pressure.

"Yep."

"Then Arlanda?"

They ran out of fries.

"Shall we get some more?" Anders asked.

Erik shook his head and turned to the young men.

"Have a good day, boys. Look out for each other," he said, gesturing for them to leave.

The youngsters got up and slouched out. Outside they started shouting and fighting again, then disappeared.

"Great lads!" Anders said.

"Sweden's future," Hasse said.

Erik coughed into his elbow. Hasse drank through a straw, looking at Erik and Anders. Anders settled down and began.

"You've already spoken to Gunilla, she's told you about the project. We wanted to meet you."

"I've heard about you, Erik, but not about any Anders," Hasse said.

"Anders is a consultant . . . ," Erik said.

"So what does a consultant do?"

"Consults," Anders said.

Hasse found a fry between his legs on the chair and ate it.

"And Strandberg?" Hasse said. "You've got the same name. Is Gunilla your missus, or what?"

Erik looked hard at Hasse.

"No," he replied.

Hasse Berglund waited for more, but nothing came.

"OK, like I care. I'm just happy to be involved, because I'm guessing that's what this is about, a job offer?"

"I think so. What do you say, Anders?"

Anders didn't answer. Hasse looked from one to the other.

"Come on, I'm stuck in a fucking airport, I need to get out of there before I shoot someone. I'm very flexible, I told Gunilla."

Erik tried to find a comfortable position on the fixed plastic chair, and let out a rattling cough.

"OK, it's like this. . . . We work as a team. We don't question Gunilla's decisions, she's always right. If the results don't come at the rate we might want them to, at least they come eventually. Gunilla knows that, and that's why we do as she says. If you don't understand your role in what we do, you don't ask, you just carry on and keep your mouth shut. Are you with me?"

Hasse swallowed the last of his drink, the ice cubes rattling at the bottom of the cup.

"OK," he said flatly as he let go of the straw.

"If you've got any complaints, if you think you've been unfairly treated, or if you've got any other whiny union questions, well, then you're out on your ear."

Erik leaned forward, took Hasse's untouched apple pie, and helped himself to a big bite. As usual, it was too hot and he chewed on it with his mouth open as he went on.

"We work with simple equations, we don't like complicating things. If you do the job well, you'll be rewarded."

Erik finished Hasse's apple pie. Hasse's expression didn't change. Erik took a napkin from the table and wiped the fevered sweat from his brow, then blew his nose noisily.

"You'll be transferred to us shortly. Keep your mouth shut about this, don't go yapping about it to any of your colleagues, just be goddamn grateful, OK?"

"Ten-four," Hasse Berglund said in his best TV-cop voice, then gave them the thumbs-up and a crooked smile.

Erik stared intently at him.

"And none of that fucking shit with me."

Erik stood up and walked out. Anders pulled an innocent face, shrugged his shoulders, and followed him.

He had been pretty shaken up after his meeting with Gunilla and Anders. The pills weren't working the way they should. Gunilla and Anders were in cahoots. They were onto something, something he wasn't allowed to be part of. They were questioning him. They didn't trust him.

His nerves were gnawing away at him. He had hurried home, picked up the prescriptions he had stolen from Rosie, and gone to the nearest pharmacy. There was a line, moving slowly, the old woman behind the counter was in no hurry. A knot of anxiety pressed at his stomach. The pharmacist started asking questions about one of the prescriptions. He answered tersely and monosyllabically, told her he was Rosie's son, that he didn't know, he was just supposed to pick them up. He kept scratching his cheek.

When he got back home he checked the online pharmaceutical directory. Lyrica was like a fucking Kinder Egg, three gifts in one: it prevented epileptic fits, neuropathological pain, and anxiety. Rosie took the pills for her nerves. It said 300 mg on the bottle, the strongest available, *bingo*. He took two, washing them down with some stale water from a glass on the desk. The second prescription was nasal spray, so he threw that in the bin. The third, the one that had looked different and that the pharmacist had asked about, was Ketogan. He looked it up in the directory. Addictive substance. The utmost care should be taken with prescriptions of this drug. He was already addicted, the school nurse had told him that. And inside Lars's head a thought took shape: If that was the case, then these pills wouldn't be dangerous for him. *What the hell could possibly go wrong?*

He kept reading. Ketogan was a powerful drug, used for very severe pain. *Very severe pain?*

He tore open the box. Fuck. Suppositories. You've got to do what you've got to do. Lars pulled down his trousers, squatted down, and shoved one of them up his backside, then another . . . and then another. He pulled up his trousers and went out into the living room. Life gradually changed into something soft, composed, and undemanding. He wandered aimlessly around the room, feeling a sudden and immense gratitude for everything in his life. It all fell into place, his feelings were where they should be, neatly partitioned, secure, incapable of making a fuss or throwing up any questions for him to get caught up in. He sat down in a corner. The wooden floor felt soft and Lars lay down, it was like a waterbed made of cotton balls. He looked out across the horizon of the floor. It was so beautiful, so intricately beautiful, imagine that a floor could be so wonderful, so incredibly wonderful in all its flatness. . . .

He lay there enjoying everything that he could understand yet not understand. When he slowly began to bottom out he took a few more of each drug. The world became interesting for a while. His fingers started talking to each other, started to explain the true nature of existence to him, the nature that lay three steps behind the laws of physics, two steps behind God's creation . . . one step behind the creation of God. . . . Then Lars fell asleep.

The alarm clock sounded like an air-raid siren. Several hours had passed and the feeling of emptiness had expanded into a huge black hole that was swallowing all the light in Lars's universe. He got on weak legs and topped up with a random mix of drugs. The black hole withdrew and life became easy again.

He drove to Stocksund. All the radio stations were playing really good music and he bopped weirdly along to it.

He found a good hiding place for the car, put on the headphones, got himself comfortable in the car seat, and listened to her. How she went around her house all alone, how she prepared food, how she talked to her friend Clara over the phone, how she laughed at something on television.

He felt like going in to see her, to share what she was doing, or just sit alongside and watch. Darkness came, the house was completely silent. Longing started to tug and pull at him.

At half past one in the morning Lars took off the headphones, put on a dark woolly hat, carefully opened the car door, and started walking toward her house.

He crossed the street, smelling the scent of the honeysuckle without actually knowing what honeysuckle was, crept into her garden, and made his way soundlessly up to the veranda.

The skeleton key worked just as well this time. It pressed in the little metal tumblers in the lock. Lars carefully pushed the handle of the terrace door, nudged it open slightly, and took a can of lubricant from his pocket. He sprayed the oil on the hinges inside the door, two quick squirts. The door slid open without a sound.

Lars stood silently in the living room, then bent down and took his shoes off, listening, but all he could hear was his own heartbeat thudding inside him. Slowly and cautiously he began to go upstairs. The old wooden staircase made small creaking sounds. A car passed by out in the road. Lars compared the sounds, possibly the same decibel level. His steps wouldn't wake her up.

The door to her bedroom was ajar. Lars stood still, taking calm, regular breaths, letting his breathing go back to normal, then took a step onto the soft carpet. A smell hit him, faint, thin, as if it were drifting about the room like invisible silk...*Sophie.* There she lay. As if in a fantasy she was lying on her back, her head on the pillow, slightly askew. Her hair was like a backdrop to everything, her mouth was closed, her chest calmly rose and fell. The covers went up to her stomach, she was wearing a lacy nightdress. His eyes were drawn to the shape of her breasts, and stopped there. She was so beautiful. He wanted to wake her up and tell her: *You're so beautiful.* He wanted to lie down beside her, hold her in his arms, and tell her everything was all right. She'd know what he meant.

Carefully he pulled out his camera, switched off the flash and sound, then found her through the lens. Without a sound he took thirty or so close-ups of Sophie as she slept.

He was about to leave when his eyes were drawn once again to her breasts. Lars stared, as fantasies from the depths of his troubled soul started to take shape. Lars crept closer to her. And closer. In the end he was standing right next to her face. He could see her skin, the little wrinkles around her eyes, her lines.... He closed his eyes, he smelled, he wished....

She moved in her sleep and let out a little sound. Lars opened his eyes, backed away carefully, and silently left the room.

He was breathless by the time he got back in the car. He felt as if he'd slept with her, a feeling of having been inside her for the first time. He felt strong, safe, happy. He knew that she felt the same. She must have seen him in her sleep, in her dreams. It was so obvious, he was her angel of salvation, in her life without her knowledge, who made love to her when she was asleep, who protected her from evil when she was awake. He took some more of the prescription drugs, the world around him took on a different hue, his tongue seemed to grow inside his mouth, and sounds became blurred.

Lars drove carefully back in toward the city, passing the Natural History Museum in the pale light from the streetlamps. And saw a huge fucking penguin that was staring quizzically at him.

Sophie had been having nightmares, she couldn't remember what they were about, but she woke up with a sense of unease. A sense that she had been subjected to something, a feeling of disgust. She got out of bed, she'd overslept. She could hear the sound of the vacuum cleaner downstairs.

It had been ages since she last saw Dorota. She usually came when

Sophie was at work, but she had the day off today. She was pleased to see her again when she went downstairs. Dorota was kind. Sophie liked her.

Dorota waved from the living room, where she was vacuuming. Sophie smiled back and went into the kitchen to get some breakfast.

"I'll drive you home later!" she called.

Dorota switched off the vacuum cleaner.

"What did you say?"

"I said I can drive you home later, Dorota."

Dorota shook her head.

"You don't have to, it's so far."

"No, it isn't. But you always say it is."

Dorota was sitting in the passenger seat with her handbag in her lap. They'd already crossed the Stocksund Bridge and turned off at Bergshamra.

"You're very quiet, Dorota. Is everything OK, are your children all right?"

"Everything's good, the children are fine. . . . I miss them, but everything's good."

They drove on a bit farther.

"Maybe I'm tired," Dorota said, looking out the window.

"You can take some time off if you like."

Dorota shook her head. "No, work's fine. I'm not tired like that, just tired in my head, if you can say that?"

Dorota tried to smile, then her eyes settled on the world outside again, at everything going past. Her forced smile vanished. Sophie kept looking between Dorota and the road.

Dorota had lived in Spånga for as long as Sophie had known her. It was almost twelve years since the first time she came to their house. They'd developed a friendship. This was the first time Sophie could see that Dorota wasn't herself. She was normally happy, talking about her children, laughing at things Sophie told her. But this time she was withdrawn. Sophie looked again. She seemed sad, possibly scared.

Sophie pulled up outside Dorota's door on Spånga Square.

Dorota stayed in her seat for a moment after undoing the seat belt, then turned toward Sophie.

"Well, good-bye, and thanks for the lift."

"I can tell something's troubling you," Sophie said. "If you want to talk, you know where I am."

Dorota didn't move, just sat there without saying anything.

"What is it, Dorota?"

She hesitated.

Sophie waited.

"The last time I came to clean there were two men in your house when I arrived."

Sophie listened.

"At first I thought they were relatives or friends of yours, but they turned nasty, threatened me."

A chill swept through Sophie.

"They said they were police, that they'd cause problems if I told anyone."

Sophie's mind was racing.

"I'm sorry, Sophie, I'm sorry I didn't tell you, but I didn't dare.... But I changed my mind. You have always been so kind."

"What did they do? Did you understand why they were there? Did they say anything?"

Dorota shook her head. "No, I don't know. One of them tried to be nice, the other was terrible, cold and... I don't know. He felt evil. They didn't say what they were doing there. They went after they spoke to me."

"Where did they go?"

"Out."

"Through the door? How did they get in?"

Sophie could hear the fear in her own voice.

"I don't know. They went out through the terrace door. That's all I know."

Sophie tried to think.

"Tell me everything they said."

Dorota tried to remember.

"One of them said his name was Lars. That was the only name I heard."

"Lars?"

Sophie didn't know why she repeated the name.

"Lars what?" she went on.

Dorota shrugged her shoulders lightly. "I don't know."

"What did they look like? Try to be as exact as possible."

Dorota hadn't expected this reaction from Sophie. She put one hand to the side of her head, staring down into space.

"My memory's so bad."

"Try, Dorota."

Sophie's tone was abrupt. Dorota could hear how desperate she was.

"One of them, the one who said his name was Lars, was about thirty, thirty-five, I don't know. Fair..."

She thought, searching her memory.

"He looked scared. Worried."

Sophie listened.

"The other one was more ordinary, hard to describe. Maybe forty, maybe younger. Dark hair with some gray. He seemed kind but he was so mean. His eyes were kind. Dark and round. Like a boy's." Dorota shivered. "Ugh, he was horrible."

Sophie could see how scared she was. Sophie leaned over and hugged her.

"Thank you," she said as they embraced.

They looked at each other once they'd let go. Dorota patted Sophie on the cheek.

"Have you got problems?"

"No... No, I haven't. Thank you, Dorota."

Dorota looked at her.

"The mean one took my ID card, he said I wasn't allowed to tell anyone. Promise you won't do anything silly. He meant it. He knows who I am."

Sophie took the woman's hand in hers.

"I promise, Dorota. Nothing's going to happen to you."

Sophie drove away from Spånga. She followed the traffic, changed lanes, kept to the speed limit. She found herself in a vacuum where there were no thoughts or feelings. Then a crack opened up somewhere. A terror was welling up inside her. A sense of being helpless, at the mercy of powerful forces. The fear grew, spreading through her, an innate maternal horror of not being able to protect

Albert, of being helpless. Then it vanished. Suddenly and abruptly, it simply winked out of existence. The vacuum returned. She drove through the traffic, her feelings shut off. Then something else bubbled up. Fury. A bright red anger poured out, like water from a burst dam, roaring through her whole body and filling her to the breaking point.

13

His tiredness had shifted into a sort of nervous wakefulness. Jens felt wired as he drove into Munich. He hadn't slept in two days, running on nothing but willpower.

The address Mikhail had given him turned out to be in a sleepy residential area with identical houses from the '60s packed tightly together. Small lawns, built-in garages, low quality. Jens stopped at number 54, got out of the car, and looked around. Not a person in sight. He went up the paved path and checked the front door, it was unlocked. He opened it and stepped cautiously inside the house.

"Hello?"

No answer. There was no furniture apart from an old sofa in what was clearly meant to be the living room. Faded, striped wallpaper from a bygone age, little brown patches of damp on the ceiling and floor. He looked into the kitchen. A table, two chairs, a coffee machine, quiet as the grave. Jens turned around and glanced back at the front door, which he had closed behind him. Toward the bottom of the frame were two electrical contacts, the sort you see in shops, which set off a buzzer somewhere whenever the beam of light is broken. He inspected the amateurish setup, following the wire to where it was connected to a thin telephone cable that ran untidily along the top of the wall.

With a sudden sense of urgency he rushed upstairs: two rooms and a bathroom. He checked the cupboards, keeping an eye out for hidden cubbyholes in the walls and floors. He ran back down and went through the same procedure in the kitchen, living room, and the back room facing the yard. Nothing. Jens considered getting out of there, realizing that he might have been lured into a trap. But which was worse—the Russians if they didn't get their goods, or the German bastards who might be on their way right now? The answer was the Russians. He had to get his weapons back.

The cellar door was hard to open, it had swollen with damp. He tugged and pulled at it, but it didn't budge. Jens backed away, took aim, and kicked it. After another couple of kicks the door finally gave way.

As he took the flight of steps in three strides he was hit by a strong sense of damp from the dark cellar. Jens felt along the wall, trying to find a light switch. As the seconds passed, he found no switch, stumbled over something, and made his way farther along the wall. A different smell hit him, a smell he recognized—the smell of something dead. He had noticed it at his place out in the country, when mice had found their way into the walls and died there. The same smell, but more pungent, stronger. He swallowed the urge to throw up, and began breathing into his elbow, still feeling along the wall with his other hand.

In the far corner of the room he found a switch, the fluorescent lights flickered groggily into life, and Jens saw a body. He was in a garage with no cars in it, the room bathed in a thin, cold light. The dead body was lying on the boxes containing his weapons, in the middle of the floor, laid out across them on its back. Its face was swollen, pale-yellow, waxy. Jens stared at the body, frozen to the spot. He didn't know what to do, and was trying to suppress the foreboding that was welling up inside him.

He heard the front door open and close up above, and the footsteps in the empty room echoed down into the cellar. A pair of shoes appeared on the top step.

"Come up," Mikhail grunted.

When Jens went up the stairs Mikhail grabbed him, checked him for weapons, found nothing, and pushed him away.

On the old sofa sat a young man in a suit and a white shirt with the top button undone. By the window facing the street stood an older man with his back to Jens, more correctly dressed, more stiff.

"I understand that you claim you're nothing to do with Guzman?"

Ralph Hanke turned around.

"There's a dead body lying on my boxes in the cellar," Jens said.

"Jürgen?"

"I don't give a damn what his name is. Would you mind removing him?"

Ralph smiled. Jens noticed that the smile was mirthless, just a physical gesture in which the man turned the corners of his mouth up.

"You see, we've been chasing Jürgen for quite some time. He took us for forty thousand euros, and thought no one would notice. What's forty thousand worth today? Not even a decent car. But Jürgen couldn't help himself."

Ralph turned to face the street again.

"He caused a lot of other trouble for us.... We don't kill people for forty thousand euros.... We're not monsters."

"Could you please remove the dead body from my things, then I'll leave. I had an agreement with Mikhail here," Jens went on.

"That still applies, in principle. I just want to talk to you before you go."

Jens looked at Christian, who had been glaring at him the whole time. Ralph turned around.

"My son, Christian," Ralph said.

Jens shrugged to say that he wasn't interested.

Ralph got straight to the point.

"I want to make the Guzmans an offer. I want them to come over to our side.... We're taking care of their affairs from now on. They're going to be employees, you could say. With reasonable perks."

Jens shrugged. "You've got the wrong man. I've got nothing to do with the Guzmans. I'm just here to pick up my things, nothing else."

Ralph took a deep breath and shook his head.

"No, you're going to pass on my proposal, then call us and tell us how they received it. You're going to be the go-between. And as long as I'm in the room, any arrangements you've made with Mikhail are worthless. Sorry."

Ralph paused for effect.

"Mikhail says he's bumped into you several times. You're the prefect man for the job. If I sent an intermediary, Guzman wouldn't be interested. I want you to go back home with my question, you can take your goods with you. If you choose not to do as we ask, we'll find you." Ralph shrugged to suggest that Jens could probably guess the rest.

Jens realized he had no choice. If Mikhail hadn't been in the room he'd have taken them on, father and son, and it wouldn't have been without its satisfaction.

"What's the question?"

Ralph thought.

"It's not a question. Just say that we'd like to ask them in, they'll understand what I mean by that."

"I'll get back to you with the answer, then my part in this is over," Jens said.

"Who's the woman?"

The question came out of nowhere, and Jens tried his best to sound convincing.

"The woman?"

"Yes, the woman who was driving when you so courageously rescued Hector."

"Don't know, one of Hector's women, I suppose."

Ralph nodded. "Is that what he's like?"

"What?"

"A man who likes a lot of women?"

"I can't answer that."

"What's her name?"

Jens shook his head. "Don't know."

Ralph stared at Jens for a moment, trying to read his eyes.

"Mikhail will stay here and help you with your things," he said, then turned and walked toward the door. Christian got up from the sofa and followed him. They left the house, the door closed behind them, and everything went quiet.

Mikhail pointed to the cellar stairs. Jens looked at the monster standing in front of him. He rubbed the tiredness from his eyes, sighed, and went down into the cellar. Mikhail followed him.

They lifted the dead Jürgen off the boxes and carried him into what looked like an old laundry room, and put the body down on the cold floor. They went back out into the garage.

"How's Klaus?" Mikhail asked in a low voice.

"Better than Jürgen..."

Mikhail repeated his question.

"What do you care?" Jens asked.

"I care."

He stopped beside the boxes.

"We drove him to the emergency room, he'll be OK."

Mikhail went over and opened the garage door. The room filled with daylight. They each took hold of one end of the first of Jens's boxes, picked it up, and carried it out to his car by the sidewalk.

"He's a good person, Klaus."

They put the box in the trunk.

"What's your definition of a good person?" Jens asked.

Mikhail didn't answer and they went back inside the garage and moved the second box. Jens closed the lid of the trunk.

"Give me your number," Mikhail said.

Jens gave him his temporary cell number. Mikhail sent his own contact details. Jens's phone buzzed.

"Call this number when you've spoken to the Guzmans. Make sure you get this sorted out. This whole thing feels fucked-up," Mikhail said, then went back into the house with his rolling walk without saying good-bye.

Jens drove out of Munich, heading toward Poland. The most direct route was through the Czech Republic, but he wanted to avoid any unnecessary border crossings. He kept going, up through Germany, hoping to find a straightforward crossing somewhere. He found one by the German city of Ostritz and slid into Poland without any problem.

He called Risto and told him that things had got pretty messed up, but that he was now on his way. He asked Risto to persuade the Russians not to make a big deal of the delay, said that he'd be prepared to take a small reduction in the fee, but that he wasn't prepared to take any shit from them. He'd be in Warsaw in seven hours, and gave Risto the name of a hotel where he could be reached the following day. Risto said he'd see what he could do.

It was dark out, it felt like this part of the Polish countryside had no electricity. Thick darkness everywhere. He didn't meet any cars, saw no houses lit up in the distance. He had a fleeting sense that he was all alone in the world. *Du-dunk, du-dunk*. It sounded like a train as the tires hit the gaps in the concrete road surface. The noise was monotonous and hypnotic. His eyes never got used to the dark. The headlights only lit up a narrow corridor ahead of him and the road looked exactly the same the whole time, as gray and featureless as the darkness beyond. *Du-dunk, du-dunk*. In the end it turned into a lullaby. Jens started to nod off at the wheel and opened the window, and tried to stay awake by singing out loud. It didn't work and he stopped singing, but thought he was still singing, although the song was just carrying on in his head. His head began to nod again. *Du-dunk, du-dunk*... then suddenly a different sound somewhere. A persistent sound. His cell!

The ringtone saved him from driving off the road into a field. He was on his way into a ditch and had to twist the wheel to get back onto the road again, then sighed to get over the shock.

"Hello?"

"Did I wake you?"

"Yes, you did. Thanks."

"It's Sophie."

"I know."

"Where are you?"

"Driving."

He closed the window and slowed down so he could hear better.

"I think I need some help."

"What sort of help?" he replied.

"Someone's been in my house."

"Are you calling from home?"

"No. I'm in one of the few remaining phone booths."

"Good."

Eons of silence.

"Did you feel threatened?"

"Yes... but not desperately."

"I'll be home in a day or two, give me a call then. If anything happens before that, let me know."

"OK."

She stayed on the line, as if she didn't want to hang up. He listened to the sound of her breathing.

"I didn't know who to call."

"Take care," he said, and ended the call.

Everything was starting to get a bit much. He found a packet of cigarettes in the door pocket, lit one with the lighter set into the dashboard, then opened the window again and blew the smoke out. He breathed in the rural Polish air, lightly spiced with the smell of brown coal from a nearby power station.

Change of cars. Lars had switched the Volvo for a Saab. An old, dark-blue 9000 that he was driving out to Stocksund, with the recording equipment in the back.

He parked, made sure he had decent reception, then switched to voice activation, locked the car, and walked to Stocksund Square. He caught a bus and got off at Danderyd Hospital, slid into the subway and got a train back to Central Station.

He stood by the doors of the subway car, holding on to a bar in the ceiling. The bastards were trying to get rid of him, he was sure of that. Gunilla's behavior supported that theory—the way she ignored him, kept him at arm's length, giving him endless surveillance jobs, not discussing or commenting on his reports. Treating him like some unknown, fleeting acquaintance—he hated it. And now some retarded racist moron had turned up in their offices on Brahegatan. Gunilla had introduced him as the group's new asset. Hasse Berglund: former rapid-response cop, former airport police officer, and overweight loser from what Lars could see. She had said that he would be helping out, but with what, exactly? Was he going to take Lars's place? What had Gunilla and Anders been talking about in Humlegården? What was going on? The more he thought about it, the more confused he got. *Fuck,* his brain wasn't working like it should. He closed his eyes and tried to concentrate, creating little squares in his head, like little boxes where he could put various occurrences that belonged together. He ended up with three boxes, one for Gunilla, one for the surveillance, and one for Sophie. So far, so good. He put various events in the different squares, but then he began to worry, switching events between the boxes. He got angry when he lost his concentration, realized he was standing there muttering, and opened his eyes.

A dad with a stroller was looking at him with concern, and quickly looked away. Lars closed his eyes again and tried to find his way back to the boxes, but was distracted when someone nearby blew their nose. A voice said *"Technical College"* over the loudspeaker, then added something about changing there for trains to Roslagen. It was hopeless, and Lars gave up as the squares disintegrated in his head.

The doors opened and a drunk entered the car, and started to shout at a young woman who was sitting reading a book at the far end of the car. Six months ago Lars would have gone over, shown his police badge, and forced the man off the train. Now he didn't care, he couldn't give a damn, and just looked down at the floor as the drunk roared and the woman suffered.

He was sitting on the floor in his office, sketching on a sheet of paper, writing down everything that had happened, asking himself questions: Gunilla, Sophie, what happened on the road at Haga. What did Gunilla know that he didn't? Lars wrote and scribbled on the sheet: names, arrows, question marks. *And Anders...* What was Anders Ask doing there with Gunilla?

More questions, no more answers. He wrote, he thought, he wrote some more, the page got messy, too much writing, too many question marks.

Lars got up from the floor and looked at the two pictures on the wall: a monkey in a Hawaiian shirt sitting on a toilet with a roll of toilet paper in its mouth. He'd had it in his room when he was little, it had always moved with him. Beside it was an enlarged photograph of Ingo Johansson in shorts and boxing gloves, leaning forward slightly, ready to go on the attack. Lars had been given that by his dad for his eighth birthday. *Ingo's not your average fucker, you need to remember that, kid.* Lennart used to drink four Rob Roys before dinner, and liked play-boxing far too hard, and used to say the Jews ran the world and that Olof Palme was a communist, stuff like that.

Lars took the monkey and Ingo off the wall and put them on the floor, then grabbed a thick marker from the desk. He stood in front of the wall and began to transfer what he had just written on the sheet of paper onto the wall. He wrote, drew, created, then backed away and admired his work, thinking hard.... There was something missing.

Lars printed a picture of Sophie from the computer, stuck it in the middle of everything, then backed away and took another look. She stared at him and he stared back. Something that he hadn't realized began to take shape. Lars scratched his head hard with his nails, and his heart beat fast within him. He printed out more pictures from the computer, pictures of everyone involved in the case, and stuck them up on the wall, like a halo around her. He wrote their names, what they had done, what they hadn't done....He drew red lines between all the faces in an attempt to find what connected them.

The lines all led to Sophie.

Hector had called. His voice sounded almost submissive, as if he were being careful, anxious about scaring her or making her uncomfortable. He had asked for her help. She realized it was just an excuse to meet up.

Hector was lying on the sofa in the living room of his apartment in Gamla stan. Sophie was sitting by his plastered leg examining the crack at the top of the cast. She tugged carefully at it.

"I can't say. You ought to go back and get a doctor to look at it."

"Take it off," he said.

"You've got at least another week left."

"I'm not in any pain, I can move my leg inside the cast, so it's probably too late now anyway, isn't it?"

"How long has it been like this?"

"Since that night."

That night...No one wanted to talk about that evening, least of all her.

"Are you sure?" she asked.

"About what?"

"About taking the cast off. It might be too early, you could end up with complications."

He nodded. "Take it off."

"Pliers, scissors?"

"In the kitchen, second drawer down, pliers in the toolbox under the sink."

She got up and went into the kitchen, and started going through the drawers. She found a pair of scissors, then opened the cupboard under the sink. She pulled out the toolbox, opened it, and found what she was looking for: a pair of pliers with straight blades. But they were very small, it was going to take a while.

She went back out into the living room. He was lying on the sofa watching her. Sophie sat down beside his leg again and started to cut the cast from the top, bending it back as she went. She could feel him looking at her.

"You could have done this yourself," she said.

She went on clipping.

"You weren't supposed to get involved in this," he said.

"Aron made that very clear to me," she said curtly.

"He's the one worrying, not me."

She looked at Hector. "And I'm supposed to believe that?"

"Yes."

"You're not worried?"

He shook his head. "No, not remotely."

"Why not?" she asked.

"Because I know you."

"No, you don't."

"Because you like me," he said.

She looked at him, not liking those words, not liking his manner or even the smile on his face.

He must have seen her reaction. The smile faded. She went on cutting.

"I'm not a bad person," he suddenly said.

She didn't answer, did her job, noting a sort of desperation in him for the first time. It wasn't much, but it was there, like an atmosphere in the room. A hint of panic that he was trying to hold in check.

"Your husband?" he asked. He was trying to sound normal. Like they were back in the hospital and playing twenty questions with each other.

The pliers were chewing their way slowly through the cast.

"You never talk about him," he went on.

"Yes, I do. You've asked me about him before."

"Maybe, but you never say anything."

"He's dead," she whispered, concentrating on wielding the pliers correctly.

"Yes, but something?"

"That's none of your business."

"But I'd still like to know."

She stopped cutting and looked up at him.

"What for?"

"What are you so frightened of?"

Anger flashed through her.

"Yes, what am I so frightened of, Hector?"

He didn't catch the sarcasm.

"Were you happy together, you and David?"

What was he after? She put the pliers down.

"I don't understand, Hector."

"What don't you understand?"

"This. What do you want?"

"I want to know who you are, what you're all about. Where we're going..."

She felt suddenly uneasy.

"Where we're going? I don't know....Don't you think the situation has changed?"

"No, I don't think so."

She realized she was staring at him. Maybe he was emotionally damaged. Incapable of understanding her fear at what had happened, at Aron's threat. Maybe he lived in a completely different world. Maybe Gunilla's warnings were true.

The thought scared her. She felt suddenly uncomfortable being there with him. Felt an impulse to get up and walk out, a strong urge to flee, leave him there. But she couldn't. Instead she pulled herself together and tried to keep the conversation going to mask her anxiety. She carried on cutting the cast.

"No, we weren't particularly happy," she said quietly.

Sophie tried to get a grip on her memories.

"David was self-absorbed," she began. "He was that sort of person, an egotist. It took me a few years to realize. Then it turned out that he'd been unfaithful. I wanted to get divorced, but then, while I was busy making plans, he was diagnosed. He begged and pleaded with me to stay. I suppose he must have known I'd look after him. The illness got worse and he was terrified of dying and demanded vast amounts of understanding and attention. It hit Albert worst of all, because he didn't understand."

She looked up at Hector.

"David behaved badly...," she went on. "That's how I remember him."

She went on cutting the cast. Hector said nothing, didn't nod.

"And Albert?"

"He cried."

Hector waited for more, but nothing came. Sophie twisted the cast open and lifted it off, covering his bare leg with a blanket.

"There, Hector, you're free again." She tried to smile when she noticed how impersonal she sounded, and went to get up.

"Wait a moment," he said, putting his hand on her arm.

His expression had changed, he seemed to revert to his old self again, was more relaxed, and there was something that could have been sadness in his eyes.

"I want to apologize," he said.

Yes, she could see a tension in him, something like regret. He sounded genuine. She recognized him again.

"What for?" She sat down.

"For my manner, and for my behavior."

Sophie said nothing.

"I could tell from the way you looked just now. You backed down and tried to stay calm, but you were wondering who I was. I think you might even have been scared. And I'd truly like to apologize for that."

Sophie listened, both horrified and fascinated that he could read her like that.

His transformation seemed to have made him tired. He ran a hand through his hair.

"From the moment Aron and I were dropped off, that night when it all happened, I've had a strong feeling that something was broken, something I couldn't mend. Maybe your faith in me, your hopes, your trust. I don't know... That's why I've been behaving so strangely today. I was scared of losing you, basically. I don't want that to happen, I want things to be the way they were before."

She said nothing.

"You never have to be scared of me," he said.

14

Svante Carlgren usually left home at about seven o'clock each morn-ing. If he wasn't going away on a trip he usually got back home at the same time twelve hours later. His life was hectic, at least that was the impression he hoped to give, with business trips, meetings, a lot of responsibility, a lot of work to be done. But really the exact opposite was the case. He was surprised that he seldom felt stressed, that he actually did so little. He lived for his work, for his career, for his triumphs. But it was easy, almost too easy. The responsibility didn't lie in actually driving anything forward, just in trying to maintain order in what was actually going on in the great Ericsson behemoth. He couldn't honestly say he knew what was going on there, but it didn't seem to matter much. He had reached a level he was content with, and he wanted to stay there, that was the only thing that interested him.

When he was about to turn in toward his house a car appeared from the opposite direction and followed him up the drive. Svante looked in the rearview mirror. He didn't recognize the car, there was no one in it but the man driving.

Svante parked, got out of his car, and frowned toward the visitor who had pulled up a few yards behind him. The door opened and a man in a suit got out, slim, black hair, prominent features, no tie....

"Can I help you?"

"Are you Svante Carlgren?"

Svante nodded. Aron walked purposefully up to him, pulled a photograph out of his inside pocket, stopped and looked at it, then handed it to Svante. He took it and looked at the picture. He found himself staring, wide-eyed, at a picture of himself.

All the energy drained out of Svante Carlgren, he wanted to say something, to react—anything. But it was as if he had frozen solid, incapable of doing anything at all. Maybe it was the paralyzing effect of realizing he'd been tricked, maybe it was the sense of complete impotence, or possibly the sheer humiliation.

Aron held up another picture. Svante in a pair of briefs that were far too small for him, snorting cocaine into his brain through a silver tube from a glass table. Svante didn't take the picture, just looked at it, then he turned away and walked toward the house. Aron followed him.

Svante stopped at the drain board, his back to Aron, and poured himself a glass of wine without offering any to his visitor. Aron sat down on a kitchen chair, crossed his legs, and rested one arm on his thigh.

"It's fairly straightforward, really," he began. "We're a special-interest group who'd like you to give us information about how things look in the company before each quarterly statement, and before any occasion when you might be thinking of going to the capital markets...and any time anything significant is about to happen....We want to know if things are going well or badly, we want to know every major piece of news before it's made public. We want to know what you hear, what you see, what the internal talk is." Aron was speaking quietly but clearly.

Svante tried to laugh but couldn't pull it off.

"You're blackmailing me to make money out of Ericsson?"

Svante took a sip from his glass of wine.

"I'm sorry, you've picked the wrong man, I don't have access to that sort of information." Svante took another gulp and went on. "You have a rather simplistic view of things. I don't know how you came up with it, but I'm afraid that isn't how the real world works."

Aron didn't say anything.

"In real life, that's not how it works," he repeated, taking another sip of wine; he was now halfway through the glass. "Besides, every big company has an entire department devoted to protecting bosses from this sort of thing. You're going to get a serious telling off, my friend."

Svante allowed himself a smile.

Aron looked around the kitchen, which was pretty cheap in comparison to the exterior of the villa. The plates and glasses on the spotlit shelves were recent reproductions made to look like antiques. The pictures on the walls were prints of a vase of flowers and huntsmen in red jackets riding through an English landscape at dawn. There were dried flowers in the window, and the kitchen table and matching chairs were poor reproductions of something Victorian. He wondered if it was Svante Carlgren or his poor wife who possessed such startlingly bad taste.

"You can choose who we send the pictures to first. Your wife, your children, or your colleagues."

Aron kept looking through the photographs. He stopped at one, looking at it from various angles, as if to imply that he couldn't quite make out the subject. Aron showed it to Svante, who glanced quickly at it.

"This is all on film as well, with sound."

Svante's feigned confidence crumbled and he took on a resigned and beaten look.

"Who do you think?" Aron asked.

Svante looked at him uncomprehendingly.

Aron waved the pictures.

"Your wife? Your children? The people you work with? Who gets to see these first?"

"I can pay you for the pictures, but I can't do what you're asking. I simply don't have the access to do that."

Svante's tone of voice was different, softer.

"Just answer the question."

Svante patted his hair.

"Which question?"

He was off balance.

"Who's your choice?"

"No one... I'm not choosing anyone! I want to resolve this somehow, there must be a way."

"I didn't come here to bargain with you. Answer the question, then I'll leave."

Svante was shaken, his brain was working feverishly; who could help him out of this?

"Why did you pick me, I haven't done anything. I'm an honest man...."

Aron leafed through the pictures.

"If you want to show you're playing nicely, contact me when you get details of the next report or anything at all that will affect the standing of the company. If I don't hear from you, I'll send the pictures to your workmates, starting with the people you're in charge of."

Aron stood up and put the bundle of photographs on the kitchen table, turned the top one over, and pointed at a cell-phone number written on the back. Then he left the kitchen, and the house.

Svante emptied his glass and watched through the kitchen window as Aron got into his car and drove away. He picked up the phone and started to dial a number that he knew by heart, a number that was to be used if anything like this happened. The company's own security department had procedures in place for all manner of possible and impossible situations, from theft and espionage to blackmail and kidnapping, and they kicked into gear the moment anyone called the number.

He never dialed the final digit.

Anders was sitting in his car, a Honda Civic, with his cell to his ear.

"His name's Svante Carlgren. Some lower-management type at Ericsson, married, son and daughter no longer living at home, that's all I could get."

There was silence on the line.

"Stick with Carlgren, find out what Aron was doing there," Gunilla said.

Jens called Risto from his hotel room. Naturally, the Russians wanted to jerk him around. He knew it.

"They aren't coming...and they want medium antitank guns," Risto said.

"Sorry?"

"They want an antitank gun each because you're late."

"Antitank guns?"

"Yes."

"You're kidding."

Risto didn't answer.

"Tell them to go to hell," Jens said.

"That's probably not such a good idea."

Jens was tired. Annoyed that everyone was fucking with him right now. He put his left hand over his eyes.

"Yeah, but tell them to go to hell."

"Normally I would, but we're talking about Dmitry here. He's... how can I put it? Impulsive. They seem to be getting more and more worked up about you with every passing day. They've decided what they think, they say you're arrogant, that you think you're better than them."

"I am."

"Admittedly...They're giving you one week. Then they want their antitank guns."

"But surely they can see that that's impossible?! Antitank guns, what a joke! You know that, I know that, everyone knows that."

"I'm afraid that doesn't make any difference."

His left hand was massaging his forehead now. "Forget it. I've got the weapons they ordered, they can come and get them."

"They won't accept that."

"I don't give a shit."

Risto was silent. Jens sighed.

"What would you have done, Risto?"

"Try to find a financial solution. Give them the weapons, give them their money back. You lose on the whole deal, but then you're out of this."

"Why?"

"Because these boys are a gang of crazy junkies who are capable of anything. It was wrong of me even to try to set this deal up, I'm sorry."

The very thought of Dmitry made him feel even more bitter.

"No, tell them we had an agreement, that I was willing to lower the price for the final delivery because of the delay. But that's all. I'm sticking to that, I'm not interested in anything else."

"OK," Risto said, and hung up.

Jens sat down on the bed. His eyes fell on a picture that was supposed to be modern art. It was a black triangle floating above a blue cube. Even the picture made him angry.

He lay back on the bed, staring at the ceiling. Things hadn't gone the way he'd expected them to recently, he was tired beyond imagining, and his willpower was starting to flag. Jens breathed out, closed his eyes. He woke up with a start a quarter of an hour later. That's what it felt like anyway, but the fifteen minutes turned out to be many hours.

He showered, had a quick breakfast, then set off for home. After what felt like a hazy eternity he drove across the Öresund Bridge. He was nervous, he had two boxes of automatic weapons in the back of the car. He did the only thing he could, and adopted perfectly ordinary Scandinavian eye contact with the bearded local in a cap at the border. That turned out to be enough, the beard raised a two-finger salute to the brim of his cap, as if to say *You're OK*. Jens glided through with no problem and felt sick the whole way up to Stockholm. His nerves weren't the way they usually felt. Was it the stress, his age, or just the realization that he'd been playing with fire his whole adult life and that he was about to get seriously burned?

Several hours later he flew across the Essinge Highway around Stockholm, on some level glad just to be back in one piece. Instead of turning off toward the center of the city he kept going north, turned off at Danderyd Church, and drove past the high school. Just behind that, in among the pine trees, scrawny firs, and ugly office buildings was a storage unit he'd rented for years.

He unloaded the weapons, and to his delight found a pocket

flashlight he'd been trying to find for years. It was hanging from a hook right at the back. He loved that flashlight. Not too big, not too heavy, a good beam of light, and it was neat—silvery, made of aluminum—damn near perfect. He spun it in the air, caught it by the handle, then locked up behind him, feeling a bit happier. Maybe because he was home again, maybe because he'd found his flashlight.

She backed out between the gateposts. She drove around the block a couple of times to see if anything looked unusual, but there was no sign of anything. She headed in toward the city, car windows down, and drove all the way down Birger Jarlsgatan to the junction with Engelbrektsgatan, and pulled into the underground garage on David Bagares gata. She emerged and walked toward Engelbrektsplan, put her phone card into a public phone, and dialed a number.

"Yes?"

"It's me again."

"Hello."

She waited to give him time to say something. He didn't.

"Are you home now?" she said.

"Yes."

He was terrible on the phone, abrupt and impossible to gauge.

"Can we meet?"

Twenty minutes later they met up on Strandvägen, on the quayside. He was already sitting there on a bench when she walked up. He saw her, stood up, kept his distance, no hug or weird handshake. She found that a relief.

They sat down on the bench. It was a warm evening. He was wearing jeans, a tennis shirt, and sneakers. She was in pretty much the same, but the women's version. People were strolling past them, sober and drunk alike. The city was lively even though it was a weeknight. She took out a newly bought pack of cigarettes from her pocket, pulled off the cellophane, and got one out.

"Want one?"

He took one, she lit hers and passed him the lighter. They took a few puffs, and she pointed toward the Strand Hotel, on the other side of the water.

"I worked there once."

The hotel glowed luxuriously.

"I'd been traveling in Asia. When I got home I got a job in reception.... I was twenty-two, twenty-three."

He sat with his legs apart, looking at the hotel, and smoked some more.

"Tell me about the people who were in your house."

She thought. Trying to figure out what to say and what not to say.

"Two men claiming to be policemen were in the house a few weeks ago. My cleaner caught them red-handed when she arrived. She's got her own key. They threatened her, said she'd be in trouble if she told anyone."

Jens was sitting with his arms resting on his legs, looking down at his shoes.

"How did they threaten her?"

"I don't know."

"Why's she telling you now? Why didn't she tell you when it happened?"

"She was scared."

He nodded to himself.

"Did they take anything?"

She shook her head.

"So what were they doing there... what do you think?"

Sophie thought for a moment, then looked at him.

"I don't know."

He tried to read in her eyes if she was telling the truth, but found nothing that could help him decide. Instead she looked the way he remembered her.

"What?" she said.

"Nothing."

She smoked the cigarette down to the filter, then crushed it under her shoe.

"How do you know Hector?" he said.

She knew the question would come.

"He was in my ward... in the hospital. He'd been in a road accident. We became friends."

"Good friends?"

"Fairly... fairly good friends."

"And what does that mean?"

"Like I said, fairly."

They sat in silence, each of them aware that their first encounter at the restaurant concealed many more secrets than either of them was willing to reveal.

"And this has got something to do with Hector?"

"I think so," she whispered, still thinking.

Jens noticed and let her think in peace.

"But I don't know. I don't know anything."

"What else is there in your life that could have led the police into your house, if we assume that they were from the police?"

She kept pulling at the thoughts flying through her head, then got up from the bench and walked over to the edge of the quay.

"Have you changed over the years, Jens?"

He didn't answer the question. She turned around and looked at him for a moment, then hugged herself, trying to find the right words.

"There's someone in the police who's after Hector, he doesn't know. She, the police officer, has asked me to give them information about him...."

Sophie looked at Jens with a look that said she hoped she hadn't said too much.

"Have you said anything about that night?" he asked.

"Of course I haven't," she said quietly.

"So what have you said, then?"

She tried to gather her thoughts.

"Little things...nothing much. Names, places, people. But she called and asked about that evening....I don't know if she knows something."

Jens's surprise was genuine.

"What did she ask?"

"What I was doing that evening."

"And you said...?"

"I said we were going to have dinner, but that Hector had to go to a meeting and I went home."

"Did she imply anything?"

Sophie shook her head. Jens thought for a moment. Then he looked up.

"What else?"

She didn't answer.

"Sophie?"

"Yes?"

"Go on."

She hesitated.

"Aron told me . . . ," she continued.

"Aron told you what?"

"Something along the lines that I should keep my mouth shut."

"A threat?"

She nodded.

"And Hector? What does he say?"

She sighed. Didn't want to talk about Hector.

"What else?"

"No, that's enough."

She looked pained. Her voice changed, its tone lower. Her whole being seemed to shrink.

"I'm in the shit, Jens. . . . I don't know what to do."

He was having trouble looking at her.

"Can you help me?"

He nodded curtly, as if he had already answered that question.

"So, who was in your house? Hector's gang or the cops?"

She still had her arms wrapped around herself.

"The police, if you ask me."

"Why?"

Sophie shrugged. "I don't know. . . ."

She was pale and tired.

"But you must have some idea?"

"Maybe they were trying to find out something about Hector. . . . Something I haven't told them . . ."

"But something else has struck you, hasn't it? The most likely explanation, assuming that they're after information."

She looked at him.

"Yes . . . But how am I supposed to know? Take the telephone apart, check the lampshades . . . is that how it works?"

He nodded, even though she was being ironic.

"That's pretty much exactly how it works."

They tried to make sense of the conversation in their heads, then after a while he looked up.

"Can you take the day off work tomorrow?"

"Yes..."

He could see how worried she was. Sophie turned and began to walk off toward Nybroplan.

He watched her go from the bench, her walk hadn't changed. He had been so fond of her back then... so long ago. He remembered it now, he remembered his suppressed feelings. How they met that summer a whole lifetime ago. How they found each other, how they talked about everything it was possible to talk about. How they got drunk, ate dinner late out on the terrace, and slept in every morning. How they would take his parents' car and drive off to get breakfast. How he there and then decided for the first and only time in his life that he would be capable of mowing the lawn in the garden they shared until old age got the better of him. And how that feeling completely terrified him. How, against his will, he had managed to get rid of her.... And he couldn't remember a thing about the period that followed.

Jens took out his cell phone, selected a contact from the list, and called the number. An old man answered.

"Hello, Harry, can you tell who this is?"

"I certainly can, good to hear from you again."

"Are you busy first thing tomorrow?"

"Nothing I can't change."

"Come 'round my place at seven o'clock and I'll make you breakfast; bring your equipment and some overalls. Have you still got the company van?"

"Sure, it's all just the same."

"Same here... Look forward to seeing you then."

Jens ended the call and looked out across the water of Nybroviken.

Why had he been so quick to say he would help her? She was involved with Hector Guzman, she was being watched by the cops and had just witnessed an attempted murder where he himself had been present. Hector and his gang were ruthless when things heated up. They had powerful people, like the Hanke group, after them, they smuggled coke, and God only knew what else they were involved in—and there, in the middle of all that, Sophie.... Was that why he had agreed to help her, because he knew that world? Or was it because she was Sophie? Under normal circumstances he would have headed for the hills the moment he saw her. Run away, without really knowing why. That's what he always did with women. But here he sat like a total idiot in his crappy tennis shirt, offering to help her....

Jens hid his face in his hands. Christ, he was tired. He leaned back on the bench, wishing things could be the way they used to be. It had all been easier then, easier to push his feelings aside, easier not to give a damn.... That was probably why everyone always said things were better before, because when they got older they couldn't cope with the deluge of the past. Everything finds its way into the light sooner or later.

His cell vibrated in his pocket. He took a deep breath to shake off the slight pressure in his chest.

"Yes?"

He listened to the soft voice at the other end. Hector Guzman sounded friendly as he asked if Jens was the sort who drank coffee in the evenings.

Lars Vinge took forty or so photographs of Jens Vall as he was sitting on the bench by the water. When Jens got up he turned directly toward the telephoto lens, and Lars got some great, clear close-ups. He left his position in a doorway on Skeppargatan and hurried back toward the garage on David Bagares gata to get there ahead of Sophie.

It was almost eleven o'clock, darkness had fallen. Jens went in through the front door and up the stairs. There was a sign on the door: THE ANDALUCIAN DOG PUBLISHING COMPANY LTD.

Jens was sitting opposite Hector in his office. A window was open, the evening was still warm, and sounds rose up from the street below. Occasional laughter, noisy youngsters going past, "Volare" was playing in a nearby apartment.

Hector's desk looked rather old-fashioned, and his chair was a leather-clad '50s design on wheels. It seemed very comfortable.

Hector was thinking.

"Before we talk, do you want anything? You look tired."

"You offered coffee on the phone."

Hector got up and left the office and Jens followed him, through a small conference room and a library packed full of books. Hector gestured as they passed through.

"These are some of the books we publish. A lot of them are translations from Spanish, but there are some original Swedish titles."

Eventually they reached a kitchen.

"The office is on this floor, and I live directly above." He pointed to the ceiling.

The kitchen was small but tastefully furnished, quality throughout. They stopped and looked at each other. Measuring each other. Jens was taller but he thought Hector felt bigger, as he somehow encompassed more than his physical body alone. If they had been younger they would have stood back to back.

Hector looked away and started to set up the espresso machine.

"What's he like, Ralph Hanke?"

"I don't know.... Arrogant, theatrical..."

Hector put two cups under the machine, pressed a button, and the contraption made an unpleasant noise as it began to grind coffee beans somewhere inside itself.

"Milk?"

"Just a little."

He poured a splash of milk into the two cups, then handed one to Jens.

"So, tell me."

"I arrived at a nondescript house in some Munich suburb and found my goods in the cellar. They'd draped a dead body over the boxes."

Hector raised his eyebrows as he drank.

"Then that big Russian, Mikhail, turned up with Ralph and his son, I don't remember his name."

"Christian...," Hector said.

"Ralph wanted me to mediate between you and them."

"And what do you think about that? Being the go-between?"

"I don't think anything."

Hector nodded.

"There won't be any mediation. Those men have stolen our goods, tried to kill me twice, they've made threats and God knows what else.... Their main aim with all of this is to force us to become part of their organization."

"Yes, that's pretty much how he put it," Jens said.

"OK. Go back to them and tell them to drop this whole business once and for all, and say that their failed attempts ought to have shown them what they're up against. If they don't back down now we'll take it as a declaration of war."

Hector turned away and rinsed his espresso cup under the tap. He suddenly looked very dark, his anger had found its way out and settled in his furrowed brow. He turned off the water and looked at Jens once more. Hector's darkness felt like a physical presence in the room.

"Every time things have heated up recently you've popped up. And I'm supposed to think that's coincidence? And now here you are, as some sort of go-between. That doesn't seem very plausible, does it?"

Jens didn't answer. Hector looked at him, then shrugged.

"But on the other hand you seem unassuming...calm."

Jens didn't bother to contribute.

"Get back to Hanke with our response."

Hector left the kitchen and went back to his office.

"If you're fucking with me, you're a dead man," he said without turning around.

In the stairs on the way down to the street Jens dialed the number he had been given by Mikhail. Roland Gentz answered at the other end.

"Yes."

"I was told to call this number and pass on a message from Stockholm. Have I reached the right person?"

"Yes."

"Hector says that you've already gone too far, that you need to back down.... If you try anything else this will escalate beyond anyone's control."

"I understand, thanks for calling."

The line went dead.

* * *

Jens walked through Gamla stan, trying to get a grip on everything that was happening, trying to allocate scores, where one was biggest, most important for the things that had to be dealt with first, and ten was for things that could wait, things he could deal with later. He found that there were tons of ones and twos, but was unable to give them any sort of internal ranking. Jens shook off the idea and went to buy breakfast. He found an all-night store selling fresh bread, freshly ground coffee, and homemade marmalade. He bought the best of everything, wanted to be able to offer Harry a decent breakfast in a few hours' time.

Albert had gone to school. The doorbell rang at half past eight in the morn-ing. She went and let in Jens and a man who introduced himself as Harry, both of them dressed as workmen.

"Good morning, madam," Jens said.

He imagined that handymen were positive, decent, a bit rough around the edges, both feet on the ground—that was how they were depicted on television, at any rate.

"Welcome, come in."

They went into the house. Jens played at being a handyman, Sophie a client. Harry kept quiet and made his way to a corner of the living room where he crouched down and opened his toolbox. Sophie was pointing randomly at things.

"To start with, I'd like a door leading to the garden here, with a French door in place of that window, and steps down to the garden as well."

Jens was looking around.

"Of course."

As they talked Harry held an oval plastic gadget to his eye and looked around the room. He got up and walked around, searching with the little gadget while simultaneously taking readings from a meter in his hand. Sophie and Jens carried on playacting.

Harry wrote something down on a piece of paper. Jens took it, read it, and handed it to Sophie. *No cameras*. They went on, but Sophie's imagination was starting to wear thin. She couldn't very well pretend she wanted the whole house rebuilt. Jens took over and explained what could be done and what wouldn't be possible. He kept using the wrong terminology; he wasn't exactly a natural handyman, far from it.

Harry searched again with a different instrument; he walked up to a lamp and the needle jumped. He had located a hidden microphone. He turned toward Jens, gave the thumbs-up, and took out a little Swedish flag on a stand and put it next to the lamp. He moved on, found another one in the kitchen, and left a flag there as well. Upstairs he found microphones in her bedroom, in Albert's room, and on the landing. Little flags dotted all over the place. Harry checked the phones and found two more. Jens's mouth was dry after all the talk of home improvements. Sophie's face was pale.

Harry pulled out a miniature camera. It looked like the clip of a ballpoint pen. He fastened it to an almost invisible electrical cable that he had placed around the edge of the ceiling, checked that it worked on a tiny television monitor no bigger than his hand. He saw himself on the gadget, backed away, and checked the image again. Harry passed the monitor to Sophie, who took it. He wrote on a piece of paper:

> *Motion sensitive. The camera starts up if any movement is detected, check it every day, keep the monitor hidden, no more than eight yards from the camera.*

Before they left, Jens gave Sophie a pay-as-you-go cell phone and a handwritten note telling her to leave the house in half an hour and call him.

Harry and Jens were driving in the van.

"What do you think?" Jens asked.

"I think that whoever's bugging her isn't short of resources. I saw microphones like that in London last year when I was over there buying supplies. They're tiny, so small they're almost invisible to the naked eye, and they're fucking expensive. The downside is that you have to stay fairly close, the range is pretty limited, two hundred yards, I think. And considerably less in a residential area with trees and houses all 'round. The people using them probably have a receiver in a parked car, which they keep collecting recordings from."

Harry was driving and talking as he went.

"Whoever installed this stuff knew what they were doing. There's probably more there than what we found. Let her know that she needs to be careful when she uses her computer, her cell... pretty much everything, really."

"If you had to take a guess, who would do something like this?"

Harry looked straight ahead.

"No idea."

"Does it record?" Anders wondered.

The caretaker shook his head.

"No, but it takes pictures. Like I said, it's old. The idea is that it takes photographs at thirty-second intervals when there's an ambulance in the bay."

"Why?"

The caretaker shrugged.

"I suppose so reception can see when an ambulance arrives, but I don't really know...."

Anders and the caretaker were sitting at his desk looking at the pictures from the night when the man with the gunshot wound was brought in. The photographs were crooked close-ups of the car's windshield.

"Why has it been set up like this?"

"How the hell should I know?"

Anders sighed. He could see the top part of a dark-colored car, half the windshield, and part of the roof. He could see an arm on the wheel, a grainy right arm, possibly a man about to get out of the car. Anders sighed again. No picture of the car as it was leaving the ambulance bay, and in the last photograph it was gone, empty.

"I want all the pictures, even if they look similar."

Eva had scanned the pictures into the computer. Anders, Gunilla, and Erik were staring at the screen.

"What sort of car is it?" Gunilla wondered.

No one answered.

"Compare it with"—Gunilla looked down at her notes—"a Toyota Land Cruiser, 2001 model."

Eva began to type, looking for images of Land Cruisers on the screen. She found one she liked, ran it through a 3D program, and adjusted the angle, comparing it with the photograph.

"They look the same," she said.

Eva opened another program and tapped in scales and measurements. The calculations were incomprehensible to the others. A tool that she was steering with the mouse measured parts of both vehicles. She looked at the results.

"In all likelihood, it's a Toyota Land Cruiser, 2001 model."

"The nurse is playing rough," Anders whispered.

"We don't know that for certain," Gunilla said.

"Plenty of other people have the same sort of car," Erik muttered.

Silence fell as they each followed their own thoughts. Gunilla broke it.

"Let's have some scenarios, assuming that it is Sophie's car."

Anders began.

"The only sign of life we have from the vehicle is an arm on the third picture in the sequence. The arm isn't Sophie's, it's a man's, and he's about to get out of the vehicle. It can't be Hector, the tone of skin is too pale. It could be Aron. It could be the partner of the man who was shot...or someone else entirely. Either way, Sophie could have driven 'round the block from the restaurant and picked them up there, there's a way out from the back, I've checked."

"So what about Lars?" Gunilla interrupted. "Why would Lars claim that she drove home?"

"Maybe he thought she did. Maybe he lost her when she went 'round the block to pick the others up? Missed it, basically."

"But then he would have said she drove around the block, and he didn't. He said she drove out onto Odengatan, and that he followed her."

"Maybe he's lying?" Anders said.

"Why would he lie?" Gunilla asked.

He didn't answer.

"Anders, why would Lars lie?"

Anders shook his head. "I don't know...."

Erik screwed up his mouth, then tugged at his bottom lip.

"I think we should examine her car before we start trying to come up with theories. If an injured man was transported in it, we'll find evidence," he said.

Gunilla turned toward Eva.

"Check all vehicles of that model and color in the Stockholm area, I want names of their owners. Anders, I'd like you and Hasse Berglund to get better acquainted."

"We're already acquainted," he said.

15

Anders Ask and Hasse Berglund had driven over to the technical division that afternoon. Gunilla had told them to pick up a box from reception. It didn't need to be signed out, just collected. Anders tucked it under his arm and left the building, nodding to some old cops he recognized. They nodded in acknowledgment.

They ate pizza at Hasse's favorite place, Pizzeria Colosseum in Botkyrka. Hasse had a Colosseum special with the works, Anders a Hawaiian. They drank Falcon, which Hasse claimed was the only beer worth drinking, everything else tasted like piss... fox piss, apparently, whatever that tasted like.

Drunks teetering on the brink of homelessness were drinking from a carafe of red wine in one corner of the restaurant. They kept veering from subject to subject, yelling at one another as they discussed education, health care, company directors, and *that bastard, what's his name, the foreign minister... Carl Bildt.*

Hasse stood up, went over to them, and asked them to keep the noise down. The hoarse, ravaged-looking woman with red hair shouted that she'd stopped taking orders from men years ago...it was against her principles...and he should make no fucking mistake about that. One of her friends started to snarl something incoherent at Hasse, who went back to his pizza and sat down.

"Why do you even bother to get involved in stuff like that?"

"I don't know." Berglund sighed, taking a bite from a large piece of pizza with strings of cheese hanging off it.

"So tell me all about Mommy, then," he said with his mouth full.

Anders cut a piece of pizza.

"There's not so much to tell, we've known each other a long time. She's rescued me from total humiliation a few times. I got the push from the security police."

Anders took a bite.

"Why did you get the push?"

"They caught me with my hand in the cookie jar," he said in between chews.

"What sort of cookie jar?" Hasse asked.

Anders finished his mouthful.

"A gang of Eritreans we had under surveillance out in Norsborg. I was going to install cameras there one evening, and found a paper bag full of money under the sink. I stuck my hand in, filled my pockets.... One of my cretinous colleagues reported me."

"And she helped you?"

"Yes, somehow or other... At least I only got the push, not prison."

"Why?"

"Why what?"

"Why did she help you?"

"In exchange for me doing a few jobs for her, staying loyal."

"And are you?" Hasse said, mid-mouthful.

Anders nodded. "Yes, I am."

"How sweet."

Hasse drank some beer. The drunks started shouting at one another again. Hasse looked over, but Anders gestured to him to let it go.

"So what happened?" Hasse asked.

"I left the security police with my tail about as far between my legs as it would go. I did a few little jobs for her during the years that followed, then everything got messed up again." Anders chewed.

"There was a group of us who wanted to make a fast buck. We

doped a few horses at the races out in Täby.... It was a fucking mess, two of them died, we were standing there when the inspectors came around, I still had the syringe in my hand."

He chuckled at the memory.

"Gunilla came to the rescue on that occasion as well, it was pretty stupid, but she always seemed to turn up and put things right whenever I messed up.... So I owe her, basically."

Hasse finished his beer and had foam on his top lip when he put the glass down.

"You started babbling something in the car... about us sticking together."

Anders took a bite and shrugged.

"Oh, it was nothing."

"Go on, tell me," Berglund said.

Anders shook his head. "It wasn't important."

"So tell me, then."

Anders thought for a moment as he chewed. He finished his beer and glanced over his shoulder.

"It was an investigation that Gunilla and Erik were running. I was freelancing. We were about to get Zdenko, the so-called King of the Racetrack, you know. Big gangster, working out of Malmö. He had a girl, Swedish, no brain at all. A blonde from Alingsås, twenty-eight years old. Patricia something..."

Anders seemed to get sidetracked for a moment, then pulled himself together.

"Gunilla had brought her in before, she had something on her, I don't know what. We put a wire on her but didn't get anything from that. Then suddenly she disappeared. Zdenko went free, although he was later shot and killed out at Jägersro Racecourse."

"Where did she go?"

"Don't know, she just disappeared. Vanished."

"What?"

Anders cut a piece of pizza.

"Vanished, I said. She disappeared, was reported missing, but there was never any sign of her again."

"Dead?"

Anders took a mouthful, looked at Hasse, chewed, shrugged his shoulders.

"How did you get away with that?"

"It wasn't that hard, we erased everything we had about her, it was as if she never existed in our investigation. That's how Gunilla works. She's always worked like that, using people. She sees it as a natural part of the job, involving people she needs to involve, even if they don't want to take part."

Anders looked up.

"And keeping people she doesn't need on the outside, that's why she succeeds in most of what she attempts to do."

"How?"

"How? Well, I'm sitting here, aren't I, the bad cop from the security police, the horse murderer. And you, a mostly terrible rapid-response cop with mood swings. That's enough, isn't it?"

"How did she get Zdenko's blonde to play along?" Hasse asked.

"I don't know.... She was probably promised something, or threatened with something."

"Like our nurse?"

"No, not quite... That was something else, I never did find out what. Either way, it's over now, finished."

The drunks were now arguing about the Palestinian question in the background.

"We made it through unscathed that time," Anders went on.

"And by that you mean what, exactly?"

Anders washed the pizza down with beer.

"By that I mean what I said before, that we have to stick together. It might turn out to be heaven or hell, but we need to have an exit strategy in case everything goes to heck."

"To heck? What kind of lame phrase is that?"

"She's taking a lot of risks right now."

"I think she knows what she's doing." Hasse leaned back in his chair, cleaning his teeth with his tongue.

Anders shrugged. "Sure, but you understand what we're doing?"

"What?"

"The group she's built up is shapeless, it's like a shadow within a much bigger organization. That's what she wanted, and that's what she's got.... This isn't just some ordinary job we're doing. This is on the verge of judicial anarchy. She does whatever she wants to get results. She's found a way. One day someone higher up will tire of it.

I'm just saying that if you see or hear anything unusual, talk to me. And I'll do the same for you. OK?"

Hasse suppressed a hiccup.

"I'm an old rapid-response cop who got exiled to the airport. That's on a par with being sent to lost property. My career was fucked, I was supposed to hang around rotting out there until I hit sixty-five. Then I was supposed to drink myself to death and die alone in some shitty apartment somewhere. But I got a phone call that changed all that. You wouldn't get any odds on that, so I'm thinking of doing as I'm told, I'm thinking of doing exactly what the boss tells me."

Hasse looked out across the room and burped quietly into his hand.

"Well, you know what I mean," he concluded.

The drunks had gotten onto immigration policy now, none of them was racist, *but*...The red-haired woman even knew some immigrants who were decent people, but the fact that they came over here and took jobs from honest Swedes, she didn't like that at all. Hasse stretched.

"When do we have to be there?" he asked.

"Three hours."

"Another round?"

Anders couldn't think of a good reason to say no. They ordered another round. Hasse drank his down in one gulp, Anders drank half, Hasse gestured for more.

"And two Jägers as well!" he called.

For a while they couldn't think of anything to talk about, and just looked out across the room. The drunks were talking nonsense, panpipes were playing "I Just Called to Say I Love You" over the speakers up in the ceiling. Anders drew the Olympic rings on the table with the bottom of his wet beer glass.

"What sort of exit strategy did you have in mind?" Hasse asked.

Beer and Jägers appeared before them. They drank the shots in one gulp.

"Two more!" Hasse said before he had time to put the empty glass down. The waitress in the black T-shirt was already long gone.

"She heard, didn't she?"

"I think we should try to be a bit strategic."

"Don't talk crap, Anders. . . . And—"

Hasse burped mid-sentence. He grinned.

"Anders And!" he exclaimed.

Anders looked quizzically at Hasse, who went on in a slurred voice: "Donald Duck's called Anders And in Norwegian. That's you, Donald Duck!"

Anders didn't respond, and Hasse let out an odd laugh.

"It's a fucking good name for a cartoon character. Anders And . . ."

Anders looked at Hasse, bemused by his strange sense of humor.

"What shall I call you? Donald Duck or Anders And?"

Anders drank the last drops from his glass.

"Anders And," he said in a tone of resignation.

"That's settled then. Where were we?"

"We need to keep our backs clear."

"And how do we do that?"

"We deny everything point-blank, but we have to deny it together."

"OK, let's deny it point-blank," Hasse said, and raised his glass.

They left Botkyrka and the Colosseum, bought a six-pack of beer from the gas station, and headed back toward the city along the Essinge Highway.

"I like driving when I'm drunk," Hasse said.

Anders leaned toward the open window, letting the mild evening air hit him in the face.

"OK, that Lars guy, he's a bit of an idiot, isn't he?" Hasse asked.

The wind was stroking Anders's hair.

"He's just an idiot. Ignore him."

They killed time by driving around the city center, drinking beer, checking out the people on the streets, and listening to an old Randy Crawford album.

Hasse did a tight turn around the Sergels torg roundabout, shifting down the Volvo's gears and putting his foot down, driving around it three times. The centrifugal force threw the men to the right. Randy Crawford sang, Anders emptied his can, burped loudly, and threw it out into the fountain in the center of the roundabout. Hasse didn't want to let the side down, so he did a truck-driver's horn gesture and broke wind noisily.

At two o'clock they headed out toward Stocksund.

They were sitting in the Volvo a block or so away from Sophie's house, connected wirelessly to the equipment in Little Lars's surveillance car, which was parked by a clump of trees. Anders had headphones on.

"I think they're snoozing nicely now. Shall we?"

They got out of the car and walked up the road, Anders carrying the box from the technical division under his arm, Hasse with a can of beer in his hand. The sun was somewhere just over the horizon. The nights were never properly dark at this time of year.

"I hate summer," Anders said.

They each pulled on a black knitted hat. Anders looked at Hasse.

"Terrorist?"

Hasse chuckled. "Where did you do your national service?"

"The interpreting unit. You?"

"Arvidsjaur," Hasse replied.

"Of course..."

They crept into the gravel drive where the Land Cruiser was parked, stopped, and listened to the silence.

Anders switched on a flashlight and looked around the interior of the vehicle. It looked clean.

He opened the box and took out an electronic gadget. He pressed a button and a digital counter started working its way through a spectrum while Anders held it toward the car. The counter started with low-frequency sounds and gradually made its way up the scale. The neighbor's car unlocked some thirty yards away, its lights flashing in the night. They laughed quietly.

The digital gadget worked. Sophie's car unlocked. Anders put the gadget back in the box and carefully opened one of the rear doors. He took an ultraviolet lamp from the box, switched it on, and swept it over the seats. He found nothing unusual, even though he checked everywhere—floor, sills, seats, roof—the whole car. No blood anywhere, it was all incredibly clean.

Anders closed the door and went around to the baggage compartment. He opened it and looked in, searching all around it with the lamp. Nothing there, either. He switched the light off and sniffed the air, trying to identify the smell. There was a faint hint of bleach, and something else strong, something chemical... then another familiar smell. He took another sniff, was it glue? He looked at the mat covering the floor of the baggage compartment. Wasn't it slightly too small? He lifted one edge and put his nose to it. Damn, it was glue.

"Hasse!" he hissed.

Hasse wandered over lethargically.

"Smell this."

Hasse leaned in and sniffed.

"Glue?"

Anders nodded. "Look at this mat, it's not the original, it's too small."

Hasse shrugged and took a swig of beer. He didn't care much about anything when he was drunk. Anders took a sample of the glue and snipped off a piece of the mat. He put them in separate little plastic bags and sealed them. He photographed the rest of the vehicle carefully, then locked it with the digital gadget. The neighbor's car locked as well. Everything was back to normal.

Gunilla had called him and told him to break off his surveillance at eight o'clock that evening, and to head into the city, to the Trasten restaurant, instead. She'd never asked him to do that before. Nothing was happening there, and after a while he realized that something else was going on, and drove back out to Stocksund again.

Lars had kept his distance, in a neighbor's garden, hidden among the bushes. He had seen them walking up the road, half drunk and fearless, he could hear them chuckling at some remark about terrorists. What the hell were they doing there?

The telephoto lens had given some decent pictures, the camera clicking off clear close-ups of both Anders Ask and big Hasse Berglund. He waited until they had left, not moving, until he was sure he was alone. He pulled a sheet from his notebook, wrote *Be careful* on it in his scratchy handwriting.

Lars dropped the note in Sophie's mailbox.

Back home in the apartment Lars transferred the pictures of Anders Ask and Hasse Berglund to his computer, printed out a couple of them, and pinned them up. He sat down on his office chair, rolled back, and looked at his handiwork. The wall had grown, as if it had a life of its own.

Sara was standing in the doorway. She'd just woken up, and was squinting as she looked at the wall. It was entirely covered with names, pictures, words, arrows, times, underlining, question marks. Total confusion, an insane confusion. Her eyes moved to Lars as he sat there staring. Vacant, pale, bad skin, greasy hair—he looked ill.

"You need help," she said.

He turned toward her.

"You need to move out."

"I'm going to, as soon as I find somewhere to go. I've spoken to Terese, she might be able to help me."

He glared at her.

"Do you think I care?"

She seemed sad, and glanced back at the wall.

"What is all this, Lars?"

Lars stared contentedly at his grandiose achievement.

"Life on a wall . . . All of fucking life!"

She didn't understand a thing. He stood up and went toward her on unsteady legs. He smiled, and she brightened up, maybe he was going to give her a hug. . . .

Bang! He hit her hard in the face. Her legs crumpled and she fell to the floor, badly shaken. Suddenly he was sitting on top of her, his face contorted. He was screaming, saliva flying from his mouth, screaming that she was never to set foot in his office again. If she did, he would kill her.

PART THREE

16

"Carlos Fuentes sought medical attention on Saturday night."

Gunilla stopped, thinking about the words before she took off her coat.

"The same night?"

Eva nodded.

"He claimed he'd been attacked by a gang of teenagers."

Gunilla hung her coat on a hanger.

"Has he been questioned?"

Eva gestured to a bundle of papers on the desk in front of her.

Gunilla read through the interview, conducted by a patrol at 1:48 Sunday morning. There was nothing remarkable about it. Carlos had crossed Odenplan and was walking up Norrtullsgatan when he was suddenly attacked by three unknown youths. He couldn't give a description, the youths had run off. Gunilla checked through the medical report, Carlos had lost two top teeth, and his face was bruised and cut. She read it once more.

"No marks on his body," she said.

Eva looked up from her computer.

"Sorry?"

"He was attacked by three youths, and it looks like they all went for his face. He's got no injuries on his body, arms, or legs."

"That's impossible, surely?" Eva said.

Gunilla was staring at the report.

"Yes, it is...."

She sat down on a chair, read the report from the beginning, all the way through. When she was done she stood up and went over to the whiteboard on the wall, picked up a marker, and wrote the date on which the man with the shotgun wound had been left in the ambulance bay. Above the date she wrote *Two unknown men to Trasten.* Then she wrote *Hector?* And *Sophie's car?* She wrote *Man shot* and she wrote *Carlos Fuentes beaten up.* The phrases formed a half-moon above the date. Beneath the date she wrote *Unknown man in Sophie's car? Car recently cleaned?*

She took a step back. There was no evidence that it was Sophie's car in the ambulance bay, there was no evidence that these events had anything in common. On the other hand, with all due respect to coincidence... sometimes that just wasn't a credible explanation.

"Eva?" she said.

Eva Castroneves looked up.

"Carlos was beaten up the same night, and Anders has identified one of the two men who went into the Trasten as the man who was shot and is now in the hospital, with seventy percent certainty, as he put it.... The mat in the back of the car is too small, and was recently glued in, and he could smell cleaning fluids.... Can we rule out coincidence?"

Eva looked at the whiteboard without replying.

Gunilla turned back to the board again, thinking and trying to find a connection for a long while. Eva went back to work. After spending an age just staring, Gunilla woke up and went over to her desk, took off her necklace, and unlocked the middle drawer with the key attached to the necklace. She pulled out a black notebook, locked the drawer, put the necklace back on, and left the room.

Gunilla walked out into Brahegatan, turned left, and kept going until she reached Valhallavägen. She walked a bit farther until she found a good place to sit down, a bench opposite the Stadion subway station. She sat there for a while.

Amid the sound of the traffic and other atmospheric noises she closed her eyes and let her inner world take precedence over the outer. Gradually the noise of traffic faded, as did the wind in the trees, the whole world around her. Gunilla was concentrating hard; nothing got in, nothing got out. She opened her mind's eye. She saw Sophie Brinkmann before her, she saw the expression on her face, heard her tone of voice, saw her hand gestures, small and insignificant. The right hand tucking her hair behind her ear, the index finger stroking one eyebrow, the palm lying flat on her right thigh. Gunilla saw a small jerk of the head, she saw three different smiles: the honest one, the polite one, the questioning one. She heard three different tones of voice: the natural one, the hesitant one, the *unconsciously dishonest one*.... She compared her meetings with Sophie Brinkmann against one another, compared her tones of voice, expressions, and phrases. She saw the look on Sophie's face when Gunilla said she felt guilty for no longer having parents. She heard Sophie's tone of voice replaying inside her, it was genuine and quietly spoken... evasive. She remembered the look on Sophie's face when she made it clear that she controlled her, and then asked *How does that feel?* Then Sophie had sounded different, she had been lying. Gunilla could hear her voice, and compared it with the phone call in which Sophie assured her that she had driven home from the restaurant before Hector disappeared. It was the same tone of voice, the same tone of lie.

Gunilla saw a linear scenario play out inside her: Hector disappears from the restaurant for some reason, Sophie and Aron help him.... She's lying about something. Is she lying all the time? Has she always been lying?

Reality came back, the sound of her own breathing, the sound of the light breeze in the treetops, the sound of traffic and people.... Gunilla Strandberg blinked a few times and opened her eyes.

She opened the black notebook in her lap, wrote down everything she had just concluded, all the thoughts and reflections, all the insights... all the *instincts*. The whole book was full of similarly indistinct realizations.

She read through what she had just written, over and over again—the image cleared. Sophie Brinkmann was evidently doing what she herself wanted to.

Gunilla stood up and walked back to the office, called her brother Erik, and said she wanted to test out a theory with him.

Albert felt elated as he walked away from her house, with the taste of her chewing gum still in his mouth. They had only been together for two weeks. Now they were a couple. Her name was Anna Moberg, and he had always liked her.

A car drove up beside him as he walked. It kept the same slow pace as Albert. He looked at the car, at its driver, wondering if he wanted something, but the driver's window was closed. He carried on walking, then stopped.

The car went on a couple of yards, then it stopped as well. Albert crossed the road behind the car and quickened his pace. The window wound down.

"Hey!"

Albert turned around, and saw a thickset, unfamiliar man in a windbreaker behind the wheel.

"Albert Brinkmann?"

Albert nodded.

"Come here, I'd like to talk to you."

Albert was on his guard. "No, I'm going home."

Albert could hear the nervousness in his voice and tried to hide it by adopting a firm stance, but his body wouldn't obey him. The man in the car waved him over with his hand.

"Come here, I said. I'm from the police."

Albert walked nervously toward the car. The man held up an ID badge.

"My name's Hasse, get in the back."

Albert hesitated.

"Get in the back," he repeated in a low voice.

The backseat was upholstered in velour fabric. He could smell food, maybe hamburgers. Hasse Berglund looked at Albert in the rearview mirror.

"You're in a fucking precarious position, kid."

Albert said nothing. There was a short, muffled, synchronized sound as the central locking sealed all the doors. The man turned around and looked Albert in the eye.

"Don't pretend you don't know what I'm talking about."

The man had a round face, short hair, and a double chin. Albert caught a glimpse of something mad in his pale, watery eyes.

The blow came out of nowhere. Hasse clipped him on the head with the palm of his hand and Albert's head hit the door window. For a second he didn't know what was going on, then the pain kicked in. Albert put his hands to his head.

"What are you talking about? You've got the wrong guy," he muttered.

He was close to tears, his whole body shaking.

"No, Albert, I never get the wrong guy."

Hasse had turned around and was staring straight ahead.

"I've just had a word with a young lady, or should I say a little girl. Fourteen years old, and she says you forced yourself on her at a party two weeks ago.... And do you know what?"

Albert was looking down at his lap, one hand on the side of his head, where it hurt.

"And do you know what?" Hasse roared.

Albert forced himself to look the man in the eye.

"No?"

"I believe her. And there are three more lads who are prepared to give statements, and we've got a medical report as well. Fourteen means underage. That's not the sort of thing that society takes lightly... not at all."

Albert's fear faded slightly.

"Well, then you've definitely got the wrong kid. My name's Albert Brinkmann, I live in Stocksund, over there."

He pointed toward his house. Hasse settled himself back in his seat.

"Were you at a party on Ekerö...," he said, looking down at his notebook. "Kvarnbacken, on the fourteenth of this month?"

"I don't know what the place was called."

"But you were at a party there?"

Albert didn't want to but nodded anyway.

"But I didn't meet any girl there.... I'm going out with a different girl."

"So you're a horny little creep?" Hasse said in a conspiratorial tone of voice. "Aren't we all. But when it turns into something else, that's when I come into the picture and put things right. That's my job, see?"

The car was starting to get stuffy.

"I haven't done anything," Albert whispered.

Hasse licked his front teeth, folded down the sun visor, and inspected his smile in the mirror.

"We're going into the city, to Norrmalm. We've got the witnesses there, they need to get a look at you. If it's the way you say, you'll be free to go. OK?"

Albert tried to make sense of it.

"What's her name, then, this girl?" he asked.

Hasse Berglund flipped the sun visor back up, started the car, and drove off toward the city. He never answered Albert's question.

"There you are, you've got a call, it's Albert."

She smiled to her colleague and went into reception, sat down on a chair, and picked up the receiver that was sitting on the desk.

"Hello, darling."

At the other end she could hear her son crying like a baby. Incapable of explaining what had happened. She listened, tried to calm him down, and said she was on her way.

At the police station she was left to sit and wait in an empty corridor several floors up in the building. She sat alone in the silence. In front of her one office door was ajar. It was empty inside, the room wasn't in use. Then there were steps along the corridor. A big, bearded man holding a plastic folder was walking toward her. He stopped and introduced himself as Erik, then sat down beside her on the bench. She could smell stale sweat on his clothes.

"Your son, Albert. He's explained to you what this is all about?"

The man's voice was dull and ordinary.

"It's a misunderstanding. . . ."

Erik wiped his eyes and scratched himself on the forehead. He seemed tired and overworked.

"Evidently he attacked a girl."

"No, he didn't," she said. "I want to see him now."

Erik cleared his throat.

"You can see him shortly."

"Now, or do you want me to get a lawyer?"

"That won't be necessary."

She didn't understand. "What do you mean?"

"Like I say, that won't be necessary."

"What?"

"Calling a lawyer."

"Then I want to see him."

He raised his hand slightly from his leg.

"Don't be in such a hurry. Nothing's set in stone. Let's just have a little chat first, OK?"

She looked at him, his beard hid all his facial expressions.

"Maybe it's like you say," Erik began. "That Albert hasn't done anything. I just don't think you should see everything in black or white. Your son has been in here.... We're police officers, we know what we're doing."

She tried to understand what he meant.

"Here, read this.... That ought to give you an idea of the situation."

He handed her the plastic folder. She took it and opened it, then leafed through its contents. It contained witness statements, three in total. She read the accounts of what Albert had done that evening.

"Of course, it's a terrible thing for such a young lad, and it's probably like you say, but... Well, he's here now, and we've got these witness statements. This is a serious matter."

Erik stood up from the bench and stretched his heavy frame, and a bone cracked somewhere. He looked toward both ends of the corridor, they were still alone.

"The boy can go home with you now," he said in a low voice. "Don't mention this to anyone, it would only cause more trouble for you and your son.

Erik walked away. Her eyes were glued to the big man as he left her. Beyond her inability to understand what was going on, a scenario was beginning to emerge, a scenario based on lies, betrayal, threats, and manipulation. She was interrupted by footsteps farther along the corridor, and she saw Albert walking toward her, unaccompanied by any police officers. Alone and confused, he made his way down the empty corridor. She stood up and he hurried to reach her. His whole being seemed to be trembling with fear and despair.

Erik Strandberg had had a good day. He had stood and stared at Albert be-hind the one-way mirror in one of the interview rooms, watching as the boy tried to find a comfortable position on his chair. Imagine, such a young boy, unable to understand why he was there. Terrified, panic-stricken. It was almost fascinating.

It had all gone like clockwork. Little Albert had come close to shitting himself. His mom the nurse was as white as a fucking sheet. That whole fear thing was so weird, he thought as he walked along Vasagatan. Some people just seem to drown in it.

Erik found a kebab shop and slipped in and ordered. The Turk behind the counter wanted to talk football scores and weather. Erik didn't answer. The man got the hint and piled up the meat in silence. Erik sat down on a high stool by a narrow counter facing the street, sighed, and unfolded the evening paper that he'd stolen from the staff room in the Norrmalm Police Station. He leafed through a few pages, some celebrity he didn't recognize had evidently gone gay. Erik had an almost permanent feeling that he understood less and less of the world he lived in.

"Albert?"

She looked over to him as she leaned against the kitchen counter. Albert was sitting there staring at the table, refusing to look up.

Unable to help herself, she went over to him and slapped his right cheek with her hand. The slap was so hard that it scared her, and she took a shocked step back, then came to her senses and went up to him with her arms open. He stood up to meet her. They stood there hugging as she stroked his hair.

"I haven't done anything," he said in a hoarse voice.

She heard the child in him, the terror of the innocent.

"I know," she whispered.

"So what was all that about, then?"

She thought about his question, believed she had an answer, but she wasn't about to tell him.

"Nothing... It's over now, they made a mistake...."

She could hear how she was repeating herself, and thought about the microphones picking up her words and presumably carrying them straight to Gunilla Strandberg.

"But they had witnesses?! Rape? What kind of—"

She hushed him.

"Try to forget it now, sometimes it just happens. Everyone makes mistakes, even the police."

She patted him on the head.

"He hit me," Albert said quietly.

Sophie blinked as if she had been struck. She forced herself to stay calm, went on patting his head.

"What did you say?"

"The policeman in the car, he hit me in the face."

Suddenly she couldn't see anything of the world outside, just something inside her, something beginning to glow. Like a little spark of color. The color started to make itself felt, started to burn, crackle, exert pressure... expand. And turned into a vast, colorful fury. Not the same fury that had grown out of her anxiety. This was a fiery rage that filled every cell of her body, spreading out and taking over, forcing out everything else. Strangely enough, it made her calm down, find her focus.

"We won't tell anyone about this. Promise me that," she whispered.

"Why not?"

"Because I say so."

Albert pulled out of the hug, a look of confusion on his face.

"Why not?" he repeated.

"Because this is different," she whispered.

"What do you mean?"

Albert waited for an answer that never came. He grew uncomfortable, turned, and walked out of the kitchen.

The phone rang. Her mother, Yvonne, asking the usual how-are-you questions. Sophie replied with the usual fine-thanks answers.

"Are you coming on Sunday?"

Yvonne sounded like a martyr as she asked the question. Sophie tried to sound the way she usually did.

"Yes, at seven. The same time we always come."

"Yes, but you usually come at half past seven. It doesn't really matter, but if we're going to eat—"

Sophie interrupted her mother.

"We'll be there at seven, or half past."

She said good-bye and hung up. And cracked. Sophie threw the phone on the floor. When it didn't break she picked it up and threw it again, then stomped on it. She clenched her jaws but didn't get the cathartic feeling the release was supposed to give her. She just felt the same fury and impotence that had been there before the phone hit the floor.

Albert was staring at her from the living room. They looked at each other. Sophie bent down and picked up the pieces of the broken phone.

The windows were open, Jens was vacuuming the apartment, pushing the head of the machine over floors and rugs. He was trying to find some calm, and it occasionally appeared when he did the cleaning. But not today, and besides, it was already clean, he had done the vacuuming the day before. The sound of things flying into the machine was appealing, the way they rattled through the tube into the bag. It made him feel a sort of satisfaction about the fact that what he was doing was fulfilling a purpose. But there were no such noises today. Just him and the vacuum cleaner going around the apartment like an old married couple.

He thought he could hear a noise over the music from the stereo and the roaring motor. He listened but heard nothing, and went on cleaning. The sound again. He switched the vacuum cleaner off with his foot and listened again—the doorbell was ringing out in the hall.

Sophie stood in the kitchen. She was speaking clearly, concisely, and carefully. Explaining what had happened with Albert and the police. He was finding it incomprehensible.

"The police say there are witnesses, and that the girl's fourteen," she went on.

Jens could see how upset she was. It colored her whole face. She looked older all of a sudden, thin . . . frightened.

The espresso maker on the stove started making noises, building to its crescendo. But he didn't hear it, he was too busy trying to make sense of what Sophie had said. In the end it was Sophie who pointed it out to him. The hissing sound entered his head and dispelled his thoughts. He took the pot off the heat.

"Could it actually have happened?" he asked as he took two cups down from a shelf.

She shook her head as if his question were crazy.

"You're quite sure?"

She flared up. "For God's sake, of course I'm sure!"

Jens looked at her, unabashed by her short outburst.

"But could anything similar have happened?"

Sophie was about to launch into him.

"No, hang on, Sophie. Could anything small, insignificant, something completely harmless have happened?"

Sophie wanted to say no, but she stopped and took a deep breath.

"I don't know...," she said weakly.

Jens let her think for a few moments.

"Come on," he said, taking the cups and heading toward the living area in one corner of the apartment.

He gestured to her to sit on the sofa, put the cups down on the coffee table, and sat down in the armchair opposite her.

"Could it be something as innocent as an approach from Albert to the girl, a bit of flirting?"

"I don't know," she said.

"What does Albert say?"

She looked up, then down again.

"That there was no girl like that there. He didn't meet anyone, didn't talk to anyone. That he'd gone to the party because another girl was supposed to be there."

"Who?"

"His current girlfriend, her name's Anna."

"Could she provide an alibi?"

"No, my son wasn't brave enough to go and talk to her."

"And what does he think?"

"He thinks everything and nothing. His first thought was that some boy he'd fallen out with wanted to get him in trouble.... But he also believes what I told him."

"And what did you tell him?"

"That the police had made a mistake."

"And he bought that?"

She didn't like the question, and didn't answer. Instead they sat in silence, sipping their coffee, each of them thinking hard. Jens wasn't getting anywhere, he needed help making sense of it.

"So the police had Hector under surveillance when he was in the hospital?"

"Yes?"

"And you and Hector became friends, and the police noticed?"

Sophie nodded, unsure of where he was going with this.

"They contacted you and asked you to inform on him?"

She didn't answer.

"Then they started bugging your whole house?"

She didn't like his tone of voice.

"And began to watch you?"

She looked down at her hands. Twisted a ring so it was facing the right way.

"And now they're threatening your son with a rape charge?"

He leaned back in the armchair.

"That sounds pretty ambitious," he said.

She looked at him, trying to figure out if he was being sarcastic.

"So what do you think?" he asked.

"Maybe."

"Maybe what?"

"Maybe it's ambitious."

"It looks like they're concentrating their fire on you rather than Hector.... Why would they do that?"

"I don't know."

He changed. As if he suddenly couldn't be bothered to be understanding anymore. As if he didn't have time for her.

"You're being threatened by the police, bugged, you're sleeping with a suspected criminal, and you're being forced to act as an informant because the police have found a way to get at your son?"

Sophie defended herself automatically.

"No, absolutely not."

He cast her a weary glance.

"I'm not sleeping with him and I don't know that he's a criminal.... And I haven't informed on him yet."

"Do you have other friends who get taken off into the forest to be executed on a Saturday night?"

"Stop it."

"No, Sophie, you stop it. What do you think this is? You can't just invent your own reality based on the way you want things to be. What you're being subjected to isn't remotely normal. This police officer seems utterly ruthless. And you're already an informant, even if you can't see it yourself. The moment the police started asking you questions, you became an informant. What you have or haven't said won't make the slightest bit of difference to Hector and his associates when they find out about it."

Jens was about to go on, but stopped himself.

"Why would the police do this?" he asked.

"I don't know."

"What do you think?"

"Control. They want to force me into a corner, make me do things I don't want to.... I don't know."

She turned to him.

"I'm not creating my own reality. But I'm not going to prejudge anyone. It's like crossing a minefield, the slightest wrong move..."

She looked down at her hands again, at her fingers and the rings on them. The diamond ring from her grandmother, the engagement ring she'd never taken off. She began to talk quietly.

"Hector, the police... I've done what I thought was right. I haven't had anyone to turn to. I haven't had any idea who I am in all of this. Only that I've had to follow some internal voice that's hardly whispered a word to me throughout it all. I've been listening to the silence for so long, crying for help. But now all of a sudden this is about my son, all about him, nothing else matters anymore."

He was relaxed again, seemed heavy and hoarse.

"Who else knows about this?"

"No one."

"No one?"

She shook her head. "No one."

"No one you see socially? No friend you can call on when things get tough?"

"Well, yes..."

"But she doesn't know anything either?"

Sophie shook her head. "No..."

Jens thought for a moment.

"Good," he said in a low voice, then looked up at her. "Why not?"

She looked at him quizzically.

"Why haven't you told anyone about this? Surely it would only be natural to turn to someone else with something like this?"

"That's what I'm doing now."

The sound of a propeller plane high up in the sky came through the open window.

"And now you want to take Albert and run away?" he went on.

"I don't know what to do."

"If you could choose?"

"Then I'd like all this to disappear."

"I can understand that. How would you make it all disappear?"

She shrugged and said nothing.

"Sophie!"

"I don't know. What sort of stupid question is that?"

"You must have some idea! You must have thought about it, at least once?"

At first she didn't answer, but she knew what he was getting at.

"I can't make any sense of it, I can't see a way out. No matter how I look at it, someone's going to get hurt. And I don't want that. I haven't done anything, nothing at all, I don't want to sacrifice anyone."

"But surely the sacrifice is obvious?"

She met his gaze.

"Yes... of course it is."

"So why don't you give him up? Do what the police are asking. Give them whatever you can, let them catch him—then it's all finished. You and your son can get back to your normal lives."

She looked at him critically.

"Is that what you'd have done?"

He shook his head.

"No. It wouldn't end there, I'd be on the run for the rest of my life, from both the cops and Hector's gang. They wouldn't give up."

"Right," she said flatly.

Sophie pulled out a scrap of paper and handed it to Jens. He took it and read: *Be careful*.

"Where did you find this?"

"In my mailbox."

"When?"

"This morning."

"Before they picked Albert up?"

She nodded. He looked at the note again, as if he might understand something that wasn't written there.

"Who wrote it?"

"I don't know."

Jens was at something of a loss. He put the note on the coffee table and leaned forward in the armchair, legs apart, elbows on his knees.

"If I were you, I'd be gathering as much information as I could about the greatest threat, which right now is the police. Then I'd find a way to confront them."

"How?"

He shrugged. "By confronting them, I just mean finding a way to get them off balance.... Maybe by finding something out."

"Then what?"

Jens got up from the armchair and headed off toward the kitchen.

"I don't know...."

17

Carlos, wearing a brand-new tracksuit, was eating soup. He could only have fluids. He was sitting in his best armchair with a towel over his knees. The television was showing a film with Terence Hill and Bud Spencer. Bud was hitting the bad guys with an open hand to the accompaniment of exaggerated sound effects. Terence's dubbed dialogue had been atrociously lip-synced. Carlos chuckled at the fight, which made his face hurt.

The doorbell rang out in the hall.

Anders and Hasse smiled amiably at him when Carlos opened the door.

"Carlos Fuentes?" Hasse asked.

Carlos nodded. Hasse was waving his police ID.

"I'm Cling, this is Clang. Can we come in?"

"I've already spoken to the police, they came to the hospital."

Hasse and Anders pushed past Carlos and made their way to the kitchen. Carlos watched them.

"What do you want?"

* * *

Cling and Clang were sitting on kitchen chairs. Carlos was standing up, leaning against the counter.

"And you don't remember what any of them looked like?"

Carlos shook his head.

"How old did you say they were?"

Anders asked the question. Carlos thought for a moment.

"Teenagers..."

"Thirteen or nineteen?" Anders asked.

"More like nineteen, maybe seventeen."

"Seventeen?" Hasse said.

Carlos nodded.

"And they attacked you, just like that, these seventeen-year-olds?"

Carlos nodded again.

"Dear me," Hasse said.

Carlos couldn't tell if he was making fun of him.

"But surely you must have seen something? A face..."

Carlos shook his head.

"It all happened so quickly."

"Nationality? Swedish?"

Carlos pretended to think.

"I think they were immigrants, they were wearing hoods."

Carlos scratched the end of his nose lightly.

"It's always those immigrants," Hasse said.

Anders looked through his notebook, just for the sake of it.

"And you were on your way home from work?"

"Yes..."

"Where do you work?"

"I own a restaurant, Trasten."

"And everything was OK at Trasten that night? No trouble? Nothing out of the ordinary?"

Carlos shook his head, and touched his nose again—quickly, almost imperceptibly.

"No. The restaurant shuts at eleven, so I went down to lock up. A quiet Saturday night."

"Of course it was, Carlos." Anders smiled.

Carlos tried to smile back.

"Tell me, where are you from again, Carlos?" Hasse asked.

"Spain... originally from Málaga."

"Isn't the king named Carlos?"

Carlos couldn't make sense of the question.

"No, his name's Juan Carlos...."

"Well, then he is named Carlos, isn't he?" Hasse said.

Carlos wasn't following.

"So nothing happened?" Anders asked again.

Carlos looked at Anders and shook his head.

"Everything the same as normal?" Hasse asked.

Carlos's gaze flitted between them.

"I just said it was!"

"Don Carlos! Wasn't there a porn star called that?"

Carlos looked at Hasse, unable to figure out if he was expecting an answer to that.

"I don't know," he said quietly.

Anders was looking intently at Carlos. "Have you ever studied psychology?"

"What?"

"Have you ever studied psychology?"

Carlos shook his head. "Psychology? No."

Anders pointed at Hasse.

"We have, we're psychologists. Cling and Clang's school of psychology."

Carlos was completely lost now.

"One of the things they teach you is that one of the most obvious signs that someone's lying is that they touch the tip of their nose."

Carlos touched his nose.

"Just like that. You keep rubbing the tip of your nose, Carlos, because right at the end there's an irritating little nerve that itches every time we tell a lie."

"I'm not lying," he said.

"How do you know Hector Guzman?" Hasse asked.

"Hector?"

Anders and Hasse waited.

"He's an old friend, he eats at the restaurant sometimes."

"How would you describe him?"

"Nothing special, an ordinary man."

"What's an ordinary man like?"

Carlos rubbed the tip of his nose.

"Just ordinary. Works, eats, sleeps... I don't know."

"Did you see Hector on Saturday?"

"No."

"But he was at the restaurant, wasn't he?"

"Not when I got there. I got there late, to lock up."

"Did he have company that evening? Do you happen to know?"

Carlos shook his head. "No, I don't know."

"A woman? Sophie?"

Carlos shook his head, grateful that he didn't have to lie.

"I don't know," he said flatly.

Anders got up and walked over to Carlos. Examined his wounded face. Carlos felt invaded, but tried to express the exact opposite. Hasse slid up behind Anders, and they both stared.

"Their aim was good...," Anders whispered.

Carlos was uncomprehending.

"The teenagers, when they attacked you. They only hit you in the face?"

Carlos nodded.

"No other injuries?"

Carlos shook his head.

"You need to wear this."

Anders held up a microphone.

"You can have it in your pocket or wherever you like, but no more than thirty yards away from this."

Anders showed him a little box. Carlos was shaking his head desperately.

"I'm afraid the decision's out of your hands, Carlos. Wear the microphone and keep your mouth shut. Make sure it's running whenever you're around Hector and Aron, fill it up with information."

Hasse and Anders left the kitchen and headed for the front door.

"You can't do this," Carlos whispered.

Anders turned around.

"Of course we can. We can do whatever we want. Even other stuff."

"What other stuff?"

Hasse walked quickly up to Carlos, grabbed him by the neck, and hammered his fist into the side of his head several times. The blows sounded meaty and hard as they struck him on the temple, ear, and cheekbone. Carlos slumped to the kitchen floor. He sat there bewildered, his eyes flaring as he watched Cling and Clang's silhouettes disappear out the front door.

Carlos was trying to calm down. His pulse was racing too fast. He felt a sudden tightness in his chest, his breathing grew labored, his heart beat faster, and he felt giddy. He managed to get up unsteadily and made his way to the bathroom. His heart was thudding in his chest. With trembling hands he managed to tip five pills from the bottle of heart medication. He swallowed three and stood there with both hands leaning on the washbasin, taking deep breaths, feeling his heart rate slow down. Carlos looked in the mirror. A beaten man in every sense. He concluded that he had two options, and possibly a third at some point in the future, but two for the time being: Hector or Hanke. The third possible option for the future was the police, but he couldn't figure out what they knew and didn't know. He had to do what was best for himself now. Carlos weighed Hector against Hanke: who was strongest, who was going to win? He had no idea, he didn't even know what the conflict was about, he just knew that he had sold out his boss and had been beaten up as a result, and now the police had contacted him, and they seemed to know more than they wanted to let on to him.

Carlos looked at his ravaged face. Hector had done that. Maybe they were quits now.

Carlos turned away from the mirror and left the bathroom. No, they weren't quits in any sense. He knew that in his heart. But his heart wasn't the issue anymore, this was now about a great deal more than that. He went into the kitchen, opened a bottle of wine, and drank a large glass. He wouldn't call anyone for the time being; he'd give it a bit longer, see how things developed. Then he'd decide whose lap he wanted to sit on.

There was a mass of papers on the table. Hector was reading. On a chair opposite him sat Ernst the solicitor. Aron was sitting at the end of the table checking everything through twice.

"I've registered the companies in the West Indies and in Macao,"

Ernst said. "The companies are registered as investment firms, owned by you, Thierry, Daphne, and your father. You have fifty-one percent, Adalberto has forty-five, which will come to you in the event of his death. The reverse applies should you predecease him, your share would go to him. Thierry and Daphne together own four percent and are listed as subscribers of the company. They've signed over power of attorney, which I've got here. . . ."

Ernst pushed four sheets of paper across the table.

"This gives you total control of payments in and out of the companies."

Hector quickly signed the documents.

"What happens if both Dad and I die?"

"Then someone else will inherit everything. That's up to you to decide. I've got the papers here; you just need to fill them in and sign them once you've decided who that person, or those people, should be."

Hector glanced through the power of attorney. He picked up the papers, folded them, put them in an envelope, and placed them in his briefcase.

Aron's cell phone rang.

"Yes?"

"We won't manage to hit our targets," Svante Carlgren said, and hung up on him.

He had called the number, he had given them information. Now they thought they had him. But that was wrong, he'd got himself a reprieve.

Mostly he just felt bad when he thought about the way that damn whore had deceived him. He wanted to get hold of her head and smash it against a wall, and tell her that no one, absolutely fucking no one had ever managed to get the better of Svante Carlgren. But she had. He sighed deeply and felt that he had been crushed. He also wanted to kill the man who had threatened him, he wanted to kill him truly and properly. Recently he had been able to think of nothing except how to get out of this predicament. He had weighed up his ideas, contemplating different groups: the Russian mafia, biker gangs . . . weren't they who you called when you were in the shit? But neither of them would be able to help him, he could see that. He'd thought about shooting the man himself with his shotgun, the Purdey that he kept for hunting pheasant. Well maintained, in the gun cabinet in the cellar. Shoot the bastard in the face—two shots ought to be enough. But Svante knew that this wouldn't work either; he'd get caught, everyone who acted in anger did.

Svante Carlgren dialed a number, an internal number for Östensson in the security division. Östensson picked up with a breezy "Yep?"

"This is Svante Carlgren."

"I see! Good morning."

"I'm calling with a question, it isn't about the company, but a friend who needs a bit of help."

"Oh?"

"Is that all right?"

"Yes . . . I don't see why not."

"You worked for a private security company before you came to us, didn't you?"

"That's right."

"How does that work?"

"It depends what you mean."

"Did you used to track people down?"

"Among other things, yes."

"Were you flexible?"

"Can you be more specific?"

"Were you flexible, I can't be more specific."

Östensson was quiet for a second or so too long.

"I suppose I'd say that we were."

"I've got a friend who needs help."

"So you said."

"Can you give me a name?"

"Zivkovic, Håkan Zivkovic."

"Thank you."

"Svante."

"Yes?"

"You're not trying to tell me something?"

Svante laughed.

"No, like I said . . . I want to help a friend who's got himself in trouble, but I understand that you have to ask."

Svante hung up and dialed Håkan Zivkovic, and introduced himself as King Carl XVI Gustaf. He said he needed help finding a man whose name he didn't know, but described him and gave details of the car he had been driving.

"We'll do our best to help you, but your anonymity will cost you extra."

"Why?"

"Because it will."

"I see."

Håkan gave Svante the number of a bank account and Svante promised that the money would be in Håkan's account the following day.

In a practically empty apartment out in Farsta seven trustworthy individuals were sitting in front of computers and short-selling Ericsson shares through 136 different agents via encrypted connections. They spiced up their transactions with various financial options to provide extra leverage on the falling price of Ericsson shares. They were finished by five. Shortly afterward the stock market closed, and Ericsson's value had remained largely unchanged throughout the course of the day.

Aron and Hector oversaw the whole business. They split up and slept badly that night, then reconvened with the seven trustworthy individuals in the same apartment the following morning.

The morning news was on the television set in the apartment. The female anchor sounded serious as she discussed Ericsson's inaccurate forecasts in Asia and other things that none of them really cared about. The silent nervousness that had set in after the previous day eased slightly. When the stock market opened at nine o'clock, Ericsson's shares fell sharply. They set to work buying back the shares and got rid of the options and warranties they had bought the day before. They looked happily at the computer screen showing the behavior of Ericsson's shares—the graph looked like a ski slope. They made an enormous amount of money.

18

At nine o'clock in the evening the doorbell rang. He was standing outside with a paper bag from the market in one hand and a bottle of bubbly in the other. Hector's smile was genuine, as if he had won something. A whole host of thoughts was flying through her head. *Albert... Jens is somewhere around... the microphones... Not now...*

"I've brought food," he said, holding up the bag in his left hand.

She tried to smile at him. "Hello, Hector. What brings you out here?"

"I didn't want to eat alone."

"Aron?"

"He's here somewhere."

Sophie looked over his shoulder.

"Come in."

They were sitting in the kitchen. She had laid out glasses, plates, and cutlery. Hector had unpacked the food on the table. They picked at the food in the tubs, drank the Champagne, and chatted idly. Sophie was constantly aware of the microphone fixed to the kitchen lamp above them. The situation was wearing on her nerves, but to her relief he was the same as usual. A friend who had popped in with some food. He made no attempt to make veiled references, he was generous, inspiring a sort of calm. He looked more at her mouth than her eyes when she spoke.

"See how easy it is," he said.

She took a bite.

"What's easy, Hector?"

"Sitting here like this, you and me." His tone of voice was different now, more serious.

She started to get worried, and gave a little smile.

"Yes . . . it's easy."

"Sophie?"

"Yes?"

He tried to find the right words.

"I've been thinking of getting a present for you, maybe some jewelry. . . ."

She started to interrupt, but he held his hand up to indicate that he wanted to finish first.

"I'd like to offer you something personal, a trip, or tickets to the theatre, or a walk and lunch, I don't know. But every time I make my mind up, I start to worry. Worries that say that this jewelry, or that play, or whatever it is, isn't you. That you're something else, something I don't know, something I can't have, no matter how much I try. So I don't dare. I don't dare make a mistake because I'm frightened of losing you."

She was staring down at her plate, took a bite of something, deliberately not making eye contact with Hector.

He whispered to get her attention.

"When are we going to have a serious conversation? Talk about us, about everything that's happened. . . ."

"Hello?"

The voice came from behind them. Suddenly Albert was standing there in the kitchen, like a gift from heaven, looking curiously at Sophie, then Hector.

"Hello, Albert."

"Hello?"

"This is Hector."

"Hello, Hector," Albert said neutrally, taking a plate from the cupboard and cutlery from the drawer. Hector's eyes followed him. Albert sat down at the table without any awkwardness, and briefly met Hector's gaze.

"Hector? Isn't that a dog's name?" he asked as he put food on his plate, with a little spark behind his eyes.

"Yes," Hector said. "It is, it's a dog's name. And Albert? I seem to remember we once had a donkey named that."

Then they started talking and joking, as if they knew exactly what each other's sense of humor was like, as if they'd always known each other—a sort of affinity that they probably weren't even aware of themselves.

Hector laughed, Albert laughed and talked. Sophie looked on with a cheerful smile and a sense of great dread.

It was a warm evening. Jens was sitting on a bench in Stocksund Square. A group of dressed-up youngsters wearing graduation caps went past. A girl with a bottle in a brown paper bag was having trouble keeping her balance in her high heels. She shrieked as she spoke, but the others didn't seem to be listening to her.

Jens was waiting for more darkness, but it was taking its time. He waited until the intoxicated youngsters were out of sight before picking up his flat black rucksack, standing up, and making his way through the narrow streets toward Sophie's house. He passed it at a distance and made his way up a hill, into a garden where he had a good view of the whole area. The family didn't seem to be home. Little evening lamps shone in different parts of the house—that seemed to be the rule out here when houses were left empty. Jens went up to the bushes at the top of the lawn, slid in among them, lay down on his stomach, pulled a pair of binoculars from his rucksack, and scanned the area.

He located the Saab, adjusted the focus, and saw a man in the driver's seat. The car was parked on its own, among some trees. He wouldn't have noticed it if he hadn't been looking. Jens looked around the car with the binoculars, trying to find anything unusual.

He widened his search and checked a larger radius, looking for any other people. Nothing.

His plan was simple, to get closer, photograph the man from a distance, and then identify him with Harry's help. That was where he'd start.... The man in the car was most likely a cop. But Jens couldn't work on probability anymore. He needed solid facts to make any sense of this whole business.

Jens lowered the binoculars and looked toward Sophie's villa. He could see movement through the kitchen window and raised the binoculars again.

Hector Guzman came into focus. He was the last person Jens expected to see there. Hector, Sophie, and Albert were sitting around the table. *Hector?* That must mean that Aron was somewhere nearby? Where? Jens checked the area again, quickly and intently. The man in the Saab was to the west of Sophie's house, Jens to the north. He looked south and east: no parked car, and no Aron anywhere. Back to Sophie's kitchen. Hector was out of sight. Then the Saab again, and back to the eastern part of the area. If Aron was here, then the situation had changed dramatically.

And he was here. Jens saw him through the binoculars, walking along a road off to the east. He was strolling along, on a direct collision course with the cop in the Saab. Jens followed Aron through the binoculars, working through possible scenarios in his head. He concluded that there was only one thing to do. He looked at Aron, then at the Saab, trying to figure out the distance, and how much time he had as a result. It was a matter of seconds, no more. And he couldn't take the most direct route... and he'd have to stay hidden. And Aron was good at hearing people creeping about. *Fuck*.

Jens got to his feet and began running along the hillside, parallel to Aron, who was walking along the road below. He speeded up, and as a result made more noise. But that was a risk he had to take, he had to get there first, ideally well in advance. And he had to approach the car from behind in order to get himself under cover by the time Aron got there. So he ran in a broad circle, the distance was about twice as far as it was for Aron. He needed to move more than twice as fast as Aron... and silently.

Jens ran through the undergrowth, across several gardens, then found himself parallel to the car parked below. He tried to find Aron, couldn't see him, and began to swerve down the hill in a wide arc. Jens was heading due south, down a slope covered in dew-damp grass, with the Saab to the west of him. He slipped and slid, somehow stayed on his feet, and rushed toward the Saab. Now he could see that Aron was heading straight toward him and the car. Jens had some twenty yards ahead of him where he would have no cover at all. He crouched as best he could and hurried toward the car from behind. He hoped the man inside was busy, that he wouldn't look in the rearview mirror... and that he was sufficiently low to escape Aron's notice.

Jens aimed at the back door, praying to God that it was unlocked. He grabbed the handle and pulled—*Thank you!*—then threw himself into the backseat, keeping his head low behind the driver's seat.

"Drive away from here now!"

The man was calm and still.

"What?"

"Start the car and drive, Guzman's bodyguard is heading this way right now!"

Jens raised his head a little and saw Aron approaching. The man behind the wheel seemed slightly retarded.

"Look left!"

The man did so. And then he seemed to realize.

The Saab started up and tore off. Jens stayed as close to the floor as he could. He opened his rucksack and pulled out his Beretta 92, then jammed it into the man's side.

"Move the rearview mirror."

It took a few seconds for the man to understand, then he twisted the mirror on the windshield.

They drove around for a while. The man seemed strangely calm.

"Give me your wallet."

"I'm a police officer," he said groggily.

"What's your name?"

"Lars."

"Lars what?"

"Vinge."

Jens stuck the barrel of the gun behind his ear.

"Your wallet."

It was on the dashboard. Lars reached over for it, then bent his arm back so Jens could take it.

"Your phone..."

Lars gave him his cell. Jens put everything in his pocket. Then he asked for the man's gun, which he unloaded. He put the magazine in his trouser pocket and dropped the pistol on the floor.

"Where are we going?"

"Just drive."

And Lars did. From his position behind the driver's seat Jens couldn't figure out where.

"Who are you?" Lars asked.

Jens didn't answer.

"Why did you warn me?"

"Shut up."

They circled aimlessly around the streets for a quarter of an hour before Jens told him to stop.

Lars pulled over to the edge of the road and stopped. Jens reached forward and took the key from the ignition.

"Keep your eyes straight ahead," he said, then got out of the car, leaving Lars with a thousand questions. Jens hurried away from the Saab and into the undergrowth of a nearby garden.

When he was out of sight he stopped and looked around. They were back in the area where Sophie lived. Her house was two blocks away. The cop had been driving around and around in circles.

Jens made his way quickly back to his car in the square. He wanted to get away from there, didn't want to risk bumping into Aron or Hector. He got behind the wheel and headed off toward the Inverness junction and onto the main road. He pulled the identity card from the wallet, police ID: *Lars Vinge*. He looked at the photograph, it was the same guy. He put the ID card back in his pocket, took out Vinge's cell phone, and began to look through the contacts. He found a few first names: *Anders*, *Doctor*, *Gunilla*, *Mom*, *Sara*... but that was all—an unusually thin list of contacts. Jens checked the last numbers dialed and the last calls received. Lars didn't use his phone much, there were just a few calls to *Gunilla*. He looked at the list of missed calls, three from *Sara* and two from *Unknown Caller*.

As Jens drove over the Stocksund Bridge, he opened the window and threw the car keys and magazine of bullets over the railing.

—

Albert had left them and gone into the living room.

"That's a fine boy you've got there," Hector said. Then he started talking about the importance of finding the right attitude toward the world around you at an early age, that everything sorted itself out if you did, everything fell into place. He compared Albert to himself.

Sophie interrupted him.

"I want you to go now, Hector."

He didn't understand.

"I should go?"

She nodded, and he searched her face.

"Why?"

"Because I want you to. I don't want you to come here again."

Hector looked at her carefully, frowning, his hands folded.

"OK," he said, trying to sound as if her words didn't really mean much. He got himself together and stood up. But instead of leaving he stood beside the table.

"I don't know what I've done."

She avoided his gaze.

"You haven't done anything. I just want you to leave."

He was clearly sad. But he didn't make a big deal of it, just made a call, muttered something in Spanish, and left the house. Aron drove up in the car.

She remained sitting at the kitchen table, she didn't know how long.

There was a look of disappointment from Albert when he came into the kitchen and sat down opposite her. "Do you want to die alone, Mom?" She didn't answer, just stood up and started to clear the table.

"What are you so scared of?"

"I'm not scared, Albert. I make the decisions about my life, got that?"

She could hear how sharp she sounded, how wrong she sounded.

"So who was that?"

"I've told you."

"Really?"

She didn't reply to that, either. She felt like saying: *For God's sake, Albert, please, just shut up! People can hear every word we say!*

But she just pointed toward the living room in some misdirected adult attempt at punishment. He was too old for that sort of scolding, and didn't understand it. Instead he just sighed, stood up, and walked out of the kitchen.

Sophie poured the fizzy wine down the sink.

The apartment looked like an old storage space, pillars holding up the rela- tively high ceiling—large, open, sparsely furnished. Harry lived in a ramshackle attic apartment on Kungsholmen. He'd lived there for as long as Jens had known him, fifteen years or so. Harry was self-taught and had worked as a private detective for the whole of his adult life. He spent the '70s and half of the '80s based in London, then for some reason decided to move home again.

He'd only just woken up and was dragging himself across the large open space in slippers and a checkered dressing gown. His thin, straggly hair seemed to have a mind of its own, way beyond Harry's control.

"The coffee's on but it'll take a while because I keep forgetting to clear the lime scale out of the fucker." Harry's voice was hoarse and rough, as if he needed to clear his throat.

The electric coffee machine over in the kitchen corner was bubbling alarmingly. There were four computers up and running. Harry shuffled over to them, scratching his scalp.

"What have you got?" he said, then coughed.

They both sat down at the desk.

"ID card and a cell phone."

Harry held out his hand. "The ID card."

Jens put Lars Vinge's ID in Harry's hand. Harry inspected it from every angle. He held it up to the light of a reading lamp on a shelf behind his monitors.

"It's genuine, so in all likelihood the guy's a cop. Did you see his face?"

"From the side, it was the guy in the picture."

Harry let out a big yawn and started tapping at one of the keyboards, glancing at the ID card.

"How did you get this? I thought you said you were going to try to get some photographs."

"The situation changed."

"Shit happens," Harry said, still tapping away, clearly not interested. He pulled out a box by his feet and took out a badly battered leather diary, dropped his reading glasses from his forehead, and began leafing through it. The pages were covered in tiny handwriting. He turned to Jens and nodded toward the coffee machine, which had fallen silent. Jens got up and walked over to it.

Harry found what he was looking for, typed a user name and password into a web page, and pressed Enter. Then he keyed in "Lars Vinge," followed by his date of birth and ID number. A page started to load and soon Vinge's passport photograph appeared. Jens came back with two mugs.

"Lars Christer Vinge, beat cop, Husby Police Station," Harry said.

Jens leaned over and read the screen.

"What site is this?"

"The cops' personnel database..."

Jens sat down as Harry read on.

"He was with the Western District until a month or so ago. Now he's in crime, connected to the National Crime Division...."

"I don't know much about the police, but can they really go from one to the other just like that?" Jens asked.

"No idea...they're police, who the fuck cares," Harry muttered, taking a sip of coffee, then put the mug down and started tapping at the keys again.

"This is going to take a while," he said.

Jens didn't move. Harry typed, looked at Jens, went on typing, then turned to look at him again.

"There are toys over in the corner, off you go."

Jens got the message.

There was a table tennis table folded up against the wall, and Jens opened it out and started hitting the ball to himself. It felt good concentrating on the sound of the ball. It was hypnotic. Jens wasn't thinking about anything, just kept the ball bouncing between himself and the wall. He shut himself off, all his concentration was focused on just one thing, making the bastard ball realize that it stood no chance against him. But evidently it did, because Harry called to him, Jens lost his focus, and the ball won. It bounced from the table and rolled off across the floor toward its own vacuous freedom.

Harry had several sites open in small windows on the screen when Jens sat back down on his chair.

"Lars Vinge's a pretty invisible character, there's nothing very interesting about him. He's a cop, he's moved from the Western District to National Crime. I've checked his medical records and managed to find a recent visit. The old records aren't online, so doctors' appointments before 1997 are difficult to dig out. Anyway, he saw a doctor recently for back pain and trouble sleeping. He got prescriptions for oxazepam and Citodon, from what I can see here.

"And what are they?"

"Oxazepam's a sedative, addictive. It's benzo, people get seriously fucked-up on benzo."

"And the other one?"

"Citodon's a painkiller, looks like acetaminophen, tastes like acetaminophen.... But this is codeine. Gets metabolized as morphine."

"How do you know all this, Harry?"

"None of your business," he muttered, tapping away at his keyboard, clicking with the mouse, searching through the flat, two-dimensional world in front of him. He seemed to be regretting his impolite response.

"My ex got hooked on prescription drugs. She used to have a whole pharmacy at home. A whole pharmacy that only made her worse and worse with each passing day."

"What happened?"

"In the end neither of us could recognize her anymore."

"That's a shame."

Harry turned to Jens, and looked him in the eye.

"Yes, it was a shame," he replied, his voice open and honest, then he went back to the computer.

Jens was looking at Harry from the corner of his eye. Harry was usually pretty tight-lipped about his private life.

"So we're dealing with a detective with a prescription drug problem?"

Harry shook his head.

"No, no, it isn't necessarily a problem. You're not fucked the moment you take the first pill.... Most people can cope if they only use them short-term, and take them in small doses."

"What else?"

Harry shook his head.

"Nothing, except that he isn't married, lives on Södermalm, and wrote some sort of report on ethnic divisions in Husby while he was a beat officer, or a neighborhood officer or whatever the fuck they're called these days.... He's licensed to drive a taxi, his finances are fairly limited, and according to his charge card he sometimes buys films off the Internet and food from a budget supermarket."

Jens skimmed through the scant information on the screen.

"I need more detail. Is it possible to find out what he's working on at the moment? Who he works with... and why?"

"You can always phone and ask," Harry said.

"Will they tell me?"

"Probably not."

"OK. Look up a woman, another police officer, Gunilla Strandberg."

Harry got to work on his keyboard.

"Who's she?"

"The boss, I think, Sophie's contact."

Harry stopped on one site, scrolled down, and read.

"Gunilla Strandberg, on the force since '78. Looks like the usual career path... beat cop in Stockholm, inspector at some police station in Karlstad for a few years in the mid-'80s... back to Stockholm, National Crime, became a superintendent.... On paid leave pending the outcome of an investigation in 2002, two months, then back to work."

"What sort of investigation?"

"Don't know, this is only the police personnel database. Nothing but the bare facts."

"Can you get into some other site, one with more detail?"

"No."

Harry switched windows and searched for her name again. He clicked to open several pages, shrank them, and lined them up next to one another on the screen.

"Unmarried, lives out on Lidingö. One brother, Erik... Nothing interesting in her medical notes.... Looks like she's never been ill."

Harry went on tapping at the keyboard.

"She's got a few notices for nonpayment of bills, but her finances look pretty good. She's a member of Amnesty and has standing orders for Human Rights Watch and UNICEF.... Possibly a member of the Peony Society, her name came up in an old register of members."

Harry stretched.

"She's a fairly wealthy old bag who's a bit disorganized when it comes to bills, is hardly ever ill, and likes peonies. No more than that."

Lars wasn't shocked, he wasn't even trembling. That was the way it was these days with Ketogan at hand. He felt devoid of emotion. Even when the cold steel of the barrel of the pistol was pressing against his skin—*nothing.*

He didn't know what to call his current state. Maybe surprised? Yes, that was probably it, *surprised.* Surprised that an unknown armed man had forced his way into his car and taken his cell, ID, and car keys. *Surprised.*

He stared out into the night with his mouth open, then tugged at his bottom lip. He knew how strung out he was, he could feel it. Mostly because of the pills, but also because of everything that had happened. It had all gone with lightning speed, within the space of just a few weeks he had ruined everything. The little he had of a proper life was now gone. His relationships were in tatters, his emotional life was in a state of anarchy, and now the machinery itself was starting to fuck with him. His soul was dead and buried somewhere deep inside his own personal hell. Not even his thoughts were his own anymore. As if the only thing left inside him was something that someone else had shoved in there. He didn't recognize himself. It wasn't him anymore... but it wasn't anyone else, either. Who was that man? Not one of Hector's group. Maybe a friend? A friend helping Sophie? But why?

He let go of his lip. Stared ahead of him. *Surprised* was probably the wrong word, actually—he hadn't felt anything at all.

Lars let the hours pass. He just sat there. But something started to dawn on him in his drug-addled confusion, a little glimpse of meaning. His phone was gone, his wallet, the magazine of his pistol, the keys to the car... all gone, together with his personality and soul... together with his previous life. Maybe it was a sign? A sign of change? That now was the time to start again, start afresh, from scratch. Figure out what was really going on around him, pick a side.

It suddenly struck him that he was free to take this in whatever direction he wanted. Lars saw time stretching out ahead of him, saw in his mind's eye what he ought to do from now on, what he was obliged to do.

He reached his arm back and pulled out his magazine-less service pistol from the floor behind the seat, jumped out of the car, and went around to open the trunk. He closed the little case around the surveillance equipment using the Velcro strips, then took it out and walked a little way toward a garden, putting it behind a birch tree. Lars sat down and pulled the laces from his sneakers, tied them together to make a longer cord, then went back to the Saab, opened the cap of the gas tank, dangled the shoelace in as far as he could, pulled it out, sniffed—*Gas, what a fantastic smell....*

He dipped the other end in as far as it would go. Just a few inches of the shoelace were visible. He looked over toward the tree, trying to figure out his escape route. Three, maybe four seconds. No, longer. Five, six.

He pulled out a lighter and ignited the gas-soaked end. The shoelace burned fast, quicker than he had anticipated. Lars ran like never before, taking long strides, panic raging at the back of his head.

The explosion was muffled and thick, as if someone had dropped a heavy carpet on the whole area. The pressure wave felt like a warm, burning squall on his back as he threw himself to the ground on top of the bag of surveillance equipment. He looked back from where he was lying. The pillar of flame stood straight up for a few seconds. The flames along its top edge formed a mushroom shape where they seemed to want to burn downward and inward. Then it vanished in the semidarkness of the evening. The Saab was in flames. It snapped and crackled and popped. The rear window was gone, the lid of the trunk was hanging from one hinge. The plastic was beginning to melt, glass cracked, the rear left-hand tire was squirting out rubber as it burned. He stared wide-eyed at the fireworks.

Sophie had dreamed that the boiler in the cellar had exploded. She bumped into Albert outside her bedroom.

"What was that?" he asked.

"I don't know."

She went downstairs but nothing looked any different. She went down into the cellar, looking around, sniffing for any wrong smell, but there was nothing there, either. She heard Albert's voice calling her from outside.

When she got out she saw a glow above the trees one block away. A strong, yellowish glow.

They started walking in that direction.

A large group of people were standing watching the fire. More were on their way from the surrounding streets. Sophie could see it was a car, an old Saab.

Albert met up with a friend, and they started laughing and joking. She stared at the burning car and heard the fire-department sirens in the distance, over the crackling sound of plastic, rubber, and metal.

He was standing right behind her.

Lars had gotten to his feet after the explosion and had been about to leave the area when a thought suddenly struck him: she was bound to come and look. He had stopped, turned around, and tucked himself away in the darkness. He had watched as people came out from the neighboring houses. Lars had hidden the bag, roughed up his hair, then went back.

Now he was a homeowner who had been woken by the blast, got dressed, and gone out to see *what was going on*.

He hadn't seen her at first, which made him impatient. Lars tried to calm himself down by listening to what other people were saying. They were mostly joking. Someone asked for a light. A man said something about Saab, shares, and bankruptcy. Lars didn't get the joke but everyone else seemed to. More people joined the crowd to watch the spectacle. And then he saw her.

She had come down the road off to one side behind him. He had glanced in that direction, saw Albert walking ahead of her, saw her beautiful apparition. He smiled, then realized he was smiling. He stopped, turned around, and stared into the fire, and saw her from the corner of his eye as she stopped a short distance from him. Lars had slowly moved closer to her through the crowd.

Now he was standing right behind her, staring into the back of her neck, the part of her that he found so attractive. She had her hair tied up loosely, her neck was bare. He wanted to reach out a hand and stroke it, massage it, press his finger into the little hollow.

"Sophie?"

A woman in a dressing gown came up to her. "This is crazy! What happened?"

Lars listened intently.

"Hello, Cissi, I don't know, the explosion woke me up."

"Me too..."

He had spent so long listening to her on his headphones, had seen her through his telephoto lens, had stood beside her as she slept, but he had never seen her like this—normal, awake, *Sophie.* He continued staring at her little movements, the small ways she moved and acted, and smiled again.

Cissi pulled a packet of cigarettes from the pocket of her dressing gown.

"I remembered to bring these, do you want one?"

"Thanks."

They lit up, then watched the burning car.

Cissi tore her eyes away, turned around, and found herself looking straight at Lars's odd smile. She looked him up and down.

"And what the hell are you grinning at?"

Sophie turned around as well and caught sight of Lars. They stared at each other. He looked down at the ground, turned around, and quickly made his way through the crowd and disappeared.

Cissi took a puff on her cigarette.

"Who the hell was that creep?"

Sophie knew.... She knew who he was. She felt scared. She had thought he would be sturdier, bigger, more like a policeman, whatever they were supposed to look like. Not like what she had just seen, with an insipid, searching gaze, weird posture, hollow eyes.

"I don't know," she said, trying to find him in the crowd. But Lars Vinge had vanished.

The wall. The confusion of pictures, names, arrows, notes. Complete chaos. He let his breathing calm down. Concentrated on the pictures of Sophie. He backed away, saw a flicker of a connection; he wanted to reach out and touch it, but lost it and... *Fuck!*

Lars wrote on the wall: *Man 35–40, Swedish, armed, calm*. He drew an arrow to Sophie. He backed away again, looked, tried to remember. Did he recognize the voice of the man in the car? His eyes slid to the photograph of the man Sophie had met on Strandvägen. Thoughts were bouncing around inside his head. Time flowed onward, his concentration wavered. His reasoning refused to stay with him.

Lars went into the bathroom, prepared a new dose. This time he thought he'd managed to mix a painkiller cocktail. He gulped down the pills, looked at himself in the mirror, lazily humming "New York, New York." Lars was pale, saggy, and he had little yellow spots around his mouth—he liked what he saw.

The wall again, Lars carried on working, looking, searching. He scratched at his spots, his legs were in constant motion, he was grinding his teeth like some fucking ruminating elk. Was there some pattern that he wasn't seeing? A code embedded in everything he had written on the wall? Had he subconsciously created a code containing the answer to everything he didn't understand? Maybe that was it.... The divine answer to everything? Maybe it was there, amid the chaos on the wall? Maybe there were other answers too? Lars could feel his drug-fueled intelligence racing. Then it stopped. As if Ingo Johansson had stepped out of the picture leaning against the wall, taken a step forward, and hit him with a heavy right hook to the face.

Lars sat down on the chair, his neck hanging, unable to think or even move. He was mentally knocked out, his brain sluggish with painkillers. He was drooling from the side of his mouth. He stared down at his legs, saw the grass stains on the knees of his jeans...like when he was a little boy! Lars laughed at the thought, grass stains on his knees! The dose had been too high. Tiredness made its way through his neck and shoulders and out into his body, his chest, stomach, legs, feet—to every corner of Lars Vinge. He slid off the chair and ended up on his knees, then fell forward and put his hands out to stop himself. His wrists and lower arms hurt as he landed.

He saw a single cable that wasn't attached to anything beneath the desk. Lars stared at the cable. It suggested a number of associations that flickered past.

He topped up with Ketogan and benzo...and something else as well. A decent enough overdose. But the dose didn't give him what he was looking for. Instead it felt as though something outside him was exerting great pressure on him, at least that was how he experienced it. He couldn't move, couldn't think, he was heavier than the mass of an exploding star. And then Ingo popped up again. This time he made some Gothenburg joke, jabbed from the left, feinted, and followed up with a heavy right uppercut. Everything went black.

The phone was ringing, dragging him back from a dense, soundless darkness. Lars looked at the time, he must have been gone for many long hours. The phone rang again. It was persistent and discordant. He got up on his knees. The phone was shrieking now. Leaning on the desk, he got to his feet and walked unsteadily over the wooden floor. The base of his spine and his knees were aching.

"Hello?"

"Lars Vinge?"

"Yes?"

"My name is Gunnel Nordin, I'm calling from Lyckoslanten Care Home. I'm sorry to have to tell you that your mother passed away this morning."

"Oh... That's a shame."

Lars hung up and went out into the kitchen without knowing why. Maybe he was looking for something. The phone rang again. He looked around, hoping that this would help him remember what it was he needed. The phone kept ringing. He looked up at the ceiling, then down at the floor, then all around him, turning 360 degrees. The phone went on ringing. No, he couldn't remember what he was looking for, although his brain was racing.

The ringing carried on. He picked up the receiver.

"Hello?"

"I'm calling from Lyckoslanten again. Gunnel Nordin..."

"Yes?"

Lars glanced down at his feet.

"I don't know if you understood what I just told you."

"Yes, you told me Mom died."

His cheek was itching, as if he'd been bitten by a gnat. Irritated, he scratched hard with his fingernails.

"Do you want to come over? See her before they take her away?"

He looked at his nails, there was a bit of blood on them.

"No, no, that's fine, take her away."

Gunnel Nordin was silent for a moment.

"I'm afraid I must ask you to come and finalize a few things, sign some papers, collect Rosie's belongings. Can you come sometime this week?"

"Yes... that ought to be OK."

Lars was still wandering about, looking for something.

"There's one more thing I should tell you...."

"Yes?"

"Rosie... your mom took her own life...."

"Oh... OK."

He hung up again. What the hell was it he was looking for?

Lars opened the fridge, and the chill that hit him felt pleasant. He stood there for a long time, it sounded louder this time. He stared at the condensing unit right at the back, listening to the way it clicked.

The phone started shrieking again, boring into him, shredding his peace of mind. He heard himself scream, a scream from the abyss, full of fury that seemed to come from the deep.

"Yes?"

"Lars, what happened yesterday?"

Gunilla's voice.

"Yesterday? Nothing, as far as I know."

"Your car's gone up in flames."

"My car?"

"The Saab out in Stocksund, it went up in a fire last night."

"How?"

"We don't know. Witnesses say it exploded. When did you go home?"

"About eleven."

"And the equipment?"

"Left in the Saab. Where's the car now?"

"It's been taken away, to the Täby Police Compound. They're going to take a look at it, but you know how long that takes."

He didn't know.

"Who could have done this, Lars?"

Lars acted bewildered.

"No idea... Hooligans, kids... I don't know, Gunilla."

"How much recorded material did we lose?"

"Nothing of any value, I've been sending you everything, after all."

Gunilla stayed on the line for a moment, then hung up.

Jens wanted to go on sleeping but the sound of the phone ringing wouldn't let up. He reached for the receiver, knocking his old alarm clock onto the floor. He just managed to see the position of the hour hand, which, together with the sunlight filtering through the curtains, suggested that it was the middle of the day.

"Hello..."

"Did I wake you?"

"No, no, I was up."

"Can we talk?"

Jens tried to put everything back in place inside his head. "Are you calling from the phone I gave you?"

"Yes."

"Hang up, I'll call you back."

He threw off the thick white duvet and put his foot down on the soft carpet. His bedroom was as light as the inside of a cumulus cloud. White everywhere, except for one painting, which was a muted deep red: a Mark Rothko copy that he was very fond of. Jens stretched, stood up, and walked out of the room. He was wearing nothing but his ivory cotton boxer shorts, big and loose, with buttons, handmade in Turkey. He had bought twenty pairs from the tailor. In his opinion they were the best clothes he had ever bought.

He continued into the kitchen, opened a drawer, and fished out a new SIM card, tore off the plastic, and inserted it under the battery in his cell phone, then called Sophie.

"A car was burned out here last night," she said as soon she answered.

He was still slightly groggy from sleep. "Burned out? How?"

"I was woken by an explosion at about half past twelve. Albert and I went out, there was a car on fire, a Saab. Then the fire department turned up to put it out."

"A Saab?"

"Yes."

"How odd."

"That's putting it mildly.... Is this anything to do with you?"

"No."

Jens thought back through the evening. "I was there a few hours before. But you know that, I told you."

"What happened?"

"There was a man sitting in the Saab, a police officer. I was going to creep up on him and take some pictures. It was all supposed to happen without anyone noticing anything. That was the plan."

"But?"

"But plans rarely work out the way you want them to."

"So?"

"I saw Hector in your kitchen. Then Aron came walking up the road. He was heading straight for the man in the Saab."

Sophie waited.

"So I had to get rid of the policeman. If Aron had become suspicious of him, and found the surveillance equipment in the car—well, you can figure out the rest."

"What happened?"

"I jumped in the Saab and forced him to drive off."

"Then what?"

"I got out a few blocks away and made my way back into the city."

"That's all?"

"Yes, that's all. I got his name," Jens said.

"What's his name?"

"Lars Vinge."

"What does he look like?"

Jens went out into the hall, took out Lars Vinge's ID card, put it on the hall table, took a picture with no flash, and sent it over to her.

They were silent at both ends of the line. He could hear her breathing, then her phone beeped.

"That's him. I saw him last night, he was in the crowd watching as the car burned."

Her response surprised him.

"Are you sure?"

"Yes. And he was the one driving the Volvo the night Hector went missing. I've seen him somewhere else, too.... I'm not sure where, maybe on Djurgården. Did he see you?"

"No, I stayed hidden behind the driver's seat." Jens thought. "He must have set fire to the car himself."

"What for?"

"Maybe he felt a bit stupid once I'd taken his things."

"What did you take?"

"His phone, wallet, and the magazine of his gun...and the car keys. All the things he cared about."

"What happens now, Jens?"

He could hear how worried she was.

"Are the police more dangerous now?" she said.

"We might be lucky."

"How do you mean?"

"He's trying to keep this quiet, Officer Lars. Not telling anyone, maybe he feels ashamed. And that's why he set fire to the car."

"Or maybe not," she said quietly. "What if your actions have made everything worse, especially for Albert? Have you thought about that?"

"Yes, I have. But I weighed that up against you getting found out by Aron and Hector. That would have been worse."

He could hear steps outside.

"What are you doing today?" he found himself asking. He regretted it the moment he said it.

"I'm going to work."

He tried to find something else to say, but failed.

"Good-bye, Sophie."

She ended the call.

19

Sara had been waiting in a café across the road, sitting where she had a view of the door and could see when Lars came out. Her eyes followed him as he walked off down the street. She thought he looked different somehow, he seemed oddly stiff—as if he were ill.

Sara waited until he had disappeared from sight. Then she got up, went out onto the sidewalk, looked quickly in both directions, then crossed Swedenborgsgatan. In the elevator she took off her sunglasses and looked at her reflection. The bruise from when he had hit her covered her whole right eye. Some of the blue was turning almost green now. She looked terrible.

Sara unlocked the door with her keys and stepped inside the apartment. There was a pile of unopened mail by her feet, and a chair full of saucepans in the middle of the hall floor. There was a stale, musty smell.

She went into the office, it was dark and messy. An unmade mattress on the floor. The sheet had somehow ended up in the middle of the wooden floor. A stained pillow with no pillowcase, a blanket lying beside the mattress. Plates with remnants of old food, glasses, bits of paper towels... *My god.*

And all the work? A chaos of papers and pictures everywhere. And *the wall,* covered in manic notes. Sara took a deep breath, pulled out a chair and sat down, and just looked at the mess. A wave of sadness suddenly washed over her, sadness that the man she had been so fond of had lost his grip. That this was his life now. Sadness at the sheer... *collapse.* But the sorrow was short-lived, she wanted to feel sympathy but couldn't—instead she felt hatred, she hated him for what he had done to her. Sara looked at the photograph of a woman named Sophie, then a picture of a man who was evidently named Hector. More names, more pictures, Gunilla, Anders, Hasse, Albert, Aron... and a man without a name; he was sitting on a bench by the water, it looked like Strandvägen. Sara let her eyes roam over the wall, not understanding any of it. And the words! Words everywhere, words written in small writing wherever there was space, some scribbled out—manically scribbled out. Some of it was in big, looping letters, as if he had written it in different moods.

She switched on his computer. She'd known the password for ages, from back when they shared the machine. She pressed Enter. While she was waiting for it to start up she opened the desk drawers. Messy, no apparent logic. In the bottom drawer she found a folder that someone had drawn a flower on. She opened it. Printouts of photographs on A4 paper. A whole folder full of pictures of the same woman. She turned and looked at the wall... Sophie. Sara leafed through the folder. Hundreds of pictures of Sophie in various situations. Sophie cycling, Sophie in the kitchen, the picture taken from outside. Sophie walking, Sophie working in the garden. Sophie going through the entrance to a big building, possibly a hospital... Sophie driving a car and... Sophie asleep. *What the...?* A close-up of her sleeping face. The picture must have been taken in her bedroom, from close quarters. *This is really sick, this is obsessive.*

She kept on going through the drawers and found a pair of silk panties; they weren't hers, they were some expensive label. She put them back and found a notepad. She opened it up and leafed through it. Poems... Lars's appalling handwriting. Awful poems, flowery language: *summer meadow... thirsting for the well of the deepest love... Your beautiful hair blowing warmth over the evils of the world... You and I, Sophie, against the world...*

Sara stared at them with a feeling of disgust. The computer had finished loading. The desktop was full of folders with dates below them. She opened one of them. The folder was packed with audio files. She clicked on the first one and sound started coming from the computer's speakers. Sara listened; to start with it was mostly just background noise, then after a while she heard steps on a wooden floor, a door opening somewhere, time passed, a television was switched on and the female anchor's voice—she recognized it—could be heard in the distance. She left the file running, playing the nondescript sounds, and stood up to look at the faces on the wall.

She knew Gunilla was Lars's boss, but the others? Anders and Hasse might be colleagues.

Everything spread out from Sophie. She followed the lines, read Lars's notes. A pattern started to emerge.

"Albert, come on, food's ready!"

Sara started, the voice was coming from the computer, it was clear, sounded close to her. Sara listened as someone took plates out of a cupboard, was that Sophie? Silence followed, then the file ended. She went over to the computer, selected another file, and heard a telephone conversation, Sophie talking to someone she knew, laughing, asking questions. The conversation was gossip, it sounded like Sophie was talking to a girlfriend about someone who'd made a fool of themselves at a party. Sara clicked on a different file. Sophie questioning a boy about World War II, he knew the answers to all the questions except for one about the Molotov-Ribbentrop Pact. She looked at a picture of a teenage boy on the wall, Albert. He looked confident, alert, and happy. She clicked on another file, music from a stereo somewhere. Another file, Albert eating sandwiches with a friend, a succession of sick jokes and bursts of laughter. Then another file. Nothing but background noise again, then something that sounded like a slap. A conversation between the boy and Sophie. She heard the words *rape*, *witnesses*, *police*. Sara listened intently, then listened again—five times to the same clip. *Oh my God . . .*

She copied as many of the audio files as she could onto a USB memory stick. She took a camera from her pocket and photographed the wall, the pictures, the poems. . . .

She copied everything she could before she left.

He had picked up his V70 again. It was standing where he had left it a week earlier, in a garage out in Aspudden.

Lars skidded to a halt outside Lyckoslanten Care Home. He had been driving faster than he had realized, and had to brake sharply when he realized. *Unaware of speed driving through the city?* He slid over the grit-covered road, and managed to stop the Volvo just before it hit a parked car. Two youths walking past gave him the thumbs-up. Lars hesitated too long. A thumbs-up in response would have been too late.

He found a nurse inside the care home, told her who he was, and that he was there to go through his mother's belongings. The nurse nodded and said she'd unlock the door for him. He followed her, she had a big backside, he couldn't take his eyes off it. The nurse unlocked Rosie's room and Lars stepped inside.

"Come down to reception when you're done, we need your signature on a couple of forms."

He closed the door behind him and went straight into Rosie's bedroom, opened the door where she kept her prescriptions, and took them out. He glanced through them: Xanor, Lyrica, Sobril, Stesolid, Ketogan.

Lars tucked the prescriptions inside his jacket and went into the bathroom. Depolan in the bathroom cabinet; Ritalin, unopened; a few other bits and pieces; blister packs of Halcion and Fluscand. He reached for a jar on the top shelf and read the label: Hibernal.... He recognized the jar, it looked old. *Hibernal*... A memory flickered past and vanished as quickly as it had come. He put everything in his pockets. There was something on the middle shelf, behind the jar with the toothbrush, another old bottle. Lithium—*a classic*...

There was a knock on the door. Lars tidied up, and for some reason flushed the toilet.

A man with a beard and black shirt was standing outside. The little white square in his collar was shining up into his face.

"Lars Vinge? I'm Johan Rydén, priest."

Lars glared.

"May I come in?"

Lars stepped aside and shut the door after the priest. Johan said in a friendly tone: "I'm sorry for your loss."

It took Lars a moment to realize what the man meant.

"Thanks..."

"How are you feeling?"

How are you feeling? How are you feeling...?

Lars couldn't think of anything other than the fact that he wasn't feeling anything. But he could hardly say that, could he? He met the priest's gaze. Something began to grow inside Lars, something he felt comfortable with: a lie.

Lars sighed. "Yes, how does it feel when a loved one passes on...? Empty, sad...tragic."

Johan nodded slowly, as if he understood exactly what Lars meant. Lars bowed his head and went on.

"It's an odd feeling, losing your mother...."

Johan was nodding frantically as Lars shook his head.

"But...I don't know," he said quietly, pleased with his performance.

Lars looked up at Johan the priest's face, which radiated humanity, worthiness, and trust. Fuck, he must really have practiced that in front of the mirror at home.

"No, how could we know, Lars?"

Lars looked sad.

"Your mother chose to end her own life.... You shouldn't feel burdened by that. She was ill, she was tired, she had lived her life."

"Poor Mom," Lars whispered.

He searched in Johan's eyes, saw that the priest believed him. The priest believed in Lars...and in God.

Lars left Lyckoslanten without looking back. He drove to the nearest pharmacy and picked up everything on the prescriptions, hoping the old woman behind the counter wouldn't see on her computer that the intended recipient was dead. She didn't. Full speed ahead for a new top-up.

He introduced himself as Alfonse. He was young, maybe twenty-five, and smiled confidently as if he thought that this whole life business was enormous fun.

"Hector," Hector said as Alfonse shook his hand.

Alfonse looked around the office and sat down.

"Books?"

"I run a publishing company, I'm a publisher."

Alfonse made little noises with his mouth and smiled.

"A publisher . . . ," he said quietly to himself.

Hector examined Alfonse and thought he could detect a family resemblance.

"You look a lot like your uncle."

Alfonse gave Hector a theatrical look, as though the comparison offended him.

"I certainly hope not."

They smiled at each other.

"How is Don Ignacio?"

"Splendid. He's just bought himself a new airplane, so he's happy as can be."

"I'm pleased to hear it. Pass on my greetings and congratulations."

Hector adjusted his posture in the chair.

"Let's talk about the reason for your visit, then I'd be only too happy to invite you to dinner, if you don't have other plans?"

"Thanks, Hector, but not today. Stockholm's full of compatriots that I have to see."

"How long are you staying?"

"There's a certain lady in this city that I have a terrible weakness for, I'm staying with her. This morning it struck me that it's so nice waking up there and having breakfast with her that I shall be staying longer than planned."

"Then I'm sure we'll find time to have dinner."

"More than likely. And I'm sure we can reach agreement on the purpose of my visit."

Their eyes lingered on each other's. Alfonse's tone changed.

"Don Ignacio is worried," he said in a low voice. "He's wondering why you've stopped placing orders. We understand that your supplies in Paraguay must be exhausted by now, but he hasn't heard from you or your father for a long time. We want to know that everything's under control . . . we want to know what's happening, and naturally to reassure ourselves that you are all well and not suffering any anxieties."

Hector took out a cigarillo.

"We've had some problems with our supply line."

Alfonse waited while Hector inhaled the tobacco smoke.

"It was hijacked."

"By whom?"

"Germans..."

Alfonse looked at Hector.

"Really?"

Hector blew the smoke out.

"It's a complicated story, we've just regained control but we're going to let the route lie low for a while until things have been sorted out."

"How long?"

"Don't know."

Alfonse nodded.

"Don Ignacio will be happy to hear that all is well with you, but, now that I have reassured myself that you are OK... Well, let me put it like this: Don Ignacio believes that there is an agreement. Under the terms of this agreement, we supply you with vitamins and the transport of these to Ciudad del Este. It's a rolling process. Now for some reason it has stopped. Don Ignacio doesn't want to go so far as to describe it as a breach of contract, but... Well, you understand."

Hector stretched.

"I don't see it as a firm agreement. We didn't agree on any specific time scale.... We agreed on a price. Don Ignacio has always received his money from us, hasn't he?"

"And he is grateful for that, very grateful."

"And we are grateful that it is so straightforward doing business with you," Hector said.

Alfonse was well dressed and polite. He was good-looking, he had the South American thick dark hair and sharp features, and his prominent chin and cheekbones lent him an appealing air of toughness. In all likelihood, women found him attractive. He made a laid-back impression in spite of his almost permanent smile. But behind that Hector could see madness. He could see madness in someone from a mile away. He had seen it the moment Alfonse walked through the door. He had seen it in Don Ignacio Ramirez the first time he met him a decade before. He liked that quality in others; it made him feel a sort of empathy for them, a kinship. Hector decided he liked Alfonse.

"Then we have a problem," Alfonse said.

Hector shrugged his shoulders.

"I don't know that it's a problem, see it as a pause."

"That word doesn't exist in our vocabulary. Don Ignacio is counting on your money, in return for his services. If you want to take a pause, as you put it, that doesn't affect the terms of our agreement."

"But we have no such agreement, my dear Alfonse."

"Don Ignacio considers that we do, and when he considers something to be the case, it usually is. . . ."

Hector thought for a moment.

"Can I offer you anything?"

Alfonse shook his head. "What problems do you have, are they anything we can help you with? These Germans, perhaps we could help, if they are causing problems?"

Hector considered the offer, knowing that the Colombians' help would be costly in the long run.

"No, we can manage, it's a small problem."

"Tell me . . ."

Hector smoked his cigarillo.

"For reasons that we don't know they stepped in and took over the whole operation, bribing and presumably threatening our associates. Then we went in and took everything back, but things got a little heated. The captain of the ship we have been using wants to lie low for a while."

Alfonse weighed this up for a moment.

"In that case there are two options," he said.

Hector waited.

"Either you pay and we replenish your stores in Paraguay and you move it onto the market before the next delivery from us."

"Or?"

"Or else we contact your German friends. They seem to be more interested in doing business than you."

Hector and Alfonse sized each other up. Hector sighed, smiling at the fact that he had fallen into the trap so easily.

"Let's carry on as usual," Hector said. "You send new supplies, I'll send the money, just give me a bit of time."

Alfonse made a gesture of gratitude.

"So, how are you going to spend your time with your fellow countrymen in Stockholm? Do you need any tips?" Hector asked.

"No, they've already booked a table, we're going out to eat somewhere."

He looked at his watch.

"Then we're going dancing at a club, the name of which I can't remember. Would you care to join us?"

"Thanks, but I shall be detained elsewhere."

"So we'll be able to conclude our business before I fly home?"

"Whenever suits you."

Alfonse stared at Hector for a moment.

"You seem to be a good man, Hector Guzman."

"As do you, Alfonse Ramirez."

Alfonse left Hector's office, stepped out onto the street, and turned right. Hasse Berglund let the stylish Colombian get a little way ahead before standing up, folding the newspaper he had just been looking through, and following him.

Gunilla's cell phone buzzed in her pocket. She didn't recognize the number on the screen.

"Yes?"

"Is that Gunilla Strandberg?"

"Who's this?"

"My name's Sara Jonsson. I'd like to meet you."

"Do we know each other?"

"Not really. My ex-boyfriend works for you."

"Oh?"

"Lars Vinge."

The penny dropped. *Sara Jonsson…* Gunilla knew she was some sort of writer. Lars had mentioned her in his interview. Gunilla had checked her out: Sara Jonsson, freelance journalist, mainly cultural stories, seldom published anything.

"Of course, was it anything in particular?"

"Yes."

"And what's that, then?"

"I want to meet you for a talk."

Gunilla considered her tone of voice. She sounded tense and nervous. And was trying to hide it behind a rather indecisive decisiveness.

"Where would you like to meet, Sara?"

"We can meet on Djurgården, by Djurgårdsbrunn."

"OK . . . When?"

"In an hour."

"So soon?"

"Yes."

"See you then."

Gunilla smiled as she ended the call, but the smile faded as quickly as it had come.

Erik and Gunilla parked in front of the Värdshuset restaurant. Sara Jonsson was waiting outside. She was wearing a cheap, washed-out blouse from some mass-market clothing chain, dark sunglasses, and a skirt that stopped at her knees. She had forgotten to shave her legs and her unbrushed hair was pulled into an untidy knot on her head.

Sara's hand was cold and clammy when they shook hands. Her anxiety was clearly visible—her sunglasses only provided partial protection.

"Well, Sara, shall we go in and sit down?" Gunilla asked.

"No. I'd rather we walked."

"Why not, it's lovely weather."

They started to walk toward the little bridge over the canal.

"How long have you and Lars lived together?"

"We're not living together anymore."

"I'm sorry to hear that."

Sara was off somewhere else. Gunilla and Erik could see it, and they exchanged a quick glance.

"I don't know where to start," she said once they had crossed the footbridge.

Gunilla waited patiently.

"Lars has changed."

"In what way?"

"I don't know, and it doesn't really matter, but because of that I started looking for answers."

Sara was still nervous.

"He still works for you, doesn't he?"

Gunilla nodded.

"Then you know he's been away a lot, working nights, sleeping during the day.... We lost touch with each other."

"And you'd like me to alter his roster...?"

Sara shook her head.

"This isn't about that, like I said, we're not living together now...."

There was a note of hurt in her voice.

"Why not, if you don't mind me asking?"

Sara stopped and turned to look at Gunilla, taking off her sunglasses. Gunilla looked at her eye.

"What happened?"

"What do you think?"

Gunilla inspected her black eye.

"Lars?"

Sara didn't answer, put the sunglasses back on, and kept on walking.

"I started looking through his things, his private things. Trying to find an explanation for why he'd changed."

Gunilla listened.

"The more I looked, the more I realized that he was doing something outside... how can I put it? Outside his actual authority."

"How do you mean?"

"I mean that I've got an idea of what's going on."

"Oh, so what's going on?"

Sara was walking with her eyes on the ground, then looked up.

"I'm a journalist."

"Yes, I know."

"As a journalist I have a responsibility to report abuses of power."

Gunilla raised one eyebrow.

"Goodness, that sounds very noble."

Sara took a deep breath.

"I know what you're doing. You're bugging people, threatening them, stalking them."

"Now, I'm not altogether sure I know what you mean," Gunilla said.

"I mean Sophie, I mean Hector."

Sara had no idea how everything fit together. She only had the names, she only had the hazy information that she'd gotten from listening to the computer files. An awareness that some sort of bugging was going on, as well as a bit of information about Gunilla's previous cases that she'd gotten from police records—but she knew no more than that. But she wasn't about to let Gunilla know that. This was her scoop, this was going to lift her out of the relentless dullness of the culture pages to something better. She was going to be an investigative reporter, a person on the side of justice, exposing abuses of power to ordinary citizens. She felt more at home there, it was more *her,* it was more Sara Jonsson.

Gunilla managed to conceal her surprise.

"I can tell you that we're investigating a number of different cases, some of which are at a highly confidential stage of investigation, and any attempt to leak information would be a criminal offense. If you want information, you'll get it, but in the fullness of time, not when it could jeopardize our investigations and the officers working on them."

Sara pulled out her next trump card.

"Albert. The witnesses, the police. Rape. He's fifteen years old!"

Gunilla was staring at her. Sara examined her face for any sign of a reaction. Had she guessed right? Maybe.

"What did you say?"

"You heard what I said."

Erik tried to rescue the situation.

"We're in the middle of a case. We're working under the strictest confidentiality. Certain aspects of this investigation are highly sensitive. Whatever you've seen or heard, you need to keep it to yourself until we give you the all-clear to publish anything," he said.

Sara kept calm. She had a feeling that she'd hit the right spot, and looked intently into Gunilla's eyes.

"Bugging, illegal surveillance, Sophie... Where exactly are you going with this?"

Gunilla was staring at Sara with something like sorrow in her eyes.

"Well?" Sara's nerves had settled, and she pulled out her ace. "Patricia Nordström, does that name mean anything to you?"

Gunilla tried to maintain an unconcerned expression but ended up with a smile that lacked any joy, stiff and unnatural.

"Patricia Nordström disappeared five years ago," Sara went on. "She disappeared while you were working with her. There's nothing in the records to suggest that her disappearance had anything to do with that gangster Zdenko, the one they called the King of the Racetrack, she disappeared while *you* were working with her. Does that apply to Sophie now? Is she going to disappear too?"

Sara was gambling everything. She really had no idea what she was talking about, she just knew that there was something rotten in all this, and she'd probably known it ever since Lars started working on the case. Moving from beat cop to National Crime overnight, that was unlikely. And he changed from Lars into someone completely different, which was just as unlikely. . . .

Gunilla didn't seem to be able to look away from Sara. Then she turned and walked away. Even Erik was surprised, and could do nothing but follow her.

Gunilla was upset when they pulled out of the garage to drive back in toward the city.

"Stupid, stupid girl," she said to herself.

Erik was silent behind the wheel.

"Why now?" she went on.

Erik knew she wasn't expecting any answers from him.

"Doesn't she understand?"

Gunilla was staring straight ahead.

"Is this the same old story again?" she went on.

They passed the Kaknäs Tower.

"How could she have found all this out?"

Gunilla sighed, and fell deep into thought.

"Damn," she whispered to herself.

"Patricia Nordström? How did she find out about her?" Erik asked.

Gunilla folded the sun visor down.

"That's in police records. There were a few little details that I never managed to get rid of. I don't know how she's managed to get hold of them, maybe she just requested to see them. But it doesn't matter. She's figured something out that she's not supposed to figure out."

"With Lars's help?"

"I don't know, I doubt it.... You saw what he did to her."

Gunilla thought for a moment.

"What did she say before she mentioned Patricia?"

"Bugging."

"Before that?"

"Albert."

"How could she know about Albert?" she asked.

Erik didn't have an answer.

Gunilla sighed and folded the sun visor up.

"We'll hold back on Lars. We'll keep him at a distance, as usual. But Sara..."

Erik turned onto Strandvägen.

"Maybe it's time for Hasse's initiation," she said.

Erik muttered in agreement.

"Damn," she whispered to herself again.

Ralph Hanke was in a terrible mood. As usual when this happened, he main- tained an impenetrable silence. Anyone around him felt it like the electricity from a high-tension cable. Everyone kept their distance.

He gazed out across central Munich through the picture window on the seventh floor. It was misty. The undersides of the gray clouds were almost at the same height as him. A few floors up and he wouldn't have been able to see a thing—which might actually have been a good thing. He often stood and looked out at this view when he couldn't make sense of his thoughts. He rarely noticed anything, just thought better when he had the world beneath him. Today he was wearing a cardigan. That rarely happened, but when it did he liked it. Maybe because it meant he was escaping his suit, could feel a bit freer. But the cardigan also seemed to have another effect on him. It created a particular mood in Ralph. His thoughts became clearer, his mind colder, more angry, like today. And a clear, cold thought in an angry mind made life's decisions much easier to take.

The intercom buzzed.

"Herr Hanke?"

His secretary's calm voice filled the room.

"Herr Gentz is here."

The door to the office opened, Roland Gentz came in and walked across the parquet floor, sat down in an armchair, and took some documents out of his bag. They never said hello to each other. They never had. Not through impoliteness, just a tacit agreement that this was the sort of men they were when they were working—men who didn't bother with pleasantries.

Ralph didn't move from the window. The dull weather, combined with all his problems, was making him long for a drink. He looked out over the city.

"Do you want a drink?"

Roland looked up from his papers, surprised at the question.

"When did we stop drinking during the day?" Ralph asked.

Roland thought.

"Sometime during the '90s... Around the time we stopped wearing ties, I think."

Ralph walked toward his desk.

"Two good things," he said with a sigh. He sat down.

"Well?"

"Sure, why not?"

Ralph pressed the intercom.

"Frau Wagner. Two single malts, no ice."

"Yes, Herr Hanke."

Ralph assumed a patient posture, knitting his hands together. Roland leafed through his papers.

"We've been paid for those three shopping malls in Britain. We're still having trouble in Hamburg, with the bridge project.... Something to do with the hydraulics, it's going to take time. We're on track to get the contract with the Americans, but we're going to have to be patient, everyone wants in on it."

Ralph wasn't really listening, he'd spun his chair around and was looking out the window again: Roland went on talking in the background. After a few minutes Ralph interrupted him.

"Never mind all that.... What's happening in Sweden?"

"Sweden? Nothing new..."

"What's the latest?"

Roland thought for a moment.

"Mikhail's partner is in the hospital...."

"Will he talk?"

Roland shook his head. "No."

"How do you know?"

"Mikhail says so."

"They've been very quiet."

Roland didn't answer.

"And the go-between, the man with the guns?"

Roland adjusted his position in the chair.

"Can I tell you what I think, Ralph?"

Ralph looked out over the city.

"Go ahead."

"Why don't we just drop all that? It's getting in the way of our other business, it represents a risk factor that gets bigger with each passing day... and as a project it's utterly insignificant.... Can't we just let it go and concentrate on what's really important?"

Ralph turned his chair to face Roland.

"What's the name of the man we bought?"

Roland wondered if Ralph had heard a word of what he'd just said.

"Carlos, Carlos Fuentes."

"Who is he?"

"Some background character who owns a few restaurants. Some sort of cover for Hector, I don't know exactly how."

"Let's use him a bit more."

"I think he's used up."

"How?"

"He was the one who got Hector to come to the restaurant so that Mikhail and his partner could pick him up. They're not stupid enough to think that that was a coincidence."

"Is he dead?"

Roland shrugged. "Maybe..."

There was a light knock at the door. Frau Wagner came in with a tray and two thick-bottomed whiskey glasses. She served the drinks, then left the room.

They didn't drink at once, sniffing at their glasses. Ralph drank first, and Roland followed him. They swallowed and savored the aftertaste in their mouths. That was where whiskey was at its best—a taste that conjured up false memories and dramatically beautiful feelings about something that was beyond the reach of human hands. Maybe that was why a certain type of romantic was susceptible to ruination by drink.

They put their glasses down.

"Have we got anyone in Spain?" Ralph asked.

"How do you mean?"

"Have we got anyone like Mikhail in Spain?"

Roland shook his head. "No."

"Sort something out. I want a sleeper there, someone we can call on at short notice."

"For what?"

"For when we need force. Ideally two, three men."

"I don't agree," Gentz said quietly.

Ralph didn't respond. The sounds of central Munich could be heard far below them.

"The woman, then? Who's she, what do we know?"

"Nothing... Just a woman, do you want me to take a closer look?"

Ralph thought, raising the glass to his mouth.

"Yes, do that."

20

***A** white peony had just opened up. It was improbably beautiful, big* and broad, symmetrical and dreamlike. Tommy Jansson looked at it. He was sitting back in one of Gunilla's white-painted wooden chairs. The table in the arbor had been set, a little corner of the garden that smelled of old-fashioned roses and clematis.

Tommy Jansson, departmental head of the Intelligence Division within National Crime, the department in which Gunilla had been employed for the past fourteen years. In formal terms he was her boss, an old tough guy who drove an American car and had a .357 in his holster. His attitude toward life was like a child's, his attitude toward work strictly professional. She valued him highly as a boss, but also as a friend and colleague.

Gunilla put down a plate of freshly baked cinnamon buns. Tommy waited until she had sat opposite him.

"I hear they call you Mommy."

Gunilla smiled.

"Who says so?"

"Your brother. I called him on the way over here to get an idea of how things are going for you all."

She made herself more comfortable.

"Why did you call him?"

"Because I did."

Gunilla poured English tea into Tommy's cup. He took a sip before going on.

"A bit of time has passed now. People are starting to wonder."

"Oh?" Gunilla said.

"The prosecutor's waiting for you to send some material over."

"You know how I work, Tommy; you know I don't like to let anything go until it's watertight, so that some stressed-out prosecutor doesn't misunderstand and misuse it, and the whole thing ends up going nowhere."

"I know, but I've got people pestering me. I can't keep covering up for you all the time."

The birds were twittering in the trees, the area was very quiet. She peered at him.

"Covering up for me?"

"You know what I mean."

"No, I don't."

Tommy looked at her.

"It isn't just the prosecutor asking," he went on. "But she's airing her theories. It's unsettling people."

"Berit Ståhl?"

Tommy nodded.

"What's she saying?"

"Do you really want to know?"

Gunilla didn't answer. Tommy tried to find a more comfortable position on the wooden chair.

"She's saying she can't understand why you've been given such a free hand."

"And what do you say to that, Tommy?"

"I say what I've always said, that you're one of the best I've got."

"And what does she say?"

Tommy took a sip of tea, resting the cup on his thigh.

"That there's nothing to suggest that."

"To suggest what?"

"She's been through all your cases from the past fifteen years, and claims that the percentage of your cases that have led to convictions is way below the average."

Gunilla sighed.

"That's exactly what I'm trying to say. What else?"

"That's all."

"No, it isn't."

Gunilla didn't take her eyes from Tommy. He looked down.

"She says that the reason you work the way you do, with your own group, without any oversight, in a separate location and so on, is a way for you to build up something you can be put in charge of when the police department is reorganized in a few years' time."

"I see. And?"

Tommy shrugged.

"That's what she's saying."

"That I'm ambitious?"

Tommy sighed.

"Nobody cares...yet. But if she continues making noise, she's going to make people nervous, and they'll start asking questions."

Tommy went on in a low voice.

"If you're floundering, Gunilla, if you haven't got as much as you wish you had, I want you to tell me. I've protected you before, and I'll do it again in the future. But if I find out that you're not being straight and open with me..."

"Don't worry," she said quietly.

He rubbed his ear with his knuckles.

"I'm not..."

She let out a laugh. "Of course you are."

He didn't answer.

"Stick to the agreement we had at the start, Tommy."

"What agreement's that?"

"That I don't need to report back," Gunilla said.

"Who's saying I've come out here for a report?"

"Why else are you here? For the buns?"

"Yes, the buns."

Neither of them was smiling.

Tommy considered what had been said. Then he carried on thinking; she was like him, they thought the same way, had the same opinions. It wasn't anything they talked about, there was a lot they didn't need to say. They knew that they generally shared the same attitude toward things.

Tommy broke the deadlock.

"I want to know where you are, and when you think you'll be able to provide us with concrete evidence from your investigations. And I also want to know if you need anything."

A chill came over her.

"You bastard," she said.

He pretended not to understand.

"What?"

"I know what you're trying to do, and you won't succeed."

"What are you talking about, Gunilla?"

"If you think you can gather information now so that someone else can take over, you're very much mistaken."

Tommy shook his head.

"I'm not here to fire you."

"That's not what I said. But I know what you're up to."

"So what am I up to?"

"You're protecting your own position, gathering information, and if it looks like things aren't going the way you want, you'll replace me. I've seen you do it before."

Tommy was starting to get annoyed.

"Look, stop this game now."

"You stop, Tommy. I mean what I say, I'm not going to change. We've got an agreement. No one's going to change that... least of all Berit Ståhl."

"Oh, just ignore her," Tommy said.

Gunilla relaxed.

"Thanks..."

He shook his head.

"No, you don't have to thank me. You seem to have misunderstood our agreement."

They could hear children laughing in a nearby garden.

"What do you mean?"

"That it's mainly about me and the other bosses."

Gunilla didn't reply. He looked at her intently.

"You're sitting in the shit," he said.

She wrinkled her nose.

"What sort of language is that?"

"Aren't you?"

She shook her head.

"No, I'm not," she said in a low voice.

They'd had hundreds of similar conversations over the years, all of them circling the same basic point—Tommy wanted control, and she didn't want to let go of it.

"How's Monica?" Gunilla asked. Her tone was gentler now.

Tommy looked out at the garden.

"She's good, no obvious symptoms yet."

"What do the doctors say?"

He met her gaze.

"That they don't know. But that they do know. More or less."

"Which means?"

Tommy lowered his voice.

"That the illness is there, that ALS is incurable, that Monica will start to show the first symptoms before too long."

Gunilla could see how upset he was. He looked down into his teacup.

"Do you know what the worst thing is?" he asked quietly.

Gunilla shook her head.

"I'm more frightened than she is."

Silence settled again. Just the sound of insects buzzing, the wind in the trees, birds singing.

Tommy drained his cup and put it on the table, then stood up. He was back to being a boss again.

"I'm behind you, Gunilla. But make sure you ask for help if you need it."

Tommy left the arbor and headed off toward the gate. She watched his back as he went. A bumblebee was hovering behind her.

It was half past two in the morning. Lars picked the lock of the terrace door, it opened easily now. He took off his shoes, took two steps into the living room in his socks. Everyone in the world was asleep. He did what he had come for, crept over to the floor lamp beside the sofa, and looked closely at it. He found the little threadlike microphone that Anders had installed, and carefully removed it with his thumb and forefinger. He put it in the little plastic bag he had in his pocket, and retreated toward the terrace door. A thought struck him and he stopped. The thought wasn't framed in words, it was more like a feeling, something along the lines of: She's lying up there... *oh my God.*

Lars made his way upstairs, genuinely drawn up there. He crept up, silently and carefully.

The door to her room was ajar. Lars put his ear to the gap and listened. Low, soft breathing from within. Slowly he pushed the door open, it all happened without a sound. One careful step and he was standing on the carpet.

There she lay, in almost the same position as last time, on her back with her hair over the pillow, just a few yards away from him. Doubt crept up on him. What was he doing there...? He was about to turn back...but...He stared at her, at her beauty, felt his longing grow inside him, his doubts vanished. Lars wanted to cuddle up next to her, tell her he was feeling bad. Maybe she'd want to comfort him. A sound woke him from his fantasy. Thin fluttering, catching sounds. The noise was coming from behind the curtain. A moth. Its wings were beating against the glass in a tortuous desire to get out, toward the faint light from the streetlamp.

Lars's pulse was calm, his breathing was calm.... Very slowly he got down on his knees and crept toward her on all fours. Carefully, carefully, soon he'd be able to detect her scent. He was getting hard, and imagined putting his hand over her mouth...climbing on top of her, and... *No, not like that.* Lars cursed himself. But he could just... *No, he couldn't...could he?* He fought against the idea, but as on every other day of the week, impulse got the better of Lars Vinge on this occasion as well.

Kneeling carefully he unbuttoned his trousers, pulled the zipper down, and put his left hand inside. He didn't want to do it, but he couldn't help himself. Lars closed his eyes, making love to her in his imagination. She was groaning his name, begging for more, stroking his back, telling him she loved him. The moth's wings fluttered against the window. Lars was kissing the empty air when he came inside his trousers. The feeling of emptiness that followed was all-consuming.

He made his way cautiously down the stairs, crept across the living room, and left the house the same way he had entered.

They couldn't even look at each other. Anders's hand was hanging low, Hasse sighed with every other breath. They were sitting in Anders's Honda, parked up on Bastugatan. Hasse broke the silence.

"Have you done it before?"

Anders stared out into the night, then nodded.

"What's it like?"

Anders didn't want to go into it.

He felt in his pocket. Held out his hand to Berglund, white pills.

"What are they?"

"They help. Take two."

"I never take pills."

"Are you thick, or what?"

Hasse didn't understand.

"What?"

"Take them!"

Anders shouted the words, then sighed and leaned against the door, still staring out into the night. Hasse took the pills and swallowed them.

Time passed slowly. It was sucking its way through thick, heavy walls, as if time itself wanted them to suffer. As if time wanted to give them a choice. Anders hated that feeling. He looked restlessly at the clock. Five minutes before the appointed hour he opened the car door.

"Let's go."

They left the car, walked to the door, let themselves in with the correct code, and made their way up the stone staircase.

Dahl, it said on the door. *S. Jonsson* was written on a piece of paper taped underneath.

They listened for noises. Anders started picking the lock. He wasn't trembling, didn't hesitate at all, the pills were working. The lock opened. They conjured forth total silence, listening for the slightest sound that shouldn't be there.

Anders put his hand on the door handle, pressed it down slowly until the door slid open a crack, waited a few seconds, then opened it just enough for them to be able to slip through.

Anders and Hasse stood stock-still in the hall. To their right was a small kitchen, narrow, with a table folded down by the window, two folding chairs, not much storage space. It was a one-room apartment, and a small one at that. Anders took a step farther in. A television, a sofa, a coffee table, a picture, a floor lamp . . . a bed behind a curtain. She was lying there, they could just make out the faint sound of her breathing.

They took off their shoes and crept soundlessly into the room. Anders crouched down and unrolled a Gore-Tex sleeve, revealing a syringe nestling on a piece of soft cloth. He picked it up gently and unscrewed the plastic cap protecting the needle.

Hasse kept behind him. He was no longer breathing so heavily, the pills had gone to work on him as well. Anders stood up. He met Hasse's gaze, *Let's do it*. They began to move silently toward the bed.

Sara was sleeping on her stomach, making little snoring sounds. Hasse moved toward the top of the bed, carefully pushed the curtain aside, crept in behind it, and stood over her upper body, ready to grab her if she woke up. Anders sat down silently at the end of the bed. He would have to lift the covers, and he tested it tentatively, raising it just an inch or two. She didn't move. Anders lifted the covers a few more inches, Sara went on sleeping soundly. He couldn't see any feet, and lifted a bit farther, and Sara kicked instinctively in her sleep. Anders started. One foot rubbed the other; she muttered something, it sounded stern, like she was telling someone off. Then silence again. Anders and Hasse looked at each other. Anders took a deep breath, concentrated, put the syringe in his right hand, his forefinger and index finger on the plastic wings, his thumb on the plunger. Her recent movement had left one foot outside the duvet. Anders nodded to Hasse that he should get ready. Hasse stood with his legs wide apart, his arms held out in the air.

Anders looked at the syringe. The liquid was transparent, unpleasantly transparent. He waited, as if hesitating, as if wondering what he was doing. Anders put the thin needle against the sole of Sara's right foot and pushed it in about half an inch. She reacted to the pain; Anders caught her foot and held it as Hasse pressed her arms down on the bed with all his weight. She screamed into the mattress as Anders injected the liquid into her system. She struggled and shook; Anders lost his grip of her foot, with the needle still in it. She was kicking instinctively with both feet. The needle broke and the syringe flew off. Hasse was using all his strength to try to hold her down.

It took several long seconds for the drug to make its way to her heart and make it stop beating. Sara stopped screaming, she stopped kicking. It became more silent than either of them could ever have imagined.

The men stared at the woman lying on her stomach on the bed, then glanced briefly at each other. Hasse let go of her and backed a step away from her.

"Holy shit," he whispered. "She went all limp!"

He backed farther away.

"Completely limp...," he said, his eyes fixed on Sara. "Is she dead?"

Anders stood up and looked at Sara. She was lying in almost the same position as when they arrived. Her head on the pillow, her hair a bit mussed up, her face to the left. She was staring at the curtain.

"Yes...she's dead."

They stood there, not moving, not for any particular reason, just a feeling of not wanting to leave, of wanting to stop time, to wind it back, to make it undone. They stared at their perverse accomplishment. Hasse swallowed hard, and Anders pulled himself together.

"Find the syringe, it's here somewhere."

Hasse didn't understand at first, and looked questioningly at Anders.

"The syringe, find the syringe!"

Hasse started looking. Anders sat down beside Sara's foot again with a miniature flashlight in his mouth. He took off his glove and carefully stroked her sole. He found the little broken needle, and pulled it out with his thumb and forefinger, like he was pulling a splinter out of a child's foot on a summer's day.

Hasse found the syringe a short distance away. They did a circuit of the apartment, searching carefully through boxes and cupboards. Anders found Sara's camera in a jewelry box, as well as her notes and a diary, and tucked them all inside his jacket.

They cleaned up after themselves, left the apartment, and drove through the Stockholm night. Anders put his phone to his ear.

"It's done," he said.

Gunilla spoke quietly, possibly out of respect, possibly because she had just woken up.

"You know this serves a higher purpose. Much higher than you are aware of at the moment."

Anders didn't answer.

"How are you feeling?" she said.

She really did sound like a mom. Not his mom, someone else's mom.

"Like last time."

"That had a higher purpose as well. And those purposes are intertwined, you know that, don't you? This had to be done, everything was at stake."

Anders remained silent.

"It was either her or us, Anders. She knew about Patricia Nordström."

He started. "What?"

"Yes."

"How?"

"Don't know, she must have dug something out of the register."

"What about Lars? What does he know?"

"No idea. Possibly more than we think."

"Is he dangerous?"

"What do you think?"

"My instinct says no. . . . But who knows?"

"Yes, who knows. . . ."

He heard her sighing.

"How was it for Hasse?" she asked.

Anders looked at Hasse's slouched head and empty face as he steered the car through the night.

"OK, I think."

"Good," she said quietly.

They drove around the city, breathing, staring. . . . Neither of them wanted to go home alone. Hasse was uptight. Anders could tell, and patted him on the shoulder a couple of times.

"It'll pass."

"When?" Hasse muttered.

“In a few days,” he lied.

Hasse drove on through the city night.

“Can you tell me the whole story now?” he said.

“What do you want to know?”

“Everything,” he whispered.

“Like what?”

“Start with why you killed the blonde, the King of the Racetrack’s bird. That was you, wasn’t it?” His voice was low, almost a whisper.

Anders realized his right leg was twitching restlessly. He stopped it.

“We didn’t have any choice. She’d seen one of our men finish off one of the King of the Racetrack’s thugs.”

“Why did you finish him off?” Hasse asked.

Anders wiped his eyes.

“It was total fucking chaos.... I can hardly remember exactly what happened.”

Anders looked out through the window. The buildings they were passing looked suddenly threatening.

“There was one guy who was close to Zdenko, so we targeted him first. We wanted to turn him, make him an informant, but he played both ways. He shafted us so fucking badly. I had complete confidence in him; Gunilla and Erik did, too.... But he was loyal to his boss. We’d misjudged everything. By the time we realized it it was all falling apart, we were on the brink of losing the whole damn thing. So we starting to work on Patricia Nordström, Zdenko’s bird. She helped us get what we wanted. I set up a nice little suicide for the traitor.”

Anders cleared his throat.

“But she saw it all. Got hysterical, started screaming and shouting, saying she was going to the police.... The whole thing was totally fucked-up.”

“What did you do?”

Anders looked at Hasse, let the silence answer for him.

“How?”

Anders didn’t like remembering.

“Like the journalist, tonight’s been like some fucking déjà vu.... But before that I shot that bastard Zdenko through the head out at Jägersro.... I was wearing a wig. The story you read in the tabloids about gang wars and all that crap was pure bullshit. We lifted as much of his fortune as we could get our hands on.”

"What happened to the blonde?"

The indistinct outlines of the city were starting to solidify as the first rays of sun appeared on the horizon.

"She's way down at the bottom of the sea," Anders said to himself.

The feeling of unease was there again when she woke up. She felt she wanted to get away from the bed, as if the room were somehow infected.

Sophie made herself a cup of tea, went over to the cellar steps, pulled the monitor out of its hiding place, and switched it on. Same routine every morning. She was holding it in front of her as she walked back to the kitchen, sipping the warm tea. Suddenly an image appeared. It was night, a streetlamp in the distance was casting a thin glow over the living room. A man in dark clothes walked past the camera toward the stairs, then the film stopped. It had lasted four seconds. She froze to ice and put the teacup down so she didn't drop it. All the energy had drained out of her. Another clip started, the same man coming from the opposite direction, from the stairs and into the living room, where he vanished from the picture.

What she felt was no ordinary fear welling up inside her. This was something else. A terror that made her feel sick, dizzy, and weak all at the same time. She watched again, the recording was dark and grainy. Hostile and threatening. She located the scroll function, rewound the clip, and froze the picture. The man was caught in a pose with one leg in front of the other. His hair was wet, sweaty.

There was no doubt about it, it was Lars, Lars the police officer....

Svante Carlgren was shaving in front of the bathroom mirror when his new cell phone rang. He knew who it was, only one person had the number. He held the cell a little way from the shaving foam on his cheek.

"Carl Gustaf," he answered.

"Håkan here..."

Svante took another stroke with the razor. "What's on your mind?"

"I need more info about your guy."

"What for?"

"Because I've used the usual channels, searched, and checked with my sources, but haven't come up with anything yet. We were hoping it would be someone we were already aware of, but that doesn't seem to be the case."

"I've already paid you. And now you're calling to say you haven't got anything."

"I didn't say that."

"Yes, you did." Svante was shaving between his nose and upper lip.

"I need a better description from you."

"I've already told you what I can."

"We need to meet, I want you to look at some pictures. Then we can put together a clearer profile of the man."

Svante was sitting in his car in the garage of Villa Källhagen. He had the window open, a few people were strolling between the inn and the Maritime History Museum. He was unconsciously drumming his fingers on the steering wheel—he hated waiting.

An SUV pulled in ahead of him. Håkan got out. Gray shirt, cropped hair on top, shaved at the sides. His eyes sat deep in his skull, as if they were permanently in shadow. A shorter man got out of the passenger side, same hairstyle, older.

"Shall we take a drive in my car?" Svante asked through the open window.

Håkan shook his head.

"We're going to take a walk."

Svante got out and held out his hand. Håkan seemed nervous, shook his hand briefly.

"This is my colleague, Leif Rydbäck," he said with a gesture. Svante shook hands with the shorter man.

The trio began to walk from the garage toward the water.

The telephoto lens captured clear pictures of the men. Anders took twenty or so photographs from the backseat of his car. He knew who the guy with cropped hair and the gray shirt was, and the smaller one as well, but...damn, he couldn't remember their names. He'd seen them before. The tall one had been a bit of a gangster, but that was a long time ago now. Anders searched his memory. He had it on the tip of his tongue. Something to do with an investigation into the restaurant mafia and a load of suspected terrorist idiots, he'd had something to do with that. Not as one of the terrorists, but some shady figure who started making threats against a gang of Syrians who owned several restaurants around the city.... What the hell was his name? And the little one? Anders thought and thought...the names wouldn't come.

He called Reutersvärd, an old colleague from the Security Police. "What the hell was his name?"

"Zivkovic, Håkan Zivkovic. Supposed to have gone straight. Runs his own security company, does surveillance jobs for various insurance firms, watches people, almost exclusively on the orders of jealous partners who want photographic evidence of their worst fears. He still has some of his old lowlife contacts, gives them little jobs every now and then. But always within the bounds of what we consider OK."

"Which lowlifes?"

"Swedish. The ones we always checked but always knew were harmless. Conny Blomberg, Tony Ledin, Leif Rydbäck, and that ugly harelipped bastard, Calle Schewens..."

"Which one's short, nose like a potato, cropped hair, about fifty?"

"Sounds like Rydbäck."

"And Zivkovic still hangs out with them?"

"Don't know about hanging out, but they do small jobs for him sometimes."

"Any of them prone to gossip?"

"Yes, Rydbäck's happy to talk for a bit of cash and other favors. Stay away from Ledin and Schewens, though, too aggressive, more likely to shoot a cop. I don't know anything about Conny Blomberg except that he self-medicates his ADHD with hash and gets turned on by transvestites with tits."

"OK, thanks, Reutersvärd. Speak soon."

Reutersvärd didn't want to hang up, wanted to do a bit of small talk, asking Anders questions about what he was up to these days. Anders said he was on his way into a tunnel and cut the call off.

He watched the three men as they walked toward the Maritime History Museum. Looking at their backs, the way they behaved toward one another. Zivkovic was explaining something, Svante was keeping his distance but was listening, then it switched around—Svante explained something, Zivkovic listened and kept his distance. Leffe didn't seem to be listening, he just stayed close to Zivkovic the whole time.

Anders pondered the scene in front of him—Svante Carlgren, Håkan Zivkovic, and Leffe Rydbäck taking a walk together on Djurgården? Why? Did Svante contact Håkan and Leffe after Aron Geisler went to see him? Were Aron and Svante Carlgren working together somehow? Did they know each other? So why Zivkovic and Rydbäck? Were they going to do a job?

The men were getting farther away from Anders. He rubbed his stubble, against the grain, as his brain worked on theories.

Was Aron Geisler blackmailing Carlgren? It would have to be something really serious, or else Svante would have gone to Ericsson's internal security division, or directly to the cops. But he hadn't. So was Håkan Zivkovic going to help Svante track down Aron instead? Maybe . . . But that would never happen, Anders knew that.

He caught some of the short whiskers on his chin and tugged at them as he examined his theory. It was worth testing.

He started the Honda and swung around toward the city again. When he got stuck in traffic on Strandvägen he set about the laborious task of sticking his head into the underworld and trying to get hold of a phone number for Leffe Rydbäck without going through the usual channels. It took a long time and a hell of a lot of favors before he got anything. Leffe answered after a few rings with a short noise that Anders didn't understand.

"Rydbäck?"

"Who wants to know?"

"Anders Ask here."

A short silence.

"Don't know any Anders . . . Ass."

Anders heard Leffe getting into a car, probably with Zivkovic.

"Sure you do. I was with the Security Police when you messed up with the Syrians and their restaurants. I was one of the team that caught you and that idiot Håkan what's-his-name."

"I remember you, you were a cocky fucker... and ugly."

"And you were a stupid fucker, Leffe. A kid could have done that better. What the fuck were you thinking?"

"What do you want?" Leffe muttered.

"This might be a shot in the dark, but I've got a question. Your answer might be worth some cash, interested?"

"No harm in asking."

"Some clowns have shown up in the city trying to blackmail various business executives. Aron Geisler and Hector Guzman. Guzman's some sort of publisher, works in Gamla stan. Do you know them?"

Anders heard Leffe put his hand over the phone and start whispering. The hand vanished from the phone. Leffe was making an effort to sound calm and collected.

"No, I don't think so. What did you say their names were again?"

"Hector Guzman: G-U-Z-M-A-N, a publisher in Gamla stan. The other one's Aron Geisler." Anders spelled out his surname as well, and could hear Leffe's pen working hard against a piece of paper.

"Sorry, no idea... And, Ass?"

"Yes?"

"Go home and fuck your mother."

"Okey-dokey."

Leffe ended the call.

Erik was feeling sad. That happened sometimes. Suddenly he would get quiet and introverted. Difficult to reach. Maybe it was a common way of handling sorrow at the approach of old age. But where Erik Strandberg was concerned, he had been sad like this ever since he was a child, since their parents died. He'd never really mourned them, probably hadn't known how you did that. Gunilla hadn't either, but she'd found something else to grab hold of. Something that kept her away from depression and other types of darkness. She didn't know what it was, hadn't felt any need to know, either. She was strong, and that was the way she wanted things to stay.

Gunilla looked at her brother as he sat in the gloomiest corner of the living room. The sun was shining outside, but he had found the darkness.

She went out into the kitchen and prepared a light lunch that she knew he'd appreciate. Herring and potatoes, flatbread, dark beer, and a small schnapps straight from the freezer compartment. Then coffee and a slice of tart, and, when he was depressed like he was today, a newspaper for him to pretend to read so he didn't feel obliged to make conversation with her. She buttered the bread carefully and patiently so that it didn't break into smaller pieces. Erik liked the butter to cover the whole thing, right up to every edge and corner. She put the herring plate, glass of beer, flatbread, and the ice-cold, syrupy schnapps on a tray and carried it into the living room, where she put it down beside Erik's armchair. Gunilla patted her brother on the cheek. He grunted something.

The phone rang. Anders gave her a clear and concise update of the meeting between Zivkovic, Rydbäck, and Svante Carlgren. And told her about his blackmail theory, and the fact that he had called Leffe Rydbäck and leaked Hector and Aron's names, and their location.

"We'll have to wait and see if I was right," he said, and ended the call.

She told her brother the news. He didn't answer, just went on crunching the flatbread. Gunilla went over to the window. The world outside was green.

"We need to get ready," she said.

She looked out across the garden.

"I'm going to miss the plants, Erik. The peonies, the roses... the whole garden."

He'd just picked up the misted-up schnapps glass in his right hand.

"We need to pin the nurse down," he said in a hoarse voice, and downed the schnapps in one gulp.

Her gaze was fixed on the roses over by the wooden fence.

"How?"

He put the glass down and answered gruffly.

"Make sure she doesn't get any ideas, she needs to mind her own business until we're completely ready to go...."

Gunilla heard what he was saying and absorbed the idea as she walked across the living-room floor and out through the terrace door.

The strength of the sun blinded her when she emerged onto the veranda.

Lars had shaved, combed his hair, dressed properly. Everyday proper— neatly ironed and clean.

The microphone he had taken from Sophie's living room was in a little sealed plastic bag. He put it carefully into his pocket, went into the bathroom, and loaded up with a perfect combination consisting of a powerful dose of Ketogan up the ass, a cocktail of benzo for his stomach, and Lyrica to swim through his nervous system. He was calm, cool, and clear. He leaned closer to his reflection, the coating on his teeth looked like recently shed snakeskin. He opened the bathroom cabinet, squeezed some toothpaste onto his toothbrush, and started to brush as the cocktail started to kick in seriously. The brush felt like cotton balls on his teeth, it was wonderful, everything was wonderful. Nasty feelings and problems were somewhere on the other side of the universe. He rinsed with lukewarm water, everything was perfect. The jar of Hibernal was there in front of him in the cabinet. He picked it up, looked at it, and shook it slightly. It sounded like maracas. He shook it a bit more, maybe this was what Cuba sounded like? He put it back.

Lars sailed down the stairs, then floated in the car to Brahegatan, where he slid through the police station, up the stairs, and into the office.

He nodded to everyone there, trying to read the mood of the room. He saw Hasse and Anders sitting on their chairs and waiting. Erik over at his desk looked tired, he had his eyes closed as he massaged the bridge of his nose with his thumb and forefinger, possibly trying to ease a headache. Hasse and Anders... Lars looked at them again, they seemed tired as well, but in a different way. Hasse looked utterly shattered, empty, and vacant... his head was low. Anders was sitting with his arms folded, legs straight out, staring at some indeterminate point in front of him.

Lars sat down on a chair, the padding was soft. Eva Castroneves came over to him with a cup of coffee in her hand.

"I didn't know if you wanted milk?"

He looked at her uncomprehendingly and she couldn't be bothered getting into any sort of misunderstanding so just held the cup out to him.

"Here."

He took it without saying thank you.

"You're welcome," she said quietly.

"Thanks," he whispered.

She sat down on the chair next to him.

"How are you doing?" she asked.

He looked at her. Was she different? Happier? Why was she sitting next to him?

"Fine, I think. It's going slowly, but well... It feels like we're making progress now."

She nodded.

"That's what I think too."

He couldn't take his eyes off her. She shuffled on her seat.

"I've changed my mind, I will have some milk," he said, getting up and going to the kitchen.

Lars opened the fridge, took the little plastic bag out of his pocket, put the microphone between his thumb and index finger of the hand holding the coffee cup, added some milk, and walked back out again. He looked around the room: Erik had found an evening paper that he was idly leafing through, Eva was staring out in front of her, Anders and Hasse hadn't moved, arms folded, pensive.

Lars went over to one of the movable investigation bulletin boards and pretended to read some documents as he let the threadlike microphone slip into the soft felt that covered the board. He turned and meandered around the room, looking at things, drinking his coffee—as if he wanted to stretch his legs before the meeting began.

Outside in Brahegatan, a few buildings farther down, Lars had parked a rental car. A Renault. Under a blanket in the baggage compartment lay the surveillance equipment.

The door opened, Gunilla frantically entered the room and apologized for being late. Eva Castroneves stood up, picked up her handbag, and went up to Gunilla. Lars watched them as they whispered to each other over by the door. He saw the smiles and then heard a laugh between the two women. He was surprised to see Eva lean forward and kiss Gunilla on both cheeks. Then she went over to Erik, smiled at him, patted him on the cheek. Erik said "Bon voyage" in a hoarse voice, and Eva left the office.

Gunilla gathered her thoughts.

"I'm going to split you into two teams. Anders and Hasse number one, Lars and Erik number two."

Gunilla read from a sheet of paper.

"Erik and Lars, go and pay Carlos Fuentes a visit, you can set off at once. Anders, you and Hasse stay here."

Erik got up with a groan and left, and Lars followed him, not quite sure what was going on.

Once Lars and Erik were out of the room Gunilla turned to the bulletin board and wrote *Albert Brinkmann* and *Lars Vinge.*

"Two topics for discussion."

—

End of the school year. Sun, birch trees, no wind.

Thirty or so of his schoolmates had met up early that morning in a park by the water. They had some sparkling wine. Everyone got a bit drunk, someone started crying, someone threw up.

They walked to school in a group. He had been walking with Anna. They split up before going into the hall. Now he felt like turning around and looking for her in the crowd of people, but didn't. Instead he sat there on his bench listening to the singing and bad flute playing. The headmaster made a speech. He told them bullying, drugs, and racism were bad, then it was all over.

Albert and his friend Ludvig were crossing the schoolyard. The big, rust-red school building behind him with its two wings was beautiful, more so today seeing as it was the first day of summer vacation. He could see Anna a short way off in a group of girls, smiled at her, she smiled back.

There was a buzz from his pocket as he and Ludvig were unlocking their bicycles. He read the message. *Tonight we can be together. xxx.*

Albert looked around, Anna was gone. He put his cell back in his pocket, couldn't stop smiling. *Damn, life was good.*

Albert and Ludvig cycled down the slope with the wind in their hair and summer everywhere. They lined up alongside each other, pedaling hard. Ludvig swung off in a wide arc, away from Albert and onto another road. He shouted something that Albert couldn't hear properly, then something about Gustav providing food but not drink.

Albert waved and carried on straight ahead. He struggled to get up a hill, then slid into a narrow lane to get home faster. He heard the car behind him, and pulled over to the right to let it drive past. But it stayed behind him at the same low speed. Albert glanced over his shoulder. A Volvo, Hasse behind the wheel.

A mass of thoughts ran through his head. That he would miss the best evening of his life, and all that had happened the last time he encountered the man behind the wheel, that he should try to escape....

And he did, he fled. He swung into the middle of the road and pedaled as fast as he could down the narrow slope. The cycle accelerated, the wind whistling in his ears together with the sound of the Volvo accelerating somewhere behind him.

He tried to figure out an escape route and realized the cycle wasn't going to be any help. Halfway down the hill he slid sharply into someone's garden. He let the bike carry him as far as possible over the lawn, leaped off it at speed, and started running, quickly looking back to see the car reversing back up the hill again. Albert took his chance and started running down the hill instead, as far away from the car as he could. The Volvo stopped reversing and headed back down the road at full speed.

Albert had gotten a head start. He ran for a while before swinging to the right. The whole time he was trying to fool the car. The Volvo seemed to hesitate. He heard it stop abruptly. A door opened, Albert glanced back, a man had jumped out of the passenger seat and started running after him. He didn't recognize the man, but he was fast. Albert put his body into overdrive and ran for all he was worth. He could hear the Volvo again, parallel to him, somewhere below him. It was driving fast, in a high gear.

"Stop! Police!" the man behind him shouted as his swift steps got closer.

Albert took a leap and jumped over a fence into another garden. The lawn sloped downward. He let the gradient increase his speed. He ran past two children who were playing on a swing. A boy and girl of about five or so. They waved cheerily at him. He turned sharply. Ran back the way he had come, then right, continuing along another road, across another garden, across another road, then swerved left and ran off along a meadow. He kept going even though his lungs, legs, and heart were screaming for oxygen. He looked back, the man was gone. Albert saw a clump of trees in a garden and aimed for it. Lactic acid was pumping through him. He reached out with one arm to a fence and vaulted over it, and landed in something that looked like an arbor, then lay still, concentrating on not breathing too loudly.

The throbbing of his heartbeat in his ears and his heavy breathing shut out all other sounds. Albert closed his eyes, pressed his face against the soil. He tried to get back to normal by catching his breath. A car passed. He looked up cautiously. A Cherokee, a blond mom driving, she looked tired, a child was crying in the backseat. His breathing was getting back to normal. He listened for steps, the other man's steps. He must have lost him somewhere. Albert was just about to get up when another car approached from the left. He raised his head slowly. The Volvo passed him out in the road. Hasse behind the wheel... then footsteps running down the road.

"He's somewhere around here," the other man shouted.

The Volvo disappeared with a roar. Albert kept his face down. What was he thinking? That he could run away from them?

The footsteps out on the street were close. Steps that didn't seem to be able to make up their mind. Steps that hesitated, walked a little way, ran back, stopped, walked on again, stopped.

Albert was focusing intently with his ears, heard steps again, if only lightly, as the man walked up and down on the street in his rubber-soled cop shoes.

"Albert?"

A calm, low voice, nearby. Albert tried not to breathe.

"Albert, you're here somewhere.... You can come out now. Your mom's had an accident.... We're here to pick you up. Don't be scared. Just come out. You mom wants you with her. She needs you."

Albert had his face to the ground. The man's steps moved away slightly. The Volvo came back, stopped.

"Albert!" the man shouted.

"Come on, Anders..." Hasse's voice.

"He can't have had time to run across the meadow before I got here, that's not possible, he's here somewhere."

"Get in!" Hasse was impatient.

A car door closed, the car disappeared. Albert lay still, they might come back. He was debating with himself whether to stay where he was or get up and find a new hiding place. Where had they gone? Just around the corner, ready to pick him up when he showed himself again? Or had they driven off, given up?

He decided to stay where he was. An eternity passed. There was no sound of the car. He looked up and checked his limited field of vision, then carefully pulled his cell phone out of his trouser pocket, put it on silent. He wrote a text message to Sophie with trembling fingers:

Police chasing me, hiding, same policeman as before.

And he sent it off, then felt like crying. He hadn't been frightened during the chase itself, or while he was lying hidden, he'd just been driven by some sort of self-preservation impulse, a survival instinct. But now came the fear, the terror, and the sense of being all alone.

A car again. He tried to listen to the sound of the engine in case it was the Volvo, but he couldn't tell. The car came closer. Albert looked at his cell: no message.

Erik had said they should stop for a hot dog before going to see Carlos. Which they did on Valhallavägen, near Eastern Station. Just the two of them, Erik and Lars. They had never been on their own together before, and certainly not while each of them was holding a hot dog.

Erik had asked a great deal of questions. The questions were about Lars. If he liked working with them, how he thought the investigation was going. Even camouflaged questions and a concealed attempt to find out how much Lars really knew about what they were doing. Lars could tell where Erik was going. He hated the bastard for it, hated them all for the way they'd treated him. Because he didn't know anything for certain, he had no problem answering truthfully. But Erik didn't seem happy with that. He wanted clear answers. Answers that could help him pin Lars down.

He threw the rest of his hot dog in the trash when Erik got back in the passenger seat again. Lars was driving the Volvo and turned left down Odengatan. Erik shut his eyes and massaged the same spot between his eyes. He seemed to be sighing out the pain, squinting against the daylight outside the car.

"And the nurse, how are things going with her? Do you think she knows anything?"

"No," Lars replied.

"Why not?"

"Because there's nothing to suggest that she does. I've spent a lifetime listening. . . . Not even a hint."

"Does she know we're listening to her?"

Lars turned toward Erik.

"Why would she?"

"I don't know, but we're not getting anything from her."

"Maybe she hasn't got anything to give us?"

Erik shrugged.

They pulled up in a no-parking zone outside Carlos's apartment on Karlbergsvägen.

Before Erik opened the car door he turned to Lars and studied him for a moment. The study stretched into a silent, protracted stare.

"What is it?" Lars mumbled.

Erik didn't seem to find the situation uncomfortable. On the contrary, he seemed to be enjoying it.

"You're a fucking clown, Lars Vinge, you know that, don't you?"

Lars didn't answer. He was still going on prescription painkillers. That always made him more self-confident. He could maintain eye contact with Erik. But Erik snorted at that.

"You're trying to outstare me?"

Lars looked away.

Erik cleared his throat. It sounded rough, and ended up as a series of coughs. He gasped for air.

"Gunilla said you wanted to widen your horizons a bit, get some different jobs. This is one of them, you ready for it?"

Lars nodded.

"Sure?"

"Yes."

"OK, watch and learn, and keep your mouth shut. That last point is the most important."

He got out of the car. Lars didn't move, took a deep breath, then followed him.

The elevator was out of order. Carlos lived on the fourth floor. They started to go up the stairs.

Erik was puffing and panting. On the third floor he stopped and grabbed hold of the handrail. His breathing was labored, his face bright red. With an irritated wave of the hand he gestured to Lars to keep on going.

Erik, headphones over his ears, was listening to the little box that Hasse and Anders had left behind on their previous visit.

"There's nothing here. Just static and shit!"

He looked up at Carlos.

"Why?" he went on.

Carlos licked his lips.

"I don't know. I was wearing it but Hector didn't talk to me."

Lars was sitting on one of kitchen chairs watching all this.

"He's going to fall, and you're going down with him," said Erik. "I'm giving you a chance here, Carlos. A chance to get out of this mess a free man. But for that to happen, you need to help us. Understand?"

Erik's tone was patronizing, as if he were talking to a child. Lars looked at the bruises on Carlos's face. "Have you been beaten up?" he asked.

Carlos looked at Lars with a questioning expression.

"Shut up, Lars," Erik said.

Erik held up the microphone again.

"Wear it all the time. We'll be back in two days, and by then it needs to be full of info. . . . There you go."

Carlos looked at the microphone that Erik was holding out, then down at the floor, as if he were searching for options.

"Take it," Erik said.

Carlos shook his head. Erik's patience ran out.

"Take it, man!" Erik's voice cracked halfway through.

Lars stood up. "Are we done?"

Erik turned toward him.

"Didn't I tell you to shut up?"

Lars smiled insolently at Erik.

"Shut up yourself. You can't do anything properly. Do you think this is a good strategy?"

Erik looked at Lars in surprise. His blood pressure went up, his face got redder.

"You fucking little cocksucker," he said in a low voice, and was about to go on when he suddenly stumbled. He muttered something inaudible. His voice sounded thick and muffled. Lars and Carlos looked at him in surprise. Erik tried to say something, he was squinting as if the light had suddenly gotten too bright. Erik rubbed a hand over his head, blinked, stumbled, and grabbed the back of one of the kitchen chairs.

"I can't see properly," he said.

"What?"

Erik's left arm began to tremble, and he looked at it in astonishment.

"What the fuck?" he whispered quietly to himself.

His gaze moved from his own shaking arm to Lars, then to Carlos. He made a guttural, incomprehensible sound, then projectile vomited. One of his legs gave way. He fell to the left, taking the chair with him, and hit the floor hard. He ended up lying in his own vomit, screwing his eyes up.

Carlos stared. Lars stared and leaned over cautiously.

"How are you feeling, Erik?"

No answer.

"We have to call an ambulance," Carlos said.

Lars held a hand up at him.

"Erik?" he whispered.

Erik was gasping for breath as he lay there on the floor. Carlos grabbed the phone off the kitchen wall, and was about to dial the emergency number. Lars drew his pistol and aimed the gun lazily toward him.

"There now, put it back."

Carlos stared into the barrel of the gun, hung the receiver up again, and took a step back.

"He can't die on my floor!" Carlos said.

"Of course he can."

Lars crouched down with the pistol hanging from one hand between his legs, staring at Erik in fascination. Waved his other hand in front of his eyes.

"Erik?"

Erik moved his eyes slightly, looked at Lars. Lars could see something pleading in them. The muscles in his thighs started to ache and he stood up and turned to Carlos.

"The police officers who were here before?"

Carlos looked at Lars, unsure what he was getting at.

"There were other police officers here before, they gave you the microphone. Tell me!"

"Two men came 'round the other evening, one big one and one... ordinary one. They asked questions.... They threatened me."

"Why?"

Carlos looked at the pistol hanging from Lars's hand.

"I don't know. Put the pistol away."

Lars looked at the pistol without putting it away. "But I'm not even aiming it at you."

Carlos put his left hand over his eyes.

"What did they ask?" said Lars.

"About Hector..."

"What did they ask about Hector?"

Carlos put his hand down, looked at Lars.

"If I'd met him at the restaurant that evening."

"What evening?"

Carlos gestured to his battered face.

"And did you?"

Carlos shook his head.

"How did they threaten you?"

"I don't know."

"How could you not know that?"

"They hit me."

"What else?"

Carlos looked confused. Lars clarified.

"Did they mention anyone else?"

"Like who?"

"A woman?"

"What woman?"

"Sophie?"

Carlos thought, nodded.

"Yes, they asked if I saw her that evening."

"And did you?"

Carlos shook his head.

"What did you tell them?"

He looked at Lars as if he was stupid.

"That I didn't see her!"

"So what happened at the restaurant?"

Carlos looked away. "I don't know."

He said the words as if he was tired of repeating the same thing over and over again.

"I want you to let me know if they contact you again."

"Why?"

Lars pointed idly at him with the pistol.

"Because I say so."

Carlos thought.

"What do I get out of it?"

Lars looked closely at Carlos's injuries.

"Nothing. You escape getting beaten up again, I guess."

Carlos shook his head.

"So what do you want, then, Carlos?"

"Protection, if I get in trouble."

"OK, agreed, but part of the deal is that no one finds out that any time has passed between the old man hitting the floor and us calling for an ambulance."

Lars gestured with his pistol for Carlos to leave the kitchen.

He pulled up a chair, sat down, and looked at Erik Strandberg's rigid body. The old bastard was slowly suffocating. Lars looked into his eyes to reassure himself that he, Lars Vinge, would be the last thing Erik Strandberg ever saw in this life. Erik died after a long and painful struggle, Lars didn't miss a second of the drama. The corpse looked odd, the face was drooping weirdly. Erik was lying dead in his own vomit. Lars felt a certain satisfaction at that.

Albert lay there, pressed to the ground, it smelled of soil and grass.

He had received a text from Sophie. *Stay where you are. Keep hidden.*

He heard steps out on the road, saw the second man, the one named Anders. Where Hasse was, he had no idea.

Albert made up his mind to run again, knew he had the advantage then.

There was a rustling sound a few yards away from him. His heartbeat was pounding in his ears. The man, whichever one of them it was, was standing close by. Albert had no choice. He got up quickly and started to run. He hadn't gotten more than ten yards when he ran straight into an outstretched arm, was hit in the throat, and pulled to the ground. Strong hands held him down, a heavy knee on his chest pressed the air out of him. Albert could see Hasse's contorted face as the fat man snarled curses at him, saliva running from his mouth.

With a hard stranglehold around Albert's neck Hasse started punching him in the face. Hard blows to his eye, nose, mouth. He stopped hitting but kept his stranglehold and squeezed. The air soon stopped. Albert could feel that the oxygen in his head was running out, that the life was running out of him. His mind was screaming for more.... His eyes could no longer keep themselves open.

Just when it felt like he was about to lose consciousness, Hasse let go. Albert rolled onto his side, retched, and tried to get his breath back.

Hasse dragged him up from the ground, holding his arm tight.

"I've got him," he shouted.

At that moment Albert managed to break free. He set off again. His legs were driving him forward even though he couldn't feel them. He had the taste of blood in his mouth, and every joint in his body ached. He got out onto the road and heard the car accelerate behind him. He managed to get into a garden. His steps were slow and heavy, his balance poor. The whole time Albert could see Hasse from the corner of his eye, running parallel to him. When he realized that Hasse was managing to keep up with him Albert leaped over the fence to run out onto the road in the hope of meeting someone, maybe stop a car... get help.

He emerged onto the road, tried to increase his speed. The Volvo came from the left, at high speed, didn't even try to brake. The blow was hard. The car struck him on the kneecaps and Albert was thrown into the air, where he performed a half somersault over the roof of the car and fell, after his long, silent flight, onto the blacktop, his back hitting first, then the back of his head, with such force that the back of his skull shattered. Everything went black.

Sophie had called, sounding upset, incoherent. It had taken a while before he realized what she was saying. He threw himself into the car.

Her son was lying in some bushes in a garden with two cops circling around him. She had said that they mustn't get hold of him, she'd repeated that to him several times. Jens had tried to calm her.

He wasn't far away when the ambulance overtook him at high speed. He followed it. The ambulance stopped a block or so farther on, beside the bloody body of a boy lying alone in the middle of the road.

Sophie bit off part of the nail on her little finger. None of her nails looked the way they usually did. They were short now, uneven.

She was standing in an empty patient's room at work. She'd been walking aimlessly around the room ever since she got Albert's text. Now she was just waiting.

An image flickered past inside her, Albert in the garden, playing with Rainer. The image vanished as quickly as it had arrived. She didn't understand why she had suddenly come to think about the dog. Rainer had been a golden Labrador, and Albert had loved him dearly. They had bought the dog when Albert was two, possibly as a substitute for a brother or sister. Albert had chased the dog around the lawn from the age of six, summer and winter alike. By the age of nine he had learned to read the dog's movements, its way of thinking. He caught it every time. She had stood in the window watching. Albert concentrating, Rainer boisterous.

Albert was twelve when Rainer died. He cried until there were no more tears to cry.

The cell phone rang, rousing her from her thoughts.

"Yes?"

She heard what Jens said, heard his clear, factual tone of voice. Her legs gave way under the weight of her despair and horror. She managed to grab the windowsill, and clung to it as if it were the only lifeline in her fall into the darkest of all dark holes. Then everything went black. The next thing she could remember was running down a corridor. She took the stairs instead of the elevator, ran down service corridors, through the entrance lobby, and into Accident & Emergency.

She got there just as the ambulance was pulling into the bay. She ran over, shoving aside the nurse who had just opened the back door of the ambulance.

She saw Albert lying on the stretcher, his face smeared with blood. His head was locked in place, with a broad strip over his forehead and his neck in a plastic collar. His torn clothes from the last day of school were covered in blood. She was about to clamber up into the ambulance when a nurse caught hold of her and pulled her away.

The exhaust fumes in the garage were stronger now that it was warm out- side. She had the window open.

Gunilla was waiting in her Peugeot in the garage at Hötorget. She watched Anders's Honda in the rearview mirror as it drove up and stopped behind her. Anders opened the passenger door and sat down heavily in the seat beside her.

"Everything went to hell," he said in a low voice.

"Is he going to be all right?"

Anders rubbed the back of his neck. "I don't know. The car hit him hard, he landed on his back."

"Did anyone see you?"

"No."

"Are you sure?"

"Yes."

Gunilla was sitting quite still.

"The car?" she asked.

"We've washed it, fixed it so it hit another car. It's parked and secure."

Gunilla leaned her face into her hand. The silence was making Anders impatient.

"I took the boy's cell. He'd sent Sophie a text. She knows it was us."

Gunilla said nothing.

"What do we do?" he asked.

She sighed. "I don't know.... Right now, I don't know."

He looked at her, had never seen her like this.

"You know what we have to do," he said.

She looked up at him, then put her face in her hands again.

"Gunilla?"

She didn't respond.

"You know what we have to do?"

"Let the boy be," she said.

Anders was halfway out of the car.

"Why?"

"Because I say so."

He thought for a moment.

"OK, for the time being. But if he wakes up, he'll have to be gotten rid of, you must see that?"

Gunilla was staring ahead of her.

Anders jumped out of the car and slammed the door behind him. She heard the little squeals of the tires on the polished concrete floor as the car left the garage. The sound died away and everything was silent. She tried to think, to find a path, a direction.... Her cell interrupted her thoughts when it started ringing in the pocket between the seats. Gunilla answered. It was Lars, who told her that Erik had just died. She understood what he said, but asked anyway.

"Which Erik?"

21

Sophie was sitting at Albert's bedside, holding his hand. He was even more tightly restrained than he had been in the ambulance: straps, neck brace, clamps, and a surreal metal crown on his head that held him perfectly still. Both legs were in a cast from the thighs down to the ankles.

The doctor came in, her name was Elisabeth, Sophie knew her slightly. Elisabeth stuck to the facts.

"We believe that Albert's damaged his twelfth thoracic vertebra. It's been driven into the marrow but we don't know what sort of state it's in."

Albert looked like he was sleeping.

"His skull was fractured. Because we dare not move him at the moment, we don't actually know very much. Just that there's pressure on his brain. We want to reduce that pressure. As soon as it's possible we're going to move him to Karolinska."

Throughout all her years as a nurse she had tried to calm patients' relatives by saying that injuries often looked worse than they were. And that had been true, that was often the case. But now the opposite was true, Albert's injuries were worse than they looked. Much worse.

Dear God, please, help us now....

Jane came into the room, took a frightened look at Albert, and hugged Sophie.

Jens had called several times on the secure cell phone. In the end she had answered. He sounded stressed.

"You need to get away from there now...."

"I can't leave him."

"Of course you can. I spoke to the ambulance staff, Albert didn't have his cell on him. The police may have taken it, they'll have seen your messages.... They know that you know. And when they find you, they'll hurt you."

"No, I'm not leaving him...."

"I've called for help. Two friends will take turns sitting with Albert. They'll guard him, protect him."

Sophie had a hundred questions.

"Leave now, Sophie!" He almost spelled it out.

Jane was standing behind her when Sophie ended the call.

"What's going on, Sophie?"

She didn't answer.

"It isn't just Albert's accident, is it?"

Sophie considered telling her. She'd always told Jane everything. And Jane had done the same with her. Truth, honesty. The glue that bound them together. She looked into her sister's eyes, fighting against the impulse to tell her.

"Not now, Jane. I have to get away from here, don't ask me why. Don't leave Albert for a moment. Two men will be coming. Let them stay."

Then she turned and walked away, unable even to say good-bye to Albert. She just left. Jane stared after her.

Sophie was packing a bag in the bedroom. She was rushing, trying to think what she'd need—the cell with the direct line to Jens was the most important thing, then her other cell, the charger. She tipped everything into her handbag, hurried into the bathroom, and started to fill a toiletry bag. There was a noise downstairs in the living room. She stiffened, kept very quiet, and listened. Nothing. She carried on, putting in toothpaste, toothbrush, creams... anything that was within easy reach. Another noise—a click, a door closing. She stopped breathing and just listened. Nothing. *Was it just her imagination? No...*

She crept over to the bathroom window and peeped out. There was a Honda parked out on the road by her gate. She left the window and crept out of the bathroom. Now she could hear the parquet floor downstairs creaking. An icy chill swept through her and she stood utterly still.

"Check upstairs."

A low male voice, then steps approaching the stairs. She just stood where she was, trapped on the upper floor. What should she do, hide? Fight? With what? There were at least two men against her.

Footsteps on the stairs. She tried to think of a weapon, couldn't think of anything. The steps were getting closer. Then a thought struck her—the fire escape ladder outside Albert's window. Sophie left the bathroom and made her way toward Albert's room as the steps got closer. She made it at the very last moment and shut the door silently behind her. Sophie hung her handbag diagonally across her chest, opened the window, climbed up on the rickety desk, and was just about to climb out when the door flew open behind her. A strong hand grabbed her collar. She was dragged backward and down onto the floor, landing hard on her back. Hasse Berglund was kneeling on her chest, a hand around her neck. His cheeks hung as he leaned over her. He looked like a dog. She met his staring, watery eyes, could see he was enjoying this.

"Anders!" he called.

Sophie stretched her hand across the carpet under Albert's bed, feeling with her fingers. She got hold of the end of the old telescope and grabbed it like a baseball bat.

"Anders!" he called again, turning his face away from her for a moment.

Sophie hit him with all her strength. The telescope struck Hasse Berglund on the side of the head. The blow was so hard that he let go of her throat and toppled over on his side, temporarily confused and weakened. Sophie struggled loose, kicking the big man to free her right leg from under his body. She could hear quick steps from the stairs. Sophie scrambled to her feet, hearing Hasse muttering something behind her. From the corner of her eye she could see him regain his strength and start to turn toward her, reaching out an arm to grab her. She leaped up onto the desk and threw herself headfirst through the window. She managed to grab the rusty ladder with her right hand, slid a short distance, and tore a deep cut in the palm of her hand. Sophie lost her grip and fell backward helplessly for a second before landing on her back on the lawn. All the air went out of her and she lay there for a moment. Even though her whole body was telling her to lie still and get her breath back, she forced herself to get up on her feet. She hurried awkwardly over to her car, which was parked on the gravel drive in front of the house, managing to pull the key from her pocket as she ran. Her body ached painfully. Sophie unlocked the car with the remote. She just managed to get in behind the wheel and lock the doors when the men came rushing out of her kitchen door. The overweight one was bleeding from his ear. The other one looked boyish in spite of his age, dark, round deer's eyes—just the way Dorota had described him.

She turned the key. The car started. The boyish one drew a pistol and aimed it at her. The overweight one shouted at her to turn the engine off and get out of the vehicle.

Sophie put the car in reverse and slammed the pedal to the floor. The tires sprayed gravel as the car shot through the gateposts. Sophie wrenched the wheel and lurched out onto the road. She went on reversing at high speed toward the parked Honda. The gears were shrieking at having to go backward so fast. She steeled herself for the impact. The Land Cruiser backed right into the front of the Honda; the collision was hard and brutal, she was thrown backward and hit her head on the seat, feeling dizzy for a moment. She changed gear and drove forward fast. A quick glance in the mirror, the front of the Honda was demolished.

The men were standing in the middle of the road. Weapons drawn, aimed at her. She pressed the accelerator pedal to the floor, the automatic transmission downshifted. Sophie crouched below the dashboard for cover and headed straight for them. Anders and Hasse leaped out of the way.

* * *

She headed into the multistory garage at the shopping center in Mörby, and parked on the top floor, where she locked the car and hurried out into the mall. Then she stopped, hesitant. Should she take the subway or head out to the buses? She thought quickly. The subway station in Mörby was the end of the line, there was only one way in and out. If the train didn't come and the men were on their way, she'd have no hope of escape.

She bought a ticket from the machine and hurried out to the bus stops, hiding in the waiting crowd of people, looking the whole while in the direction the buses came from, occasionally glancing back toward the main entrance to the mall, where she imagined the two policemen were going to rush out at her at any moment. Her heart was beating so hard that she thought it was going to burst through her chest.

Then, at last... a large, red, articulated bus turned in toward her from the junction and stopped with a hiss in front of the waiting passengers. The number of the bus meant nothing to her, but she didn't care. She moved with the line and got on board, showing her ticket to the driver, who waved her past. Sophie moved toward the back and sat in a vacant pair of seats, then leaned over and prayed that the bus would leave soon. But it didn't, it stood there with its doors open, waiting for the scheduled departure time.

Her breathing was getting harder, shallower. Panic was building and she had to summon up all her strength just to stay on the bus, not run off, even though her whole body was screaming at her to go.

Finally the doors closed and the bus set off from Mörby. She could breathe out. It carried her toward Sollentuna. Sophie got off at Sjöberg, where she walked among the identical-looking houses and called for a taxi. It arrived fifteen minutes later, and she asked the driver to take her into the city center, Sergels torg.

She paid cash, jumped out on Klarabergsgatan, and went down into the square. She disappeared into the crowd, made her way into the subway station, and caught a train to Slussen. There she changed platforms and took another train back to Gamla stan, and from there she headed off on foot toward Östermalm.

He met her in the street, waiting outside his door. She didn't cry, just let herself be embraced and rested her head on his shoulder.

They took the elevator up to the top floor. He looked at her in the mirror, not knowing how to comfort her, or if he should even try. He didn't know how to do that sort of thing, had no training in it, because that was pretty much what he'd spent his whole life avoiding. Now he wanted to be able to do it, now he wanted to know what to do to comfort her. But it was too late, he'd only mess things up if he tried.

She asked for antiseptic. He gave her what he had. Sophie bandaged her bleeding hand and went into another room. He could hear her talking to her sister on the phone.

Jens made food for her. She ate in silence, withdrawn, and he let her be.

There was a smell of formaldehyde in the room. Gunilla was standing there looking down at her dead brother. Erik Strandberg was lying on one of the mortuary's shiny metal trolleys, it was as if he was asleep. She felt like waking him up, telling him it was time to go to work now, that this was going to be an ordinary day, then they'd have dinner somewhere, discuss the case, talk about all the things they always did.

What do you do when you see your brother for the last time? Do you try to find something to remember? Do you try to remember something you've forgotten? Outside the hospital she sat in her car looking out through the windshield without registering what she was seeing. The scream came. She screamed from the depths of her body until the air in her lungs ran out. Then came the tears, and then the grief, rolling through her consciousness like great gusts of wind. The pain felt like it was going to suffocate her; she felt alone, a vast feeling of abandonment that refused to let go. It was joined by a shapeless sense of impotence. And from that feeling an image gradually emerged, an image that showed that her total isolation had put her in a position in life where she had nothing to lose.

Then she was done. She opened the window to let in some air, took a few cautious breaths, and wiped her eyes and the makeup that had run down her face. She put her makeup on again in the mirror of the sun visor, sat herself up, took a deep breath, started the car, and drove off.

That night she came to him. She crept up next to him on the sofa where he had made a bed for himself, into his arms. She lay there for a while, letting herself be held. Then she pulled away and went back to her bed. Jens watched her go, tried to get back to sleep, but couldn't. He got up, called Jonas at the hospital—he was watching over Albert, said everything was OK.

In the kitchen he lit a cigarette and smoked it out the window. His cell vibrated on the counter, the screen showed a Moscow number.

"Yes?"

"Your friends have left for Sweden." Risto's voice sounded as untroubled as ever.

"To Stockholm?"

"Yes, they're on their way...."

"When did they leave?"

"Don't know. I'd guess at yesterday."

"Fine, let them come. They'll never find me."

"They know your name...."

"They know my name's Jens, that's all."

"You traveled to Prague under your real name... That first meeting with them..."

Jens remembered. He did that sometimes when there was nothing at stake.

"They got it from the hotel."

"OK... Thanks, Risto."

Jens ended the call and stood there thinking.

"Fuck...," he whispered quietly.

"What is it?"

He turned around. Sophie was standing there looking at him. He tried to give her a reassuring smile.

It was twenty past three in the morning when Lars put the key in the rental car that was parked on Brahegatan.

He drove off through an apparently dead city, saw just a few people, most of them drunk. He was drunk himself, but that wasn't something he bothered to consider. Hammered, wired—*encapsulated*—had become his general state of being.

He parked the car three blocks from his apartment, took the surveillance equipment out of the back, put it under his arm, and lumbered home.

In his office he transferred the files to his computer, put on the headphones, and listened to the sequence from Brahegatan where he himself had been present—he heard Gunilla ask him and Erik to go and see Carlos. The sound was bad, it didn't quite reach the microphone. Footsteps on the floor, a door closing. His and Erik's footsteps. Lars listened intently, then heard the unmistakable squeak of a marker on the bulletin board.

"Two topics for discussion." Gunilla's voice.

Silence, then Gunilla's voice again: *"Before we talk about the boy, I want us to go back to that night. Lars knows more than we thought. Erik's trying to question him now."*

"Patricia Nordström, does he know about her?"

That was Anders's voice. Lars wrote "Patricia Nordström" on a piece of paper.

"I don't know, I don't think so."

"But she knew?"

"Yes," Gunilla said curtly.

"She?" Lars tried to make sense of it all.

"Have they found her?" Hasse asked.

"Yes, a girlfriend found her," Gunilla said.

"Cause of death?"

"Heart failure, just as we wanted."

Lars wasn't understanding any of this.

"No question marks?" Anders said.

"No. No question marks . . . not yet."

A cough from Hasse, and Gunilla went on: *"It's important that he doesn't find out anything right now. I'd like to get rid of him, but if he is holding something back, I'd rather have him here with us in ignorance."*

A few seconds of nothing, the sound of the pen on the board. Lars pressed his hands over the headphones, concentrating.

"We have to find the boy, bring him in again," Gunilla said.

Lars tried to understand—the boy?

"Why?" Anders said.

"We need to pin Sophie down. I get the feeling she's going to do something drastic soon. That mustn't happen, not at this point."

Gunilla's voice sounded hollow.

Lars was thinking. The boy?... Albert! What did they want with him?

"Isn't it the last day of school today?" Hasse said.

Then unclear muttering from Anders and a quiet answer from Gunilla; he couldn't make out the words. Then the sound of chairs scraping on the floor as Hasse and Anders stood up.

He switched off the equipment, trying to think about what he'd heard, trying to think about Albert. While he and Erik had gone off to see Carlos, Anders and Hasse had gone after Albert. Had they succeeded? And why? What did they want with the boy? Lars's brain was working at top speed. Was there anything about Albert that stood out in the surveillance of Sophie? He closed his eyes, searching feverishly inside himself. A thin, indistinct memory drifted past, he tried to capture it. That didn't work; it disappeared, but not entirely. Something had stuck... something small and fragile. He screwed up his eyes and went over to the computer, trying not to lose it, and typed in the search terms *Albert*, *Sophie*, *kitchen*. A mass of files showed up in the search window. Lars looked at the dates and started listening from the top of the list. There were conversations over breakfast, conversations over dinner, conversations during the day while Albert was doing his homework. There were conversations in the evenings, Sophie on the phone. Albert on the phone. And there were a lot of background noises that set off the voice-activated equipment only for it to shut down again shortly afterward. He listened through file after file, fast-forwarded, searched. *Shit,* there was something he remembered, he just couldn't recall what.... Something that only his subconscious had registered. And the more he listened, the weaker his indistinct recollection became.

After two and a half hours he hadn't even listened to half of the files. Lars clicked on another one, listened once more, fast-forwarding through the silences. A fridge opened and closed, Sophie's voice said *Albert.* Silence followed... and then the unmistakable sound of a slap.

Lars pressed lightly on the headphones, the sound became clearer, the details audible. Footsteps on the floor, someone standing up from a chair.

Lars listened.

"I haven't done anything."

Albert's voice sounded muffled, as though he were pressing into his mother's shoulder.

"It's over now, they made a mistake."

Lars didn't remember this, he remembered hearing it, but didn't remember it like this, not this way.

"But they had witnesses?! Rape? What kind of—"

Lars heard Sophie hushing him.

"Try to forget it now, sometimes it just happens. Everyone makes mistakes, even the police."

There was silence again. Lars went on listening.

"He hit me."

"What did you say?"

"The policeman in the car, he hit me in the face."

There was a long, drawn-out silence in the headphones, the file came to an end. Lars stood up, gathered his thoughts, then wrote what he had just heard up on the wall. He worked feverishly until long into the night. The pieces of the puzzle were finally starting to fall into place.

As morning dawned he was woken by a phone call. Gunilla wanted to meet him.

He stared at himself in the bathroom mirror, found a personality that might work. He took it easy with the drugs because he had, after all, been present when her brother died.... That meant you were likely to be a bit off form.

"What happened?"

She had her hands in her lap. It was warm, seventy-five degrees in the shade. They were sitting at an outdoor café on Östermalmstorg; she was restrained, as if she were bracing herself to hear something that might affect her emotionally. Lars looked down at the table, then up at Gunilla.

"We got there, Erik was doing the talking... suddenly he collapsed...."

A breeze swept across the square, but brought no relief from the heat.

"How?"

"Does it matter?"

"Would I be asking otherwise?"

Lars began. "He said he couldn't see properly. One arm started to tremble and shake. He said something incomprehensible, then he fell."

"What did he say?"

"I didn't hear."

"What did you do?"

"I rushed over and checked his pulse."

"And?"

"He was still alive, and I called for an ambulance."

"Then what?"

"I sat down beside him."

"Did he say anything, did you say anything?"

"He was unconscious, but I kept talking gently to him."

"What did you say?"

"I said everything was going to be all right, that the ambulance was on its way, that there was no need for him to worry."

Gunilla looked away, took a deep breath.

"Thank you."

Lars didn't respond.

"And the other man? Carlos, what did he do?"

"He got scared, went off into another room."

"How far had you got in your conversation with him?"

"Not very far. Erik said he wanted results. We didn't get any further...."

Gunilla looked at the people around them.

"It's starting to come together now, the evidence is starting to mount up. We all need to concentrate on what we're doing now. No mistakes."

Lars took a sip of his glass of water.

"Has anything happened that I don't know about?"

A sad look crossed her eyes, then she shook her head, apparently to herself.

"It's terrible, Sophie's son, Albert, was hit by a car yesterday.... His back's broken, he's in intensive care, the whole thing's just terrible."

He wanted to scream. But instead he concentrated on staying calm. He thought about a tree slowly growing, about a stone being shaped by the sea... about anything that happened unbelievably calmly.

"Oh... Who did it?" he said, sounding precisely as unconcerned as he had hoped.

Gunilla shrugged her shoulders.

"Don't know, it was an accident... hit and run."

"That's terrible. Anything else?"

He was trying to sound cold and professional.

"No, I don't think so."

Gunilla watched Lars Vinge as he headed off toward Humlegårdsgatan. She thought that he had changed, that his previous uncertain and feeble attitude had turned into something else. Not more confident... but stiffer, quieter. He was introverted without being fretful, however that worked.

She let Lars go, took out her cell, and quickly called Hasse Berglund.

"Would you mind cleaning up everything at the nurse's house? Anders can tell you where the microphones are located. Everything needs to go, we mustn't leave any trace at all."

She ended the call, then spent a while just watching the people around her, finding them all interesting. She smiled toward a curly-haired boy in a white shirt and black trousers, who took a few seconds to realize that she wanted to pay her bill.

Lars left Östermalm and drove to his bank on Södermalm, waved to the young clerk with the greasy skin, and asked to look at his safe-deposit box.

He opened the box and put in copies of the surveillance files of Sophie Brinkmann and the recording from the police station, photographs, printouts, summaries... everything. He left the bank and drove out toward Stocksund. *Watch over her...*

* * *

He checked that she wasn't home, then parked two blocks from the house. A quarter of an hour later a car blew its horn briefly. Lars looked to his left as Hasse drove past, giving him the finger. Lars let the air out of his lungs and leaned his head back. Time passed, maybe five minutes, maybe ten, and Hasse came rolling toward him from Sophie's house, slowed down, and lowered the window, leaning out toward Lars, his left hand hanging outside the door.

"As soon as you see her you call me, Anders, or Gunilla. You don't do anything at all yourself. . . . Got that?"

Lars nodded.

Hasse drummed his hand on the outside of the car door, then stuck his finger up again. This time so clearly that Lars couldn't miss a second of his protracted *Fuuuck Yooou* as he rolled away. The sound of tires on the grit covering the road. Then silence again.

Lars remained sitting in the car, staring out at nothing. Birds were singing but he didn't hear them. Some children were playing somewhere, happy laughter and shouting, but he didn't hear that, either. All he could hear was his own thoughts. He was working hard, but soon got tangled up. His cell rang in his pocket. He answered with a muttered "Hello?"

"Lars?"

"Yes?"

"This is Terese."

Sara's friend, she was sobbing down the line.

"Can we talk for a bit? I can't bear going 'round with my own thoughts. . . ."

Lars wasn't following.

"Thoughts about what?"

Terese was crying.

"What is it, Terese?"

Silence. "You don't know?"

"What?"

Terese sobbed that Sara was dead, that she'd suffered heart failure the night before last.

The universe turned itself inside out, the sky split apart. He opened the car door and threw up on the street.

Mikhail had gotten the call in the middle of the night. Klaus sounded tired but in good humor.

"Can you come and get me?"

"How are you feeling?"

"How does anyone feel when they've had a bullet in their guts?" Klaus said.

"I don't know. Only how it feels to get a bullet in the thigh, shoulder, chest... and grenade shrapnel in your ass."

They laughed. Mikhail hung up, packed a bag, and headed off to the airport early the next morning. He took the first flight to Scandinavia. He ended up in Copenhagen, where he caught another flight to Stockholm.

The same routine once again. Renting a car in a false name at Arlanda, driving to the weapons nut in Enskede and picking up a new, untraceable pistol. Then he drove to the Karolinska Hospital.

Mikhail was tired of Volvos, blond people, and the façade of social welfare—he was tired of Sweden.

Hector was talking to Adalberto over a secure line. Adalberto told him that the money from the Ericsson job was secure. Hector did the calculations in his head, as did Adalberto.

"Hector, before we go on... Hanke tried to contact me. A Roland Gentz called, asking for my opinion on their proposal."

"What proposal?"

"That was my question too...."

"And?"

"They're not backing down."

"Where are we at the moment?"

Adalberto was silent. Hector could hear him drinking from a glass, heard him crunch an ice cube between his teeth.

"I've got lawyers suing them from all directions. I want to fight the battle on that front instead. This business with guns and cars is starting to feel a bit tiresome. But take care. They seem to be up to something.... That man, Gentz, made threats. He was very clear."

"We have to deal with them sooner or later, Dad."

"Later. Let's see how my new move develops."

Hector lit a cigarillo. Adalberto drank some more.

"I've spoken to Don Ignacio. He's calmed down, told me that you and Alfonse got on well together."

"We're going to meet up before he goes home.... Go through the details."

Adalberto muttered something that Hector couldn't hear, then went on. "Leszek and I have been doing some work, the pipeline will soon be running again. The captain's changed ships."

Hector thought.

"What does that mean, the captain's changed ships?"

"Nothing clever. Like I said, he's changed ships. Sold the old one, bought a new one. The same deal applies. The goods are being driven from Ciudad del Este and he'll pick them up in Paranaguá in a week. A new cargo will be arriving in Rotterdam at the end of the month. We're up and running again."

"Is that good or bad?"

"I don't know. But we didn't have any choice, did we?"

Hector didn't answer that. "How's Sonya?"

"She keeps to herself."

"How are *you*, Dad?"

Adalberto didn't answer at once, as if the question had unsettled him.

"No better than I deserve...," he said quietly.

Hector smoked in Stockholm, Adalberto sipped his drink in Marbella. They just sat there for a while in each other's company.

Hector hung up, and thought for a while on his own. He was interrupted when the doorbell rang out in the hall. Aron went past the office.

"Are we expecting anyone?" he asked.

Hector shook his head and took a revolver out of the desk drawer. Aron took his, fitted with a silencer, from the bookcase. They went toward the door.

Aron could see two men through the peephole. He didn't recognize either of them and waved Hector over, who looked through and shook his head. Aron gestured to Hector to stand back.

He tucked his gun inside the waistband of his trousers, opened the door, and smiled amiably at Håkan Zivkovic and his sidekick, Leffe Rydbäck.

"Yes?" Aron said.

They both had cropped hair and were wearing sneakers and cheap clothes from a cheap men's clothing chain, and stupid bulletproof vests that bulged beneath their jackets. The sidekick had a potato nose, was a head shorter than Zivkovic, and very nervous, which he was trying to hide beneath a constant scowl.

"We're looking for Aron or Hector." Zivkovic sounded cocky.

"On what business?" said Aron.

"A proposal."

"If you wouldn't mind putting your proposal in writing and sending it to us, we'll get back to you. Thanks."

He was about to close the door when Håkan Zivkovic shoved it open. Aron let the men push their way in; they were nervous and threatening.

They got into the hall, and Håkan shoved Aron with both hands. It was an odd shove, as if it was intended to make Aron scared, get him off balance. Hector stepped forward.

"Hello. How can I help you?"

Zivkovic and his sidekick lost their thread. The sidekick drew a pistol and held it nervously.

"Shut up and sit down. We do the talking," Zivkovic said.

Aron and Hector allowed themselves to be threatened. They went into the living room and sat down on the sofa. Zivkovic and his sidekick remained standing.

"Now, listen to me," Zivkovic said, taking a few steps around the room.

Aron and Hector looked at him, the poor bastard was really rather tragic.

"You've made threats against one of my clients."

"Oh, who?" Aron asked.

Zivkovic's gaze darted about.

"That doesn't matter."

"It must, surely?" Hector said.

Zivkovic hadn't expected to be questioned.

"No, it doesn't."

"Who?" said Hector.

The sidekick waved his gun at them.

"You know perfectly well who I'm talking about."

"No..."

Zivkovic fixed his eyes on Hector.

"Leffe will shoot if I tell him to, he's killed people before."

Hector looked at the sidekick in astonishment.

"Leffe? Have you killed people before?"

Leffe tried to look fierce, and nodded. Zivkovic resumed his commanding march around the room.

"Withdraw your threats, or you'll be in serious trouble. You have my word on that. We know who you are, and where to find you."

Zivkovic didn't like the fact that the men were smiling. Hector raised his hand.

"OK, it's time for you to leave," he said calmly, standing up.

"Sit down, for fuck's sake!"

Zivkovic was shouting like a soldier. Aron stood up beside Hector. They were smiling at his presumption, they were smiling at his total ignorance of who he was dealing with. Zivkovic was about to say something when Aron pulled out his revolver from behind his back. It happened fast. The silencer made a puffing sound as he fired two shots into Leffe Rydbäck's bulletproof vest. Leffe fell backward, dropping his gun in the fall. Hector launched himself forward at the same moment, grabbed Zivkovic by the neck, and pulled him to the floor, then hit him hard in the face, twice. Hector pressed his knee into Zivkovic's cheek and turned his head toward Leffe, who was lying on his back a short distance away, gasping for breath.

"Now watch what happens when people come into my home with guns in their hands," he whispered.

Aron yanked open Leffe's bulletproof vest and tugged it off him, pulled up Leffe's head and tucked the vest down behind him. Leffe didn't understand what was going on.

Aron pressed his pistol to Leffe Rydbäck's heart and fired two shots. The bullets went through his body and got caught in the bulletproof vest. The floor escaped damage, Leffe died on the spot. Zivkovic screamed like a small child and started crying.

"Who are you?" Hector asked.

Håkan was staring at his dead friend with tearful eyes.

"My name's Håkan Zivkovic."

Hector removed his knee and rolled Zivkovic over.

"Are you scared now, Håkan?"

Zivkovic couldn't get a word out.

"You weren't a minute ago.... You were cocky and threatening.... Funny how things change, isn't it?" Hector took a firm grip of his throat. "Talk."

"He never said his name," Zivkovic hissed.

"What did he look like?"

Zivkovic described what Svante Carlgren looked like.

"And what was the purpose of this visit?"

Hector squeezed his neck tighter.

"To frighten you. To let him go, leave him be."

Hector looked at Zivkovic, the color was starting to drain from his face.

"And if we didn't?"

"Then we were going to shoot you."

"That didn't work... did it?"

Zivkovic shook his head.

"Go back and tell him what happened here, in detail. Make him understand that we're never going to leave him alone, nor you either.... Remember that, Håkan Zivkovic."

Hector let go of Zivkovic, who stood up and left the apartment without looking at his dead friend.

Håkan Zivkovic came out the front door and went off along Själagårdsgatan at a half-run. He was pale, his nose was bleeding.... He was on his own and had been roughed up.

Anders called Gunilla and told her what he had just witnessed. There was silence on the line.

"On his own?" she said, as if the question would give her more time to think.

"Yes."

"So maybe your plan worked?"

Anders didn't answer.

"And the other one's still up there?"

"I'd rather not think about what state he's in."

"OK... then it's high time. Isn't it, Anders?"

"I'd have to agree with that."

22

The German had woken up half an hour ago, causing a great commo-tion on the ward.

The doctor's name was Patrik Bergkvist. He had curly hair, was thirty-eight years old, and wore a helmet when he cycled to work. Dr. Bergkvist was sitting on the edge of the bed looking into Klaus's eyes with a small flashlight he kept in the top pocket of his white coat. Klaus looked back as a nurse hovered in the background. Patrik was trying out his schoolboy German.

"Do you remember your name?"

Klaus looked irritated.

"Yes."

"What's your name, then?"

"None of your business."

Patrik tried to keep his composure.

"Oh? Why's that?"

"None of your business."

Patrik wasn't prepared for that response. His patients usually treated him with respect, and he didn't like losing face when there were nurses present. He switched off the flashlight.

"We've removed the bullet. You were lucky, it didn't cause any permanent damage to your internal organs. You'll have some discomfort for a while, though."

"Danke," Klaus said quietly.

Patrik nodded.

"The police want to talk to you. Do you feel up to that?"

"No."

"I'm going to call them anyway, I think you're up to it."

Dr. Bergkvist left the room, went into the little office that was squeezed between two hospital rooms, and found the number that the police had left. He called it and someone named Gunilla Strandberg answered. She turned out to be a very pleasant woman.

"How bad is he?" she asked.

Patrik Bergkvist rambled on with his expert doctor's talk. She interrupted him when she decided he was just showing off.

Klaus was sitting up in bed leafing through a Swedish gossip magazine. He looked at pictures of King Carl Gustaf, Queen Silvia, Carl Philip, and Madeleine, all standing on a lawn in front of a white palace somewhere, waving. Victoria and her husband weren't there. Maybe they were away on some trip. He recognized all of them. Rudiger, his boyfriend, was crazy about the royal families of Europe.

The door opened. Anders nodded slightly as they walked into the room. Klaus looked him up and down. Then looked in disgust at the porcine Berglund following closely behind.

"Are you feeling OK?"

Anders's German was good. He pulled up a chair and sat down.

"Who are you?" Klaus asked.

Hasse pulled out his police ID.

"You were shot?" Anders asked.

Klaus continued paging through the magazine. Kikki Danielsson was sitting at a pine kitchen table in her lovely home.

"What's your name?"

Klaus looked up, showed no intention of answering.

"We can help you, that's why we're here."

Anders was demonstrating great patience as Klaus turned another page. Someone named Christer, with a very big head, was holding his tiny little wife. Christer was evidently very fond of Elvis Presley and liked to spice up the usual dismal Swedish décor with shiny gold bathroom taps. Anders leaned forward and gently took the magazine from Klaus's hands.

"I've got some other things for you to look at."

Anders put the magazine aside and pulled a folded A4 envelope from inside his jacket. He opened it and looked through a number of photographs. Klaus waited, glancing quickly at Hasse, who was standing over by the window. Anders pulled out a picture of Hector and held it up in front of Klaus.

"Do you recognize this man?"

Anders looked at Klaus, who was looking at Hector. Klaus shook his head. "No..."

Anders held up a picture of Aron Geisler, Klaus shook his head. Anders held up a picture of Sophie Brinkmann, Klaus shook his head. Anders held up a picture of a random criminal from the police archive. A reaction from Klaus, as if he had spent a microsecond too long searching his memory. Klaus shook his head.

"He knows," Anders said to Hasse in Swedish.

Anders reverted to German again.

"You're lying there with a gunshot wound. We know you were driven here by someone. Who?"

Klaus shrugged his shoulders.

"Who shot you?"

Klaus didn't answer.

Anders changed tack.

"Let's start again. Who dropped you off here at the hospital?"

Klaus glared blankly at him.

"If you tell us how you got here, what you know about Hector Guzman, we'll let you go, in return for possibly having to testify at some point."

Klaus let out a big, relaxing yawn, reached for the gossip magazine beside Anders, and started to look through it again. Then he looked up and smiled at Anders.

"OK, as soon as the doctor says you're well enough, we'll lock you up in prison until you decide to talk."

Klaus was still smiling when Anders and Hasse left him.

Anders and Hasse walked down the corridor. The door at the far end opened. A large man came walking toward them with a sort of rolling gait. The corridor looked like it was one size too small for him.

They met halfway. The big man didn't so much as glance at them, just marched past purposefully.

Anders stopped after a few steps, and looked back at him.

"Anders?" Hasse asked.

He turned toward Hasse as if he was still stuck in a thought, a memory.

"What is it, Anders?"

Anders turned around again and looked at Mikhail, who was opening the door to Klaus's room.

"It's him...."

"Who?"

"The big guy, that's his partner, the one I saw going into Trasten."

"Are you sure?"

"No..."

"But?"

"But what the hell..."

Anders drew his pistol and walked back toward Klaus's room. Hasse drew his, and followed him with long strides.

Mikhail had opened the door of the cupboard, pulled out Klaus's clothes, and tossed them on the bed. The door flew open behind him. He turned around, saw a man, saw an arm, saw a raised pistol. Mikhail reacted instinctively. He shot out his hand, grabbed Anders's arm, and pulled it toward him. A shot went off. Klaus screamed. From the corner of his eye, another man with a drawn gun; Mikhail was still working on instinct. He twisted Anders around, still with his hand on the pistol, pulled it free, and aimed the barrel at Hasse, his finger squeezing the trigger.

"Mikhail!" Klaus shouted. "They're police!"

Mikhail eased his grip on the trigger.

"Drop it" was all he said to the fat one.

Hasse didn't hesitate, dropped his gun to the floor. Mikhail threw Anders across the room, and gestured to Hasse to go and sit beside him.

"The bastard shot me," Klaus said, holding his shoulder, as blood pumped out steadily.

Mikhail looked at the chaos in the room, weighing his options, then tossed the pistol to Klaus, who picked it up in his left hand. Mikhail picked up Hasse's gun from the floor and left the room.

He marched down the corridor as some nurses tried to take cover behind a trolley, and searched through every room and cupboard. In one office, beneath a desk, Patrik Bergkvist sat huddled up. Mikhail bent over, felt with his hand, grabbed his curly hair, and pulled him out.

"I need tranquilizers or narcotics. I need bandages, needle and thread, and equipment for removing a bullet from someone's arm."

Patrik Bergkvist nodded to everything. Mikhail took the man by the neck. They headed toward a storeroom.

Klaus was covering Hasse and Anders with the pistol. The door opened. Mikhail pushed Patrik Bergkvist inside, and he went straight over to Anders Ask.

"No, not him. Him!"

Mikhail pointed at Klaus and his bleeding arm. Patrik hurried over and started to examine the wound. Mikhail opened a flimsy blue garbage bag he had in his hand. He took out a glass bottle of thiopental and loaded two syringes. He drove one into Anders's thigh and injected the drug. Anders started swearing angrily before he slumped to the floor. Mikhail did the same with Hasse, who whimpered as the needle drove into his flesh. Within a minute they were both sleeping soundly.

Patrik Bergkvist had temporarily stemmed the flow of blood with a tight ligature around the wound.

"This man needs to be operated on at once."

"How fast can you do it?"

"One hour."

"Forget it."

Mikhail filled the syringe. Patrik Bergkvist shouted "No" over and over as Mikhail took his arm and squeezed the narcotics into his system. The doctor was slurring hysterically, trying to say he needed to be supervised by an anesthesiologist, that he needed oxygen. Then he fell to the floor, arms by his sides, hitting his cheek hard and slipping into unconsciousness.

Mikhail helped Klaus out of the bed and supported him as they hurried out of the hospital.

They got into the rental car outside the main entrance. Mikhail headed into the city.

"Where are you going? We have to get to the airport!" Klaus said.

"Not like this, you'll die."

Mikhail dialed a Stockholm number on his cell.

The telephone rang. He recognized the voice at the other end. Mikhail sounded stressed, and was offering a deal. Which was worthless, of course. Pretty much: do me a favor now, and I'll owe you one. Jens said no. But Mikhail didn't give up, and pleaded in a way that surprised Jens. The man sounded almost humble. But this was Mikhail, there was no way....

"Sorry, that's impossible."

Silence down the line.

"I'm begging you.... You're the only person who can help us. My friend's dying here...."

Was that something human he could hear in Mikhail's voice? Someone was dying. Could he coldly hang up and never think about what he could have done differently? Could he just say no and go on with his life? He looked at Sophie, who was sitting on the sofa. *Hell.*

He gave Mikhail his address and hung up, bitterly regretting his decision. Ten minutes later someone banged on the door. They both recognized the bleeding Klaus as Mikhail carried him into the living room.

"What happened?" she asked.

"He's been shot in the shoulder," Mikhail replied.

Klaus lay on the sofa.

"Quick, Jens, get me some warm water and towels, and anything you've got in the way of medicine."

Jens disappeared from the room. Mikhail emptied the contents of the plastic bag on the coffee table. Syringes, needle and thread, thiopental, antiseptics, bandages. He was about to take the bandage off when Sophie stopped him.

"Hang on, I've got this," she said, sitting down beside Klaus, removing the temporary bandage around his upper arm and looking at the wound in his flesh.

"I need tweezers, or a narrow pair of pliers or something," she called to Jens.

She felt Klaus's pulse, it was shallow and fast.

"Where did you get this?"

She gestured to the things on the coffee table.

"Hospital," Mikhail replied.

Sophie loaded a syringe with thiopental. A low dose, she didn't know how much she should use.

"You decide," she said to Mikhail. "Either we operate on him without anesthetic or I give him a small dose of this, but it's risky."

Klaus let out a whimper of pain.

"Give it to him," Mikhail said.

Sophie pressed the drug into the man's arm. Klaus's pain vanished at once as he drifted off among the clouds. Jens came back with water and towels, together with what he had found in his poorly stocked bathroom cabinet.

Half an hour and a considerable quantity of blood later, Sophie had managed to pull the bullet out and stop the bleeding. The bullet had shredded the muscles in the arm, but the bone seemed to be intact. She cleaned the wound, sewed him together, doing whatever she could with the meager means at her disposal. Mikhail kept an eye on Klaus's breathing.

"Thank you," he said as she gathered up the things on the coffee table.

"This is only temporary, he needs proper care."

She went off to the bathroom to wash. Jens caught Mikhail's eye.

"We'll leave as soon as he wakes up," the Russian mumbled.

The men heard Sophie turn on a tap in the bathroom. Neither of them had anything to say.

"Are you hungry?"

Jens didn't know why he asked. Mikhail nodded.

They ate a cold spread at the kitchen table. Mikhail sat leaning forward with his left arm around his plate, shoveling the food in with his right hand.

"What are you both doing here?" Jens asked.

Mikhail chewed, gestured toward Klaus on the sofa.

"I came to get him," he said, chewed, then swallowed. "He woke up in the hospital yesterday and called me. I flew up."

"What happened?"

Mikhail stretched.

"The police arrived, we had to get away...."

"Who shot him?"

"The police..."

Sophie came out into the kitchen and looked at Jens and Mikhail, who were eating in silence. She didn't like what she saw.

"Is he going to have another go at Hector?"

Mikhail seemed to understand the question and shook his head. She kept her eye on the Russian as she said to Jens: "I want you to ask him for something."

Carlos was out of breath. He had come as soon as Hector called. Now he was standing in Hector's bathroom looking at Leffe Rydbäck's body as it lay crookedly hunched up in the bath. Hector was standing behind him.

"You need to cut him up into pieces and take him to the restaurant. Then grind him up in the mincer."

Carlos had his arm over his mouth, the urge to vomit in his throat. Aron came up behind them with two paper bags in his hands, forced his way past, and spread a towel out on the bathroom floor. He opened the paper bags and took out two handsaws, different sizes, and put them on the towel. He carried on with dishwashing gloves, a plastic apron, shower cap, vinegar essence, pruning shears, disinfectant, a roll of freezer bags, a circular saw with a freshly charged battery, protective goggles, a breathing mask, chlorine powder, a white plastic bucket, and a Steel Eagle hammer with a rubber handle. Finally Aron pulled out a vanilla-scented Magic Tree air freshener, ripped the plastic off, and hung it up on the shower head.

"You ought to get going before he starts to smell," he said.

Carlos hesitated, then bent over and picked up the apron, shower cap, and dishwashing gloves and slowly began to put them on. Aron pulled a folding knife from his trouser pocket and opened it up. It had a ridged black handle and a short blade of air-hardened carbon steel.

"This is sharp," he said, passing the knife to Carlos, handle first. "And throw up in the toilet, not the bucket," Aron went on as he and Hector left the room.

Carlos was left standing in the hollow silence of the bathroom. Staring at Leffe Rydbäck in the bathtub. He took a few shallow breaths before sitting down on the side of the bath and taking hold of the corpse's right hand. It was cold. He held the sharp knife blade against Rydbäck's little finger and pressed. It was pretty easy, the finger shot off and bounced off the side of the bath. Carlos repeated the procedure on the thumb. Once he had worked out what he was doing the rest of the fingers came off quickly, then he moved on to the left hand.

Hector was sitting on the sofa with a newspaper. Aron was in an armchair. From the bathroom they could hear Carlos testing the circular saw like a teenager with a souped-up moped. Then the sound of the saw working through something thick. It eased off slightly, the engine idling, then picked up again. The saw fell silent, then came the sound of Carlos heaving and throwing up in the toilet. And then the whining sound of the saw again.

Time passed, Hector went on reading, Aron stared out into space. They were interrupted by steps on the spiral staircase that led down to the office. Aron stood up, drew his gun. The steps were slow without being heavy.

A woman in her fifties came up, looked at Hector, then at Aron and his raised pistol.

"You can put that away," she said.

Aron lowered the gun, but kept it in his hand.

"I must apologize," the woman said. "But you'd never have let me in if I'd knocked on the door, so I had to make my own way in downstairs via your office."

Gunilla held a finger up to her ear. The noise of the saw was coming through the wall.

"Are you doing some home improvements?"

She listened some more.

"Unless that could be Leffe Rydbäck, in the middle of being sawn up in the bathroom?"

Aron raised his gun again, but the woman seemed quite indifferent to it. She held out her ID.

"I'm a police officer. My name's Gunilla Strandberg. Please, put the pistol away, people know I'm here."

Aron hesitated and went over to the window. He looked down, then out, saw nothing.

"No, there's no one there, it's just me. I came to talk, but people know I'm here. If anything were to happen..." She gestured with her hand. "Well, you understand."

Gunilla looked at Hector.

"I just want to talk," she repeated in a low voice.

He folded the newspaper, indicated that she should sit down.

Gunilla sat down on one of the sofas. The sounds now coming from the bathroom were hard hammer blows to bones and flesh, and then the whining of the saw started up again. Hector inspected her.

"Do we know each other?" he asked.

"I know you, Hector Guzman. You don't know me."

Hector and Aron waited for more.

"And now you're wondering why I'm here?" Gunilla fixed her gaze on Hector. "Out of sheer curiosity, I think," she said.

Carlos was throwing up again. This time he shouted out as he vomited.

Gunilla waited until Carlos had finished.

"I'm curious about how much money you made from blackmailing Svante Carlgren, and from your dealings with Alfonse Ramirez, who I know is in town.... Just a rough idea, I mean?"

Hector was looking at her hard.

"What do you want?" he asked.

A curious look from Gunilla.

"I can see it on you," he went on. "You want something, answers, possibly. Isn't that what you police like most—answers?"

"No, I've already got the answers. And they don't interest me at all."

Hector looked at Aron, who in turn looked at Gunilla.

"So what do you want, then?" Hector asked.

"I want what you've got."

"Sorry?"

"How much have you earned from Ramirez and Carlgren?" she asked again.

Hector didn't answer.

"I want a share of that," Gunilla said.

Now Hector understood.

"In exchange for what?"

"In exchange for a free hand for as long I'm in the police department."

PART FOUR

23

The tears never came. He was rolling paint over the wall. The notes, the deductions, the arrows . . . the whole context. Everything disappeared behind thick, white paint.

Sara had been in his apartment. She had seen the wall, she had figured something out. Then she had contacted Gunilla. She had been murdered. And soon they would murder him as well.

He had copied everything, both digitally and in hard copy. Two sets. One was secure in the safe deposit box at the bank. The other was in the sports bag on the floor. He checked his pistol: full magazine, another in his jacket pocket. He usually carried it in a holster on his belt. Now he had it in a shoulder holster instead, he could feel the straps across his back and shoulders.

He looked around the office. The wall was as white as new-fallen snow, the room was tidy, nothing of any interest to anyone. He picked up the black sports bag from the floor. Took his laptop and the surveillance equipment and left the apartment.

Down in the street he headed toward the rental car. If he'd been paying attention, he might have seen the man sitting in a car a bit farther along. But he didn't, he wasn't paying attention. . . . He was coming down, and was mainly focused on his own pain.

Lars drove the car through the city. The traffic was light, summer vacation had started. He parked on Brahegatan, a block from the police station. He put the surveillance equipment on his lap, checked that it was getting a signal from the microphone up in the room. He moved it into the trunk and left the car with the bag and laptop in his hands.

Lars walked with his head down, crossed Karlavägen, then the small park running down the middle of the road, heading toward Stureplan.

He was nudged in the side from the left. A light nudge, he looked up, a large man was walking beside him.

"Walk with me," the man said in English, with an Eastern European accent.

Lars went cold and reached for his service weapon.

The man showed the pistol in his right hand. And gestured for Lars to give him his gun. Everything happened quickly, suddenly the big man had Lars's pistol in his jacket pocket and was steering him across the road to a parked car. Mikhail pulled open the back door and shoved Lars into the backseat.

"Lie still and keep your mouth shut," Jens said from behind the wheel.

They pulled out into the traffic.

"Who are you?"

The big man punched him in the face.

The room was terrible. Like a cabin on a boat, with a constant rushing sound from the highway up above, in spite of the soundproof windows.

Once Jens and Mikhail had left she had gotten in a taxi and headed south along the Essinge Highway and out onto the E4, toward the southern suburbs. The motel was beside the highway in Midsommarkransen. There was no reception desk, just a lobby where you checked in using your credit card—Jens had given her one.

She sat down on the bed and waited. Maybe it was more of a bunk than a bed, hard and unyielding. She kept calling Jane. Jane always had the same answer: *No change*. Sophie noticed her reflection in the mirror above the fixed desk. She saw a sad, exhausted figure—and looked away.

After what seemed like an eternity there was a knock on the door. Sophie got up and went over to open it. Jens pushed Lars Vinge inside, and the door slid closed by itself behind them.

Lars Vinge was lost. He didn't know where he was. She looked at him, he looked sick, weak and pale, dark rings under his eyes—emaciated, somehow. His nose had been bleeding, he had dried blood in his nostrils. Jens gestured for him to sit down. Lars found a chair by the table, which too was screwed to the wall.

"Can I have something to drink?" His voice was quiet.

"No," Jens said.

Lars rubbed his eyes.

"Do you know why you're here?" Jens asked.

Lars didn't answer, instead he just stared at Sophie and started to smile. He smiled as if they were old friends, old friends who hadn't seen each other for a long time. The smiling made her feel uneasy.

She'd only seen him very fleetingly before. Now she realized what sort of man he was. She didn't like him. Lars Vinge exuded a peculiar mixture of low self-esteem and unwarranted self-confidence. He was unstable, unpleasant . . . and scared.

"But you didn't have to do this," Lars said.

"Why not?"

He was looking at Sophie the whole time, his left leg was twitching unconsciously.

"You didn't have to capture me like this. . . . I was going to get in touch with you soon anyway. . . ."

"What for?" Sophie asked.

He looked down at the table.

"I'm so sorry, I heard about Albert. How is he?"

"Tell us what you know," Jens said.

A long silence followed.

"Gunilla wanted Anders and Hasse to pick him up."

"Why?" asked Sophie.

"I don't know. Something was going on. They wanted a hold over you, Sophie, they said they wanted to make sure you weren't going to start anything."

"Start what?"

"I don't know, they must have been worried about you.... Worried that you'd do something without thinking it through—after all, they'd threatened you. Sooner or later you were likely to do something."

Sophie didn't understand.

"But why now?"

Lars thought. "Something's going on—"

"Tell us everything, right from the start," Jens interrupted.

Lars looked up at Sophie and Jens, trying to think. He put his right hand down flat on the table, seemed to be trying to find a structure. Then he started to talk. First hesitantly and tentatively, but after a bit of confusion he pulled himself together, got onto the right track, and managed to stay on it. He described how he had been contacted by Gunilla Strandberg, how he had started working for her. How he had quickly forgotten the purpose of it. How he had watched Sophie, and about the microphones in her house, about his reports to Gunilla, about how he didn't know the others had kidnapped Albert. How he didn't know anything about anything, how he had been kept at arm's length.

She thought it all felt unreal. There was the man who had been stalking her for weeks, telling them things that were beyond her comprehension. The idea that she was somehow in the center of something gradually dawned on her. He talked about people who had made her the starting point for a criminal investigation that didn't seem to have any foundations. About the way Gunilla Strandberg worked and didn't work, about the fact that the man she had met in the police station was Erik Strandberg, Gunilla's brother, and about his sudden death. About their attempts to put pressure on other people around Hector, about an unhealthy obsession with making progress toward something. And about a clandestine detective—Anders Ask—and a thug—Hasse Berglund—and how the pair of them had gone after Albert.

Lars stopped talking, looked down at the table, and rubbed his finger on an invisible mark.

"You said you were starting to build up a picture.... What did that picture look like?" she asked.

"I don't know...." He scratched his forehead. "Our lives are in danger. Yours and mine, Sophie... Albert's, but you've already realized that."

He looked at Sophie and Jens.

"Was it you who put the note in my mailbox?" she asked.

He nodded.

"And you've been inside my house?"

Now he was staring at her.

"What?"

"Answer," Jens said.

Lars lowered his head, shook it. Stared fixedly at the floor.

"No . . . ," he mumbled.

"No, what?"

"No, I'm not going to answer that," he whispered.

Jens and Sophie looked at each other. This guy was seriously disturbed.

"The Saab, why did you set fire to it?" Jens asked.

"I was just starting to realize that there were a lot of things going on that I wasn't part of at all. . . . When you came and took my ID and the rest of it, I started to get an idea. I took the surveillance equipment out . . . set fire to the car, told Gunilla all the equipment had gone up in smoke."

"Why?"

Lars was drawing circles on the table with one finger of his right hand.

"I've started listening to them instead."

"Who?" Jens asked.

"Gunilla, my colleagues."

"Why?"

Lars stopped drawing circles.

"What did you say?" he asked, as if he'd suddenly forgotten everything he'd just been saying.

"Why did you start listening to your colleagues?" Jens said slowly, in a sharp tone of voice.

Lars's memory came back and he swallowed.

"Because I realized that something was going on that I . . . that I was being kept out of."

"What?" Jens asked.

"Just then everything was too messed up to make any sense out of . . . but I was right, at least."

Jens and Sophie waited.

"They murdered my girlfriend."

Lars almost whispered the words.

"Sorry?" Sophie said.

He looked up at her and Jens.

"They murdered Sara, my girlfriend."

Mikhail was driving back into the city, Sophie and Jens were in the backseat.

"Fucking hell," Jens whispered.

She could only agree. She was staring out of the window, looking at the steady stream of traffic driving past them.

Mikhail and Klaus had left, the good-byes had been short. There was a knock at the door. Jens looked at his watch.

"Mikhail must have forgotten something," he muttered to himself.

He looked out through the peephole, expecting to see two men. But outside stood three men, three men of a different sort: hollow-eyed, tired, and staring all at the same time. Gosha with his shaved head, Vitaly with a bottle of liqueur in his hand, and Dmitry, eyes wide apart. *Fuck*. He'd calculated that they wouldn't reach Stockholm before later that evening, and wasn't expecting them before that. They must have driven nonstop.

Jens pulled away from the door and went into the kitchen. Sophie saw the look on his face.

"What is it?"

Jens hurried over to the kitchen window.

"What is it, Jens?"

"They're here earlier than I expected.... We have to get away from here, now."

There was a loud bang on the door.

"Who are they?"

Jens opened one of the kitchen windows. "Never mind that. Come on, we need to leave."

"Let me say that you're not here."

"Trust me, you don't want to do that."

The banging on the door had turned into heavy thuds. The whole frame was shaking out in the hall. Jens pointed at the open window. Sophie wanted to come up with another option. The thudding became hard kicks. She could hear the Russians' agitated voices. Jens climbed out the window, turned back, and held his hand out to her. She looked at him, looked at the hand, hesitating. Then she left the kitchen and disappeared back into the apartment.

"Sophie!" Jens hissed.

A foot came through the wood of the front door, the agitated voices could be heard more clearly now. She came back with her handbag, took his hand, and stepped up onto the window ledge. The sound of wood being kicked out of the door merged with the men's shouts and yells as they made their way into the apartment.

She clambered out onto the narrow ledge. It was clad with worn, beaten tin. The wind was gusting. She clung on to the edges of the attic windows adorning the top part of the façade. It was a long way down to the street and the tin was slippery. She glanced down. The cars looked small enough for the view to give her an instant fear of dying. She looked toward Jens, but that made her feel just as giddy. The sky above her felt far too large.

"We need to get farther away. Be careful, little steps," he whispered, and began moving off to the left.

Sophie followed him. She could hear voices from inside the apartment as the Russians wandered between the rooms. Dmitry was screeching angrily, then something got broken, and the men started shouting accusations at one another. She was sweating, shaking. Her fear of heights was rising inside her like a fierce sense of nausea. Jens turned toward her and saw how terrified she was.

"Just a few more steps. You can do it," he said calmly.

They moved slowly toward the next apartment. The façade changed, they were moving onto another building. Jens stopped, trying to think of a way to proceed. The ledge got even narrower, it sloped downward, and there was nothing to hold on to, just slippery tin with a few raised edges for the three yards ahead of them before they reached the next window. She stared, it looked impossible. Jens tried it out, clinging to one of the ridges with one hand, there wasn't much to hold on to, their fingers would have to do all the work.

"I can't," she said.

Her heart was pounding in her chest. Her throat was dry, she couldn't swallow.

Jens changed his grip, slid one foot along, clinging to the ridge in the tin.

"We have to get to the next apartment."

"No, I can't," she pleaded.

Fear of dying was pressing in on her. She just wanted to sit down and wait for someone to come and get her.

With one swift movement Jens moved onto the next building. He was standing with his feet on the narrow ledge, clinging to the ridges in the tin plating. He held still for a moment to see if the technique was going to work. She stared at him. What he was about to do looked impossible. She could never do it. She looked down. Her breathing was shallow, and tears began trickling down her cheeks.

"You're crazy, you hear?" she said.

He saw her tears, the state she was in, took another step, keeping his body tight against the façade of the building, shuffling along with his feet, his knuckles white. Jens stopped and took a deep breath. When he had regained his composure he took a few more little steps. He had covered two yards and was getting closer to the next window. But not close enough to be able to reach it.

Finally he made it to the attic window. Jens stopped and clung on tightly as he concentrated, swung his leg out, and kicked as hard as he could to break the glass. Once the window was broken, he had to crouch down to open the catch from the inside. He let go with his right hand and carefully bent his legs, stuck his hand in, opened the window, and climbed inside. Everything seemed to happen in one long, considered movement.

He vanished for a couple of seconds before reappearing. This time he was sitting hunched on the windowsill, reaching as far as he could in her direction. That might give her one yard's grace, but what good was that? She straightened up, and the wind tugged at her. He waved her toward him.

"Come on, now."

She wanted to breathe in more air but she was so terrified that she could only take shallow breaths. Her heart was pounding so hard that it seemed to be absorbing all the oxygen in her body. Sophie breathed out, but the lump in her throat was still there.

"You can do it, just hold on tight with your hands," he said.

She started to hyperventilate and tears began to fall once more.

"Now!" Jens said, beckoning with his hand.

Sophie realized that she only had one option: to do what he had done, find some sort of grip and heave herself up with one leg.

"Sophie!" he hissed.

The Russians were yelling inside the kitchen. She blinked away her tears, swallowed the lump in her throat, and did it all in one movement. She grabbed hold of the protruding joint in the tin plating, and stood there with her back toward certain death. It felt like it would only take one little gust of wind and she would fall. She took a step to the left. The ledge beneath her sloped downward. She clung on tight, her fingers were white. She got ready to switch her grip to take the next step and grab the third ridge in the tin. Sophie flung out her arm, got hold of the ridge, and took a quick step to the left. Her foot started to slide, and her grip on the tin slipped. She screamed as she lost her hold.

She felt his hand grab her hair, then an arm around her neck. For a second everything went black.

They crashed down onto the floor and ended up lying on broken glass. Sophie couldn't move. She was lying on top of Jens. His eyes were wide open, his forehead wet with sweat. They looked into each other's eyes.

"You did it," he said.

He got up, pulling her with him. They hurried through the apartment, she was high on adrenaline. Jens gestured to her to stop in the hall. He called a number on his cell, then said that now he was the one who needed help. After a short conversation he ended the call and was about to make his way out into the stairwell when he realized that the door was locked from the outside.

"Start looking!" he told her.

They started searching the hall, Sophie looking through the outdoor clothes hanging up there, Jens checking the drawers of a low chest beneath a large mirror. He found nothing, neither did she. He checked in another cupboard, she looked in the drawers again, as if she didn't trust him to do it properly. Sophie glanced around the hall, along the walls, along the floor, the door frame, above the fuse box. . . . There, a hook, one solitary key. She reached for it, caught it, tried it in the lock. She turned it—*click*—the door opened.

They took the stairs down to the street in long strides, Jens held the heavy wooden door open for her. They ran to his rental car and jumped in.

Just as he swung out onto the road Dmitry came running out the door of the next building. Jens put his foot down and drove off at speed. Dmitry and his friends ran toward their car.

Sophie pulled out her phone and made a call.

"Hello... It's me."

"So I hear."

"What are you doing?"

He didn't answer at once, possibly surprised at her direct question. "Nothing much."

"Can we meet?"

"When?"

"Now?"

He was silent again.

"This is all rather sudden. I'm at the restaurant," he said.

She ended the call. Jens was weaving through the traffic.

"Are you sure?" he asked.

"No...," she said quietly.

"Why do you want to go there?"

"Have we got a choice?"

"There's always a choice."

"That's the only place we can get any protection," she said.

Jens looked in the rearview mirror, couldn't see Dmitry's car.

Hasse was sitting in his car, parked outside Trasten, glowering lazily at the world around him. He had been given clear instructions. Wait outside the restaurant, don't react to anything. Aron Geisler might come out and contact him, or possibly a man named Ernst Lundwall. Hasse was to go with the flow, go back in with them. Once he was inside, the plan was that he should call her, tell her what was going on, what the men were saying to him. But primarily this was about watching the transfer of money. Gunilla would keep an eye on things from her end, and when everything was done he was to shoot Hector Guzman and Aron if he got the chance, make it look like self-defense, then—*case closed.*

Anders was wandering around the city at random, looking for Sophie and Lars; there was a bounty on their heads now, Sophie in particular. She had to be gotten rid of, which was a bit sad.... Or not, he wasn't sure what he felt anymore. The murder of Lars's tree-hugging girlfriend had fundamentally altered him, switched something off, removed something else. But he had also been struck by a vast sense of guilt. It was there the whole time. And he wanted to kill again so that killing became a habit. Then perhaps the guilt would even itself out.

A car drove past Hasse and he followed it with his eyes, it found a space farther up the street and pulled in. A man jumped out, waited for the woman to get out of the passenger side. It took a few seconds for Hasse to realize who it was. After all, he'd only seen her very briefly last time, from behind, when he was about to strangle her. They disappeared inside the restaurant.

He called Anders on his cell. Anders got excited, told him to wait, lie low, said he was on his way.

Then another car drove past and parked farther up the street, a car with Russian plates, but Hasse didn't react to that. Hasse was instead preparing to kill two birds with one stone, or possibly three. He checked his gun, took the safety catch off, made sure there was a bullet in the chamber.

The restaurant was closed. Hector was sitting at a table with Aron, Ernst Lundwall, and Alfonse Ramirez. The table was now their workplace. Alfonse was sitting in front of a Wi-Fi laptop, Ernst was going through a mass of documents, Hector and Aron were doing calculations on a sheet of paper. They were all drinking coffee except for Alfonse, who was drinking wine.

Hector looked almost startled when he saw Sophie come in together with Jens. He was about to say something but Sophie interrupted him.

"We have to talk."

Hector stood up and indicated that they should sit down a bit farther away.

He held out a chair for her. She sat down, and he sat opposite and looked at her, waiting for her to begin.

Sophie took a deep breath, glanced quickly at Jens, who had sat down on his own at another table, then at Ernst and Aron and the stranger, who all seemed occupied with their work.

"Am I interrupting?" she asked.

Hector shook his head, and gestured hastily toward Jens.

"What's he doing here?"

Everything felt so wrong, she wished it could be different.

"We can deal with that later," she said, collecting herself and trying to find a way to begin. Sophie put her hands in her lap and prepared herself for what might turn out to be her own suicide.

"My son, Albert, is in the hospital. He was run over, his back's broken."

Hector looked momentarily horrified and was about to ask something when she held her hand up.

She started again.

"About a month ago I was contacted by . . ."

She didn't get any further than that. The door of the restaurant flew open with a bang and was left hanging from one hinge.

"Jeans!"

The voice was loud. Dmitry marched into the restaurant with a revolver hanging from his hand. Behind him came Gosha with a heavy cudgel, then Vitaly with a pistol. Dmitry spotted Jens.

"Missed me?"

Jens looked at Dmitry with distaste. Hector and Aron exchanged a glance, as if they were trying to figure out who these men were.

"What do you want?" Jens asked.

Dmitry pointed toward himself with the pistol, trying to look surprised.

"What I want? Doesn't matter . . . because now I'm here and . . . it's been a long fucking journey and I've been looking forward to shooting you, over and over again."

Sophie could see Jens tapping at his cell under the table. She glanced cautiously around the room. Aron was sitting still, the stranger was rocking gently on his chair, taking careful sips from his glass of wine. Ernst Lundwall was staring down at the table. And Hector . . . he was sitting there quite still, smiling reassuringly at her.

Jens stood up, Sophie saw him slip his cell into his pocket in the same motion.

"I've said all I've got to say to Risto, he's passed it on to you.... If you've come all the way here in the hope that we can work something else out, then your journey has been in vain."

Dmitry was staring with his mouth half open. Then he seemed to get bored, gestured to Gosha, and Gosha marched over to Jens and hit him over the head several times with the cudgel. Jens fell to the floor and Dmitry was there at once, kicking him. Vitaly kept the others covered with his pistol. Their beating of Jens was brutal and impulsive. Sophie didn't want to look.

Jens thought the kicks would stop, but they didn't. He got a sudden feeling that he was about to die, that Dmitry was so sick that he was going to kick him to death. Jens tried to protect himself by curling up. Dmitry's shoe kept hitting everywhere, in the head, neck, back, stomach. Then he changed tactic and began stomping on Jens's face.

"That's enough!" Hector shouted out across the room.

Dmitry stopped, looked at Hector, rather breathless now.

"Who are you... *nigger*?"

Sophie saw something flash in Hector's eyes. Something flaring up. It wasn't any usual sort of anger. This was something else, something beyond fury. Aron saw his condition and calmly shook his head. Even the stranger, who had been showing such restraint, looked different now.

Dmitry grabbed hold of the battered Jens, pulled him up from the floor, and looked into his badly injured face.

"Do you know how much I've been looking forward to this, your arrogant fucking attitude has been itching away at me like—"

Dmitry couldn't be bothered to finish the sentence and aimed a misjudged punch at the back of Jens's head, and Jens collapsed to the floor. Gosha had pulled out a small box and was sniffing the white powder straight from his finger. He loaded a new dose, then stuck his forefinger under Dmitry's nose. Dmitry inhaled the powder, then yelled out loud, as though he wanted to convey some sort of primitive strength to the room. He went over to Jens again, grabbed him by the collar, lifted him up, and aimed a right hook at him, putting all his strength into it. His fist hit Jens over the eye with a meaty crunch. Dmitry was panting excitedly as he straightened up from the blow, then leaned over Jens to administer a follow-up.

"Stop it!" Sophie shouted, with tears running down her cheeks.

Dmitry suddenly saw her. He looked happy, as though she were a gift he hadn't been expecting. He went over to her, looked down, took hold of her chin. Leaned in close to her face.

"Are you his whore?"

He stank of something.

"You're his whore, and if you aren't his whore...then you're someone else's. Because you're definitely a whore!"

Dmitry looked at his friends and let out a surprised laugh, as though what he'd just said had been a particularly sharp joke.

"She's someone else's whore!" he repeated. Vitaly and Gosha joined in, laughing exaggeratedly.

Dmitry still had a firm grip on her chin.

"When that bastard on the floor over there is dead, I'm going to fuck you...and everyone can watch."

Hector was quivering with anger now. He was staring at the table, his breathing was heavy, and his jaw muscles were working hard. He was positively glowing with hatred, Sophie could see his aura in the corner of her eye, burning with utter fury. Aron was keeping a watchful eye on him.

Dmitry looked affronted now, as if he couldn't remember why he was there. He drew his pistol again, and waved it toward the table where Aron, Alfonse, and Ernst were sitting.

"Who are you? What are you doing here? How do you know this bastard?" He pointed with the pistol toward Jens, who was still lying on the floor. No one answered. Dmitry marched over to the table and pressed the barrel against Alfonse's head. Alfonse remained calm. Dmitry was getting impatient and took a few steps toward Hector and Sophie, aiming the gun at Sophie.

"You, whore, talk!"

"Put the gun down," Hector whispered.

Dmitry tried to imitate Hector. He failed, he couldn't remember what Hector had just said. Instead he aimed the gun at Sophie's head. Sophie shut her eyes.

Jens moved slightly on the floor.

"Dmitry...," he spat through blood and cartilage.

Dmitry turned around and looked down at him.

"Yes?"

"Risto told me no one wanted to have anything to do with you in Moscow anymore. That you keep fucking up. Over and over again," Jens whispered.

Dmitry looked out across the room, then down at Jens again.

"What?"

"There's a type of person who can't do anything, who's incompetent, ignorant, talentless, no talent whatsoever, who tries to make up for all his failures by constantly committing more, which makes him a permanent loser. You're that sort of person, Dmitry, and everybody knows it."

Jens smiled through his pain.

"Everybody but you, Dmitry. Even your own mother. Your whore of a mother! Your whore mother, Dmitry. The woman who fucked every single bastard in your retarded home village. Even she knows it!"

Jens laughed, knew his speech had given Sophie a reprieve. Maybe it wouldn't be enough, but what could he do? His only hope was that Aron or someone else was armed and would start shooting. But that didn't seem to be happening.

Jens saw Dmitry turn his gun toward him; he looked straight into the dark barrel, wondering for a moment where the bullet would hit him, if it would hurt, how long it would take before he died. If he was going to see Grandpa Esben. If they'd start arguing the way they always did whenever they met.

Dmitry's finger was squeezing the trigger when someone cleared their throat over by the door. The Russian turned around. He saw two men, one big bastard and a thin-haired, sinewy guy with his right arm in a sling. They were holding guns, and were standing just inside the restaurant. For a moment it looked like things were going to stay like that, as if everything was going to freeze at that precise moment, as if God had pressed the Pause button. But He hadn't.

Hector realized what was about to happen. He threw himself at Sophie and tackled her. At that moment there was a coordinated thunderous noise as Mikhail and Klaus opened fire with their weapons. Gosha and Vitaly were riddled with bullets where they stood. Blood, fragments of bone, and homemade Eastern Bloc smack flew through the restaurant.

Sophie hit the floor with Hector's weight on top of her. She saw

Jens lying battered some distance away. She saw the two dead men hit the ground, their limbs limp, bodies shot to hell. She saw Dmitry, who still hadn't figured out what was happening. She saw Jens make a last, adrenaline-fueled effort and grab Dmitry's arm, drag him down, and disarm him in the same movement. Saw how Jens grabbed Dmitry by the hair, pulled him close, and let him look into his eyes before he systematically smashed his nose, eyes, and teeth with an explosion of rock-hard blows. Where Jens got the strength from she had no idea. But it was there. And nothing could make him abstain from his righteous revenge. Dmitry was gurgling, begging for mercy, swallowing his shattered teeth. Sophie turned toward the table. The gunpowder and drugs had formed a mist in the room. She saw Aron Geisler get up, aiming a revolver at Mikhail and Klaus. Sophie and Jens saw what was happening and cried out simultaneously.

"No, Aron!"

Now things got confused.

Mikhail and Klaus turned their guns toward Aron.

"They're not here for you!" she shouted.

Aron, his gun aimed at the men, didn't seem to listen. He fired two shots. Mikhail and Klaus, their guns outstretched, fired at the same time. There was terrible noise. Aron had taken cover behind a pillar. The bullets struck it, sending up plumes of plaster.

"We're not here for you," Mikhail yelled.

Aron stuck out his gun and fired two shots blind. The bullets smashed into the wall behind Mikhail and Klaus. Sophie shouted, Jens shouted, Aron fired again.

"I could shoot Hector Guzman here and now! Look, we're putting our guns down!" Mikhail called.

He and Klaus put their weapons down on the floor. Aron waited a moment, looked out twice from behind the pillar. When he saw the men prove that they were unarmed he stepped out with his revolver aimed at Mikhail.

"Why are you here?"

Mikhail nodded toward Jens, who, his face badly beaten, had his arm around Dmitry's neck and was in the process of strangling him. Aron kept his gun pointed at Mikhail.

"Explain."

"I can explain," Sophie said.

Another shot rang out through the room. There was total confusion, shouting, and yelling between Mikhail, Aron, Klaus, and Hector. Hasse was down on one knee in the doorway, Anders behind him. Mikhail recognized the men from the hospital. He grabbed his pistol from the floor and was about to fire when Hasse and Anders managed to take cover behind the outside wall.

"Police!" Hasse Berglund shouted, panic in his voice.

There was silence, then Hasse and Anders Ask showed themselves again.

"Police!" Hasse repeated.

"Hector! We had an agreement!" Anders called.

Aron looked at Hector. Their eyes met, Hector shook his head. Aron nodded that he understood, he raised his pistol and locked it onto Anders. Mikhail and Klaus were aiming straight at Hasse's forehead. Jens had grabbed Dmitry's pistol and was lying on his back with the gun in his hands, aiming down the barrel. The trajectory would pass between Mikhail and Klaus.

"I've got a perfect shot at the pig's heart," he said gruffly to Aron.

Six pistols aimed at bodies and heads. Hasse's was the first hand to start shaking.

"Drop your weapons," he said, his voice sounding thinner this time.

"No. Come inside and put your guns down. There are four of us, two of you.... Figure out for yourselves how this is going to end," Aron said.

Anders tried to salvage the situation.

"We'll back away. Leave you alone..."

"If you back away we'll fire."

Aron was firm in both voice and grip.

Sophie followed all this from her position on the floor, with Hector still on top of her. Jens was exhausted, he was bleeding heavily. She couldn't understand how he was managing to lie there with his gun pointed at the policemen.

Aron pulled the hammer back on his revolver instead of repeating himself.

Hasse put his gun down and slid it across the floor into the room, then crept in on all fours. All the guns were now aiming at Anders. He stared for a moment at all the barrels gaping at him, smiled slightly as he gave up a fleeting thought, then put his pistol on the ground and stepped into the restaurant.

The status quo had been restored. Jens realized Aron was never going to lower his gun first.

"Mikhail," he warned.

Mikhail understood, put his gun down again, followed by Klaus. Sophie felt Hector get off her, saw his exhilaration at the hatred flowing out of him as he approached Dmitry, who was lying unconscious on the floor. He grabbed one of the Russian's arms. Alfonse Ramirez went up behind him, grabbed Dmitry's legs, and they disappeared into the kitchen with the man, as if the only thing that mattered there and then was hitting back, sating the desire for vengeance.

Aron was shoving Anders and Hasse ahead of him toward the kitchen and back office.

Sophie had sat herself up and met Anders's and Hasse's gaze as they passed her. She went over to Jens, laying his head in her lap. He was in a bad way. The muscles and bones in his face were shattered, he was missing several teeth, and probably had several more broken bones in his body. When he breathed there was a hissing sound.

She was emotionally drained, felt like throwing up, wanted to get away from there, wanted to get away from herself, away from everything. Sophie sat there in the devastated restaurant stroking Jens's hair, and looked on as Klaus and Mikhail picked up their guns from the floor. Saw the bodies of the Russians in their unnatural positions. Ernst Lundwall, pale and scared, hurriedly leaving the restaurant with a briefcase in one hand and a laptop under his arm. She saw Albert's accident in front of her, she saw him lying in his hospital bed—unconscious, alone, broken. Her thoughts were spinning as she fought to hold on to any sort of sense, possibly it was the hand stroking Jens's hair that stopped her from losing her grip. Back and forth, the same movement the whole time. She concentrated on his hair beneath the palm of her hand. He was warm. She closed her eyes, trying to focus only on what she was doing, not think about the room or what had just happened. Back and forth with her hand, gently stroking Jens's hair, slowly . . .

Suddenly Mikhail was sitting beside her, examining Jens.

"We're going now," he said quietly.

Jens said nothing, his ravaged face just looked back at Mikhail.

Mikhail turned to Sophie, maybe he saw how scared she was. He had nothing to say that could help, and instead just stood up and walked toward the door. Klaus came over to her, said something in ragged English that she understood to mean that he owed her, that she had saved his life twice and that he didn't understand why. He tried to say this several different ways, but failed. Instead he picked up a pen, leaned on a table, wrote something on a napkin, and gave it to her. Sophie looked at the napkin, read *Klaus Köhler* and a phone number. She looked into his eyes. Klaus turned away and followed Mikhail, who had now left the restaurant.

Hector came out of the kitchen with his sleeves rolled up, bloody fists, and staring eyes. He looked at the chaos in the room, then at Sophie sitting on the floor with Jens's head in her lap. He was different, somehow charged. Charged with two thousand volts. Something was burning inside him, something he couldn't control. His eyes stopped on Sophie, but she got the feeling that he couldn't see her. Hector was about to say something when the stranger came out of the kitchen. Freshly washed and tidied up, he kissed Hector on the cheeks. They exchanged a few rapid words in Spanish. He walked toward the exit, smiling at Sophie as he passed her, then disappeared out past the broken door. Hector went back into the kitchen.

She hadn't told him what she had come here to say. Now Anders Ask was in there, along with Hasse Berglund. The men who had run down her son, the men who had tried to murder her...

Sophie laid Jens's head gently on the floor, got up, and walked out through the kitchen, passing Dmitry. He was sitting dead on a chair in the middle of the kitchen, his head lolling back. She could see a carving knife sticking out of his heart, one eye was hanging out, and there were several quarts of blood in a big puddle under the chair.

"Hector Guzman!" she heard Anders's voice say from inside the office.

She stopped, the door was ajar. She saw Anders sitting tied to the radiator beside the desk, Hasse alongside him. She could see Aron working at a computer. Sophie leaned forward and saw Hector, barechested, wiping his hands on a damp towel, his bloody shirt in a heap on the floor.

"We're supposed to supervise the transfer . . . ," Anders said.

Hector didn't answer.

Anders was struggling against his losing position.

"Shall we begin?" he said.

Sophie was trying to understand.

Hector opened a desk drawer, took out a new shirt, and tore the cellophane off it.

"It looks to me as if you're tied to a radiator," he said, starting to recover from the two thousand volts now.

"Just let us go, and we can finish off what you agreed with Gunilla, then we'll leave."

Gunilla? Sophie thought that nothing would ever surprise her again.

Hector waved his hand in the direction of the restaurant.

"Things have changed. There'll be no transfer for you, which I dare say you will understand after this." He unfolded the shirt with a shake.

"OK. We'll just go, we haven't seen anything," Anders said in a vain attempt to open up some sort of bargaining. Hector didn't bother responding to his suggestion. He pulled the shirt on.

"Don't be stupid now, Hector Guzman!"

Anders's words sounded angry. Aron stopped what he was doing on the computer and turned toward Anders. Hector stopped.

"Sorry?" he whispered.

Anders didn't seem to care.

"We can help you here . . . if you let us go. We can do the transaction together, we'll take the witnesses and leave the restaurant, and you're free."

Hector buttoned the shirt and looked up.

"Free?" he said in a toneless voice.

"Yes, free."

"You're a very strange man. Do you assume that everyone is as stupid as you are?"

Anders was about to reply when Hector held up his hand. Then he finished buttoning the shirt, with his chin on his chest.

"Be quiet," he said.

But Anders the terrier wasn't finished.

"Let us take the witnesses and leave, that's all I ask."

Sophie held her breath.

"Who?"

"The witnesses."

"What witnesses?"

"The woman, Sophie, and the man, her friend. They've got nothing to do with this."

Hector looked at Anders.

"How do you know that?"

"I just know."

Sophie heard a noise and turned around. Carlos Fuentes was standing there, staring at her. He looked small, marginalized, bowed somehow. She shook her head slowly to tell him to be quiet, not to give her away. Carlos's eyes were cold. He walked off.

She was sitting beside Jens again when she heard noises behind her. Hector and Aron came out. Hector in the fresh shirt, a jacket, and carrying a briefcase in his hand.

"Sophie?"

He was almost whispering.

"You have to come with me," he said.

"What for?"

He didn't have time for the question.

"The police will be here any minute, the ones in the office saw you."

She was seeing a different side of him again, he was emotionally shut off.

"Jens?" she asked

"Aron will help him."

"Where are we going?"

"We need to get away from here . . . that's the first thing."

She realized she had no choice. Anders and Hasse were sitting in the office, there were three dead bodies in the restaurant, and Gunilla and Hector were doing business together. . . . She had no chance. Had Anders told Hector about her?

Sophie looked at Hector, then at Aron, trying to detect any sign. She could see nothing but impatience and an urge to get going.

She leaned over Jens, kissed him on the head, wishing for a

moment that he would wake up, get to his feet, take her by the hand, and run off. But he wasn't going to. He wasn't going to do anything, he was severely beaten and unconscious, scarcely capable of even breathing by himself. Sophie stood up, grabbed her handbag, and followed Hector as he hurried out of the restaurant.

The smell of powder and death lingered in the room.

Carlos looked out across his restaurant. He had been in the kitchen pushing the pieces of Leffe Rydbäck through the mincer when the first shots were fired. He had stopped and hidden inside one of the kitchen cupboards. But when Hector and the Colombian dragged the Russian in and killed him, Carlos backed out and hid in the office. He had heard Hector's phone conversation with his father, how Hector had asked him to send the G5 up to Bromma Airport. Carlos had made his way back into the restaurant and hid on the floor behind the bar counter.

He couldn't figure out who was who, but he recognized the policemen, Cling and Clang. He had prayed to God while he was lying with his nose against the cold floor, prayed to Him to spare his miserable life. And God had done so. Carlos had made his way into the kitchen again, and found that woman, Sophie, eavesdropping on Hector. Then he had found another hiding place until Hector and the woman disappeared. Aron had come into the restaurant and picked up the wounded man, Jens. He had put him over his back and disappeared.

Now everything was silent, there was no one there, except the dead bodies and the policemen tied up in the office.

He looked around the inferno of blood and dead bodies, weighing things up, then, with shaking fingers, tapped a number into his cell phone.

"Gentz," Roland answered at the other end.

"This is Carlos . . . with the restaurant in Stockholm."

"Yes?"

"There are dead bodies here."

"Oh?"

"I need your help. I can give something in return."

"What?"

"Hector's location."

"We know that already."

"Where?"

"Stockholm."

"No."

"Where?"

Will you help me?"

"Maybe."

"Málaga, in a few hours."

"What do you want help with, Carlos?"

"Protection."

"From whom?"

"From everyone."

"Where are you now?"

"Stockholm."

"Get out, lie low, then call me again and I'll see what I can do.... You said people had been killed? Who's dead?"

"I don't know."

Gentz hung up. He could hear police sirens in the distance. Carlos left the restaurant.

24

The house was by itself. Looked more like a little summer cottage than the home of a detective superintendent. He had just spoken to her on the phone, she was at Brahegatan. He said he had been trying to find Sophie everywhere. She told him to come in. He said he couldn't. There had been a short silence, then she had asked what he wanted.

"Just checking in," he had replied.

Lars parked the car a few blocks away. Now he stepped inside her garden, walking under the apple trees and through the grass on the narrow gravel path that led up to the veranda.

The lock on the front door was modern, impossible to pick. He went around the house and checked the windows. All closed and locked. Lars found some steps that led down to a cellar door under the house, solid but out of the way, it had an old window with bubble-patterned glass, and possibly a latch on the inside. He pulled the sleeve of his sweater down over his arm and broke the glass, stuck his hand through, and felt. There, an old latch. He unlocked the door and went into the cellar.

Lars hurried through the rooms, scanning with his eyes as he went. A storeroom, a pantry, a recently installed geothermal system with a generator, a staircase leading to the floor above. He took it in a couple of strides, opened the door, and found himself in a kitchen that could have been taken from an English interior-design magazine. A new stove, but an old-fashioned design, a wooden floor with wide floorboards, oiled and varnished. Old-fashioned cupboards, beautiful. He kept going through the kitchen, turned into a living room, and went into an office. A desk, a lamp with a green glass shade, a filing cabinet, locked. He broke it open using a screwdriver he found in the bottom kitchen drawer. It made a noise, tin bending and twisting, but eventually it opened. A mass of documents hanging in a row. He worked through them with his fingers, looking for Sophie Brinkmann, but she wasn't there. His fingers went to G, Hector Guzman, nothing.... Just the names of tons of police officers he didn't recognize. Everything was in alphabetical order.... He went on. Wait, that was something—Berglund. Hasse Berglund. A passport photograph of the pig, Hasse, and some service reports. A note in pencil in the top right corner. *Violent,* it said. Lars looked on through the files. Found Eva Castroneves, no pencil note... instead a roughly drawn star. Like a teacher might put in a pupil's schoolbook. He checked the letter V, and found himself. He pulled the file out, opened it. The photograph was old, the same one he had on his police ID. At first the word that was written in pencil in the top right corner didn't want to sink in, as if he didn't understand it. *Unstable,* it said.

Lars closed the file and put it back. He experienced a moment of complete silence within himself as his eyes failed to register anything. Then he came back to life again.

He sat down on the chair by the desk, opened drawers: paper, pens, reading glasses, paper clips, a ruler... a few notes and coins. The bottom drawer was locked and he broke that open as well. Papers, notes, letters, he put them all in his pockets. He glanced around the room one last time before heading back down to the cellar. There he checked in every nook and cranny. He needed to pee, and sped up the search. Into the boiler room, his flashlight dancing over the walls, ceiling, floor. A cleaning cupboard under the stairs, an old Nilfisk vacuum cleaner with the hose looped over a semicircular metal hanger. Mop and bucket, cloths and disinfectant—a smell of old, unscented Ajax, hazy and fleeting childhood memories that he hurriedly shrugged off.

Into the pantry, full of tins and preserves. She could survive a nuclear war down here. The flashlight playing over the ceiling. Lars sat down and searched the floor. Got up and searched behind the tins...something shimmered. Right at the back of the shelf, behind the beans, the sweet corn, different varieties of Campbell's soup... He swept them aside with his arm and the tins went flying. There it was in front of him, the treasure he'd just uncovered. A dial, numbers around it, solid steel—an old safe, fifteen inches square, set back into the wall. But his joy was short-lived....How the hell was he going to open it? A quick glance at the time; he might have an hour, maybe less. What could he do in that time? Spin the dial at random? He tried to think...the notes in his pockets! Lars sat down, spread the notes out on the floor in front of him, the flashlight in his mouth. He read, tons of words and questions, he went on looking, no numbers anywhere.

He ran upstairs again, into the office, and grabbed as many of the folders from the filing cabinet as he could carry, down into the cellar again, and spread them out on the floor. The same trip three times. On the fourth he picked up all the old bills and papers that had been on top of the desk, and in the living room he grabbed a floor lamp.

He was on his knees, the floor lamp shining at the safe. He searched through the bills, found her ID number, stood up, and tried it, splitting it into two-digit segments. The first two counterclockwise, the following two clockwise. Locked. He repeated the process, starting with clockwise. Locked. He tried her phone number, locked. He tried her phone number and date of birth...locked. Time was passing. He still wanted to pee. And now he was sweaty, cold, and tired as well. His withdrawal was slowly worsening, his teeth were grinding the whole time.

Lars kneeled down on the floor again, opened the first file, leafed through it—information about a police officer named Sven. Sven had gotten the pencil annotation *Reactionary.* He put it aside. Opened more files—more police officers, trainees, inspectors, detectives... Small passport photos of faces he didn't recognize. Gunilla's notes in the corner in pencil. *Solitary*, *Dependent on company*, *Passive-aggressive*...All the files were set out the same, photograph in one corner, a personnel office record, notes, and a service report. He read through ten or so, trying to find anything that stood out. Nothing. He went back to Gunilla's notes again...nothing of interest. *This isn't working,* he thought. Lars stood up, stepped back, and looked at the folders. He turned the light from the floor lamp on them. The light made them look different from one another. In the filing cabinet they had all looked brown. They still did, but the different shades indicated that they were different ages. He shone the light around and picked up the file that looked palest—palest equaled oldest. He opened it, it was thicker than the others. The file contained a mass of old newspaper clippings, typewritten notes, washed-out photographs. He read a date...August 1968. He read names, Siv and Carl-Adam Strandberg, murdered on a camping trip in Värmland on August 19, 1968. *Strandberg? Her parents?* He tried the safe again, 68 08 19, locked. He tried clockwise and counterclockwise, he tried backward, counterclockwise, and clockwise. Locked. He read her parents' dates of birth, tried those the same way. Time was flying now, he'd been there almost forty minutes, Gunilla could show up anytime. Locked, locked, locked.

Sweat was dripping from his brow, his heart was pounding, his throat was dry, he badly wanted to take something, get rid of the itchy feeling in his soul....Lars went back to the file, looked through the newspaper clippings. A photograph of Siv and Carl-Adam Strandberg with their two children, Erik and Gunilla. They were standing in front of the entrance to Skansen, the open-air museum, sometime in the '60s. Siv and Carl-Adam were smiling, strict clothes, Carl-Adam with a little hat on his head; a tight, checked, short-sleeved shirt, straight trousers, polished shoes. Siv in a dress, hair piled up high, white shoes; the children smiling as well. Lars could see Gunilla in the girl's face. She looked happy. He looked at Erik, a fair-haired, laughing boy who was about to go into Skansen with his family. The boy was happy, he seemed to be glowing somehow. A terrible sense of guilt overwhelmed Lars. A feeling that it was this innocent little boy whom he had let die on the floor of Carlos's apartment. Lars stared at the photograph, breathing deeply to dispel the unease that was starting to spread. He looked on. The investigation. Lars read: They had been shot through the canvas of the tent. Shotgun. The murderer's name was Ivar Gamlin, he was thirty-one when it happened, seriously drunk, he'd beaten his wife then gone off in his car. The gun happened to be on the backseat by chance, he had claimed. He had been using it to hunt birds the day before. He just hadn't bothered to take it indoors. Lars moved on to an interrogation: Gamlin claims he has no recollection. Farther down the page: Gamlin sentenced to life imprisonment in 1969 . . . November 23, 1969. Lars tried those numbers every way he could, locked. He looked at the time again, almost half past five. He listened to see if he could hear anything. Then kept looking through the file. Gamlin applies for clemency, 1975. Rejected. Gamlin's sentence is fixed, 1979; he will be released in November 1982. Lars read quickly, skimming, leafing through. . . . There! Ivar Gamlin is murdered by another inmate, 1981. Lars went on, found a postmortem report. He scanned through the findings and got the impression that pretty much every bone in Gamlin's body had been shattered. He found another police report, a typewritten sheet of A4. Someone had gotten into Gamlin's cell at night. Cause of death was suffocation, with the help of an unknown object. The coroner's report suggested that this might have been a plastic bag. Lars thought, read once more, scanning the text. He found what he was looking for. Date of death 1981 . . . 03 . . . 21 . . . Lars tried the numbers on the dial. There was the sound of a car outside the house, tires on gravel. He kept going: 19 counterclockwise, 81 clockwise, a car-door closing, 03 counterclockwise. Steps on the gravel, 21 clockwise, steps heading toward the door. He tried the handle. Locked.

A key was inserted into the lock up above. He tried again, starting with 19 clockwise. The door upstairs opened and closed. Footsteps into the living room. He turned the dial slowly, sweat running from his brow—21 counterclockwise. He turned the handle slowly. Quick footsteps. He finished turning, *click*! The safe opened. Other people would have guessed it was God's help. Not Lars, he didn't guess anything.

Gunilla's voice through the floorboards above. She sounded upset, she was talking to someone on the phone. Lars stuck his hand inside the safe. Two plastic folders, a notebook, two bundles of thousand-kronor notes, a pistol, and a thick, official ledger with a dark-green felt spine. He took it all, tucked it inside his jacket, zipped it up silently, then made his way out of the pantry, past the stairs. He could hear Gunilla's voice more clearly now. Her tone was curt and irritated, she was saying that her house had been broken into and demanded that a forensics expert be let off other duties to come out to her.

He was moving slowly toward the exit when the cellar door above him opened and he heard steps on the stairs. Lars set off, ran through the darkness, found the door, and raced up the little flight of steps.

Instead of running out onto the road the way he had come, he swerved immediately left, into the leafy undergrowth. Twigs on slender stems whipped at his face. He'd gotten quite a distance when he heard the door opening behind him. Lars kept up the same speed until he reached his car five minutes later. He started it the moment he was behind the wheel and drove off, away from her house, away from Gunilla. Away.

It was a lounge, empty, cool, and private. They sat in separate armchairs, looking at each other. He was about to say something, changed his mind, looked away, and made eye contact with a woman behind a desk, waved her over, and asked for some water.

They drank in silence. Outside, planes took off and landed in turn, in the end the sound of jet engines became just a part of everything.

"How is your son?" he asked cautiously.

She looked at him.

"He's not good."

"What do the doctors say?"

"Nothing yet."

"Did you want to tell me anything in particular?" he asked quietly.

"It doesn't matter."

He looked at her.

"Tell me."

Sophie leaned forward slightly. "I came to tell you that Mikhail and his sidekick had asked Jens for help, that they weren't here to hurt you."

He looked at her critically.

"Why would you tell me that?"

"Because I was there when they arrived."

"Where?"

"At Jens's."

She realized how odd her lie sounded. But that didn't seem to be what Hector got caught up on.

"What were you doing there?"

"We've known each other for a long time."

Hector raised an eyebrow.

"How?"

A turboprop plane passed above them.

"I was waiting for you in the restaurant the first time Mikhail and his sidekick showed up; we were going to have dinner, you and me, and you never came back. I went into the office and found Jens unconscious on the floor. I hadn't seen him in over twenty years, it was just a massive coincidence."

Hector was looking at her closely.

"I let it go, we didn't talk for a while, then we got in touch again."

His expression hadn't changed.

"Mikhail came to Sweden to collect his friend from the Karolinska," she went on in a low voice. "The police were there, and shot his friend in the arm. Mikhail had Jens's number and called to ask for help. They came 'round to Jens's apartment, the friend with a gunshot wound in his arm. I helped him."

Hector let a few moments pass. "Then what?"

"Then I went to the restaurant, to see you."

"To tell me this?"

Now she was looking at him.

"No, we needed help, the Russians were after us.... We didn't know where to go."

The logical answer calmed Hector's thoughts a little.

"Who were they, the Russians?"

"Jens's customers."

He fell deep in thought, a darkness had come over him.

"Are you having an affair with him? Are you in love?"

Sophie shook her head. But it wouldn't have made any difference if she had said yes or no at this point. He was jealous, and also terrified of getting hurt. The weakest state for any man. The state that most of them hated in themselves, never wanted to see or experience. Hector was no exception. She realized that he was steering himself away from uncomfortable emotions by drifting further into thought. His act of avoidance seemed to fill the entire room.

"I don't trust him. There's too much coincidence about him, has been since the moment he first showed up."

"He saved our lives in the restaurant."

Hector didn't answer that, and seemed to be struggling instead to try to see her objectively.

"Who are you really?"

The question wasn't framed as a question, and she remained silent. The woman who had served them came over to say that their flight would be arriving soon. Sophie and Hector sat quietly, looking into each other's eyes. He was hoping to see something he could cling to; she remained still because anything else would have given too much away.

Hector was the first to look away, and got up.

They went and stood by a large window, watching as the Gulfstream landed, braked hard, then taxied toward the building they were standing in.

Half an hour later they were sitting in the plane, after refueling and a peculiar check-in and security procedure in which none of their luggage was inspected. Sophie was sitting in a beige leather armchair opposite Hector, separated by the central aisle. The plane taxied out to the runway and set off. Sophie was pushed back into her chair by the force of the acceleration. They climbed steeply and suddenly they were up among the clouds and the plane leveled out. She looked down as Stockholm disappeared below her. Albert was down there. She was sitting in a plane flying away from him, nothing could possibly have felt any worse than that. The sense of guilt was absolute, total, cemented into her soul. She knew she would never be able to get rid of it. She had gotten him into this. She was directly responsible for what had happened to him. If she had behaved in a different way, then perhaps...

Sophie saw islands and water, she looked out at the sky—blue, as usual. She heard Hector unbuckle his seat belt, get up, and head toward the rear of the cabin. He came back with two glasses and two bottles of beer, she declined the offer. He sat down in his seat, not bothering to use the glass, and took a gulp from the bottle.

"We'll be landing in Málaga, I'll go with you to Dad's, then I need to move on."

"Where are you going?"

"Away... The police must have issued an international warrant by now. But you'll be fine, Dad will take care of everything."

"Take care of everything?"

Hector nodded.

"What does 'everything' mean?"

There was a pause before Hector answered.

"Everything. You'll need to stay hidden until things have settled down. Dad will help you...."

The plane hit some light turbulence, the pilot increased the thrust and climbed, but neither of them paid any attention.

"But I have to get home soon...."

He said nothing to that, leaned against the window, deep in thought, puzzled, possibly worried. He was avoiding her, she could feel it, she understood. He was wrestling with the question of whether he could trust her. As was she. Wondering who she was, what her motives really were. Whether she could have done anything differently.

She looked at Hector again, he was still gazing out the window. She had seen that expression many times before, a concentration, an introversion that always seemed to rouse her curiosity. She had also seen it in him as a boy in the album he had shown her on the boat. Maybe that was what he really looked like. Maybe that was Hector?

She wanted to like him, but she didn't dare, she had seen his madness.

25

The dead bodies still hadn't been covered up. Tommy Jansson was standing in the middle of the restaurant. Two corpses in front of him and one in the kitchen, blood everywhere. Total carnage. Forensics was working frenetically, Anders Ask and a thickset man were sitting in silence on two chairs some distance away. Tommy recognized the thickset one. A rapid-response cop in the city center, if he remembered rightly. Tommy had told them to stay where they were and not move a muscle. They had refused to talk. Not a word. Anders Ask, what the hell was he doing here?

Tommy rubbed his ear with his knuckles.

"Who was first on the scene?" he asked the room in general.

Antonia Miller, a detective inspector who was standing nearby writing in her notebook, looked up.

"What did you say?"

"Who was first on the scene?"

The expression on her face suggested that he was disturbing her work.

"A patrol, I let them go half an hour ago."

"And they found those two?" he said, pointing at Anders and Hasse. "Where?"

Antonia was writing in her notebook.

"In the office, back through the kitchen, tied to a radiator."

"And what happened?"

She sighed, closed her notebook, and clicked the ballpoint pen.

"We got a call from someone in the building who had heard repeated banging sounds. The patrol arrived, saw the two bodies here in the restaurant, called it in, checked for signs of life, and secured the scene."

"Then what?"

"They searched the whole place. Found the body in the kitchen, and then those two in the office, tied up," Antonia said, gesturing toward Hasse and Anders with her thumb.

"The big one's a fellow officer," she went on, looking down in her notebook. "His name's Hasse Berglund, he showed the patrol his badge, and they checked with regional control, it checks out.... The other one has no ID at all."

Tommy looked around. Antonia opened her notebook again and went back to work.

Suddenly Anders's cell phone rang, Anders looked at the screen, let it ring. Tommy went over, grabbed the phone from his hand, and pressed the green button.

"Yes?" Tommy said in a low voice.

"What's happened, are they still there?"

He recognized Gunilla's voice, she sounded stressed.

"Hello, Gunilla."

A moment's silence. "Tommy?"

"What's going on, Gunilla?"

"That's what I'm wondering too."

"I want you to come to the Trasten restaurant in Vasastan, I believe you know where it is."

He ended the call and put the cell in his jacket pocket, giving Anders a "what are you going to do about that?" gesture. Then he took a walk around the scene. A bearded forensics officer was sitting beside one of the bodies.

"Hi, Classe," Tommy said.

The forensics officer looked up and nodded.

Tommy went over to the bar, where he stopped and turned around to get an impression of the whole premises. He saw the shattered front door, the bodies, the bullet holes and shell casings on the floor—all marked out by the forensics team. Overturned furniture, people had left in a hurry. And in the middle of all this, completely silent, Berglund and Ask? Tommy looked at them, Tweedledum and Tweedledee. . . .

"You're a couple of fucking idiots, you know that, don't you?" he said loudly.

Hasse and Anders didn't answer. Tommy glared at them for a while, muttered something else insulting, and went through into the kitchen.

On a chair in the middle of the floor sat a bloody man with a carving knife sticking out of his heart; he had no teeth left, his face was beaten to a pulp, and his right eye was hanging out. Tommy shuddered with distaste.

A female forensics officer with big biceps, whose name he couldn't remember, was brushing for fingerprints on what looked like frozen food.

"We found this in the freezer," the woman said, pointing at the meat.

"Oh?" he said, none the wiser, and saw the mass of plastic bags that had been pulled tightly over what he thought were frozen joints of meat. Some of them looked like fillets.

"So what is it?"

"Take a closer look," she said.

He screwed up his eyes and leaned over, and saw part of a human arm, and a foot.

"Fucking hell! Whose are those?"

"No one here, at any rate, they've all still got their arms and legs."

"Where did you find them?"

"In the freezer, like I said."

What a fucking mess.

"So, four dead?" he said.

The woman put a finger to her chin and looked up at the ceiling.

"Hmm, let's see, two out there, two here . . . Two plus two is four. Yes, you're right, four dead!"

Tommy didn't like irony or sarcasm, never had, couldn't see the point. He went on into the office and sat down on the chair behind the desk. Waiting, thinking, stroking his cop's mustache.

Half an hour later Gunilla was standing in front of him.

"Tell me," he said.

She looked cold, cold and stiff.

"What do you want me to tell you? You can see for yourself what it looks like out there. We've been following Hector Guzman for a month. This is the result."

"What's Anders Ask doing here?"

"How do you mean?"

He looked at her wearily. Sometimes she was like a stubborn child.

"There are three bodies in this restaurant, four if we count the foot and arm we just found in the freezer. What the hell is Ask doing here?"

"He's been working for me, on a freelance basis."

"A freelance basis?"

"Yes."

"Since when has anyone ever worked for the Swedish police on a freelance basis?"

"That feels like the least of the problems we should be talking about now, don't you think, Tommy?"

He adjusted his position on the chair.

"Why won't they talk to me?" he asked.

"Because that's what we agreed."

Tommy shook his head and pulled a face that told her to stop all that.

Gunilla looked down at the floor, then up again.

"We don't know who's lying out there. The dead men aren't known to us."

"What do Ask and the other one say?"

"Hasse Berglund was watching the restaurant; when the shooting started he called Anders, when they got in everyone was dead, and they were overpowered by Hector's gang and tied up."

Tommy thought for a moment.

"Where do you want to go from here?"

She smiled.

"Good, Tommy. I want to carry on as before, first we need to secure this place."

"You'll have to stay in the background. Antonia Miller is in charge of the murder investigation, you'll have to work together, she's lead investigator."

Gunilla stood up.

"I'll keep you informed," she said quietly, then left the office. Tommy listened to her footsteps as she disappeared.

"Gunilla!"

She stopped.

"Yes?"

Tommy was picking at a mark on the desk with his thumbnail.

"Anders Ask is your responsibility, I don't know anything about him."

She didn't answer.

Gunilla made her way through the kitchen, deliberately not looking at the dead body on the chair, and went out into the restaurant, walking along the marked-out path toward the front door. She saw the two other unknown men lying dead on the floor. Gunilla lifted the police cordon tape blocking the door and stepped out into the street.

Anders and Hasse were waiting beside Hasse's car.

"We're not talking here."

The Hotel Diplomat was bathed in sunshine. Lars Vinge had checked in around dinnertime under a false name.

The hotel was too fancy for him, no one would think of looking for him there. White sheets, down pillows, a view across the water of Nybroviken, a flag fluttering outside his window; the bathroom was like a dream, but Lars couldn't summon up the slightest enthusiasm at experiencing this level of luxury for once in his life. His energy was absorbed by two things: his attempts to suppress his own craving for Ketogan, as real as hunger to a starving man, and his relentless effort to understand everything that was going on.

He had made his way to Brahegatan that afternoon and had removed the surveillance equipment from the rental car. It had been dangerous; he had been far too close to Gunilla and the others, but anything he did right now was risky, even showing his face in daylight.

The surveillance equipment was on the double bed, together with the things he had stolen from Gunilla's safe. He had counted the money, two bundles of thousand-kronor notes, fifty in each. The gun was a Makarov, an old communist-era Russian pistol with its serial number rubbed off—for emergencies. Lars checked it: the magazine was full, eight bullets, he put it down on the bed beside him. Then two plastic folders, fairly thin, twenty or so sheets of A4 in each, then the thick official ledger and the black notebook. He read the notebook first, it contained a whole bunch of comments and thoughts, small writing in pencil. It was messy, as if Gunilla had written whatever had occurred to her, as if she was arguing with herself, as if she was writing her way to some sort of understanding. He read, trying to find a pattern, but couldn't make any sense of it and put it aside. He looked at the thick ledger and started to leaf through it, page after page about Hector Guzman. Lars read about a smuggling route from Paraguay to Europe, about murders, about the blackmail of some manager at Ericsson, about contacts in all corners of the world. There were pictures, reports of interviews, evidence. It told a story that stretched all the way back to the '70s. It contained everything about Hector and Adalberto Guzman's affairs.... There was enough evidence to convict the men ten times over in a courtroom. Hector Guzman would be behind bars for an eternity.

Lars kept turning the pages, and the more he saw, the more puzzled he became. There were also amounts jotted in the margin in ink—large amounts, eight digits, as if Gunilla had been trying to work something out. Lars was beginning to understand everything and nothing....

He put the ledger to one side and went back to the notebook, tried once more to understand the reasoning. It was difficult, it was complicated, but the more he concentrated, the more things fell into place. He read about Sophie; it said that she was the key, that she would lead the way, that she was beautiful, that she was Hector's dream woman, the woman he could never have. And more of the same, suppositions from Gunilla about Sophie's inner characteristics. Lars didn't agree with her, Gunilla had misjudged Sophie.... There were also musings about how Gunilla thought Sophie might act and react in different situations. Gunilla was probably right there, she was working along lines that had never even occurred to Lars. It was complicated, but he thought he was starting to understand what Gunilla was after.... Lars turned a few more pages, and read something he was obliged to read over and over again.

Lars is burdened by guilt. The words "burdened by guilt" were underlined. *He's malleable.* This too was elaborately worked out, as though Gunilla had been exerting her intellect to the utmost in order to understand him. The picture that emerged as Lars read about himself became slightly clearer. He meant nothing to Gunilla, he was to take the blame if anything in the plan went wrong.... What plan?

Lars took a few deep breaths... turned a few pages at random. *Tommy can see how perplexed I am.* Tommy?... Tommy Jansson in National Crime?

He wrote Tommy's name on a sheet of paper.

Lars plugged the surveillance equipment into a socket, put the headphones on, and lowered the volume. Scratchy, quiet noises that didn't mean anything. The voice activation was sensitive, it reacted to most things, a door slamming somewhere, a car alarm going off in the street, someone walking down the corridor outside the room.

He waited, listened, his right foot twitching impatiently. The sound of the door to the room opening. He looked at the time on the surveillance equipment—four hours ago—footsteps and voices that he recognized. Gunilla, Anders, and Hasse, chairs being pulled across the floor. Gunilla's voice was strained, she was talking about the break-in, then Hasse muttered something in a low voice. Lars concentrated, it was about Trasten, that Hasse had been waiting for a chance to go in, that Sophie had turned up with an unknown man, that three unknown men, probably Russians, had gone into the restaurant. The sound quality was poor, maybe because of the air-conditioning struggling to supply cool air. Lars pressed the headphones to his ears: just more inaudible talking from Hasse, then, after a while, it got clearer.

"Then what?" Gunilla's voice.

"There were two men lying dead on the floor when we went in. The third member of the group was the one who was found dead in the kitchen. The German from the hospital and the big Russian were in the restaurant."

"And Sophie? Where was she?"

"In the same room."

"And Ramirez has left the country?"

"Yes."

Lars heard a sigh from Gunilla.

"And the money? The transfer?"

There were several seconds of heavy silence. Anders cleared his throat: *"I tried, but Hector was being unreasonable."*

"What do you mean, 'unreasonable'?"

"He said that things had changed as the result of the shooting and the dead bodies...."

"And Carlos... the owner? Where's he?"

No answer.

"Aron?"

"No."

"That lawyer? The one who looks after everything, Lundwall?"

"Don't know." Anders was whispering.

"What did you say to Antonia Miller and Tommy?"

Lars wrote "Antonia Miller" on his sheet of paper.

"Nothing," Hasse said.

Lars paused the equipment and got up from the bed, went over to his laptop on the desk, logged in, went online, and tapped in the address of one of the daily papers. A big photograph of Trasten. He read the article, nothing of interest, police reluctant to say anything, unconfirmed sources suggest three people dead. He moved on to the evening tabloids. SLAUGHTER was the headline on one of them, UNDERWORLD SHOOT-OUT on the other. Same thing there, no information, just unconfirmed reports of three dead.

Lars shut the laptop, looking in front of him. He realized they were going to try to murder him, that he had a price on his head now. He felt scared in a way that he didn't recognize; the fear led to one feeling, which led to another, which led to a third—terror and panic were the main ingredients, and this mixture revived the little devil that stuck pins in his soul, shouting at him to take some medication... *for God's sake!* And all the while, behind that: the pain, the physical pain that sent little cramps throughout his body... cramps that twisted and squeezed Lars Vinge's entire nervous system.

He took a bar of chocolate from the minibar, then walked aimlessly around the room, eating and taking deep breaths. The chocolate didn't taste of chocolate, it tasted of sugar and fat. He ate it anyway, the sugar helped the withdrawal cravings for all of twelve seconds.

Lars stopped at the window and looked out across the water of Nybroviken. He saw the bench where Sophie and Jens had sat talking. Where he had photographed them from his position over on Skeppargatan. It felt like another life. What had he realized since then?

One of the Vaxholm boats sounded its whistle three times and backed away from the quayside. His thoughts were somewhere else, on some other level, deep down where he couldn't reach them. Lars went back to the bed and started again. He read through the thick ledger, looked through the files, read through the notes. A mass of numbers, maybe amounts—big ones, millions. He went through all the documents, a bank with a French-sounding name based in Liechtenstein. Huge amounts. Lars kept going, more figures. The account-holder's name wasn't on the withdrawal slip, just a number.

Lars scratched his scalp hard, thinking, then leaned across the bed and got the black notebook and started to read... started to read carefully. Five years before: *Handelsbanken Uppsala, three million kronor,* it said in pencil, then a bunch of strange words and reflections. He kept reading, *Christer Ekström* and a bunch of figures, up in the multimillion class. Strange reflections there, too. Lars went on: *Zdenko,* it said, the King of the Racetrack—every police officer knew who Zdenko was, he died in Malmö five years before, shot out at a racecourse. Lars kept going, more names, more amounts.

Something was trying to get out of Lars, up, out, into the light, to be born; it was a thought, an idea, an idea that he hadn't even come close to. It started to work its way up from the depths of his unconscious, the thought that was the answer, the answer he had been seeking since he had written the first words on the wall back home in his office, it seemed obvious when it came to him. He put his feet down on the floor, took two steps across to the desk.

He surfed quickly, logging onto the internal police server and typing in search terms from the first piece he had read, then found them in the text that appeared on the screen: *Handelsbanken... Uppsala Robbery... Two men convicted... Third suspect found dead one year later... Eight million kronor still missing... Investigating officer: Erik Strandberg.*

He typed *Christer Ekström* in the search box. He read that the financier Christer Ekström had narrowly escaped prosecution due to lack of evidence. Head of preliminary investigation: Gunilla Strandberg.

Lars typed in *Zdenko* and found masses of information on the police server. He identified a preliminary investigation stretching over several years, with Gunilla Strandberg as the officer in charge. Lars read: *Zdenko was murdered by an unknown man at Jägersro in Malmö. . . . Zdenko's money in Sweden has not been located.*

He leaned back, staring at something that his eyes didn't register. If his mind hadn't been so tired, his body suffering such abstinence, and his heart so dark, he would have burst out laughing. But there wasn't even a glimpse of humor left in the world for Lars Vinge.

26

When they landed in Málaga and made their way through passport control he walked a few steps ahead of her. They emerged into the heat and headed toward a multistory garage.

Their footsteps echoed metallically under the low concrete roof of the garage as they walked toward a small car parked by itself among the pillars. Hector took a set of car keys out of his briefcase and gave them to her.

"Would you mind driving?" he said.

She got in the driver's seat, adjusted the position of the seat, started the engine, put her arm on his seat, turned around, and reversed from the parking spot. Her eyes, which had gotten used to the gloom in the garage during the short time they were in there, were dazzled when she got back out into daylight. She followed the signs, found the exit ramp, and pulled out onto the highway.

They let themselves be carried forward, let the new world show itself to them. She could feel herself relaxing, turned toward him, and was just about to say something when a sudden ear-shattering noise hit the car. He was quicker than she to realize what it was.

"Faster!" he shouted.

As if in a haze she accelerated, driving like a maniac, cruising between the cars. More shots were fired, she ducked, glass rained down on her, she saw the motorbike, the car drove into the barrier—chaos.

Hector kicked out his window, leaned out, and fired. How many shots she had no idea, but after repeated thunderous noises the weapon just clicked. She got the impression that he was venting his shock rather than seriously thinking the shots would hit their target. He dropped the magazine on the floor and pulled another one from the open glove compartment, swearing quietly to himself as he loaded the pistol.

There was a rattling sound close to them and a shower of bullets, the rear window exploded in an inferno of glass. She screamed, and in the corner of her eye she saw him move oddly.

"Hector?"

He shook his head.

"I'm OK," he said, and aimed the gun through the broken back window, fired four shots, and the motorbike pulled back again.

Sophie kept on driving, angry horns blasting as she swept past other cars at high speed. She peered off into the distance ahead of them and thought she could see a traffic jam building up. Their options were shrinking.

"What should I do?" she shouted.

Had she already shouted that? She couldn't remember. He didn't answer, just kept staring backward. The line up ahead was getting clearer. Hector made a third call on his cell, searching for the motorbike the whole time. Finally he got an answer.

"Aron. Listen, I can't get hold of Dad or Leszek. We're being shot at on the way from the airport, we're driving toward Marbella, Sophie and I, in the car."

Hector listened as Aron asked questions.

"I don't know. Two men on a motorbike...Listen to me. Tell Ernst that the power of attorney goes to Sophie...."

Hector listened, got annoyed.

"It's my decision! Power of attorney goes to Sophie Brinkmann, and you are hereby a witness to that. Get hold of Dad or Leszek. Warn them!"

Hector ended the call. She looked at him; he waved away the question that she hadn't asked, coughed, and turned around. The motorbike was coming at them again; he emptied his pistol once more, the rider braked, the same story each time. He grunted something to himself that she didn't understand, and inserted a new magazine.

"Slow down, draw them in, then put your foot on the brake when I say so." His voice was hoarse, he was dripping with sweat.

Their pursuer was unshakable, zigzagging between the cars behind them, lying low on the curves. Hector aimed, fired two shots, and was countered by a hail of bullets at the same instant; Sophie screamed, they both ducked instinctively. Hector stuck his head up and the gunman behind the driver aimed again and fired. The shot whistled past them.

"Now!"

She slammed her foot on the brake, the car's tires shrieked, Sophie and Hector fought against being thrown forward.

For a short moment the world stopped, their thoughts hung there weightless inside the car, their fears got a brief respite, their eyes met...and then they were sucked back to reality: the sound of the submachine gun rattling, the sound of the bullets hitting the car, the sound of the motorbike, the sound of the world around them. Everything merged into the same audio picture. Hector threw his arm up and aimed at the driver, who swerved quickly and assuredly, overtaking them on the inside.

"Drive!" he shouted.

Now the situation was suddenly reversed, Hector and Sophie were chasing the motorbike. The gunman kept looking back, Hector leaned out of his broken window, fired two shots, the motorbike kept going toward the traffic jam. He was holding the pistol in his right hand, letting it rest against his palm, then aimed and fired three more shots, one after the other.... Missed again. The line was getting closer, Hector emptied the magazine again.... Nothing happened.

The motorbike was about to slip in among the cars. He put the last magazine into the gun, took half a breath, aimed, held his breath, and fired repeatedly, emptying the magazine.... As if by some miracle one or more of the bullets found their target, the motorbike suddenly lurched sharply to one side, tipped over and up onto its front wheel, throwing the driver and gunman off as it spun around. The driver slammed into the barrier in the median, back first. The gunman was thrown over it, onto the opposite lane of traffic; a truck tried to brake and swerve but failed, and bounced over the man.

They were yelling as if their football team had just scored. It was absurd, but it was the same feeling, the same sense of release. . . .

Sophie veered off up an exit ramp at the last moment, her hands were shaking and her breathing was shallow. She wanted to throw up.

He was working intently. Neat piles on the bed, reports, transcribed surveil- lance recordings, all the material transferred onto various forms of memory devices. Masses of photographs of Sophie, Hasse, Anders, all of them. Bank papers from Liechtenstein, together with Gunilla's cases, her notes. Anyone who read them would understand what was going on.

He was sitting at his computer, transferring the surveillance files from Brahegatan to a USB stick, gathering everything he had.

Lars looked over at the bed, he had done a good job, he felt satisfied. He hadn't had that feeling for a long time. His internal reward system was shrieking for attention. The minibar was first prize. He drank a beer. It was cold, slipped down his throat in a matter of seconds. He waited awhile, then worked his way back through the whole fridge, stupid little bottles of spirits, a half bottle of red wine, a half bottle of white, Champagne. *Party time.* It all went down.

Lars glared out across Nybroviken, the minibar was empty, he was drunk. But the intoxication soon began to fade, and it wasn't giving him what he needed. Alcohol was overrated. One leg started twitching nervously, he was grinding his teeth, trying to keep his hands still. Lars walked around the room, scratching at his scalp; this room was making him itch so badly, he wanted to get away from there, wanted to get out.

With the sports bag in his hand he walked quickly along Strandvägen, staying close to the buildings, then turned right into Sibyllegatan and made his way up to Brahegatan and the rental car. He put the equipment in the back, checked that it was getting a signal from the microphone up in the office, then locked the car and headed back the same way. But instead of turning left onto Strandvägen and going back to the hotel, he walked quickly along Nybrokajen, up Stallgatan, past the Grand Hotel, and across to Skeppsbron. He was heading toward Södermalm with a sense of purpose.

It was dark inside the apartment, it smelled musty, there was still a faint smell of paint. He went straight into the office, unlocked the drawer, dug out what he wanted, pulled down his trousers, and did what he was good at—shoving in a few suppositories and pulling up his trousers. He didn't bother to fasten them, and sat down on the office chair, spinning around slowly . . . at the same rate that well-being began to caress his senses. But the pleasure was short-lived, and merely flickered past. He repeated the procedure, squatting down, another one, then took something else, rifling through the drawer, gulping down whatever he could find. Fear, angst, resentment, and melancholy all lit up, then vanished just as quickly. Everything became soft again, no corners or edges for his warped feelings to catch themselves on.

Lars got down from the chair and lay on the floor, but he didn't fall asleep—he just switched off for a while.

It was as they were approaching Marbella that she noticed how pale he was, almost white, with the sweat on his face like a lacquered film. His breathing was labored and shallow, she put her hand on his forehead—cold and clammy.

"Hector?"

He nodded without looking at her. She let her hand slip down over his neck and throat, he was soaking.

"What is it, Hector?"

"Nothing, just drive."

She looked down at his body and asked him to lean forward.

He hesitated, then leaned forward cautiously some five inches or so. She saw blood all over his back, the seat, and dripping onto the floor.

"Dear God!" she said. "Where's the nearest hospital?"

He coughed.

"No hospital. Drive me home, there's a doctor there."

"No, you have to get to a hospital, you need an operation."

Now he roared: "No! No hospital!"

She tried to stay calm.

"Just listen to me, you've lost a lot of blood, you need proper care... otherwise you'll die."

He looked at her, trying to stay just as calm.

"I won't die.... There's a doctor at Dad's, he'll look after me, if I go to the hospital I'll end up in prison... and die there. So there's nothing to discuss. You drive, I'll tell you the way."

She drove fast through Marbella and passed out the other side, heading upward for a while before turning back down toward the sea again. Hector had given her directions to start with, then he began to nod off. He explained where to go, where to turn off, described the whole route to her, then he got groggy and slowly started to fade. She realized what that could mean.

"Hector!" she shouted. He waved his hand to show that he could hear her.

"You mustn't fall asleep! Do you hear me?"

She kept looking between Hector and the road ahead. Sophie drove fast. One hand on the wheel, the other on his shoulder, shaking him.

"Do you hear me?"

He nodded weakly, then drifted off again.

A car was coming toward them on a bend and she swerved quickly, and the car's horn disappeared in a Doppler effect behind them. She shook Hector, talking loudly, trying to get him to listen to her. He couldn't keep it up, and sank into unconsciousness. She shouted at him, she slapped him, he was out of reach. Sophie tried to memorize the directions he had just told her.

Dusk was starting to fall as she drove up a long road that wound its way to a house between neatly trimmed grass lawns. The garden was bigger than she could imagine, it was like an endless park. The vast sea spread out to her left as she pushed the car to its limits.

There were three vehicles outside the house, an ambulance and two private cars, the door to the villa was wide open, she sounded the horn, ran in, shouting.

A man came rushing down the stairs with blood on his arms and clothes, but he still looked strangely composed.

"Hector's been shot, he's lying in the car," she said loudly and breathlessly.

The man turned on the stairs and hurried up again, called something in Spanish, then came back with another man, just as bloody, just as composed. The men ran to the ambulance, pulled out a stretcher, hurried over to the shot-up car, lifted Hector out, and pushed him inside the house; Sophie followed as they carried him up the stairs.

The first thing she saw when she got upstairs was that the windows of the dining room had been shot out, there was broken glass all over the floor. Leszek was lying on a dining table, two men were operating on him. A dead body was lying on the floor under a sheet, and at the far end of the room an unknown bearded man in a checked shirt and jeans was sitting dead against the wall with a pistol in his hand. He had a bullet hole in his neck, and blood all over the wall behind him. She tried to make sense of it.

One of the men tore off Hector's clothes; the other looked through a big bag, searching for blood plasma, reading the different blood groups. They worked quickly and calmly. The man standing next to Hector was a doctor.

"I'm a nurse," she told him.

He looked at her, then around the room, and pointed at Leszek. She went over. Leszek had been sedated, he had a large flesh wound in his shoulder. It was bloody, dirty, and messy; everything at that moment was about saving lives. None of the focus on hygiene and other luxuries that she was used to. One man was standing beside Leszek, pulling out fragments of a bullet with a pair of tweezers, the man beside him was checking the drip and keeping the wound clear. Leszek's doctor had heard what she had said, and pointed toward a bathroom. Sophie went over, washed her hands carefully, not looking at her reflection in the mirror.

They worked furiously, the broken windows filled the room with salty sea air, she stood between Leszek and Hector and responded as the doctors and nurses called for her help. She made sure they all had what they needed.

"Hector's lost a huge amount of blood," the doctor said. "We're replenishing it as best we can; he's got two bullets in his back, it's hard to say anything about his condition."

Sophie sewed Leszek back together, bandaged his shoulder, then her work was done, there was nothing more she could do for anyone. She went to wash her hands again, and didn't look at her reflection in the mirror this time, either.

Outside in the room everything was silent. Hector's doctor was operating, his assistants working alongside him.

Sophie summoned her strength and went over to the person under the white sheet; she knew who it was, she knew that his son wasn't yet aware that his father was dead. She lifted the sheet carefully and saw Adalberto, looking almost peaceful. She lifted it a bit more, coagulated blood across his chest. She lowered the sheet again.

"What happened?" She addressed the question to Leszek's doctor, who was smoking a cigarette toward the other end of the room. He shrugged.

"We arrived... Adalberto was dead. Him too." The doctor pointed at the bearded man who was sitting against the wall, a bloodstain had followed him down.

"Leszek was wounded but conscious. I don't know what happened, it doesn't matter. The devil's been here, that's enough." He took a drag and the cigarette flared.

"Who are you all?" she asked.

He blew out the smoke.

"Who are you?"

"I'm a friend of Hector's."

For some reason he didn't want to look her in the eye.

"We're doctors and nurses, freelancing today, employed yesterday. We've had an agreement with Adalberto Guzman for a few years... a retainer agreement, in case anything like this should ever happen."

They were interrupted by a sound from the floor below, by the stairs—everyone in the room exchanged glances, scared glances. Who should take charge here? Steps on the stairs, the men in the room tried to hide. Slow, hesitant steps approaching. Sophie hurried over to the bearded man, bent his fingers open, took the revolver from his cold, stiff hand, and aimed it toward the stairs. The steps were getting closer, she aimed, trying to breathe, she was going to fire. A head appeared, her aim was steady and followed the head, which gradually acquired a body, the slender body of a woman.

Sonya Alizadeh came up into the room. Sophie lowered the gun, put it down on the floor.

"Are they dead?" Sonya whispered, sitting down on a chair. "They came without warning," she said. "They shot into the house from the outside. Adalberto was hit as he sat and ate.... Then they came inside the house and kept on shooting. Leszek got one of them. Then he was hit as well."

"Who by?"

Sonya thought.

"I don't know. A man who drove off in a car."

"And you?" Sophie asked.

"I ran downstairs, hid in the cellar."

Sophie went over to her, pulled a chair out, and sat down close to Sonya, taking Sonya's hand in hers. They sat like that, looking out across the room, holding hands. A mild sea breeze was coming in through the shattered windows, caressing them. Sophie looked at Hector, who was lying on the stretcher fighting for his life.

There was a sound of small paws on the stairs. A little white dog appeared and looked around the room as if he was searching for something.

Sonya held out her hands and the dog went over to her, still hesitant, seeking, sniffing, unable to find his master. Sonya crouched down, called him over. The dog wagged his tail and jumped up into her arms. She sat up in the chair again with the dog in her lap, gently stroking his fur.

"This is Piño...."

Sophie realized she was smiling at the dog, possibly because she always smiled at dogs, perhaps because the dog's presence lent the room a bit of calm and normality.

Suddenly one of the machines that was attached to Hector started to beep, and the doctor and nurse started to work feverishly as Sophie and Sonya looked on.

"He's going into a coma." The doctor's voice was stressed.

Sophie hurried over as the doctor worked intently. He asked for things, she handed him whatever he needed, he muttered and swore that he couldn't work with so few resources. The nurse was pumping oxygen into Hector manually, and Sophie looked on impotently as the doctor gave up his attempt to stop Hector from slipping into the coma. He swore in Spanish, asked the nurse a question, a question that had no answer and was just an expression of his frustration.

"He needs to be moved."

"Why?"

"Because that's part of the agreement. He needs a respirator."

"Where are you going to take him?"

"To a safe place."

"Leszek?"

The doctor looked over at the sleeping Leszek.

"Don't worry about him."

Sophie was sitting in the back of the ambulance next to Hector's stretcher, Sonya beside her with Piño in her lap. They drove through Marbella, the town glowing outside. Sophie could only see through one of the windows in the back doors: people having fun, cars whose paintwork gleamed under the evening's neon lights, restaurants, terrace bars, motorbikes, mopeds, heat, music, young and old together.

She was holding Hector's hand in hers, wanted to say something, anything, wanted to believe he could hear her behind the walls of unconsciousness, wanted to believe he was holding her hand in his. She let go of it after a while. Took out her cell phone, called Jane. She held on to Hector's stretcher with the other hand. Jane sounded sleepy when she answered. Said she was at the hospital, that she was sleeping there. That the two men were still around. That one of them was there the whole time, working in shifts. No one else had asked after Albert or her. And she was able to reassure Sophie by telling her that Albert seemed to be doing all right. He was sound asleep.

They emerged from the town and headed up toward the mountains, out into the countryside, driving in darkness, passing the town of Ojén and then on into the darkness again. After an hour they slowed down and the ambulance stopped. Sophie heard the front doors open and close, followed by footsteps outside, then the back door was opened by the doctor and warm evening air hit her, and he gestured for them to get out.

It was an old farm, now restored, white, red roof, lights on. A compact car was parked outside, the sort of car single people have, unremarkable, with small wheels and flimsy doors. Someone was waiting for them inside. The door was opened by a woman.

Hector was carried in on the stretcher. Sophie and Sonya followed. The woman who let them in examined Hector briefly in the hall, then indicated that they should carry him into the living room. It was a large room, white stone walls, terra-cotta floor, Spanish furnishings, sober in its lack of pretension. Sophie saw hospital equipment: a defibrillator, two drip stands, a respirator, and, off to one side, a large hospital bed.

Hector was lifted into the bed. The woman rolled the equipment over and attached the drip and connected a catheter under the sheets. The doctor and nurse set up the respirator, spoke briefly to the woman, left the house, and drove off in the ambulance.

The woman checked Hector once more, then turned toward Sophie and Sonya.

"My name is Raimunda, I'm going to take care of Hector. As of this evening, this is where I work. Yesterday I was working at a private hospital, I resigned four hours ago when I got the phone call."

She was speaking quietly and clearly.

"This place is secure, only a few people know about it, and that's the way it's going to stay."

Sophie looked at Raimunda. She was thin, in her thirties, black hair that stopped at the base of her neck. There was something correct, strict about her. She felt good, stable... loyal.

Sophie whispered, "Thank you."

The cicadas were singing in the night when Sophie went off to bed in one of the rooms.

There was a buzzing noise from Sophie's handbag on the chair. She got up and went over. The phone she had been given by Jens was lit up at the bottom of the bag, down there with her wallet, jewelry, makeup, and random receipts.

"Jens?"

"No, Aron."

"Hector's been..."

"I know everything, where are you now?"

"At the farm... up in the mountains."

"Who's there with you?"

"Raimunda, Hector, and Sonya."

"Stay there. The police have sealed off Adalberto's villa. Leszek's on his way to you."

"And you?"

"I'm coming down as soon as I can, there's a warrant out for me, I need to take a detour."

"Jens?"

"I patched him up as best I could . . . he's going to be OK."

Silence.

"Sophie?"

"Yes?"

"We need to talk when we meet."

He ended the call.

27

The sun's rays were wandering slowly across the room. Gunilla fol-lowed them leisurely. He was lying on the floor with no covers, curled up like a little baby in the womb. Slowly, slowly the light made its way up over his shoulder, then hit his chin. The passage of light across Lars Vinge was like a symphony, she thought, a silent symphony. She waited patiently, as usual. The sun found its way up his cheek and eventually nudged at his closed eyes. She could see movement behind the eyelids; he swallowed, opened his eyes, stared out across the floor, closed his eyes, swallowed again.

"Good morning," she whispered softly.

He saw her sitting on the chair, looking down at him. Lars leaned up, still sitting on the floor, still drowsy, with a Ketogan hangover and as empty as a vacuum.

"What are you doing here?" he managed to croak.

"I've been trying to get hold of you, but I never get an answer, I wanted to see how you are."

He looked at her with hazy eyes.

"How I am?"

"Yes."

Lars tried to think, how had she gotten in? Had he been followed last night?

"Lars?"

He looked at her, wished he'd had more time, more time to figure out a plan of how to deal with her.

"I'm not feeling so great," he said quietly.

"Why not?"

"I don't know. I've probably been working too hard."

She looked right through him, held up a bottle of pills that she had on her lap.

"What's this?"

"Just medicine," he said.

She studied him.

"You've got a whole drawer full?"

He didn't answer that.

"This isn't ordinary stuff, Lars. . . . Are you ill?"

He felt like saying *Cancer, the late stages*. People who were in the late stages of cancer got to do what they liked. No, she already knew everything about him.

"No."

"So why are you taking Ketogan?"

"That's my business."

She shook her head.

"No, not as long as you're working for me."

Now he looked into her eyes; they were shut off somehow, empty and dead. As if someone had crawled in behind them and closed the curtains. Had she always had eyes like that? He didn't know; he just knew that she was there at that moment, that she was lethal, that she probably hadn't come alone. That his pistol was out of reach. That she may well know that he knew. Maybe she'd found the microphone in Brahegatan. Maybe he was going to die now?

Lars looked at the drugs on her lap. He thought about the time he lied to the priest in Lyckoslanten, how easy it was to lie when you made use of reality. The truth is the best lie.

"Lars? Answer my question."

He sat on the floor and rubbed his eyes.

"What do you want to know?"

"I want to know what you've been doing these past few days, I want to know why you're taking a cocktail of Ketogan, benzo, and anxiety medicine."

He let time pass.

"Sorry, Gunilla...," he whispered.

She looked at him intently.

"Sorry for what, Lars?"

"Sorry for letting you down..."

Her calmness turned into a tense curiosity.

"How have you let me down?" Now she was whispering too.

Lars took several deep breaths.

"When I was young...," he began, "ten, maybe eleven, I was given medicine to help me sleep, drugs. My mom got them on prescription.... I soon became dependent on them. Later on, toward the end of my teenage years, I got help to stop... but the damage was already done. I've managed to abstain for most of my adult life. I've avoided alcohol, never taken any strong medicines. Recently I sought help for back pain," Lars went on, "and when the doctor asked I said I was having trouble sleeping. I always have, and, well... I wasn't really thinking. He prescribed something, painkillers and tranquilizers, and I took them."

He looked up at her, she was still listening.

"It was nothing terribly dangerous, but it was like pressing a button. It made me happy... it made me happy in a way I hadn't been since... well, I don't remember when. My whole system responded to the pills, reacted and accepted them.... Then it just took off. I was hooked after a week or so.... I managed to get hold of stronger substances. I've been using them ever since."

"You said you'd let me down?"

He looked at the floor and nodded almost imperceptibly.

"I haven't been doing my job properly, I've spent the last few days lying here, knocked out.... I called you from here, said I was looking for Sophie, I lied to you."

Gunilla was looking for truth and bluff at the same time. After a while she relaxed, he could see it.

"It doesn't matter, Lars," she said. "It doesn't matter...," she repeated.

Gunilla stood up, looked at him, seemed to want to say something more. But instead she started to walk out of the room. Lars watched her go.

"Gunilla," he said.

She turned around.

"Sorry."

She considered what he had said.

"I don't want to lose this job. You gave me a chance...give me another, I'm begging you...."

She didn't answer and disappeared into the hall. Lars heard the front door open. Anders Ask walked past the office doorway, smiled at Lars, pretended to shoot him with his forefinger, then followed Gunilla out into the stairwell. The front door closed and the apartment was left in silence.

He lay there until the sound of their footsteps on the stairs had faded. Lars got up, gathered his pills, waited a bit, then left the apartment and made his way to the subway. He traveled around, paranoid, changing trains several times, trying to see if he was being followed. When he was sure he was alone, he went back to the hotel on Strandvägen and hung the Do Not Disturb sign on the door. He was trembling down to his very marrow, aware that he had just managed to cling to his life by a hairbreadth. Lars realized that time was pressing. He got to work, and began to figure out a plan of how he should proceed.

Leszek was frying bacon.

One arm was strapped up, but he was managing to do everything with the left one. Raimunda was sitting in an armchair reading a book by Annie Proulx, Sonya was asleep on the sofa, Hector was lying on his back in bed, in another dimension, perhaps.

Chopin was playing quietly from a stereo, Raimunda's choice. Hector should hear beautiful music the whole time, she had said. Sophie listened from the edge of the sofa. It was the Bernstein recording, the Second Piano Concerto...*En fa mineur.* She had played parts of it herself as a child. She had stopped playing sometime when she was a teenager, she couldn't remember why.

Sophie got up and went over to Leszek, who was turning the bacon in the pan; he was staring down vacantly into the grease, looking sad. She patted him gently on his healthy shoulder.

"Do you want me to cook?" she asked. He shook his head.

She got plates out of the cupboard, started setting the table, then there was the sound of a car outside. Leszek was quick, pulling the frying pan off the heat, taking his pistol from the spice shelf, and hurrying over to one of the windows. The car door opened, and Aron got out of the driver's seat. Leszek relaxed, went out, and met him. Sophie watched through the window as they embraced, then fell into conversation, with Leszek doing most of the talking, presumably telling Aron in detail about everything that had happened over the past few days.

Aron came in, hugged Sonya, and exchanged a few words with her. He introduced himself to Raimunda, then went and sat beside Hector, talking quietly to him in Spanish and stroking his hair. He met Sophie's gaze.

"Let's go for a walk."

They left the house and took a narrow sandy path that led up toward the mountains. Aron had his hands in his pockets. They walked on for a while, it got cooler the higher they got. Sophie looked at the ground, the gravel here was different, browner, finer than the gravel at home in Sweden, but there were still a few larger stones. She tried to avoid them as she walked.

"Any more news about your son?"

She shook her head.

"What do the doctors say?"

"I don't know," she replied.

He paused for a moment before getting to the point.

"Hector said on the phone that you were to have power of attorney, do you know why?"

She didn't say anything, just shook her head.

"Me neither. At least not at first."

Now she looked over at him.

"I've come to two conclusions, very different conclusions," he said.

They walked a bit farther before he went on.

"You've seen a lot, you've heard things, maybe you've understood things you weren't meant to understand, I don't know. Maybe Hector realized that we couldn't just let you go, maybe the power of attorney is a way of keeping you here with us, close, where you can't do any harm."

He glanced quickly at her. "That was what I thought at first. Hector knew he was injured...."

Aron waited a few moments.

"But there could also be another reason," he said. "I don't know if this still applied when he called me from the car...."

A breeze caught her hair. She pushed it back.

"Hector often talked about you, before all this happened.... About what you were like... your qualities. He appreciated you in a way that I realized he'd never appreciated a woman before."

She looked down at the ground.

"He saw something different in you."

"What?" she whispered.

Aron shrugged his shoulders.

"I don't know. But he saw something."

They had gotten a fair way up, and had a view across a valley that stretched hundreds of yards down into dark green vegetation. Aron stopped, resting his eyes on the view.

"He said that you didn't understand what sort of person you really are."

The reasoning seemed unclear.

"What sort of talk's that? That's just words," she said.

"No, not when it comes from him."

He stared at something in the distance.

"He wanted something with you. But I don't understand what, I still don't understand exactly what he meant in our last conversation."

"Do you need to?"

He looked at her.

"Yes, I do."

There was new sharpness in his eyes. Decisions were being made deep inside.

"I'm putting you in a kind of quarantine until things clear themselves up, or until Hector wakes up and can explain his choice."

"And what does that mean?"

"The power of attorney gives you a partial right to make decisions about our work. It means that you'll become initiated into and complicit in what we do, and if you're complicit, then you're no threat. Something like that."

"What about me, what does it mean for me?"

"It means that you're going to help me. I have to stay here, stay hidden until everything's settled down a bit."

"What do I have to do?"

"We can't let the world think he's out of the game, that would be disastrous for us and a lot of other people who are dependent on him. You know him, don't you?"

"What do you mean?"

"He knows you, he says. So you must know him?"

"I think so," she said cautiously.

"Then you know what he would do?"

Was that something like pleading she saw in Aron? Something beseeching that was peeping out from in there?

"Maybe. But you know him as well, Aron."

"Yes, but in a different way.... We'll do this together."

"And what about in the future?"

He thought.

"I don't know."

"What *do* you know?" she asked.

He looked at her.

"If everything goes to hell for us, you're coming down with us. Pretty much."

She thought about his words, it all sounded so absurd.

"Hector has a son," she said.

Aron nodded. "Lothar Manuel," he said.

"Why not him? Why not you? Why not Sonya, Leszek, Thierry, Daphne...Ernst?"

Aron met her gaze and shrugged. That was his answer.

She tried to make sense of her thoughts.

"What if I refuse? If I walk away from here and never look back again?"

"That won't be possible, I'm afraid," he said.

"Why not?"

"Because Hector told me that you were to have power of attorney, and that's what's going to happen."

"But I must have a choice?"

He shook his head.

"No," he said in a low voice.

She stared at him. He let her, then she looked away.

"The police know who I am," she said. "They saw me at the restaurant."

"That's a risk we'll have to take. Those police officers were after our money. They don't care about you. Leszek will go home with you, he can protect you if necessary."

"What about you?"

"I'm going to stay hidden, and tell you what to do."

She had a thousand questions, a thousand pleas.

"I'll give you an introduction into our work. We'll take a few days here in the mountains to do that, then we'll see how things develop in Stockholm." He turned around and began to walk back down the sandy path.

She stood there with thoughts flying around inside her head, unable to settle anywhere. After a while she followed him, walking slowly. Aron stopped some way ahead and waited for her. They walked back side by side.

"They beat up my son, Aron. Ran him down with a car. He's probably going to be paralyzed for the rest of his life."

Aron didn't respond.

"He hadn't done anything," she whispered. "It's not fair. . . ."

Aron had a folded document in his hand, and held out the power of attorney that Hector had signed. Sophie took the document and put it in her pocket.

They walked the rest of the way back to the house in silence.

Tailing Anders Ask had been simple. After work a quick visit to the 7-Eleven on the corner of Odengatan and Sveavägen to buy an evening paper, drink, and candy, a bit of chat with the girl behind the counter, then a pit stop at the Italian place with checkered tablecloths to pick up a pizza. Then home to his apartment opposite Vanadislunden.

Lars had gotten into the building and taken a photograph of the lock on Anders's door, an Assa that looked pretty old. The next morning he had found a similar one at a locksmith's on Kungsholmen, bought it, and practiced picking it back in his hotel room. That turned out to be pretty difficult, it took time even though he had the best tools for the job. He worked until long into the night, wishing he had been born with three hands.

The next day, as the sun rose somewhere over by Djurgården, he managed to get the lock open for the first time. Lars practiced hard all morning, over lunch, and into the afternoon, and finally managed to pick the lock in less than seven minutes.

He got himself ready and headed off to Sveavägen on foot. It was half past three in the afternoon when he stepped in through the door of the building for the second time and took the rickety elevator up to the third floor, pushed the gate back, and stepped out in front of the door to Anders Ask's apartment.

Anders had two neighbors, Norin and Grevelius. There was no sound from Norin, and a television was buzzing quietly in Grevelius's apartment. He pulled a hood over his head, took out his tools, got down on his knees on the cold stone floor, took a few deep breaths, and got to work. Lars worked methodically; it all went as it should, the picklocks found their way in and pressed the little notches inside the drum of the lock. A door opened and closed on the floor above and the elevator started to chew its way upward. Lars had to stop, pull out his tools, and hide on the stairs while the elevator made its way down again. But after that he got his seven minutes with the lock. It let out a click.

Lars pulled on his shoe covers, breathing mask, and gloves—then stepped into Anders Ask's hallway.

The apartment had two rooms plus a relatively large kitchen. He glanced into the living room. A sofa with flattened cushions, a crooked, rickety coffee table from IKEA. A glass cabinet with dusty glass figurines on one shelf. Pictures by famous artists on the walls. An enormous flatscreen television, speakers on the floor, and little treble speakers up by the ceiling. Anders liked his surround sound. Lars went into the bedroom. An unmade bed, closed blinds, a paperback on the bedside table, Arto Paasilinna's *The Year of the Hare*. Lars saw a suitcase standing by the wall. He crouched down and opened it. Clothes, passport, money . . . Anders was planning to take off.

Into the kitchen again. Lars sat down on a chair, the clock on the wall moved slowly, he pulled the mask from his mouth, let it hang from the elastic cord around his neck. The sound of traffic from Sveavägen was soporific and Lars nodded off.

After a couple more hours he woke up when a key was inserted into the lock. The front door opened and then closed again. Anders clearing his throat in the hallway, keys being put on a table, shoes being kicked off, a zipper being pulled down—the slippery sound of nylon as a jacket was taken off. A loud sigh, the smell of freshly made pizza. Steps from the hall. Anders jumped when he saw Lars from the corner of his eye, put his arms out to defend himself, the pizza box landed on the floor.

"What the fuck?! Christ, you scared me!"

Anders stared at Lars, angry and worried at the same time.

"What are you doing here?" He looked around, confused. "How the fuck did you get in?"

Lars was pointing Gunilla's Makarov at him.

"Come in and sit down."

Anders hesitated, looked into the barrel, then at the pizza box by his feet. Lars nodded toward a chair; Anders looked bewildered at first, then stepped into the kitchen and sat down hesitantly.

"How are things going with you, Anders?" Lars asked, with the barrel of the gun aimed at Anders's stomach.

"What did you say?"

Lars didn't repeat the question. Anders swallowed.

"With what?"

"With everything."

Anders saw the breathing mask around Lars's neck.

"It's all right, I suppose.... I don't get it, Lars."

He sounded scared.

"What is it you don't get?"

"This! What you're doing here... with a pistol?" Anders tried to smile.

"Oh, you know, don't you?"

"No, I don't!"

He suddenly sounded annoyed now.

"Are you angry, Anders?"

Anders held out his hands.

"No, no, sorry, I'm not angry. I'm just... surprised."

Anders's submissive smile returned.

"Come on, Lars, what is it? We can sort this out. Please, just put the gun down."

Lars stared blankly at him, kept the pistol where it was.

"How shall we sort this out?" he asked.

"However you like, you decide," Anders said desperately.

Lars pretended to think.

"What is it we need to sort out, exactly?"

Anders didn't understand. "What?"

"*What* do we need to sort out? You said we could sort this out. What?"

Anders stared at Lars.

"I don't know, whatever you're here for."

"What do you think I'm here for?"

"I don't know!"

Anders glanced down at Lars's shoe covers, and his fear rose into his throat.

"Yes, you do. . . ."

"No, I don't!" Anders's voice sounded a bit too high.

Lars let the seconds tick, a long, painful, dramatic pause. "Sara."

Anders tried to look quizzical.

"Oh? Who's that?"

Lars stared at Anders.

"Stop it," he said calmly.

"I don't know what you're talking about, Lars."

Anders was a bad liar when he was frightened. Lars pulled a face to let him know, and weirdly enough that seemed to make Anders relax. He sat silently, glancing out the kitchen window, taking deep breaths.

"It wasn't me. It was Hasse . . . and Gunilla gave the order. I had nothing to do with it."

"What happened?" Lars asked.

Anders's mouth was dry.

"Sara had worked something out from reading your wall. You'd written everything on a wall. . . . Hadn't you?"

Lars didn't answer.

"So she gave the order, Gunilla, I mean. The girl knew everything, even something that Gunilla was involved in before, some girl. Patricia something . . . something I don't know about."

Lars shook his head.

"No, Sara didn't know anything, she was trying her luck."

Anders didn't understand.

"You saw the wall, didn't you? How the hell could anyone have made any sense of that? There was hardly any notion of coherence there. I wrote it all in a kind of totally wired fucking chaos! She didn't know anything, I didn't know anything. . . ."

"But you do now?"

Lars nodded.

Something almost like pride came over Anders.

"Are you surprised?"

Lars had no answer to that, and shrugged.

"Do you understand how smart we've been?"

Lars looked up. "Why didn't you let me join in?" His voice was almost beseeching.

"We would have, Lars, of course we would. We just had to be certain. But it's not too late, is it? Come on, we can do this together."

"But you've murdered Sara."

Anders looked down at the floor.

"OK, Lars, think about this. Gunilla's our problem. Together we can change all this. You're nothing on your own, I've got access to everything. Put the gun down. . . . We'll do it together, Lars, we'll sort her out once and for all . . . OK?"

Lars hesitated, thinking, and looked up at Anders.

"How would that work?"

Anders saw an opening, a bit of self-confidence started to creep out. He looked at the pistol, then up at Lars.

"We'll gather everything we've got, put together a plan, report her, you keep quiet about me, I keep quiet about you. . . ."

"What about Hasse?"

"Up to you, Lars. We could take him out, I can do it for you. Remember, he was the one who killed your girlfriend, not me."

Lars nodded to himself.

"Yes, that sounds like a good idea. . . ."

Anders smiled with relief, slapped the palm of his hand on his thigh.

"Good! That's it, Lars! Christ, we're going to get her now, together, you and me, a team."

Anders breathed out, rocking on his chair.

"Where do we start?" Lars asked.

Anders was fast.

"The important thing is that we mustn't make Gunilla or Hasse suspicious.... We carry on as usual for a few days, we meet in the evenings, draw up plans, then we pick one and stick to it. This is going to work out fine, as long as we do it together, you and me, Lars!"

Lars hesitantly lowered the gun slightly.

"Sorry I came here like this, Anders, with a gun and everything."

Anders waved his hand, convinced that his powers of persuasion had worked on Lars Vinge the idiot. But Lars raised the pistol, let it rest against the palm of his left hand for a couple of seconds, then aimed and shot him squarely through his half-open mouth. A loud bang rang out in the kitchen. The bullet tore through Anders Ask's throat and neck and kept going, into the fridge door behind him. Then the kitchen was totally still. Anders was staring at Lars in astonishment. The chair he had been rocking on ended up in a kind of weightless no-man's-land, balancing on its two back legs for a moment before gravity got the better of it and it fell backward to the floor, taking Anders Ask with it.

Lars pulled on the face mask, stood up, went over to him, and crouched down. Anders stared at Lars, a trickle of blood running out onto the floor under his head.

"You're an asshole, Anders Ask, do you think I'm totally stupid?"

Lars could detect a faint smell of burned meat.

"Let's take a moment to consider the situation.... I live, you die."

Anders tried to say something, no sound came out, just a mouth moving laboriously, like a fish on dry land.

"I can't hear you, Anders," he whispered. "It'll be straight to hell for you. You've killed women. A boy's lying in the hospital, possibly paralyzed for life. They've probably got a special section for people like you down there."

Lars looked on patiently as Anders Ask's life ran out onto the linoleum floor. When he was dead Lars stood up, opened the kitchen window, and wiped the gun on a kitchen towel, all the while staring at Anders's corpse as it lay there. What was he feeling? Regret? No... Liberation? No, he wasn't feeling anything. Lars turned the kitchen radio on at full volume.

He crouched down beside Anders again, put the dead man's right hand on the pistol, aimed the barrel at the open window, angled his own hand away from the gun so the flash of powder would hit Anders's hand as much as possible. Lars fired. The news drowned out the bang, the bullet flew out through the window, shot over Vanadislunden, and kept going, past Eastern Station, finally coming to earth somewhere on Lidingö. Maybe the neighbors would have heard two shots, but that couldn't be helped.... Witnesses were usually wrong. Every police officer assumed that. Witnesses were basically a bit thick.

He closed the window and looked at Anders's position in the room, working out how the pistol would most likely have fallen from his hand. He put it on the floor a little way from the body. Then he went into the bedroom, opened Anders's suitcase, and unpacked it, putting the clothes back in the closet, his passport in a drawer, and pocketing the money, then shut the empty case and slid it under Anders Ask's bed.

Lars backed out of the apartment, pulled off the latex gloves and face mask, and shut the door behind him.

Lars slept soundly that night, waking up at half past five in the morning. He ordered coffee in his room, didn't feel any need for food. He waited until eight o'clock before making the call. The man at the other end was dubious, but Lars was insistent.

He had showered and ironed a shirt. The shirt was smooth and unbuttoned as he stood in front of the bathroom mirror and combed his hair into something vaguely neat. He was high, but in a controlled way, and was combing very slowly....

His shoes were polished, his trousers had been under the mattress all night. He looked respectable, and tried out his face in the mirror, he never had any problems with that when he was high. He practiced an expression. An expression that would be hard to read. Lars came up with something vacant and neutral, buttoned the shirt, took his jacket from the back of the chair and put it on. On his way out he picked up the sports bag from the bed and left the room.

Daylight was dangerous for him. But he had no choice. This had to happen during the day so that his target didn't suspect anything. He had chosen Mariatorget, an open square that he knew he could get a good view of.

* * *

He was standing in the stairwell at the top of a neighboring building, looking down on the square through a pair of binoculars. The time was now 11:44. The meeting was supposed to take place at half past eleven. He scanned the people down below with the binoculars. Mostly mothers with strollers, children on swings, one or two dads with their backs bent, holding hands with their toddlers who were insisting on walking. He looked farther away, toward Sankt Paulsgatan. People who were in a hurry, a group of laughing youths, a few elderly people sitting on benches.

Lars turned the binoculars back toward Hornsgatan, nothing there, either. Cars, people walking around aimlessly, fat tourists from the country eating ice cream by the little kiosk.

He lowered the binoculars, checked his watch—11:48, should he get going? He took a last look at the square.... And there, in the middle of his sweep, a single man on a bench. The man was sitting with one arm along the back of the bench, he had fairly long hair with a bald patch on top. The man turned slightly and Lars saw his cop's mustache. Hell, that had to be him.

Lars keyed in a number on his cell phone. Put the phone to his ear and watched the man through the binoculars, saw him feel for his cell in his pocket, pull it out, answer.

"Yes?"

"Tommy?"

"Yep." Almost inaudible.

"I'm running a bit late, five minutes."

Lars hung up. Tommy remained seated on the bench, glaring at the people in the square. He didn't call anyone, didn't give any signal. He just sat there waiting—bored, restless, and hot. Lars scanned around with the binoculars. Looked at the people in the vicinity. Looked between the trees on the far side by the old cinema, saw nothing. It seemed as if Tommy had come alone.

He put the binoculars in the bag and walked back down the stairs. Lars stepped out into the sunlight and headed toward the bench where Tommy was sitting. The next bench was empty, and Lars sat down there. Tommy glanced at him, then looked out across the square again. Lars waited and waited, nothing seemed to be out of the ordinary. Tommy sighed and looked at his watch. Lars stood up, went over, and sat down next to him.

"I'm Lars."

Tommy was annoyed.

"You're an arrogant bastard, Lars. Making me sit and wait like this, I don't like that. What do you want?"

Tommy had a Södermalm accent. *Maybe his mom had given birth to him right where they were sitting...?*

"I want to talk to you about a few things."

"Yes, so you said on the phone.... You work for Gunilla, why don't you talk to her? You're aware of the chain of command, aren't you?"

Lars glanced around, a lot of people milling about. He suddenly felt nervous again.

"Can we go somewhere else?"

Tommy snorted.

"Forget it, I'm sitting here on overtime.... Come on, spit it out, or I'm leaving."

Lars pulled himself together, looked at Tommy. Doubt hit him like a tidal wave. Was this the right man to talk to, or was he about to make the mistake of his life?

"I've got information," Lars said.

"About what?"

"About Gunilla."

The frown on Tommy's forehead was fairly set. "Oh?"

"Gunilla isn't running any investigations, it's all a bluff," he said in a low voice.

Tommy stared hard at him.

"What makes you say that?"

"Because I've been working for her for the past few months."

Tommy looked at Lars sternly.

"You don't think four dead in Vasastan counts as an investigation?"

"There's an investigation because of the murders, but she was never interested in that."

"What do you mean?" Tommy asked.

Lars wanted to give him the whole picture.

"It started when we bugged the nurse."

Tommy's irritation was still visible on his forehead.

"What nurse?"

Lars was tense. "Wait, let me go on.... Hector Guzman was in the hospital, Gunilla was there, and started to take an interest in a nurse on the ward who had evidently developed some sort of relationship with Guzman. Either way, we bugged the nurse's home, Anders Ask and I."

Tommy was listening, and the frown of annoyance gradually became one of curiosity.

"I was instructed to watch the nurse, Gunilla was certain she and Hector would end up having a relationship, which they did. As usual, she was right, but nothing came out of it, not from the bugging, or the wider surveillance."

Tommy was about to say something, but Lars continued.

"As time went on, Gunilla got more and more stressed when nothing useful emerged. She called in an old riot-squad gorilla from the Arlanda Police, Hasse Berglund, and turned him into her weapon, together with Erik and Anders. As her frustration grew, she reacted in a very odd way."

"How?" Tommy asked in a low voice.

Lars looked out across the square.

"She went for the nurse's son."

Tommy wasn't with him.

"Hasse and Erik brought him in for questioning, a faked-up interview. They'd concocted a story about the boy forcing himself on a girl, rape...."

Tommy didn't know what to think.

"That way they'd have a hold on her.... I think they were trying to get her to shop Hector in return for her son's problem disappearing, something like that."

Tommy was thinking.

"So did she do it?"

Lars shrugged.

"Don't know... I don't think so, I don't think she had anything to tell."

Tommy slapped his right thigh.

"OK, this is terrible, Lars, if what you're saying is true. Gunilla's always used unconventional methods. But now she's gone too far, no question. I'll talk to her. Thanks for contacting me."

Tommy stood up and held out his hand. "Let's keep this between us, OK?"

Lars looked at Tommy's hand.

"Sit down, that's only the start of it."

Lars gave Tommy Jansson everything he had, from start to finish. It took twenty minutes.

Tommy was glowering. His face had changed.

"Fucking hell . . . ," he whispered.

He was no longer stroking his mustache, and was scratching hard at his stubbly cheeks instead.

"Holy fuck . . ."

He stared at Lars.

"And you've got all this on tape, you say?"

"I've got recordings where she discusses Sara's murder, with Anders Ask and Hasse Berglund present. The murder of Patricia Nordström is also mentioned. There are also recordings of the conversations about how to frame the nurse's son, how they ran him down, about the illegal surveillance, her whole method of working. There are notes and accounts detailing the numerous millions that she, her brother, and Anders Ask have stolen from the investigations they've worked on over the years."

Tommy swore quietly to himself for the tenth time.

"And the boy? Is he still in the hospital?"

Lars nodded.

"He's in a bad way."

Tommy sighed, trying to fit the puzzle together.

"What are you going to do?" Lars asked.

The question seemed to hit Tommy Jansson hard, as if he didn't want to hear it.

"I don't know. . . . Right now, I don't know," he said quietly.

"You probably do know."

He looked at Lars. "Oh?"

"She's a murderer, a criminal . . . and a police officer. You're her boss, so she's your responsibility."

"What are you talking about?"

"The fact that you've got two choices."

"And they are?"

Lars waited for a couple of elderly people to walk past.

"Either you arrest her for murder, extortion, making illegal threats, breaking and entering, impeding the course of justice, bugging...well, the whole lot. And you as her boss will go down with her. At a guess you'd get caught for something once this gets examined by every police officer and journalist in the whole country. No one's going to believe that you were completely ignorant."

"But I am. I didn't know any of this."

"Do you think anyone's going to care about that?"

Tommy leaned back against the bench.

"Option two, then?" he asked quietly.

Lars had been waiting for him to ask.

"Option two is to let her go."

Lars leaned forward.

"That way you avoid problems, questions, responsibility. She just resigns. Age, grief at Erik's death, I don't know. But she has to disappear from here, go far away. In return for keeping quiet about this, I want her job...or something better in National Crime. I want you as my immediate superior. I don't want you looking over my shoulder while I work. And after a few years I want to be promoted...."

Something hard came over Tommy.

"You're a beat cop who for some inexplicable reason ended up in Gunilla's group. You have no experience, no track record, nothing. How the hell am I going to explain that when people ask?"

"You'll think of something."

Tommy bit his lip.

"How do I know what you're saying is true? Maybe you're just sitting here making it all up."

Lars pushed the sports bag toward Tommy.

"Take a look for yourself and get back to me, preferably this evening," Lars said.

Tommy was trying to think. Lars stood up and walked away. Tommy watched him go, then he picked the bag up and headed in the opposite direction.

28

F**auré's* **Requiem** ***was playing in the church, the procession past the coffin had just started. Gunilla was standing at the head of the coffin, where she laid a flower on its lid and curtsied, all according to custom. A few old duffers in badly fitting police uniforms were among the thirty or so people who had gathered to say a last farewell to the idiot Erik Strandberg.

Lars was observing the spectacle from a pew toward the back of the church. Tommy Jansson was standing in the line waiting to walk past the coffin. At least he'd had the good taste to come in just a blazer.

Lars tried to catch Gunilla's eye as she went and sat down. He thought their eyes met briefly. Or did they? Lars looked at Tommy Jansson, was he going to wobble, was he going to let on to her that he knew? But Tommy smiled amiably, sadly, and assuredly at Gunilla, and even patted her on the shoulder as he passed her. *Good, Tommy.*

When the procession was over the mourners left the church.

Gunilla was standing by the door, accepting the fabricated grief of those present. Lars gave her a hug.

"Thanks for coming," she said sadly.

"Have you got a moment?" Lars asked.

After Gunilla had listened to all the condolences they walked off to one side outside the church. They found a quiet spot under a holly.

"How are you feeling?" he asked in a friendly tone.

She sighed.

"It feels sad, but good as well, it was a nice funeral."

"I thought so too," Lars said.

The churchyard was completely still now. A mild summer breeze ruffled their hair.

"I waited half an hour before calling the ambulance. I sat and waited half an hour for your brother to die."

He looked into her eyes as he spoke to her, his voice was low.

"He had a stroke.... He was lying there on the floor. He'd be alive today if I'd called the ambulance. But I waited...."

Gunilla was pale. Lars smiled.

"He suffered badly, Gunilla."

She was staring at him.

"And imagine, Anders Ask shooting himself with your old Makarov? However could that happen?"

Gunilla couldn't make sense of her thoughts and was about to say something. Lars got in first.

"I suppose we're even now?" he said.

She didn't understand, and narrowed her eyes.

"You don't get it, do you?"

Gunilla shook her head slowly.

"Sara... You murdered Sara."

Lars stared into Gunilla Strandberg's eyes. They were shut off. Lars gestured toward Tommy.

"He knows what you've done. He's giving you until this evening to run. That's probably the best offer you've ever had. Take it."

Tommy was standing in a group of men and looked over toward

Lars and Gunilla, and nodded almost imperceptibly. She turned to Lars.

"You've got nothing, Lars. I never let you have anything. Have you got even the faintest idea of why you were ever allowed anywhere near this?"

"Because I'm malleable?"

Gunilla looked at him in surprise.

"I took one of the microphones from Sophie's house and left it in the office in Brahegatan. It's all been recorded: Albert's kidnapping, the bugging, Sara's murder, Patricia Nordström's murder.... It's all there... loud and clear. I've got your notes and bank papers as well. The amount that you, Anders, and your brother stole over the years..."

Gunilla was standing still, staring at Lars, trying to find words, thoughts. Then she turned and walked away.

Lars watched her go, then headed back toward the church. He found a bench, sat down, and pulled out his cell phone, filling his lungs with air and gradually letting it out. The bells started to ring, and he raised the phone and keyed in the number. The ringing tone sounded foreign.

She answered with a hello. He got nervous when he heard her voice. He muttered his name. Her tone was abrupt, she didn't sound at all happy that he had called. Lars apologized and said that everything had been sorted out, that she could feel safe now. She asked what he meant and he explained to her what he had done.

"I'm going to be away for a while," Lars said.

Sophie was silent.

"Maybe we could meet up and talk sometime when I get back?"

Sophie ended the call.

They made a stop-off at Ruzyně International in Prague. Leszek took her and Sonya to the VIP lounge, where they had a bite to eat and got some rest, their flight to Arlanda wasn't due to leave for another couple of hours.

Sophie tried to read a newspaper. She folded it, stood up, and walked around to stretch her legs. She stopped to look through the window onto the arrivals hall. People were milling around down there in a sort of organized chaos. This journey was approaching its conclusion, but it didn't feel like that. Instead she had a constant sense that something had only just begun, that something big was in the offing. She let her eyes drown in the sea of people below. After a while she turned away. She saw Leszek lying asleep on a sofa, Sonya leafing through a magazine. She went and sat beside them, picking a magazine off the table. Sonya looked up from hers, smiled at Sophie, then went on reading.

From Arlanda she went straight to the Karolinska. Jane and Jesus were sitting in Albert's room, both reading books. Jane stood up and greeted Sophie with a long hug.

Albert was still unconscious. Her legs wouldn't hold her any longer and she had to sit down. Albert looked so peaceful, maybe he was dreaming beautiful dreams; she hoped so, that was the only thing she hoped at that moment. She held his hand and time dissolved. The thousand and one thoughts that had occupied her in recent days, one single wish, just expressed in different ways—that Albert would be all right, one way or another.

She sat there for a long time, hours perhaps. Then she left the room. She walked down the corridor, passing a man with a goatee beard and short hair who was sitting on a chair against the wall. He was trying to catch her eye and she stopped.

"I'm a friend of Jens's," he said discreetly before she had time to ask. "I'll carry on making sure nothing happens to your son."

He looked away, as if their conversation was over. She didn't know what to say, she wanted to say something, and ended up whispering "Thank you."

She unlocked the door of the house and stepped inside. The silence that met her was audible as little creaks in the building. She walked into the kitchen and stopped in the middle of the floor. She felt like calling out to him, let him know she was home. He'd answer, from either the television room or upstairs. He would sound angry even though he wasn't, then she'd get on with putting the food in the fridge, or setting the table...or sit on a chair and read a magazine she'd just bought. He'd come down into the kitchen, joke with her. She'd ask about homework and tell him he ought to get his hair cut soon. He wouldn't answer, and she wouldn't mind.

But...no noise anywhere. No one else there apart from her. She felt like she was on the verge of collapse. She didn't want that, she fought against it, and found her way back to something deep inside.

They arrived at seven fifteen, the way guests usually do.

Sonya, Leszek, Ernst, Daphne, and Thierry were all in her living room. Leszek had taken up position by one of the windows and was keeping an eye on the garden and road. Ernst was looking at a painting. The others were looking at the photographs on the mantelpiece and talking among themselves.

She watched them from the kitchen as she finished preparing dinner. They were an odd crowd of people, but they were her crowd now, her people. Friends? No...not at all. Enemies? No, not that either. She felt alone, and she felt that she was playing her role. Perhaps that was what the others were doing as well.

They talked and ate. Sophie listened to the emotionless topic of conversation. Everyone agreed that they should lie low, wait, and see what happened with Hector. The Hankes were going to die, the only question was how and when.

29

Lars had checked out of the hotel, paying with some of Gunilla's cash.

He left the city and arrived at Bergsjögården late in the evening. He was met by two people in their fifties, a man and a woman. Warm, safe, normal. He had been expecting something else, possibly the opposite.

They asked to go through his luggage and he let them.

Lars paid for a month of treatment with the remainder of Gunilla's money, and the following morning he was sitting in a circle with eleven other men from various parts of the country, from different backgrounds, all with different appearances. They introduced themselves with their first names and nervously explained why they were sitting there, they were all hooked on prescription medication or other types of drug. They were all scared and anxious about what lay ahead of them.

The first day was good. He got a sense that he was in the right place, that he was getting help. He spoke to a counselor that afternoon.

It was a confidential conversation, at least from the counselor's side. His name was Daniel, he had once been an insurance broker in Småland and got addicted to prescription drugs. He said he knew what Lars was going through, that Lars would get help if he was willing to change his life.

Lars didn't understand much, but the overwhelming sensation was that he was in a good, humane place governed by a sort of collective common sense. A common sense that he wanted to get back.

The second day things felt harder, at least to start with. They were asked to write down the story of their own misuse of drugs, but his resistance faded when he heard the other men talk. It was open, sensitive, and honest.

Lars wrote so much that evening that his pen was red hot, and he started to feel free somehow, free and grateful. The more he wrote, the clearer the picture became, a picture that he felt he could put right. That life could possibly be different from now on, better.

He slept well that night, dreaming dreams that he recognized, and woke up looking forward to breakfast.

On the afternoon of the third day withdrawal and denial kicked in. Now Lars had forgotten the positive feeling. Daniel noticed and tried to get him back on track again. But Lars Vinge had a mocking smile glued to his face. Daniel and the other men at Bergsjögården had suddenly become his enemies. He compared himself to them. They were all idiots, members of a sect. He had nothing in common with any of them. They were weak, brainwashed, and could shove their higher power up their backsides. The desire to flee was banging and shouting inside him, and that night he escaped out of his bedroom window and found his way to the garage and his car. He was going to go home and lose himself in drugs for a few days, then he'd stop again, that wouldn't be a problem. He knew where this place was now, and it wasn't going to vanish. Besides, he had the right to do what he liked with his own life, didn't he? It wasn't like he was hurting anyone.

Lars got home to the apartment and doped himself up with drink and all the drugs he could find. His brain got sluggish and he crept around the floor looking for ants and other insects to have a chat with. He threw up in the sink, it was a nice, cleansing feeling. Then he swallowed loads of Hibernal. He knew what it was, chemical lobotomy. The pills worked just as they should. Lars sat on the floor staring out at nothing for ages, without even a hint of any feeling. He just sat there, Lars Vinge, feeling nothing, thinking nothing, expecting nothing. A great big nothing that didn't contain anything at all. Then everything went black, as usual.

The next morning he woke up on the kitchen floor with a cold feeling between his legs. He felt with his hand; his jeans were wet and cold, yes, he had pissed himself.

His cell phone rang on the floor beside him, he reached out for it.

"Hello, boy."

Tommy's voice. Lars wiped the saliva from the corner of his mouth.

"Hello," he said in a rough voice.

"Have you checked out?"

Lars tried to get his head straight.

"How did you know?"

"I keep an eye on my people, you should have said something, Lars. We take care of each other.... You're not alone, if that's what you think. How are you feeling?"

Lars rubbed under his nose with his forefinger.

"I don't know, OK, I think."

"I'm coming 'round," Tommy said.

Lars didn't have time to object.

Tommy arrived half an hour later. He had food and drink with him, in the form of a piece of sweet pastry and two cans of orangeade. They sat in the living room and talked candidly with each other, Lars in an armchair, Tommy on the sofa. Tommy said he thought Lars should try again, that the job wasn't going to disappear, that as his boss he was in a position to pay for Lars's treatment. Lars listened carefully. Tommy asked questions about Lars's drug use, about which drugs he took, how he got hold of them, which ones were strongest. Lars replied as best he could. Told the story of how he got addicted as a child, and how he lost all sense of direction when he started again with relatively harmless stuff. Tommy listened and shook his head.

"Sounds like hell," he said quietly.

Lars almost agreed.

"But we'll get this sorted out," Tommy said, and slapped his thigh with the palm of his hand, blinked, stood up, and went out to use the toilet.

Lars sat there alone, yawned, and stretched.

When Tommy returned he passed behind Lars. Lars was taken by surprise when the heavy blow hit him on the back of the neck. He was even more taken aback when Tommy caught both his hands, bent them back, and pushed him down off the chair. Lars hit his face hard on the floor, with Tommy's body on top of him. He tried to struggle but Tommy had the upper hand. Tommy was tough and strong, Lars hungover from the drugs. It was an uneven fight. Lars protested, bewildered, but Tommy told him to shut up, then took a pair of handcuffs from his belt and put them around Lars's wrists.

"What are you doing, what the hell have I done? Tommy?"

Tommy disappeared from the living room again. Lars was left lying flat on his stomach.

"Tommy!" he called. No answer. Lars listened, heard Tommy open the front door, heard it close again out in the hall. Had he left?

"Tommy? Don't go!"

Lars lay there with his arms fastened behind his back, and tried to think. He rested his cheek against the cold floor.

"Tommy!" he called again after a while, and felt his own breath as it rebounded off the wooden floor.

Lars could hear little noises from the kitchen, it sounded like two people whispering....

"Tommy, please! Can't we talk?" Lars's voice was weak. He lay there with his face on the floor. Time passed, he didn't know how long, but suddenly he thought he could see the shape of someone out in the hall. It wasn't Tommy, it was the shape of a woman. He screwed up his eyes and recognized her, Gunilla.... She was standing in the doorway of the living room, leaning against the frame with her handbag over her shoulder.

It began to dawn on him, something that his mind was hardly capable of daring to think. His breathing became labored and heavy. He sighed loudly several times, and coughed when the anxiety made his heart snag in his chest.

"What are you doing here?" he managed to say.

Tommy pushed past Gunilla and came back into the room. In his hands he had an automatic pistol with a long silencer attached to the barrel. Lars tried to cough out his fear of dying, pissed himself again, and tried to sit upright but couldn't with his arms cuffed behind his back. Instead he made jerking movements over the hard, slippery floor, like a seal on dry land. He tried to reason with Tommy, but his terror made the words weak and incomprehensible. He tried to say something to Gunilla, tried to explain that this was going too far... that he wasn't supposed to die now, that this was out of all proportion to what he had done. But she didn't seem to hear or understand what he was trying to say.

Tommy stopped behind Lars, pulled him up into a sitting position, put the silencer a half inch from his right temple, and looked at Gunilla. She nodded. Lars tried to say something else. It came out as a shrill sound of air that smelled of dark anxiety and heartrending terror.

Tommy fired, *pop, bang*—the same sound as a loud puff of air. The bullet went right through Lars's head and hit the living-room wall some distance away. A short stream of blood from Lars's left temple, thin but with heavy pressure. Gunilla stared. Lars collapsed on the floor. Tommy backed away carefully, then went quickly to work. He crouched down, undid the handcuffs, wiped the floor where he had been standing.

Gunilla felt the opposite from what she had expected. She thought she would feel some sort of pleasure at watching him die, some sort of relief, a liberating feeling after what he had done to Erik. But it didn't feel like that. It just felt empty and sad. She had asked Tommy to finish Lars off in just this way, so that the last thing he saw was her, to make him realize that he could never beat her, that it was predetermined. Maybe he had realized that, maybe not, but either way she felt different from what she had expected. There was something tragic about the fact that Lars's wretched and pathetic life should end so miserably. She was tired of everything to do with death.

"Thank you, Tommy," she said in a low voice.

He looked at her.

"How does it feel?"

She didn't answer. Tommy stood up, the cuffs in one hand, the pistol in the other, and met her gaze.

"I miss Erik," she said quietly.

Tommy sighed. Their eyes stayed on each other's. He raised the pistol. Didn't need to aim, just squeezed the trigger. And again, the same hard, short puffing sound from the gun, the recoil that jolted the silencer up about fifteen degrees. The bullet hit the right side of Gunilla's forehead.

She stood motionless for a few moments. As if she had been so shocked that the force of her surprise kept her alive for a short while before her legs buckled beneath her. She fell where she had been standing, like a puppet whose strings had been cut. Her eyes stared crookedly up at the ceiling as blood seeped from the hole in her forehead.

Tommy was breathing heavily, his heart beating hard, his mouth was dry and he struggled against feelings that were trying to get out. He tried to compose himself and suppress everything. He was muttering quietly to himself about what he was going to do, what he had memorized that he needed to do, nothing could be left to chance. Tommy looked at Gunilla, then at Lars. Just two dead objects, he told himself.

Tommy unscrewed the silencer and put it in his pocket, then put the gun on the floor, took a Q-tip out of a plastic bag in his pocket and rubbed it gently above the trigger where there were invisible traces of powder. He dabbed the powdered Q-tip on Lars's right hand, between the thumb and forefinger. Tommy planted the pistol in Lars's hand, checking how it ought to be positioned in light of Lars Vinge's suicide shot. He left the handcuffs in Lars's bedroom. The forensics team would find tiny, almost invisible chafe marks on his wrists, so a pair of handcuffs in the bedroom would lead them to the conclusion that everyone leaps to when they see handcuffs in a bedroom.

He crouched beside Gunilla's body and went through her handbag, searching for the slightest sign of anything to do with the case or the investigation. He was fairly certain she wouldn't have anything like that on her, she was just as careful as he was, but he felt obliged to check anyway.

He had contacted her after going through all the material he had been given by Lars in Mariatorget. He hadn't made any big deal out of it, just said he knew what she and Erik had been up to, and that he wanted a piece of the cake. And because she knew him, she had merely asked how much. Erik's half would be enough, wouldn't it? *OK*, he had replied.

After a self-confident Lars Vinge had told her at the funeral that he had let her brother die, she added an extra clause to the contract, saying she wanted to determine how Lars should die. That hadn't been much of a problem. It was with great sadness that he had shot her. Sadness because he felt a kinship with Gunilla. But it couldn't be helped. Tommy knew Gunilla, she'd demand his share back at some later point, that was just what she was like. He would have been looking over his shoulder the whole time. But the main reason was that he had seen the sums of money on the papers he had received from Lars. Then he realized something that he couldn't ignore. His wife, Monica. Money saves lives. . . . With all this, maybe he'd be able to buy her some care, prolong her life, maybe cure her ALS. Then there was a third aspect, which was small but oh-so-important. A vague feeling that he traced back to two-weak-beers-in-the-fridge-for-when-you-want-to-get-drunk. A sense of deficit. Otherwise he might as well let it all go. All or nothing. And when he had gotten the sports bag from Lars in Mariatorget and went through the material at home that same evening, he saw a surplus. A surplus, safely at arm's length. And it was at that moment that the path had become clear. Crystal clear.

Eva Castroneves had been stationed in Liechtenstein, as a kind of sleeping resource charged with taking care of the money from Guzman. But she had been given another task when that had all gone to hell. After a conversation with Gunilla she had transferred money to a dummy account that Tommy could access as he pleased. Now Tommy was planning to contact Castroneves and tell her to transfer Gunilla's share of the money to him as well, and to keep ten percent for herself. If she made a fuss, he'd contact Interpol, who would hunt her to the ends of the earth. He had an entire sports bag full of evidence in which her name cropped up on every other page. Eva Castroneves wouldn't cause any trouble. He was sure of that.

Tommy took a turn around Lars Vinge's apartment, double-checking that there was nothing there that had anything to do with the case. There wasn't, it was clean. He thought through everything that might be of interest to the forensics team. He knew how they worked, they were fuckers sometimes when it came to putting things together.

When Tommy felt confident, he left Lars and Gunilla and went down to the street, jumped into his Buick Skylark GS, and started it up, letting the tuned V8 engine echo between the buildings. He put his right foot on the brake pedal, moved the gearshift to D. The trimmed engine made the whole car bounce as the gear settled.

He drove away and headed home to Monica and the girls. They were planning to barbecue sausages on the terrace that night. He would nod over the fence of his row house to the neighbors, Krister and Agneta, say something amusing to Krister, who would laugh, he always did. Then Tommy would test Vanessa on the extra English homework that she had been given over summer vacation. She would tease him about his pronunciation, he would exaggerate his Swenglish, and they'd laugh. Emilie would get stuck in front of the computer. He would tell her to log off. She'd sulk for a while, but that would pass. After a bit of television Monica would suggest backgammon and coffee in the conservatory, with a slice of that Swiss roll that they were both addicted to. Monica would win the game. They would go to bed and read, a car magazine for him and something by Jean M. Auel for her. Before they turned out the lights he would pat her on the cheek and tell her he loved her, she'd say something nice back, strong in spite of the ever-present illness.... Something like that. Everything would carry on exactly as usual for a bit longer. Then he would set to work and save his wife from slow suffocation.

Tommy forced his way through the Stockholm traffic in his Buick. He calculated in his head how rich he was, indirectly at least. He made it two digits, followed by six zeros. Two relatively high digits. That was a lot to digest for a boy who was born in Johanneshov in the '50s, who had pinched Robin Hood cigarettes, listened to Jerry Williams, and thought the Phantom and Biggles were cool.

She sang softly to him, washed him, combed his hair, and dressed him in clean clothes every day. She kept on reading him the book he had been reading before the accident. She had found it beside his bed with a bookmark in it.

The door of Albert's hospital room was ajar. Jens stopped, looked in. The sight of the mother beside her unconscious son was just as sad each time. He had a pack of cards in his hand, bought from the shop downstairs, he had imagined that he and Sophie might play cards to pass the time. But now that he was standing there, it was as if a wall had grown up in front of him, an invisible wall that made it impossible for him to enter the room. That made it impossible for him to be part of her and Albert's lives. That made it impossible for him to confront his fears, once and for all, and take the step into the warmth.

She sat and read, tucked a stray strand of hair from her face. She was so beautiful when she didn't know she was being watched....

Jens turned and walked away down the corridor.

The atmosphere was subdued and tense. The men were thinking. They were sitting in the same room as always, the conference room that was Björn Gunnarsson's very own smoking room. Björn Gunnarsson was Tommy's boss, and he sucked at his pipe before breaking the deadlock.

"What do we know, Tommy?"

Tommy had been sitting there staring at the table, leaning back in his chair. He kept his eyes focused on an invisible point for a few seconds before looking up.

"Lars Vinge was unstable. Gunilla was worried about him. She mentioned it to me once in passing. I didn't pay it much attention at the time. But he was evidently very pushy, thought he deserved better than the jobs he was given. He called her, sent e-mails, was aggressive and threatening. And apparently his mother and girlfriend both died recently, one after the other. That seems to have knocked him even further off balance...."

Gunnarsson listened and smoked. Tommy went on.

"Vinge had checked into a rehab center, but bolted just a few days later. We have a call from him to Gunilla registered the same evening he came home. Maybe he called to ask for her help, I don't know. Either way, evidently she went to his apartment the following morning. He shot her and then killed himself. The indications are that he did so while he was under the influence of very strong medication...."

"What sort of medication?"

"Prescription Ketogan... He was high, he was addicted to it. Apparently he had a history of trouble. I don't know much about it, but according to Gunilla it was escalating out of control again. It might have had something to do with his mother and girlfriend."

"And their investigations?" Gunnarsson puffed at his pipe.

Tommy wiped some invisible grit from his eye.

"This is where it gets a bit strange. The office on Brahegatan contained practically nothing. It was empty, apart from a few surveillance reports, some photographs, and a few other case notes."

"Why?"

Tommy left a dramatic pause, then looked up.

"I don't know."

"What do you think?"

Tommy's face took on a slightly pained look, as though he were about to say something that was actually physically painful.

"What?" Gunnarsson asked, with the pipe still between his teeth.

"Maybe Gunilla and Erik didn't have anything, maybe they hadn't gotten anywhere.... At least not as far as she wanted to make out."

He said these last words in an almost apologetic tone, as if it hurt him to speak ill of the dead.

"What makes you think that?" Gunnarsson's voice was gruff.

"Remember that she managed to sell this way of working to us. We bought it, lock, stock, and barrel, and gave her carte blanche. Maybe she was ashamed that it wasn't turning out the way she'd hoped. Or else she wanted to keep on getting financial support, and knew that would stop if she couldn't show any sign of progress."

Tommy shrugged his shoulders. "But I don't really know," he said.

Gunnarsson let out a deep sigh. Tapped the exhausted tobacco into the palm of his hand and tossed it into the wastepaper basket beside him.

"And the murders at Trasten?" he asked.

"Antonia Miller's running that. I've let her have everything I had from Gunilla, the little that did exist, I mean. We'll have to hope that forensics can help us there."

"And Guzman, he's gotten away?"

"Yes. We've got warrants out for him through all the usual channels. His father was murdered in his home in Marbella at roughly the same time as those shots were fired in Trasten. It looks like this settling of accounts stretches much further than we thought."

Björn Gunnarsson frowned.

"Hasse Berglund?"

"Vanished," Tommy said.

"Why?"

Tommy shook his head.

"Don't know. He already had plenty of crap in his record before he was employed by Gunilla. He's probably just fled the field."

A moment's silence.

"So, where is he then?"

Tommy shook his head. "No idea."

"And Ask? What the hell was Anders Ask doing in all this?"

Tommy left another dramatic pause before he replied.

"I asked Gunilla when I saw him at Trasten. She said he had been helping with some surveillance work. Said she didn't want to overburden the force."

Gunnarsson looked up.

"She said that, *overburden the force*?"

Tommy nodded.

"So why did he kill himself, then, Ask?" Gunnarsson asked.

"Why does anyone kill themselves? I don't know, but he's not the first officer to take the shortcut. You know about his past. No one wanted to work with him, or even have anything to do with him after the debacle with the Security Police. He was tainted, used up, alone.... I'd guess he was just pretty damn tired of it all."

Tommy saw a quick nod from the man opposite. "Pretty damn tired" was a phenomenon that Gunnarsson was well acquainted with.

Gunnarsson took a deep breath.

"Don't you think there are an unusual number of question marks surrounding this whole business, Tommy?"

Tommy let a few moments pass.

"Well, yes..."

His answer stretched no further than that. The sound of traffic could be heard from somewhere below. They were sitting in Police Headquarters on Kungsholmen. Björn Gunnarsson filled his pipe again and sighed out of habit.

"How do we proceed?"

"There's not so much we can do. It's a tragedy, Björn. The work of a madman, a madman by the name of Lars Vinge. End of story. As far as Gunilla's Guzman investigation is concerned, we'll continue with what we've got. The same with Trasten."

Gunnarsson had his matches ready, and said gruffly as the pipe tapped against his teeth: "We've probably only got ourselves to blame for part of this tragic business. Gunilla wanted to work without supervision, and we allowed that. We allowed her to fail. And if she for her part could have just dropped the clever-girl routine and asked us for help when she realized she wasn't getting anywhere, then maybe the situation would be very different today."

Tommy read his boss. Somewhere in there Gunnarsson was terrified. Terrified he was going to have to take responsibility for this chaos. Just as Tommy had hoped.

"I'll take care of it, Björn. I'll make sure it all gets sorted out."

Gunnarsson lit his pipe again, took several deep puffs, the smoke was almost blue. He looked at Tommy carefully as he let the nicotine do its work on his tongue and cheeks.

"Gunilla and Erik were close friends of ours, Tommy. They had a good reputation. I want their memory to stay that way."

Tommy nodded.

Epilogue

AUGUST

She moved Albert from the front seat and down into the wheelchair. She knew he hated that. There were so many aspects of daily life that he found humiliating. But he was brave, never showed that he was weak or despairing. Sometimes it scared her, she was worried he was bottling up his grief.

But the glint in his eyes was there, she'd seen it when he woke up in the hospital two weeks before. That had dispelled all her anxiety, it was her Albert waking up, it was her Albert asking questions, who got angry when he realized what his life was going to be like from now on, who after two days started crying, and after four started joking with her for the first time. Then it was her turn to grieve. After that came his questions. She told him everything, from the day she first met Hector in the hospital, about Gunilla and her threats, right up to the point when she fled to Spain. He listened and did his best to understand.

* * *

Tom and Yvonne were being a nuisance. They stood by the car door, wanting to be helpful. They were in the way, and she asked them to go and wait inside.

Sunday dinner, there they were again, Jane and Jesus, Tom and Mom, Albert and her. Yvonne was happy and upbeat, Tom the same. Rat, the dog, was barking, Jane and Jesus were silent and kept to themselves. The terrace doors were open, the table set in the loveliest way, and the warm evening caressed the dining room—everything was as it should be... almost.

She looked around the table at her nearest and dearest. Albert was reading texts on his cell phone in his lap, Yvonne was nodding eagerly at something Jesus had just said. And Tom was smiling at her. And then Jane—Jane, who without any questions had shown such immense strength and stability. She had just rolled into action. She did that whenever anything serious happened. Then she switched from being a dizzy gadfly to calmness personified, taking charge where other people lost their grip or the plot. Jane was a rock, and hardly anyone knew.

She looked at Albert again. His phone buzzed, he read a text and replied with his thumb.

And then she looked at herself for the first time in ages. She saw a flame somewhere, a shimmering light that she recognized. The flame didn't burn, it wasn't blinding, it just lay there soft and warm inside her, rocking gently within a feeling that told her something about herself that she had forgotten. A feeling that said she could step away from her fear, away from her self-imposed isolation, that she was bigger than she had dared to see. That she didn't need to understand the fear in order to get rid of it; she could just walk away from it quietly, leave it behind, say good-bye. It didn't happen after a chain of thought where she put words to something. It was crystal clear. She was changing, shedding the skin of her personality. The change had happened gradually. She realized that she had stopped fighting against it. Everything was changing, it was always changing, everywhere throughout the universe, day and night alike, for all eternity. The change that no one and nothing could shield themselves from, not even her. She felt angry, warm, intense, empty, and determined all at the same time. And it felt completely natural.

Sophie turned to Albert, who met her gaze, and gave her a wide, heartfelt smile. She wondered why, until she realized that she herself was smiling.

They drove home at dusk. Even though it was still warm, it felt like a different season, a season when the darkness came earlier. A season when the green leaves of the trees hung heavily on thin branches, a time just before the visible change, when the leaves could no longer hold on, just before they lost their grip.

They parked outside the house and repeated the procedure, out of the car, down into the wheelchair, up the ramp to the front door. He wanted to do it all himself. He could move freely at home, where all barriers had been removed and a lift had been installed on the stairs.

Sophie locked the doors all around the house with the extra locks that she'd had fitted, and activated the alarm in the rooms they weren't going to be in.

When Albert had fallen asleep, Aron called. He told her what was going on in the world around them, asked questions, and kept her informed. She listened and spoke to him, reasoning and trying to find the best solutions to his queries. She asked if there was any change with Hector, but there wasn't. He was lying there connected to machines that were keeping him alive.

She made tea. Drank it alone, cursing herself. She would always do that, the guilt would never leave her. She wished Jens had been there. But he had vanished, gone. She had gotten a text. Something along the lines of: I'm forced to go away for a while. *Forced*... she thought. I'm forced as well. Everyone is forced.

And amid all of this, she took care of Albert and kept looking over her shoulder. That was what her life looked like.

She woke up eight hours later and ate breakfast out on the veranda. It was pouring rain. She was sitting in the cover of the balcony above, drinking her tea and listening to the water falling from the sky. Sophie heard the sound of tires on gravel on the other side of the house, footsteps approaching. When she heard the front doorbell ring she got up and leaned out from the end of the veranda.

"I'm back here!"

Around the corner came a woman of her own age, possibly a few years younger. She was fairly tall, had dark hair, and was wearing high boots and tight jeans. Trinkets rather than classic jewelry, Sophie had time to note as the woman jogged around toward her to get out of the rain.

"Ugh!" the woman said as she came up the steps to the veranda, brushing the rain off her clothes with her hand.

"Goodness! Antonia Miller, detective inspector," she said, holding out her wet hand.

"Sophie Brinkmann," Sophie said.

"Am I disturbing you?"

"No, come and sit down, I was just having breakfast."

Sophie and Antonia sat on the veranda; Sophie offered tea, Antonia accepted the offer.

"You have a nice house," she said.

The woman seemed to mean what she said.

"Thanks," Sophie said. "We're happy here."

Sophie could see Antonia wondering who "we" was.

"I live here with my son, I've been a widow for many years now."

Antonia nodded.

"I understand. I'm not married myself, I live in a two-room apartment in the city... it faces south. Every morning this summer I've woken up asking myself why I live in a sauna."

Antonia reached for a slice of bread from the little bread basket, took a bite, looking at the flowers and trees.

"I could certainly live like this."

Sophie was waiting, and Antonia noticed.

"Sorry... I'm in charge of an investigation, a murder inquiry. A triple-murder in Vasastan, at the Trasten restaurant, I'm sure you've read about it?"

Sophie nodded.

"It's a real mess.... I'm slowly feeling my way forward... That's pretty much what the job's like, feeling my way the whole time."

Antonia drank a sip of tea, then put the cup down.

"And as you've probably also read, there was another murder, a meeting between two police officers that ended in tragedy."

The rain was still falling beyond the terrace.

"Yes, I'm aware of it, and my name's cropped up somewhere, and now you're here to ask some questions."

"Yes," Antonia said.

"I'm afraid there's not much I can tell you. But I'll try to help you as much as I can."

Antonia took a little notebook from her jacket pocket and turned to a fresh page. There was something uncomplicated about Antonia Miller. She was easygoing and had honest eyes. Sophie liked her, and that scared her.

"Apparently Gunilla Strandberg's investigation hadn't gotten anywhere. She left very little material about the case... but among that material your name did crop up."

Antonia looked at her, then she asked: "How did you come into contact with each other?"

"She came to see me at the hospital where I work, Danderyd. She told me she was investigating a Hector Guzman. He was on my ward, he had a broken leg after being hit by a car. That was at the end of May, beginning of June...."

Antonia listened.

"Gunilla asked me some questions about him, but that was all."

"Did you know Hector?"

"I got to know him a bit while he was in the hospital. That sometimes happens with patients, you develop a relationship with them. We're always being told that we're not supposed to... but that's easier said than done."

Antonia was taking notes in her book.

"Then what?"

"She called me a few times, asked questions I didn't have any answers to. Hector was discharged, he invited me to lunch." Sophie leaned forward and drank some of her tea.

"He invited you to lunch?"

Sophie nodded. "Yes..."

Antonia was thinking.

"What was he like?"

Sophie kept her eyes on Antonia.

"I don't know, pleasant, well mannered... almost charming."

Antonia was taking notes.

"Leif Rydbäck?" she said suddenly without looking up.

"Sorry?"

"Leif Arne Rydbäck, does that name mean anything to you?"

Sophie shook her head.

"No, who's he?"

Antonia looked at Sophie, wrote something in her pad.

"We found three murdered men at Trasten, but also a fourth when we searched the place, he had died earlier. I've only recently had his identity confirmed, Leif Rydbäck."

"I see.... No, I've never heard the name before," Sophie said.

"Lars Vinge?"

Sophie shook her head.

"No, I've never heard that name either, who's that?"

Antonia didn't answer immediately.

"Lars Vinge was the policeman who murdered Gunilla Strandberg, even if his name hasn't been officially released yet."

Antonia went on asking questions. There were a lot of them—small, thin, and harmless. Antonia Miller didn't know anything, she had nothing to go on. She didn't know who had been working on the case. She had no knowledge of Hector, no knowledge of anything, really....But she wanted to know, wanted to be able to build up a picture. Sophie could hear it in her voice, see it in her slightly forced unobtrusive manner.

Sophie shook her head to all of Antonia's questions, totally ignorant, just like the innocent nurse that she was.

They were interrupted when Albert came rolling out onto the veranda. The suntanned boy in the wheelchair threw Detective Inspector Miller off balance slightly.

"Hello! My name's Antonia," she said rather too cheerily, standing up and shaking Albert's hand.

"Albert," Albert said.

Sophie put her arm around him.

"This is my son, he's got one more week of his summer vacation left. I've told him it's time to start getting back into a proper routine, but you don't really care about that, do you?"

And with that, she kissed him on the head.

About the Author

Alexander Söderberg has worked as a screenwriter for Swedish television and lives in the countryside in the south of Sweden with his wife and children. *The Andalucian Friend* is his first novel.

About the Type

This book was set in Sabon, a typeface designed by Jan Tschichold in 1964. It was named for a sixteenth-century typefounder, Jakob Sabon, a student of Claude Garamond. The typeface is a modern revival of a type issued by the Egenolff-Berner foundry in 1592, based on roman characters of Claude Garamond and italic characters of Robert Granjon.